# A Sweeping Saga

a story spanning a person's whole life

## Cenarth Fox

In memory of the Palawa
the first inhabitants of Van Diemen's Land

**1822**
In Britain, the first act of parliament for the prevention of cruelty to cattle was passed.


**1889**
In Britain, the first act of parliament for the prevention of cruelty to children was passed.


*Since the primary Settlement of Van Diemen's Land, various acts of aggression, violence and cruelty have been committed on the Aboriginal Inhabitants by Subjects of His Majesty.*
**Lieutenant-Governor Sir George Arthur**

# The Child

## Chapter 1

Londoners loved a good hanging and the more swinging stiffs the better. Rain, hail or shine, in 1812 massive crowds flocked to the free spectacle with traders making a killing.

The scaffold, outside Newgate Prison in Old Bailey, shot up overnight. Inside, those due to die in the morning, heard hammering as cursing carpenters whipped up the structure. It must have been hard to sleep the night before you were due to hang, and it hardly helped hearing the gallows taking shape outside your cell. At midnight, a priest from the nearby Holy Sepulchre Church rang a hand bell outside the cells of the condemned to warn them their soul was in mortal danger. Talk about rubbing it in and cheering them up.

Once upon a time the condemned were driven three miles through London in open carts to the infamous Tyburn tree. Down Oxford Street they went, the journey taking forever thanks to the curious and bloodthirsty mob grabbing the chance to gawp and barrack.

'Swing me darling,' and 'Give Satan a kiss,' they screamed.

The authorities gave the Tyburn executions away in 1783 because in summer, tens of thousands of Londoners, out for a stickybeak, became a traffic hazard, hence the gibbet being moved to Newgate.

Coffee shops and pubs catered for rich geezers to watch in comfort while enjoying their favourite thirst quencher. Vendors proclaimed.

'Best seats in town,' and 'Best coffee in London.'

Once the victims began dancing the "Newgate Hornpipe", the masses cheered and jeered. They couldn't afford Theatre Royal prices but this ballet was gratis. Mind you, a short arse saw nothing.

It turned into a family day. Parents brought their nippers who ran around like headless chickens and thieving children struck gold. A toff, eyes fixed on the scaffold, never felt his pocket being picked.

These juvenile criminals robbed from necessity. With no food in their miserable hovels, and no work except for slave wages, nicking anything you could sell became essential. And a leading light amongst those young criminals was one named Jonathon Sweeping.

Thanks to the Industrial Revolution, London's population boomed. The unemployed rural working class became the unemployed urban working class, and demand for housing lured developers.

But they scored short leases, and if your investment ceased after 21 years, why build the Taj Mahal? So up went cheap, multi-storey slums for which the struggling tenants overpaid. Okay, the roof leaked, the floorboards rotted, and the windows made it open house for wind and rain, but that was your lot, my son.

'If you don't like it, you can feck off,' being the standard response to anyone who complained. Few complained.

Sanitation saw a cesspool built beneath a privy where a bloke, short of a bob, would climb down to shovel the shit into a basket and haul it away. The poor sod would work only at night. Many residents carried their full-to-the-brim chamber pot or bucket into the street to dump their goodies in the gutters of the roads or lanes. These gutters led to such rivers as the Fleet and Westbourne, both of which flowed into the greatest river in London, the Thames, the city's open sewer. Here comes the cholera. Thank God for the rain.

Some families would get their water from these rivers or, unbelievably, the gutters. You set your bucket aside for a day or two before scraping the muck off the top. Healthy it wasn't and folk would use this "clean" water for bathing. No wonder disease thrived.

This was the home life, the background, the real life situation of the young Jonathon Sweeping, he who went stealing as the populous gawped during the public hangings at Newgate. His family history did not a happy bedtime story make.

His mother, Clara Sutcliffe, was the daughter of the blacksmith in the small Norfolk village of Little Tinker, not far from the cathedral city of Norwich. Clara's parents wanted their 15 year old daughter to have a future. Her reading and writing skills were limited but her sewing talents matched those of her seamstress mother. Mr and Mrs Sutcliffe knew Mrs Beadle, the housekeeper at Bittering Hall, the local stately home, and after church at St Felix's one Sunday, asked the woman if there was a chance their girl might find work at the Hall.

'I'll ask,' said the housekeeper, and left for the stately home.

Next week, Clara's mother bumped into Mrs Beadle in the grocer's in the nearby market town of Castle Stop as the women placed their vastly different orders.

The women exchanged greetings before Mrs Beadle dropped a bombshell. 'Oh, and your girl can start as a scullery maid on Monday. Two and six a week, all found. Seven am. Don't let her be late.'

The housekeeper turned and left leaving Mrs Sutcliffe staring at the grocer and his wife in stunned silence.

At home, Mr Sutcliffe and young Clara were told the news and happiness filled their humble cottage. Lots of advice came from the parents, and Clara's bones ached with enthusiasm.

That night, her mother told Clara how she must behave and stay out of trouble. Trouble was not defined in specific terms although Clara believed it involved sex. The innocent child drowned in vague information and warnings.

And that was how Jonathon Sweeping's mother placed her foot on the bottom rung of the ladder of life.

Bittering Hall was a stately home with its wealthy owners controlling vast swathes of surrounding land. Rent from tenant farmers kept the Marquess of Fakenham, Lord of the Manor, in a style to which he'd become accustomed. His wife, the Marchioness, ruled on matters domestic while he ran the vast estate.

Clara arrived at the back door with knees knocking and heart pounding. Mrs Beadle appeared. It was 24 seconds past 7.

'You're late,' she said and walked to the kitchen leaving Clara to follow and close the door. Other staff stopped work. 'This is Clara,' said Mrs Beadle, 'the new scullery maid.' No names of the others were given and Clara's fears multiplied. 'Put your things there and start scrubbing the floor.' She pointed at a bucket and brush and left.

No-one offered to help the new arrival. She placed her bag, bonnet and coat on a chair. 'Not there,' snapped the kitchen maid who made no effort to help. Clara quickly discovered she was on her own. She placed her possessions in the hallway, picked up the bucket and scrubbing brush and started work.

Her fellow employees spoke not a word. 'Hello, my name's So-and-So.' No, nothing. 'I'll show you where your room is later.' No, nothing.

Clara scrubbed with feeling wanting to make the right impression thanks to her mother explaining the benefits of being a good worker.

'Lord Rallison will reward you if you work hard,' she said. It was balderdash as His Lordship had little if any interest in or knowledge of the servants.

Clara attacked her work. Half an hour later she stopped scrubbing. Afraid to speak, she waited. Mrs Beadle arrived. The maid spoke softly. 'Mrs Beadle.'

The housekeeper looked at the maid who indicated with her head. Mrs Beadle looked at the floor and then the newcomer.

'Finished have we?'

'Yes, Mrs Beadle.'

'Right, come with me.'

The housekeeper set off and Clara wasn't sure what to do with the bucket and brush. The kitchen maid and the cook stared at her saying nothing but thinking, *You're on your own, sister*. Clara placed the bucket and brush where she found them, and scurried down the corridor. Mrs Beadle opened a door.

'This is your hideaway with all the cleaning equipment. If I find anything missing or dirty or not in its proper place, I'll dock your wages and tell His Lordship you're not up to snuff. You get one warning after which you're gone. Is that clear enough?'

'Yes, Mrs Beadle,' replied Clara without making eye contact.

'Right, get your apron and cap and go back to the kitchen. Mary'll tell you what to do next.'

Mrs Beadle walked into the house. Clara looked at the tiny room crammed with brooms, dusters, buckets, rags and more. She couldn't see any apron. *And who is Mary?* Her first day went from bad to worse. *And where is the apron?*

As tears welled in her eyes, she went to close the door and only then saw an apron and cap hanging on the inside. Feeling a smidgeon better, she put on the apron and cap, closed the door, and headed to the kitchen.

She found the cook and kitchen maid preparing the luncheon. The two women stared at Clara who decided to be bold.

'Mrs Beadle told me to ask Mary to give me my next task.'

The kitchen maid wiped her nose on her sleeve. 'See them pots over there.' Clara looked and nodded. 'They need to be as clean as a new penny.' Clara hesitated. 'Well don't just stand there.'

Clara moved to the pots. *At least I know who Mary is.*

'You clean them outside by the pump,' said the kitchen maid sneaking a grin at the cook.

Clara picked up the pots. At least two trips were necessary but being new and desperate to please, she tried too hard and once outside, she stumbled on the steps and dropped the lot. The others ignored her, and the noise sounded like a drunken cymbal player rehearsing in a cobbled courtyard. Dogs barked and a curious stable boy appeared. He laughed at the girl's predicament and went back to his grooming.

Once all the pots arrived at the pump, and a brush and rags were obtained, Clara prepared to clean. She looked at the first pot, big and solid and spotlessly clean. She picked up another and another. Not a skerrick of food on any of them; even their handles were sparkling. Clara knew she was being tested or teased, although many would call it bullying, even abuse.

She'd been made to carry the pots outside when they could have been cleaned inside and worse; they didn't need cleaning at all.

Her heart ached. She wanted to flee but knew her parents would be shocked and so disappointed if she ran away.

This first day in her new job helped make the character of Clara Sutcliffe. Her mind filled with instructions.

*If I can beat the bullies and stand up to their cruelty, it's as good as giving them a tongue-lashing and a poke in the eye with a stick. I'll hang in there and won't let them get the better of me.*

And she didn't. She washed the pots, dried them and took them back inside. They were stacked neatly in their correct place. Clara turned to Mary who couldn't believe how calm this new girl looked and seemed.

'I've finished the pots, Miss,' said Clara. 'What would you like me to do next?'

The cook was impressed, the kitchen maid dumbfounded. A flustered Mrs Beadle came into the kitchen. 'Sir William and Lady

Howard are coming to luncheon. His Lordship expects extra-large portions and everything must be warm but not hot. Is that clear?'

The two regular kitchen staff murmured their assent.

'Is there anything I can do to help with the luncheon, Mrs Beadle?' asked Clara, and her question stopped the large clock on the wall.

The new member of staff displayed excellent manners and a willingness to help when all hands to the pump were required. Mary reckoned her goal of humiliating the newcomer became much harder.

'Ask Cook,' said Mrs Beadle and departed.

Clara smiled at the older woman. 'Peel dem taters,' said Cook in her broad Tipperary accent.

'Certainly, Cook,' came the polite and respectful reply as Clara took the bowl and a knife, sat in a corner and began peeling potatoes. Silence became her byword and Mary quietly fumed trying to think of another way to destroy the newcomer.

Mary behaved out of fear and jealousy. It took her ages to win promotion from the position of lowly scullery maid, and anyone now in that role and showing promise, might upstage the kitchen maid and have her sent below to once again work at the grimiest level.

Cook grumbled and the two younger women made furtive glances at the older woman. Clara worked quickly and produced the pot containing the two dozen freshly peeled spuds.

'Please Cook, where shall I put them?' she asked.

A nod of her head from Cook indicated the end of the table as the older woman set off for the pantry. Clara stood back wondering what her new task would be. Mary moved to check on Cook's location then hurried to the pot and knocked it to the floor. Clara gawped.

Mary yelled. 'You stupid girl; you clumsy, useless idiot.'

Cook arrived at her usual speed—obesity regulated her travel time—and stared at the floor covered with potatoes.

'What da hell are you doin?'

Clara glanced at her accuser and wondered what she should say. She wondered if telling the truth would work for her.

*Mary is an old hand and may well be trusted. I have no credibility. But if I take the blame, will I be sacked on my first day?*

Cook panicked. Her head was on the line. 'Well don't stand dere, girl, pick 'em up.'

Clara knelt and placed the potatoes in the pot. Cook's mind raced planning to have the meal ready on time. Mary gloated. Mrs Beadle arrived. On the floor out of sight, Clara froze awaiting the chop.

'Panic over,' said the housekeeper. 'I misread the calendar. Sir William and Lady Howard are coming *next* week.' She went to leave but stopped. 'And send that new scullery maid to my room. Tell her to bring her things.' She left and Clara stood.

The three kitchen staff looked at one another. Cook spoke to Clara. 'You 'ave da luck of the Irish, girlie. Now be on y'way, an' it's da last door on da right.'

Clara placed the pot of recycled spuds on the table, collected her bag, bonnet and coat, and scurried away. Cook looked at Mary who failed again and found her insides churning with anger.

The scullery maid arrived at the housekeeper's room, knocked gently and waited.

'Come in.' Clara entered and closed the door. Mrs Beadle waggled her finger and Clara moved forward. 'Before we go to your room, I want you to be clear about how we work at Bittering Hall.'

She paused and Clara decided to speak. 'Yes, Mrs Beadle.'

'Lord Rallison is a great believer in the saying that servants may be seen but never heard. Being mostly below stairs, there is little chance you will ever be seen but woe betide if you ever make a racket. Work hard, in silence, and you might survive.'

Another pause and Clara spoke again. 'Yes, Mrs Beadle.'

'And one more thing; the Marquess has two sons. The younger, Lord Rupert is a fine upstanding gentleman with no interest in females, above or below stairs.' No euphemism was intended. 'The other, Crispin, is an Earl, a cad who treats women, especially servants, with contempt.' A pause endured. Clara didn't speak.

'Be on your guard.' The housekeeper stared at Clara feeling she'd done her duty as a superior and as a woman. 'Follow me.'

She led Clara through the bowels of the house then up a flight of back stairs, narrow and mean. Clara thought the climb would never end. It did and revealed her accommodation.

A large broom cupboard described it well, and consisted of a single bed, a chamber pot, a frightened table with a washing bowl, jug and candle, and a single nervous chair. A window near the ceiling offered little light and a limited view of the Norfolk sky.

'You wash here or in the yard. You rise at 5 and light the stove. You clean all the ground floor fireplaces and light the fire in the breakfast room and main sitting room. Once Lord and Lady Rallison come down to breakfast, you do the same with the fireplace in their bedrooms.' Clara's enthusiasm at hearing the news of her new employment situation began to come alive. *I've made it*, she purred.

'Only when all those tasks are complete may you have your breakfast, and always in the kitchen with Cook and Mary. Any questions?'

Clara struggled, afraid to ask anything. 'No, Mrs Beadle.'

'Then put away your belongings and return to the kitchen. Oh, and don't let anyone see you carrying your chamber pot downstairs. Empty it during the night.' Clara thought. *Where?*

Thus ended the induction. Mrs Beadle departed and the sound of her footsteps seemed to last forever. Clara sat on her bed. Was it made of stone? She was cold in November. What would it be like in February?


In the kitchen, neither woman looked up when Clara returned. She was about to speak when a voice sounded behind her.

'Hello, hello, and who have we got here?'

Clara turned to face a tall, young man with a smile as wide as his thin face.

'She's the new scullery maid,' said Mary with a voice of disdain.

'My name's Francis but everyone calls me Frankie. I'm his Lordship's valet, footman and self-appointed majordomo.' He held out his hand and Clara shook it.

'I'm Clara.'

'Welcome Clara, how are you settling in?'

'Quite well, thank you,' she replied much to Mary's displeasure.

'We're a happy bunch here below stairs,' said Frankie and addressed Mary. 'Aren't we, Mary?'

She snorted.

Cook interrupted. 'I've given dem potatoes you spilt to the pigs. Peel me a few new 'uns.' She indicated with her head.

Clara set to work. Frankie wandered around and poured himself a cup of tea but copped the cold shoulder.

'Do y'mind?' said Cook. 'Some of us 'ave work t'do.'

Frankie took his tea and gave Clara a wink as he left.

Cook went to the larder, which Mary knew was her excuse to have a nip of brandy from the supply she kept hidden behind the flour.

'I forgot to tell you,' said Mary. 'You have to fetch coal from the cellar when it's needed.' Clara looked at her enemy who offered a poker face. 'As you can see, it's needed.'

Clara looked at the empty coal bucket and placed her knife on the bench. 'Where is the cellar?'

'Where is the cellar, please Miss Mary?' replied the maid.

Clara repeated the question without a trace of resentment although by now she wanted to slap her fellow servant who she guessed was a year or two older.

Mary gave directions and Clara departed carrying the coal bucket. The cellar was dark and dangerous. Leaving the door open provided a little light. A large pile of the black stuff sat in the far corner. Picking up a small shovel, Clara began to fill the bucket.

She jumped when a loud noise exploded. The door slammed shut and blackness filled the cellar. 'Hey!' cried Clara now scared. She called again and heard nothing. She approached the cellar door treading warily in the darkness. She tripped and threw out her hands for protection leaving her head free to bang against an oak pillar.

Pain joined her fear. Crying came easy as she struggled towards the door. She found it by feeling, and tried turning the handle. No joy. It wouldn't budge and her calling proved futile. She gave up, collapsed on the floor in the dirt and sobbed. Then she screamed at the sensation of a rat running across her body making her misery complete.

Her greatest fear would be telling her parents she'd run away. They tried so hard to find her work, and now she planned to spurn the opportunity and would let them down.

In the darkness, she crawled back towards the coal heap, found the bucket and small shovel. She stood, whacked the bucket and shouted for help, hoping at least it would frighten the rat.

She heard nothing, stopped making sounds, and wanted to die.

'Hello?' A male voice sounded outside. It sounded again. 'Hello?'

Clara came alive. 'Hello. I'm in the cellar. Can you please help me?'

'Okay, stay there,' called the male, and Clara's heart sprinted. She heard sounds of a bolt being withdrawn then grunting, as a wooden covering creaked open and light flooded the cellar.

Clara shielded her eyes. The outline of a man appeared. 'What's wrong with the door to the corridor?' he asked.

'It's locked. I've tried shouting and knocking but no-one came.'

'Right, hang on, I'll be back.'

He disappeared. Clara wiped her tears not knowing she smeared her face with coal dust. The man returned and ordered her to move back. A ladder was lowered into the cellar.

'Can you climb out?' he asked.

'I'll try,' she said and began to climb. The ladder wobbled but Clara took it one rung at a time. She looked straight ahead at the cellar wall. Near the top, she took fright when a hand appeared in front of her face. She stopped and looked up at the smiling face of Harold, the Bittering Hall groom.

'Give me your hand.' She did and he guided her to terra firma. He studied her. She studied herself and saw the mess on her apron, dress and hands. Tears re-appeared. He spoke kindly.

'Would you like to wash your face and hands before you go back inside?'

'Yes please and thank you so much for rescuing me.'

'This way,' he said heading to the stables. 'What's your name?'

'I'm Clara the new scullery maid.'

'Well, Clara, the new scullery maid, welcome to Bittering Hall.'

Clara survived her coal cellar experience when saved by the groom. Her gratitude bubbled over as he led her to the pump and filled a bucket with water.

'Wait here,' he said. 'I'll be back in a minute.'

He returned with a cake of soap and a towel, itself in urgent need of a wash. Clara's heart glowed.

'Thank you ever so much,' she said not being sure what to call him.

'I'm Harold the groom and everyone calls me Harry.'

She scrubbed her face and hands and didn't hesitate in using the grubby towel. Alas her apron looked awful, thanks to the coal cellar.

'I gather you've had a run in with the lovely Mary.'

Clara looked at him not sure how to respond. She played it safe. 'I think I accidentally locked myself in.'

He grinned. 'I believe you, thousands wouldn't.' They shared a stare. 'Come and have a look at my hidey hole.' He took the towel and soap and walked to the stables. Clara followed.

'Thank you for being so kind, Harry.'

He stopped and smiled. 'We victims of the bullies should stick together, Clara. Come and meet the horses.'

He led her to the boxes introducing Clara to his charges. She spoke to each one while observing the young man.

He looked about 20 with no distinguishing features. Medium height, average looks, average build and a personality sort of average. She thought of calling him Harry Average. There seemed little chance the groom would ever sweep her off her feet. But boy was he kind.

'I'll be getting back,' she said, 'and thanks again for coming to my rescue.'

She started to leave but stopped when he spoke. 'You might need to take that.' He pointed to a bucket of coal. 'You'll give Miss Mary a real surprise when you waltz in carrying that. She probably thinks you're still locked in the cellar.'

'Are you sure?' asked Clara.

'Of course and good luck.'

She returned his smile, picked up the bucket, and headed back to the kitchen. When she entered, Cook and Mary looked up with Cook reacting to the filthy apron.

'Mother of God, girlie, what 'ave you been doin'?'

Mary froze, unable to speak.

'I've been fetching coal, Cook.' She put the bucket by the stove. 'I'll wash my apron right away.'

'If Mrs Beadle sees you like dat, you'll be on your way. Now go.'

In the laundry, Clara scrubbed her apron. She rinsed the garment and pegged it on the line then turned when she heard footsteps.

'Think y'self pretty clever,' said Mary with arms folded.

'Clara,' called Mrs Beadle, giving the scullery maid a reason to flee.

Mary walked to the line, looked around, picked up a handful of dirt and moved to the apron. As she went to smear the dirt on the newly washed garment, she froze.

'I wouldn't if I was you.'

Harry stood watching. Mary snorted, tossed the dirt away and, clapping her hands to clean them, went back inside, quietly fuming.

Back in the stables, Harry brushed a horse when the estate owner strode in. Harold tugged his forelock. 'Good day to you, m'Lord.'

'My sons are coming for the hunt this weekend. I require all horses in fine fettle and looking magnificent.'

'Very good, m'Lord,' said the groom again tugging his forelock.

The estate owner turned on his heel and left as Harry continued to brush the horse. 'Did you hear that, Goliath? Let's hope you don't get lumbered with the nasty brother.'

Lord Rallison's two sons were chalk and cheese. Rupert stored kindness inside his heart, and filled his saddlebags with compassion. Crispin couldn't even spell moral compass. Workers on the estate avoided the evil sibling. They dreaded the fact Crispin seemed to be, and in effect was above the law. Complaining about the brute meant a thrashing or instant dismissal. Rumour had it Crispin once killed an estate worker in a fit of rage with the body buried in secret.

Over the years, he harassed lowly female members of staff, forcing himself upon them and ordering them to say nothing. His threats were frightening. Nothing ever happened to the appalling Crispin.

As Harry brushed the horse, he wondered if he should say anything to the new scullery maid. Her slim, slight body and obvious youthful innocence would be no match for Crispin the blaggard. Once Master Evil arrived, Harry thought he might whisk Clara away to guarantee her survival. Trying to sleep, he struggled, worrying about the hunt and Lord Rallison's loathsome bastard of a son.

Upstairs in her pocket handkerchief bedroom, Clara settled down for her first night away from home. Her candle set shadows dancing. She wrapped a shawl around her shoulders and slipped into bed. The house slept. She decided to lock the door with no lock. She placed the single chair under the door knob and jiggled it to make it secure.

Blowing out the candle, she hopped into bed. Apart from Harry the groom and Frankie the valet, the others treated her with cruelty or disinterest.

Drifting to sleep, she woke with a start hearing footsteps climbing the stairs. Clara breathed quietly as the footsteps stopped. The door knob turned.

In the darkness, Clara saw nothing but heard everything. The door was pushed but stayed shut. The person outside tried to force it. Still the chair did its job.

Staying silent was Clara's plan. The door rattling stopped and a whisper sounded.

'You'll keep,' said the visitor with Clara certain it was Mary.

Having no clock and believing her being late would see her dismissed, Clara willed herself to wake, and in the dark, rose, dressed and tip-toed downstairs carrying her chamber pot and shoes. Her noiseless stockinged feet couldn't prevent every creak in the stairs saying, "I know you're there". The household was silent and dark. Creeping into the kitchen, she squinted at the large clock on the wall.

'Four thirty,' she whispered and went outside to finish her ablutions.

Now decision time beckoned. *If I go back to bed for even half an hour and fall asleep, I'll be sacked.* She began work.

She'd lit fires at home and seen her parents do it often. Goodness, her father was a blacksmith. She lit the fire in the stove, put a kettle in position and sliced a loaf of bread. She made herself a cuppa, found butter and marmalade jam and toasted the bread. What a life.

Time dragged. She put on her shoes and a clean apron and decided to make an early start. She lit a candle and carried it upstairs to the breakfast room. With brush and pan, she cleaned the fireplace. Then she set and lit a fire, feeling great as the flames roared and the coal glowed. She did the same in the main sitting room.

When Mary appeared—Cook had perfected the art of sleeping in— the kitchen maid couldn't believe the stove was lit and there were fires in the two rooms upstairs.

Clara perfected the turn-the-other-cheek routine. 'Good morning, Mary,' she said with a hint of a smile. Her enemy was smashed with politeness and respect. It was hard to fight when your opponent refused to surrender or worse, join the fisticuffs.

Cook arrived and made no comment. Her kitchen was ready to roll. It's what she expected. She looked at Clara.

'Lady Rallison has come down. Have you attended to her room?'

Clara looked nervous then surprised when Mary spoke. 'I'll show her,' she said and headed up the back stairs with Clara following. From the landing, Mary pointed. 'It's the last door on the left.'

Clara stood shocked as Mary bounced back downstairs. *Why is she helping me?* At the bedroom door, Clara knocked, waited, and heard nothing so entered. She left the door open and cleaned then set the fire. Finished, she left and closed the door. A loud male voice barked.

'Who are you?'

Clara turned, looked at an impatient Lord Rallison, and bobbed.

'I'm Clara, m'Lord, the new scullery maid.'

He stared making Clara uncomfortable. 'Clean my fireplace, and make sure you help with the hunt.'

He left for the main stairs. She bobbed again, attended to his room then took the back stairs to the kitchen.

*Have I met everyone?*


The weather did its best to make the hunt a success. Clara proved reliable. Her instructions were crystal clear.

'You fetch and carry,' said Mrs Beadle. 'Only the males serve the riders but you must have the trays ready with all glasses full. Understood?'

'Yes, Mrs Beadle.'

Harry and Frankie and two of the gardeners moved among the horses offering a stirrup cup to each rider. All drank port although Frankie knew to offer his Master and the horrid Earl Crispin a whisky. The dogs found their patience running thin. They ran around, tails aloft, champing at their invisible bit. They waited for the sound of the horn. Clara watched from a distance ensuring the next tray of drinks was ready. Lord Rallison shouted at regular intervals. His son Crispin mimicked his pater while the younger son, Rupert, showed manners and respect.

Drinks consumed, the leader of the hunt sounded the start. The riders and dogs departed. Clara carried a tray of cups inside then washed and dried them.

Harry helped and spoke quietly. 'A word of advice, Miss Scullery Maid; stay well clear of Earl Crispin; never ever confront him.'

Clara worried. This was a second Crispin warning. 'But working below stairs means I will never have cause to even speak to him.'

'You may have to prepare the fire in his room. Only do so when he is far, far away.'

Silent, Clara wondered why the groom said what he did.

He stared at her wondering how he could say what he wanted to say without terrifying the girl. 'Earl Crispin has a reputation. He treats the staff, particularly females, badly.' Clara sensed fear. 'My best advice is if he can't find you, he can't hurt you.' He paused. 'The best way to avoid trouble is to avoid the troublemaker.'

'Thank you. That's the third time you've been kind to me.'

He smiled with closed lips then returned to the stable.


Clara thought about Harry's words as she worked in the kitchen helping prepare food for members of the hunt. The day went well. The hunt was successful, the luncheon well received and with Christmas approaching, it was a busy time for all.

It was late when Cook sent Clara to bed. She was halfway up the stairs when the noise began. A male voice shouted and a wall copped a slap.

'Where are you, you little hussy. I'll find you.'

Peering aloft, she saw Earl Crispin, the worse for wear, angry at having found her room empty. Not for a second did she consider continuing her journey upstairs but quietly hurried outside to the stables.

'Harry?' she whispered. 'Are you there, Harry?'

Looking surprised and holding a lantern, he appeared in a night shirt. 'Clara? What's happened?'

'Earl Crispin is calling for me outside my bedroom.'

Harry shook his head. 'Did he see you?'

'I don't think so. What should I do?'

'Nothing. He'll run out of steam, retire and sleep it off. I'll check to see if he's gone. Wait here.'

Harry left and Clara realised her heart was racing. She sat on a bale of straw and wondered if taking this job was wise. *If the son is a brute and his parents don't know or care, how will I be safe?*

She heard rapid footsteps and panicked. Harry rushed in. 'Quick, under that straw.'

He helped her and was about to blow out the lantern when Crispin appeared.

'Hey you, groom, where's that new scullery maid?'

'Good evening, my Lord.'

'She's not in her room and I want to welcome her to the Hall.'

'The maids are not allowed in here, sir. Have you tried the kitchen or laundry?'

Crispin stared at Harry then pointed at him. 'You know I always like to welcome new maids to the estate. Make sure she comes to see me before I leave tomorrow.'

'Of course, my Lord, and good night to you, sir.'

Crispin produced a coin and tossed it to Harry who caught it. 'There's another if you tell me when she's abed.'

The wealthy son and heir left. Harry waited, blew out his lantern then whispered. 'He's gone. You can come out now.'

In the darkness, Clara appeared. They stared at one another.

'Thank you,' she whispered. She paused, then stepped forward, stood on tip-toe, and kissed his cheek. He indicated behind her.

'If you climb that ladder, you'll be safe till the morning.'

She did and was.

# Chapter 3

Christmas at Bittering Hall was always the same. The family gathered, feasting and drinking took place, and the servants ate the crumbs that fell from the rich man's table. With the Rallison sons at home for a week, Clara followed her stay-out-of-sight plan.

She settled into a routine, was ignored rather than bullied by Mary, and enjoyed her slow-burning friendship with Harry. She wrote to her parents with news of her progress, and hoped to go home for a day visit early in the New Year.

On Christmas Eve, she busied herself in the coal cellar when a voice sent a chill through her body. Earl Crispin invaded the kitchen demanding a kiss from all the females. Clara stayed put.

Once his voice faded, she ventured out. 'Where were you?' asked Mary. 'Earl Crispin always demands a kiss at Christmas and was not best pleased you weren't here.'

Clara looked at Mary's inscrutable face. Mrs Beadle entered.

'More fires to clean and light, Clara. If any guests complain of the cold, there'll be hell to pay. Do you understand?'

'Yes, Mrs Beadle.'

'And come down during the night to check on the oven.'

'Yes, Mrs Beadle.'

It was late. The back stairs were doubly freezing at this time of year and Clara shivered as she climbed. Her mind raced as she knew the brute of a brother, the son who did as he pleased, was at home and more than likely on the prowl.

Now about to turn sixteen, her body began to blossom. Her sex education was limited and what little she knew of getting pregnant made her hug herself and ponder ways to avoid trouble.

Her candle threw shadows on the walls and the same wooden steps made the same creaking sounds. Would her simple chair work as a lock on her door? She thought about going to the stables.

The silence in the house sounded loud as she reached the landing. She twisted the door handle, and went to push the door. It moved without her help half pulling her inside. Clutching her candle meant one hand was occupied. The door flew open thanks to a person inside. Clara stumbled, stifled a scream, and fell into her room.

In a flash, the door was closed, she was dragged to the invader, and the burning candle dropped to the floor.

Everything happened so quickly, it took but a second for Clara's heart to explode and her fear to run wild.

Crispin Rallison was up for what he considered a bit of fun. Females, and particularly those below stairs, were fair game. This particular wench had avoided him until now. She was to be his Christmas present. Forget the mistletoe. No preliminaries required.

'Now, my darling,' he sneered grabbing the young girl in a rough embrace and planting his mouth on hers complete with flavours of whisky and tobacco. He considered his rough stubble a bonus.

Trying to scream, resist or flee was impossible. He positioned himself between her and the door. The room became a torture chamber. His hands began to roam. Her fear caught fire. She froze.

As he prepared to throw her on the bed, she managed to scream. He loved that, thinking it part of her pathetic resistance, which it was, but her concern centred on their possible death. The fallen candle set fire to her second pair of stockings and threatened to spread.

'Fire,' she gasped and the word stopped the attacker, momentarily. He saw the flames and postponed his conquest. He stamped on the flames and as he did, Clara hopped up and grabbed the door. She was out and heading downstairs when he flew after her. She tripped and fell grabbing the bannister. Her physical pain rivalled the terror in her brain. He arrived, grinning in the dark, and helped her to stand by grasping her hair and yanking.

'I like a woman with fire in her belly.' He dragged her upstairs and back into the normally darkened room. But this Christmas was blessed with a clear sky, and moonlight peered in through the small window near the ceiling.

'How about I put some real fire in your belly?' Clara went to speak, to protest, to beg for release but said nothing as Lord Rallison's son slapped the scullery maid's face with venom. His definition of seduction involved violence and intimidation.

She surrendered. What else could she do? Forget about losing her virginity, now her life was at stake. She tried keeping her knees together. She tried to cry and failed. His weight and brutality won and the young girl suffered a brutal rape. Is there any other type? Being young and innocent, the trauma consumed her.

The law would never be involved and besides, the age of consent in this green and pleasant land was currently 12 years of age. Why, this wench has to be at least 16.

Her visitor, having satiated his lust, adjusted his clothing and left. At the door, he turned and spoke. 'Now don't you ever hide from me again, wench. Oh, and Merry Christmas, bitch.'

Time didn't exist. Physically she ached all over. Lying still on her bed brought no relief. Making even the slightest movement sent arrows of pain surging through her body.

He left her desolate, numb, and bereft of any emotion. She couldn't create tears. She sobbed inside, thought of her parents and desperately wanted to go home. But if she fled, what would she tell her parents? The truth? What then? Would she be blamed? Would her parents be angry, disown her? Surely not once the truth was told.

And if she decided to stay, how could she work with Mrs Beadle, Cook and Mary? They would know what happened. Eventually everyone would know; the rapist hardly tip-toed downstairs. He was proud of his mighty achievement.

The thought of climbing onto the roof and throwing herself to the flagstones below didn't cross her mind, it festered there.

She fell asleep having no idea of the time. A cock crowing woke her. She touched her body and winced. Feeling moisture, she wept. Struggling out of bed, she lit her candle and peed. It was red. Now she was wide awake in a nightmare.

Tidying herself as best she could, Clara dressed and crept downstairs fearing anyone and anything. The house slept.

Snow fell but she crept into the yard and tried to fill a bucket with water. It arrived bitterly cold. Using rags she washed her bruised body. The freezing water shocked her to life. And *what* a life. It now faced ruin and she could tell no one or ask anyone for help.

The Bible tells us: "In this world you will have trouble." Clara agreed with Jesus and managed to find an inner strength. The bullying she previously suffered hurt but her reaction to it and the bullies helped her now. Now she set out to survive again. She entered a brutal world where innocence and kindness fled. Her choice was plain; run away or stay and fight. She stayed.

There was no speech, no urging herself onward. She now knew how a dead person viewed life; blackness. Surely her heart was broken, and yet, while dead inside, she started her work.

When the others came into the kitchen there were greetings. Mrs Beadle carried a small gift for Cook, Mary and Clara. 'Where's Clara?' asked the housekeeper.

'She's lit the stove and fires,' said Cook.

'Here she is,' said Mary as Clara arrived carrying a bucket of coal. Her face was bruised and red.

'What happened to you?' asked Cook without a shred of compassion. The others stared.

'I slipped on the stairs,' said Clara and turned away.

Mrs Beadle held out a small wrapped present. 'This is for you, Clara. Merry Christmas.' Clara froze, nodded and accepted the gift.

'Thank you, Mrs Beadle,' she whispered.

'When you do the fires upstairs, don't forget to attend to Earl Crispin. He's very particular.'

He certainly was particular, although Clara thought more along the lines of evil and vile. A dagger plunged into her heart.

She was fit to collapse. Having to even think about the monster, or hear his name, set off a pain in her chest. The thought of having to enter the brute's bedchamber caused her brain to explode. Dizziness swamped her body. She headed outside and stumbled through the snow. The biting cold helped her stay upright. She kept walking and only stopped when her name was called.

'Clara? What are you doing out in this weather?'

She stopped and looked at the speaker. In the pre-dawn she faced Harry then collapsed. He ran, picked her up and carried her into the stable. His cubby hole was warm and he placed her on the straw and wrapped her in blankets.

'Are you ill?' Her eyes shouted pain. He fetched a small flask of rum and held it to her lips. She swallowed a little and coughed. He waited for her to speak, afraid to ask what happened.

'I need to go inside,' she croaked.

'No, you need to stay here and rest,' he said and his kindness was overwhelming. She wondered. *Is there kindness in this world?*

'Mrs Beadle will be looking for me. The vegetables need to be prepared, the pots washed and the ...' She couldn't say the words.

'What? What else?'

She struggled. 'The fires upstairs have not been cleaned and set.'

'I'll do those. When Lord and Lady Rallison come down, I'll sneak up and do them for you.' She paused, confusing him. 'What's wrong?'

'I need to attend to the rooms of Earl Crispin and Lord Rupert.'

A terrible thought popped into Harry's brain. He was unsure but dreaded the truth. He knew the girl needed protection, safety. 'You don't have to go to their rooms. I'll do them all.'

She wept silently. He lifted her upper body and hugged her and she let him hold her tight. She wanted to tell someone but couldn't bring herself to do so, at least not a man. She was a typical victim who embraced shame and blamed herself when to do so was ridiculously wrong.

He gave her a handkerchief and helped repair her teary face. Then he helped her stand and walked her back towards the kitchen.

'I'll look after you, Clara. You go back to bed and rest. I'll do your work and I'll see that brute never comes anywhere near you.'

A sinking feeling told him his kindness was far too late. He kept talking trying to sound as if everything was normal. He knew it wasn't and the pit of his stomach rumbled. At the back door, he kissed her hand and watched her slip inside. If only he knew.

# Chapter 4

Clara endured the festive season thanks largely, no solely to the kind and caring groom. He went out of his way to protect her from harm.

After New Year, the guests, including Lord Rallison's chalk 'n cheese sons, packed up and their caravan left town. Life returned to normal although not for Clara who kept reliving her night of terror.

Her body began to repair itself and she dared not ask to consult a doctor or anyone. Her problem would never be discussed.

But then, weeks later, it happened. Her abdomen moved. Lying in bed, she touched it, and the thought set fire to her brain. *I am with child.*

This was terrifying. *Is it true?* Who could she ask? What would she say? Was she damned to hellfire?

As if the attack itself was not monstrous enough, now she suffered a new and enduring agony. The joy of becoming a mother, for Clara became torture, a constant, soul-destroying fear.

She could hide her ever-swelling belly today but for how long? And where would she have the baby? And far, far worse, what would she do with the infant? Keep it? Kill it? Her mind caught fire with decisions and problems and thoughts of horrible endings.

She lay in bed, unable to sleep and with her hands on her abdomen touching the new life within. *When is it due? How can I tell my parents? What will I say?* She decided to ask to come home.

The strain, the pressure became immense. Without thinking, she slipped out of bed, crept downstairs, walked through the darkened kitchen, out into the yard and headed to the stables.

A horse neighed. She put a finger to her lips encouraging the animal to relax but froze when a voice spoke.

'Clara? Is that you?'

Harry stood there holding a lantern.

As if being controlled by a puppeteer, Clara walked towards him. 'I need to tell you something.'

They sat in his room as she told the tale. Harry couldn't speak. As she revealed the pregnancy, she wept. He copied her, silently.

'I do not know what to do, Harry. You are the only person I have told. You are the only person I *can* tell. Will you help me?'

'What a damn silly question.' Harry surprised himself. He acted calmly and with respect. He took control giving Clara hope, even a vague belief her life might improve.

'Go back upstairs and try to sleep. I will take care of this matter.'

'No, Harry, I do not want you to suffer. It is my fault and I must take responsibility.'

Clara recoiled at his anger. 'Never, ever say those words,' he hissed, 'never! Your fault? What kind of nonsense is that? You've done nothing wrong and Mr Evil must pay for his wicked crime.'

Clara's mouth opened and stayed open. He took her arm and led her outside and back to the kitchen.

'Go back to bed and stay there. I will do your work in the morning and come and fetch you when it's done.'

She looked at him through weepy eyes. She whispered, 'Thank you.' He hugged her.

'Now go,' he said and watched her cross the kitchen and disappear up the back stairs.

Harry was waiting in the kitchen when Mary came in. The fire in the stove was on song. The fire in the breakfast room had been alight for an hour.

What are you doing here?' asked Mary starting her chores.

'Clara is unwell and is to stay in bed.'

Mary stopped working. 'Says who?'

'All her fire tasks are complete and I will do whatever else needs to be done.'

Cook entered and Mary told her the news.

'What's wrong with her?' asked Cook, 'and how come you know so much? Have you been seducing the girl? His Lordship'll skin you alive when he finds out.'

'Leave the poor girl alone. I'll cover for her and will speak to Lord Rallison on her behalf. Just leave her be.'

He strode out leaving the two women staring at one another. Mrs Beadle came in. 'Why are you standing about?'

Cook spoke. 'Clara is poorly, Mrs Beadle.'

'What's wrong with her?' Neither domestic spoke. 'How do you know she's unwell?'

Cook became the spokeswoman. 'Harold told us.'

'Harold? How does he know? Are they cohabiting?'

Mary wasn't sure what cohabiting meant but had a pretty good idea. Cook shrugged. Mrs Beadle snapped at Mary. 'Tell Harold I want to see him in my room, now!'

Mrs Beadle left and Cook spoke. 'Off you go and no cohabiting.'


Harry racked his brains trying to think of the words to tell Lord Rallison about his bastard son, the one who created a bastard. Each sentence came up against a powerful answer from the landowner.

The groom heard soft footsteps and dreaded the fact that Clara had defied him and left her room. He stepped into the corridor with the horse boxes and was shocked to see Mary.

'Mrs Beadle wants to see you in her room right away.'

He stared at Mary. 'What have you been saying?'

'I think the question is have you and Clara been cohabiting?'

He too wasn't sure about the word but walked past Mary, headed inside and knocked on Mrs Beadle's open door.

'Come in and explain yourself.'

'I don't know what you mean, Mrs Beadle.'

'What is wrong with Clara and what have you and she been up to?'

'I heard she's unwell and told her I would tell you and Cook.'

'And?'

'I did her tasks this morning so the kitchen would run as usual and I'll do her other tasks till she's better. That's all there is, Mrs Beadle.'

'You know I have to report this to Lord Rallison.'

'Thank you,' said Harry.

She paused unsure about his calm, unworried demeanour.

'You know this means the sack for you *and* the girl. You might as well start packing now. I'll go and see His Lordship at breakfast.'

'May I come too, Mrs Beadle?'

She sucked in air. 'Certainly not. How dare you ask such a thing?'

'I'm afraid there's more to the situation than meets the eye.'

She fumed mainly because it appeared she might be ignorant of all the facts. She certainly was ignorant. 'What do you mean?'

Harry paused. 'I'd rather tell Lord Rallison in person, Mrs Beadle, if that's all right with you.'

'It most certainly is not.'

'Then I regret, Mrs Beadle, I have nothing more to say. Good day.'

He gave a slight nod and walked out leaving the housekeeper with red cheeks and enough bluster to dry the washing.

Harry waited outside the kitchen, kicking his heels. Mary came out and spoke to him. 'You're to do the fireplaces upstairs.'

He followed her inside but stopped when Mrs Beadle appeared. 'Come with me.' He followed her to the breakfast room. 'Wait here.'

She entered closing the door. Lord Rallison's raised voice boomed. 'Bring him here,' was heard and Mrs Beadle fetched the groom.

Harry entered cap in hand. He tugged his forelock to Lord and Lady Rallison. She ignored him, nibbled toast and read a letter. His Lordship put down a newspaper and addressed the employee.

'Mrs Beadle tells me you've been a naughty boy. You know the rules. You can pack and leave and don't even think about asking for a reference.'

Harry looked at Mrs Beadle who indicated the door with her head. The groom stood still.

'May I have a word, my Lord?' The landowner stopped, surprised at the groom's reply. 'It's about Earl Crispin.'

The fire crackled in the breakfast room but the atmosphere froze and remained frozen.

'I can still thrash you while you're on my land,' said the Marquess, getting his retaliation in first.

'What I have to say, sir, may be better said between two men.'

Lord Rallison looked at the housekeeper. 'Thank you, Mrs Beadle.'

She looked aghast but naturally did as asked. Lord Rallison made no effort to have his wife leave the room.

'This better be good.'

Harry tried deep breathing. He pressed his hands against his body to stop them shaking. 'The scullery maid, Clara, is with child, my Lord, and the father is Earl Crispin.'

The greater reaction came from Lady Rallison. 'Oh for God's sake,' she hissed throwing down both marmalade and missive. Her reaction reeked of disgust and frustration.

'There was no willingness on the girl's part, my Lord. Your son entered the maid's room uninvited and forced himself upon her.'

Lord Rallison snapped. 'How do you know? Were you there?'

'She was badly injured, my Lord. Your son hid in the room, waited until the maid climbed the stairs then attacked her. This was not the first time he tried to seduce her. Once when Earl Crispin came looking for Clara, I hid the girl in a stable. She was terrified of the man and is terrified even more now she is expecting his child.'

The landowner fumed. This wasn't the first time his selfish brute of a son attacked a servant girl although this was the first known pregnancy. 'She'll have to go. Send her back to her parents.'

'They may not accept her, my Lord. They may think she has brought great shame on the family name.'

'Well she can't stay here. This is not a poorhouse for bastards.'

'She has no money, my Lord.'

Lady Rallison spoke out. 'Pay her off and send her away.'

Lord Rallison stood. 'Wait here.' He departed and, opening the door, forced Mrs Beadle to scurry from the keyhole. He glared at her. 'Fetch the girl.' He stormed down the corridor and when he returned, Clara stood shaking outside the room beside Mrs Beadle.

Lord Rallison led the way. 'Inside,' he snapped and Harry turned to see Clara and Mrs Beadle enter. Harry smiled and discretely held out a hand. Clara moved and stood next to him.

'Make it quick,' said Lady Rallison hating the situation.

'I'll give you money,' said Lord Rallison. 'You must leave the district and never mention my son. Two coins landed on the table.

Clara hesitated. Harry spoke. 'I'm sorry, my Lord, but there may be a better way to handle the situation.'

Mrs Beadle gasped at the audacity of the young man. Lady Rallison ground her teeth, and her husband looked around for a whip. Harry remained calm and, in effect, took control.

'The solution, my Lord, is to have the child raised by a married couple who will give their name to the babe and raise it with love.'

The others were stunned. Lord Rallison scoffed. 'And where will you find this married couple?'

'We stand before you, my Lord.'

This knockout punch stunned everyone but none more so than Clara. Harry turned to her. 'If Clara will marry me, I'll care for her, and we can raise the child as our own.'

Here was a first; a marriage proposal in the breakfast room at Bittering Hall.

Clara shed a tear and joined her hand to Harry's. A stronger acceptance would never be seen. Even Mrs Beadle's heart softened.

The landowner desperately wanted to remove the problem and realised he was staring at a gift horse. He ignored its teeth.

'Right, you put your name on the church record, leave the area and never return.' He tossed two more coins on the table.

Harry hesitated sending the tension skyrocketing.

'I'm sorry, my Lord, but your offer is unfair considering the protection of your good name, and the costs we now will face.'

Puce well described His Lordship's complexion. He looked ready to strike Harry but stopped when his wife shouted. 'Ten pounds!' It sounded like an order. Her husband froze. Being told what to do by anyone was a first, and by a working class nobody in the form of his groom was unthinkable.

'And a reference too if you please, my Lord,' added Harry feeling sure he would get a thrashing. His punt paid off. Everyone knew Harry and Clara, held most, if not all the cards.

Begrudgingly, His Lordship tossed the money on the table then whispered with hatred. 'I'll give the reference to Mrs Beadle.' He roared. 'Now get out!'


Holding hands, the couple hurried to the kitchen. Having heard raised voices, Mary and Cook were all ears.

'We're leaving and getting married,' said Harry, and Clara smiled for the first time in this kitchen. He kissed his future bride and sent her upstairs to collect her meagre possessions.

The others didn't know what to say. Cook broke the silence. 'Good luck to both of you. Where will you go?'

'I fancy London,' said Harry and went to the stable to pack, leaving the kitchen crew speechless.

# Chapter 5

Despite Clara's protests, Harry insisted they go to her parents. His family lived in Northumberland, he knew not where. The couple walked to Little Tinker. It rained the whole way and when they arrived at Clara's father's forge, shock and surprise hit Mr and Mrs Sutcliffe. Their pregnant daughter appeared unannounced but thankfully, with a man willing to become her husband.

The young couple decided to say that Harry was the father of the child, or rather speak and act as if such was the case.

Clara's parents were relieved more than delighted to see their daughter about to wed even with a bairn on the way. They took the couple in, helped with the wedding plans, and the happy event was held at the earliest possible time. Clara's sister, Daisy, was visiting their aunt in Winterton-on-Sea and missed the whole shebang.

On their wedding night, the couple whispered in their room. 'I will never be able to thank you enough, Harry, for marrying me and taking care of the baby. I think you are a saint.'

He hugged her. 'You're going to have to stop saying that,' he said.

'My parents want us to stay here for as long as we like.'

'They're kind like their daughter but you know we can't. If Lord Rallison discovers we're in the area, who knows what he might do?'

'How will he find out?'

'You mean you've never heard of wagging tongues?'

She understood and thinking about their future together gave her goosebumps.

'Where shall we go and when?'

'To London and soon. Everyone's going to the cities. At the market last month, three chaps told me they were off, one to Birmingham and two to London. With Lord Rallison's reference I'm sure to find work with horses. We'll rent a cottage and raise our family.'

Clara loved the idea of living in a cottage. She'd never been out of Norfolk and, like her new husband, had an innocence and ignorance about life in London. There the population boomed leaving a dire shortage of cottages with hollyhocks around the door and, even worse, with the Great Stink getting up a head of steam.

The baby bump grew bigger and pressure to leave Little Tinker increased when Mrs Beadle saw them, and they her, in Castle Stop. She didn't acknowledge them but hurried away.

'We must go, Clara,' said Harry. 'I have three pounds and eight shillings in savings plus the ten pounds from Lord Rallison. That will keep us for a while and I'm sure to find work so we'll be fine. Will you tell your parents?'

Clara nodded through moist eyes.

Her father took the young couple in his cart. Clara's mother came too. They headed to Norwich and the departure point for the London coach. Harry went to the booking office and paid extra to have his wife seated inside the coach. He paid half her fee to sit on the bench above. No protection from the weather up there. There was much hugging and weeping as the family said their farewells.

As Harry prepared to climb aloft, the coachman called to him.

'Hey, young man, fancy a ride up front?'

A shocked Harry accepted with pleasure. He sat beside the coachman thinking all his Christmases had come at once. With a yell and flick of the reins, the four horses set off and reached their top speed of 8 miles per hour. It was 12 miles per hour in summer.

Inside the coach, each bump attacked Clara who hoped her baby would not suffer the rough and tumble of travel.

After a couple of miles, the coachman offered the reins to Harold. 'Fancy a drive, sir?' Harry looked at the older man who grinned. His teeth were filed down so as to better grip the straps.

Harry took control and proved a natural having handled horses all his working life. Only once he took control did Harry understand why the coachman offered the passenger the role. He, the coachman, took a swig of brandy from his flask, snorted snuff, and lit his pipe. A chap can't drive a team of four and enjoy life's little pleasures. *So his teeth are filed for when he hasn't got a back-up driver.*

They covered about 35 miles and stopped for the night at an inn. Harry thanked the coachman and climbed down to help his wife. She looked dreadful as he helped her inside.

'Will you be wanting your supper, sir?' asked the innkeeper. It was obvious the pregnant woman would only be wanting a bucket, and the night was spent with interrupted sleep. The innkeeper scowled, hating the fact that battered travellers often refused refreshments because the add-ons were where he made his money.

Next morning, the new team of horses was driven by a different coachman who offered no invitation to any passengers, and Harry sat upstairs at the back and copped the persistent rain most of the day.

The only break from boredom and jarred muscles came when the guard let fire with his weapon. He took a pot shot at a pig but missed.

Such were the joys of travel. Clara looked and felt dreadful as they finally reached the old, former Roman town, Londinium. Harry and Clara couldn't believe the number of people. The coach stopped outside an inn and the newlyweds were never so happy to settle in their room. Harry went downstairs and returned with supper hoping his wife would be able to keep it down. She did, just.

'We'll stay another night,' said Harold, and tomorrow I'll go and look for a job.'

'And a cottage,' said Clara wanting to settle in a place of their own.

After breakfast, Harry kissed Clara and set off to explore the city. 'Please keep an eye on my wife,' he said to the innkeeper and his wife. 'She's expecting and I need to find us a cottage ready for the baby.'

The innkeeper's wife smiled. 'I'll pop in every now and then.' Harry thanked her. 'But you won't find many cottages hereabouts.'

Harry nodded and went outside. A coach arrived with four horses tired from their run into town.

'Hello there,' called the coachman, and Harry looked up at the man who gave him control of the coach when they first left Norwich.

'Good day, sir,' said Harry.

The coachman dismounted and held out his hand. 'What are your plans in this fine metropolis?' he asked and Harry told him.

'I know the company is looking for an ostler. Are you interested?'

'Indeed I am,' said Harry, his heart springing to life.

'Right you are. Wait while I finish my business and then I'll introduce you to the foreman.'

This was better than good news and Harry couldn't wait to tell Clara. He thought about dashing inside with his news but stopped when the coachman returned.

'Come along. It's a bit of a walk.'

They set off and Harry explained his situation with the coachman reckoning the young man ideal for the company. They reached the yard with horse stalls lining three sides. Harry met the foreman, explained his experience and produced Lord Rallison's reference. The new arrival was offered a job on the spot. He could start today.

'That's very kind of you, sir,' he said, 'but I need to find a place for my wife. She is expecting a baby and I'd like to get her settled.'

'There are rooms to let all over Bermondsey.'

'Where is that, sir? I've only arrived in London today.'

'This is Bermondsey. Families live in this street. Go and look.'

'I will, thank you, sir.'

'But I need an ostler now. I can't hold this job forever.'

Harry showed his enthusiasm. 'I'll return directly, sir, I promise. Please, I can start work today.'

He ran out of the yard and along the street. There were rows of houses, two and three storeys high. They looked dreadful. No gardens, no trees in the street, only manure and urchins. Harry couldn't see any cottages. He walked up a lane and saw the backs of the attached brick buildings. Ropes were strung across the lane with washing hanging in the hope of wind or sunshine. Ancient sheets pleaded for help.

Still no gardens and the smell became worse. In the lane, children tried to play on the hard stones. A woman came out of an outhouse.

'Excuse me,' called Harold. 'I'm looking for accommodation. Do you know of anything around here?'

'See Mr Cruickshank in number five, round the front.'

'Thank you,' said Harold and went to find number five.

The door was open. He knocked and called. A middle-aged man needing a shave and a wash came out of the front room.

'What?'

'Good morning, sir. I'm looking for Mr Cruikshank.'

'Dere's one room available. Two bob a week, pay in advance. Take it or leave it.'

Harold was shocked. Getting a job was the best news and, if accommodation too, then his day was complete. But what is this accommodation?

'May I see the room, please sir?'

'Upstairs, second on the right.'

Harry stopped. 'Ah, my wife is expecting our first child and I'd prefer if she didn't have to climb any stairs.'

'Okay, the back room is one and six. Take it or leave it.' He pointed. 'Down there, last on the right.'

Harry walked along the corridor. A child screamed and another cried behind a thin wall. You could hear people spit. He came to the last door and went to open it. It needed a push. He entered a long, narrow room and found it was colder inside than out.

A single window at the end was the only light source. It looked out on the back yard overrun with washing. There was a fireplace with angry bricks. A cooking pot hung on a bar above the grate. There was a bed with a defeated mattress, a table you could put in your pocket, two chairs and two chamber pots, one filthy. Oh, and a breeze. The carpentry meant fresh air came free. It was the unwelcome lodger.

Harry stared at the room. There were no roses around the door and hollyhocks refused to even consider the address. He couldn't expect his wife to live here. But then he worried about his job offer.

If he went looking elsewhere, that would take time and the job might go to another man.

He reckoned they could live here while he looked for better accommodation. He told Mr Cruickshank he would take the room. Without speaking, the landlord held out his hand demanding the rent in advance.

Harry paid, went back to the stables, started work and endured a smorgasbord of feelings. The job was brilliant, the accommodation terrible. *I can't put Clara in such a place, at least not for long.*

Back at the inn, he put on a brave face. His plan was to go to the room tomorrow before work, tidy and repair it as best he could then take Clara there explaining it was a temporary move. With employment secure, he would look for the right accommodation. Fingers crossed.

# Chapter 6

There were few, if any rose-covered cottages for rent in jam-packed, working-class London suburbs. It was hard to even find rooms. People kept flooding into the city. Folk, desperate for a roof over their heads, snapped up anything regardless of size, style or suitability. Harry kept looking. Quality rooms were like hen's teeth. He was stuck with what he found in the sellers' market.

Landlords had no incentive to improve their property. They could subdivide the rooms and still fill them with ease.

Clara struggled, her abdomen swelling. She asked a mother next door, Mrs Judd, for advice. She'd given birth five times with only two still alive. 'You want old Glad as your helper,' she told Clara. 'She give me a hand with my last two. I'll get her to come 'round.'

She did and Clara sensed shame at the condition of her dwelling.

'Gawd, if you think this is bad, I could show you a few cesspits some muvvas call home. Now when is you due?'

'Soon,' said Clara not having any specific date.

'You send for Doctor Radley when you're about t'drop. He won't come unless it's time.'

Clara had never heard of any doctor in London.

'And I can get you a wet nurse if you needs one.'

Clara's confusion kept rising. She hated exposing her ignorance. 'How will I know?' she asked.

'Know what?' Glad realised the young mother-to-be was ignorant. 'How old is you girlie?'

'I'm sixteen.'

Glad snorted. 'Well if you can't feed the little mite, you'll need anuvva woman to feed y'baby. It's usually a woman who's just given birf, and dat woman is called a wet nurse.'

More confusion for Clara. 'But how will I know that and why won't I be able to feed my baby?'

'You'll know if you ain't got no milk. It's the way it is, love. Nipples crack, bubs can't suck; dere's all sorts of reasons. Anyway, you send for me when you're due, and I'll fetch the doctor and, if you need one, the wet nurse.'

'Thank you,' said Clara, 'you're very kind. How much do you charge?'

'It's a shilling if you're quick but half a crown for a wrong way round or a blockage, and only sixpence if it's a dead 'un.'

Clara became sick, no, more sick. Glad left, and from inside her abdomen, Clara copped the biggest kick yet.

When Harry came home, he prattled on about his work, and how the boss was pleased with the way he managed the horses. Harry always asked about Clara but like many fathers-to-be, possessed little understanding of what his wife was enduring day and night. When Clara served their evening meal of soup and bread, he noticed she was moving even more slowly than before.

'What did you do today, my dear?' he asked.

Clara went to sit and collapsed on her chair. She cried out in pain. Harry leapt to her side and asked possibly the most stupid question in the history of humankind.

'Are you in pain?'

She grasped the table and whispered. 'Send for Glad.'

'Who's Glad?'

'Ask Mrs Judd down the corridor.'

'But are you all right?'

In fear and frustration, she snapped. 'No! Just go.'

Harry disappeared. Clara struggled to stand and moved to the so-called birthing chair by the fire. She tried to lower herself sitting with a thump as Harry raced in. 'She said she's coming.'

Clara looked at her husband. 'So's the baby.'

Harry looked terrified. 'What? What do I do?'

'I think I need hot water and a towel.'

In a panic, he fussed, bumping into himself and wanted to pull out his hair. Then Glad arrived and spoke to Clara.

'Righto, let's have a look at you.'

Glad did her investigating and yelled, scaring Clara *and* Harry.

'Get the doctor, love, it's coming.' Harry froze and Clara yelled.

'Tell Mrs Judd!' Harry fled.

Footsteps sounded and a few locals arrived. There was not much free entertainment in these Bermondsey slums so a woman giving birth was well worth a gander. Without even asking, three women, one with two small children, wandered in, not to assist but to watch. Harry returned not knowing whether to offer the visitors a seat or order them out. There weren't enough chairs. There weren't *any* spare chairs. Clara continued her vocal exercises.

Dr Radley was local. He trained in London, knew the area, and had no shortage of patients. He was regarded as kind and caring but tragically, like most physicians of the time, knew little about the spread of disease. Mandatory hand washing and instrument sterilization were decades away.

Being told by a noisy child a baby was due, he set off to meet Clara Sweeping. As he strode along, a friendly dog approached. The good doctor patted the animal who decided to follow.

The child led him to the "baby house" and Doctor Radley gave the dog a final pat. A screaming woman drew the doctor to the room.

He shook hands with the expectant father and then, without washing his hands, examined the patient. He was hoping for an easy birth. Finding the baby's feet was a nightmare although having the infant lying sideways could be worse.

If he had to use crude and unsterilized implements to try and twist the unborn, he was literally taking the child's life in his unwashed hands. Due to the lack of hygiene, in this situation the medical profession was giving both mother and baby an excellent chance of infection. A safe delivery might still result in the death of either or both of the mother and babe.

Cesarean sections had been performed for thousands of years but often as a last resort and usually with deadly results. In a one-room slum, Dr Radley was relying on a large slice of good fortune.

Clara's cries were constant getting louder. Glad knew more than the doctor. 'Push,' she yelled. Clara screamed and the doctor did his best to remain relevant.

After more cries from Clara and more goading from Glad, the midwife yelled. 'Yes, here it is.' Nursing the new-born's head, Glad held the infant aloft. Harry wanted to look but feared he might faint.

'It's a boy,' said the doctor and Harry grinned like a dairy cat. The new father, step-father, looked at the spectators who shared none of his joy. It was a good education for the children. The baby howled and Glad passed the infant to his mother who wept. The doctor cut the umbilical cord and Glad helped the infant find his mother's breast.

She did as mothers have done for millennia, cradling the new-born and hoping she could express milk. There was crying from mother, investigating by the new-born, and then a shout of glee from the midwife; suckling success.

The neighbours were shown the door, Harry paid the doctor and midwife, and both left leaving the new Sweeping family alone.

Harry inspected his son. The parents looked at one another. Clara dreaded this moment. She wondered how Harry would feel once he first saw the child fathered by another man.

She relaxed a tad when Harry smiled then kissed the boy and then the mother.

'Now, Mrs Sweeping,' he said. 'What shall we call the lad?'

Clara thought about this and decided Harry should choose. She hoped it would bring him closer to the child. Naming him might help Harry think of the child as his own.

'You choose, Harry. It's a boy and I'd like you to name him.'

Harry knew the name he wanted. 'My favourite uncle taught me everything about horses. The old chap's gone now but I'd like his name to continue through our son.'

Clara warmed inside. 'Well then, what's it to be?'

'Jonathon, after Uncle Jonathon,' said Harry looking at his wife.

She smiled then kissed her baby's head. 'Welcome to the world, Jonathon Sweeping.'

# Chapter 7

In Bermondsey, the toddler Jonathon Sweeping survived, which was no mean achievement considering the slum in which he lived. Harry tried to find better accommodation for his family but anything of size and security was either miles away or miles too expensive.

Harry and Clara battled on, struggling to make ends meet. Life was tough and infant mortality common. The city's lack of proper sewage treatment helped spread disease and death.

The couple tried for another child but failed until after two years, Clara fell pregnant. But when lugging washing out to the yard, tragically she suffered a bloody miscarriage and wept for days.

She and Harry talked about going back to a rural life but he'd lost contact with his family, and hers was in Norfolk. Would Lord Rallison and his evil son do them harm if they returned to the area, especially now with His Lordship's bastard grandson in tow?

Clara thought having more money might help. 'I could get a job in the hat factory down the road, or the tannery,' she said one night.

'And who will look after the boy?' asked Harry.

'The old lady, Glad, said she'd care for him for a few pennies.'

'How much will you make?'

'I think five shillings a week.'

'For what, 12 hours a day with a fine if you take a break?'

Harry looked at his wife and his stepson, playing with a stick and a ball on the floor. The lad needed a decent bath, any sort of a bath.

And so Jonathon spent his days with a babysitter whose heart was in the right place but who fed the youngster on sugared water, bread and dripping or, as Glad called it, mucky fat. Despite this, the lad grew stronger. Other children picked on him and once he realised crying and complaining helped not one jot, he fought back. In his fourth year he learnt to stand up for himself and kicking shins became his specialty.

At night, Harry would ask the boy what he did during the day. When Jonathon related his latest skirmish, his parents exchanged worried glances with Harry feeling proud. The boy would be all right. He would make something of himself.

The years slipped by and when Clara found herself pregnant again, she kept it a secret. No good getting excited only to suffer the devastation of losing the baby. Lugging washing to and from the freezing communal laundry continued to batter her body.

Eventually her swollen belly meant the news became public. Harry was pleased and Jonathon confused when told he was to have a brother or sister. Touching his mother's tummy both puzzled and excited the boy. *Is that where babies come from?* He grew up fast.

Changes were afoot as Clara couldn't keep on working at the hat factory and so their income dropped. Harry wanted to ask for more money but knew if he did anything to offend his employer he could be out on his ear. With another child on the way, losing his job didn't bear thinking about.

Then one night Harry didn't come home from work and Clara worried. He was a good husband, not out drinking or failing to provide for his wife and child. But where was he? She heard a voice outside in the corridor.

'Does Harry Sweeping live here?'

Clara opened the door, her heart racing.

'Are you Harry's missus?' asked the man.

'What's happened?' asked Clara, frozen in fear with her son clinging to her legs.

'There's been an accident at the stables. Harry got trampled.'

'Is he dead?' gasped Clara.

'No, no, he ain't dead, but his foot's hurt pretty bad. They took him to the hospital.'

'Which hospital?'

'I don't know but if I find out, I'll come and tell you.'

'Thank you,' she whispered trying not to cry in front of her boy.

The visitor held out four coins. 'Harry told me to give you these.' He looked at her pathetic face, swollen belly and stunned child. 'I'll ask around. Good luck, Missus.' He gave a weak smile and left.

Clara led her son inside and sat, resting her pregnant body.

'Where's Da?' asked Jonathon.

'He hurt his foot, but he'll be home when the doctor helps him.'

'Can we go to him?' The child's face pleaded. 'Please, Ma, please.'

Clara's heart began to break. She was ill, her second child was due, her husband was hurt, probably badly, and now her son begged to see the man he loved and believed was his father. Getting through the night was unbearable. No family nearby, no real friends, no husband, and now the worries of no income and giving birth.

Medical science had much to discover in the early 19th century. Surgeons were decades away from setting broken bones and providing rehabilitation to benefit the patient. When faced with Harry's smashed right foot, the decision was simple—cut it off. You could see which part of his foot had been stamped upon by a large horse. Below the knee seemed okay but from the ankle down, the damage looked catastrophic.

Laudanum was used to relieve pain. People dying of inoperable cancer lived on it. Harry was doped, tied down, and the man with the saw stepped forward. The patient lost his foot and would be in bed for days until a wooden stump could be made and attached.

Harry's wages were stopped. No work, no pay was the rule, and when Clara heard the news, her spirits slid below sadness into desperation. She wanted to visit her husband but with a young boy bereft and missing his father, and she about to give birth, staying home was her only option.

Old Glad the midwife knew the Sweeping situation as she doubled as a child-minder when Clara worked in the hat factory.

Glad arrived and examined Clara. 'Let's get the baby out and then we can worry about your old man,' she said. Clara wept quietly with the midwife the only person who seemed to care.

At 6 in the morning, Clara called to Jonathon. 'Go and fetch Glad. I need her to come directly.' The boy was awake and concerned because of the tone of his mother's voice. 'And hurry,' she called. He did.

Glad arrived just in time having sent a child to fetch Dr Radley.

If a divine being existed, he, she or it smiled from above and Clara's delivery was straightforward, if there is such a thing.

Jonathon grew up fast. He stood in their draughty room while his mother screamed, old Glad barracked and Dr Radley arrived with enough germs to infect half of Bermondsey.

'It's a girl,' announced Glad. 'You 'ave a daughter, Missus.' She turned to Jonathon. 'You 'ave a sister, young man.'

He tingled. His school education was zero and illiteracy his best subject but his knowledge of life and the world around him kept growing.

The doctor stepped forward to add his finishing touches and managed to add another patient's hairs to Clara's belly. All that was missing was the birth father of the child.

Clara did well in expressing milk and Jonathon was alone with his mother and sister. She was named Kitty and Jonathon wanted his Da.

Harry arrived ten days later. It was hard to know who was the more sad, happy, distressed or relieved. Harry had a daughter, a child he fathered. Clara had her husband and Jonathon his father, although the poor man limped in on crutches with his right foot now a combination of wood and leather.

With the boy and baby asleep, Clara and Harry discussed their future.

'I can go back to work but not handling the horses,' said Harry.

'Doing what?' asked Clara.

'They said I can change the feed and water, work in the tack room, order new supplies and the like. It'll mean less money but it's better than the sack.'

Clara looked at his face in the soft glow of the dying fire. 'We need to go home, Harry, back to Norfolk. My parents will take us.'

Harry hesitated. He hated charity, knew they couldn't afford the coach fee, and wondered what work he would find back in the rural landscape. There was little there when they left, and his fear of Lord Rallison and his wicked son still lingered in the back of his mind.

'We'll talk about it in the morning.'

They went to sleep. Clara got up and fed the baby twice during the night. The mother couldn't sleep anyway as Harry tossed and turned, groaning and taking sharp gasps of breath because his missing foot gave him merry hell.

This was the new life for the Sweeping family of Bermondsey; reduced income, less food of even poorer quality, a room which welcomed the wind and damp, and a future slightly less than bleak. They struggled to survive for months.

Harry succumbed to the pain and turned to drink. He came home with a belly full of gin. There were 8,000 gin shops in London. Hundreds of houses sold it. It was cheap and poisonous but dulled his pain. He suffered from a missing foot, and the depression of seeing his family struggle. He brought his wife and future child to London, and now his job and hopeful future turned to a trough of despair.

Life grew worse and at a faster rate. In summer, the stink from the sewerage in the street and back lanes became normal and was only marginally less putrid in winter. His son enjoyed the same schooling as did he, none, and what would that mean for Jonathon's future?

His wife and daughter bonded and that at least gave his heart a lift. But then a chance meeting with a chap from Rotherhithe, who drank in the same public house, gave Harry an idea and hope. At home he told his wife.

'I think Jonathon can get a job.' She looked at him with surprise and concern.

'A job? He's not even seven.'

'That's to his advantage. Small boys are perfect as chimney sweeps.' Clara said nothing. 'I know a chap who'll give him a try. We can do something for the lad.'

'Isn't it dangerous? He could be injured or worse.'

'Not if he's trained. And this bloke has trained dozens of lads.' More silence from Clara. Harry pleaded. 'Clara, I can't offer him a job. This could mean a future for the boy and besides, Clarrie will give us five bob for the boy's apprenticeship.'

'Does Jonathon get paid?'

'Not at first, not when he's being trained.'

Clara recoiled as the news hit hard. She blurted a question. 'He works in a filthy, dangerous job and for nothing?'

Harry hushed her. 'Shhh, the boy might hear. Look, it's one less mouth for us to feed. He gets a warm bed, all his meals and when he's older, he'll have a trade. He could even hire boys to work for him.'

'If he lives that long.'

'Come on, love, let's at least try. Give the boy a chance.'

And so Jonathon Sweeping began his working life aged 7. He was lucky, some sweeps started when only four. His boss, Clarrie Pearce, started as a child sweep, and reckoned the soot he "wore" on his first day was still in his hair, what little that was left.

Jonathon held his father's hand as he and Mr Pearce discussed the boy's employment. 'With a name like Sweeping, young fellah, you'll be a natural.'

The boy didn't understand the details of his new life and was yet to form an opinion. He knew he would leave his home, his parents and young sister. He would live in a big house near the Thames with Mr and Mrs Pearce and a few other boys. He could go home to visit his family on the first Sunday of the month. Once his apprenticeship was over—no date given—he would be paid—no sum announced. And this, he was told, was a good deal. It was slavery under another name.

After the Great Fire of London in 1666, new building laws meant chimneys became more narrow with bends, meaning removing soot was a task for small humans, children. The young sweeps, mostly male, would wriggle in the confined space and climb using their back, elbows, hands and feet. It was called "Walk the chimney". To toughen extremities, these were scrubbed with salt. Many undeveloped bones were damaged. Cancer of the scrotum was unique to sweeps and those afflicted died a horrible death. Only when a sweep was trapped in a hospital chimney and a wall had to be demolished to free him, did the authorities outlaw the practice. It took a mere 200 years.

A cruel boss might light a fire to "encourage" the lad to get a move on. Climbing was but the means of getting to work as once up the chimney, the sweep would use a brush to dislodge the toxic black stuff. Down it fell via the sweep's hair, ears and clothes and, if too slow, his eyes, nose and mouth. The sweeps quickly learnt to keep their mouth shut. The waste-not-want-not boss would have the sweep collect the soot and hand it over so he could sell it keeping the funds for himself; nothing, not even a farthing for the labourer.

For sweeps, injuries were common and life expectancy lowered. Their beds were often the filthy sacks they used by day. Stunted growth was a way of life. Jonathon survived with Mr Pearce being, if not kindly, then at least rarely cruel. Like Harry Sweeping, Clarrie

Pearce knew that treating your horses, in this case sweeps, with care made them more productive for longer.

Two months after he became a sweep, Jonathon went to visit his family on his second free Sunday. His mother cried as she hugged the boy. His young sister clapped her hands with pleasure but his father lay on the bed, snoring.

'Your Da's poorly. When he wakes he'll be so pleased to see you.'

Clara thought Jonathon looked well apart from his new hair colour and darker skin. Like a typical mother, she put hot water in a bucket and ordered her son to place his head in position.

Years ago, as a scullery maid, Clara knew how to scrub. She gave her son the same treatment. He complained politely, Kitty gurgled, and his mother gave it her all.

She found pleasure as the lad now looked a bit like his former self. She fed him from her limited supply, and asked all manner of questions. She became less worried at his new situation but could see he was sad because his father would not wake and greet the boy. His sadness gnawed at her heart.

'Why don't you go and see Glad? Say hello and then come back.'

Jonathon looked at his mother. His stomach churned. 'Are you having another baby?'

Clara blanched. *How could such a young mind think like that?* 'No, no, there will be no more babies. Glad asks me how you are going so why don't you tell her about your job.'

Jonathon nodded and left.

'Jonafon,' cooed Kitty and pointed at the door. It was one of the first words she said having fallen in love with her missing big brother.

'Yes, Kitty, he's your brother and he'll come back soon.'

Once he left, Clara tried to wake her husband. More and more the pain of his missing foot, physically and psychologically, pushed him to alcohol and sleep. He dropped his bundle. His reduced pay at the stables added to his woes. His spirit died and his self-esteem slipped through the cracks and gaps in the floor through which the rats and draughts popped in for a visit.

Clara knew about the dozens of London's workhouses, a final refuge for the poor and destitute. With her husband racing to oblivion, if she couldn't move back to her family in Norfolk, her only choice would be the workhouse. At least her son was no longer her responsibility.

She gently shook her husband. 'Harry, wake up. Jonathon's here.'

A grunt and complaint was his reply. 'Stop botherin' me, woman.' He belched and turned his back. She tried again. 'Please, Harry, the boy wants to talk to you.'

Harry grabbed the grubby pillow and tossed it. It landed beside Kitty frightening her. She cried. Clara scooped up the girl as Harry's anger chilled the already chilly room. Then she heard the final nail being belted into the coffin.

'And you can tell the boy I ain't his father.'

The knife plunged into Clara's heart and for an encore, twisted itself. Never had the stepfather made mention of that fact before; in fact the opposite. Harry raised the boy as his own before tragedy intervened. His amputation, constant pain, low wage and vanishing self-esteem dragged him deep into the mire; the self-pity quicksand.

Clara carried her crying daughter down the corridor and waited on the front steps. Eventually Jonathon returned and saw both his mother and sister with moist eyes.

'What's wrong, Ma? Is Da all right?'

Clara shook her head. 'He's not, my boy, he's poorly and very sad he can't see you today.' Jonathon's chest hurt. 'But when you come next time, I'm sure he'll be better, and you and your Da can have a grand time talking about your work and all sorts of things.' She paused. Her attempt to make her son happy failed. 'Okay?'

He nodded but lied. It wasn't okay. He wasn't okay. His sadness blocked his throat.

'Come and give me and your sister a kiss.'

He did and Kitty perked up no end. She'd heard so much about her brother, it was exciting to see him and even better to receive a kiss.'

He looked at his mother and despite his tender years, knew her heart was broken. He wanted to hug them and stay with his family.

'We all love you, Jonathon,' said Clara. 'Come back soon,'

He fought hard not to cry. Clara prompted Kitty. 'Say goodbye to Jonathon, Kitty.'

'Bye bye, Jonafon,' she called and waved.

He waved and headed down the street, his heart a mess.

# Chapter 8

Harry limped around the stables. He limped from feed supply to horse box, filling the animals' food. Using crutches to stay upright, it took him twice the time a fit man could do the job. He struggled with a sack of oats but stopped when he sensed a person behind him.

'Mr Balfour,' said Harry. The look on his boss's face spelt doom. Standing beside the employer was a strapping young lad of about 16.

'It's time, Harry. You knew it might come to this. We've hired a young lad who can do all your work and handle the horses.'

Harry was speechless. Being sacked was the last straw. No job, no pay, no future and no ability to provide for his wife and daughter.

'You can stay on for a week or two and show the lad the ropes but after that, it's time to go. This is George. I'll leave him with you.'

The boss left and Harry stared at the young man who was nervous and more so at Harry's despair. The cripple did the right thing and showed his replacement the stables, horses and supplies.

'Thank you, sir,' said the lad, 'and I'm sorry to take your job.'

Harry waved a hand as if to say, "Forget it", then grabbed his coat and limped out of the yard.

At home, Clara struggled more than ever. Kitty was 2 and Jonathon 8. The boy came around only once in a while now because his father showed little interest in his son. Clara knew Jonathon's absence was due to Harry's constant misery and indifference.

The evening meal, such as it was, sat on the table. Kitty had already eaten, and played with her homemade rag doll. Clara's default position was worry but as the night grew longer and her husband didn't appear, she worried even more.

She put Kitty to bed. 'Where's my Da?' she asked as her mother tucked her into the box filled with straw and which soon would be too small for the girl.

'Hush, Kitty, go to sleep.'

The candle was long ago snuffed out. Cost cutting ruled their household. Clara crept down the corridor wrapping her shawl tight for a semblance of warmth. She peered into the street hoping from the darkness and swirling fog, her husband would limp home. He didn't and she slept alone although sleep became fitful.

Waking at odd times, she thought the sound of his hobbling footsteps were outside their door. Nothing. Before dawn she lit the fire looking at the near empty coal bucket. Kitty slept and her mother lived the life of a pauper; little money or food and absolutely no hope.

Come morning, still no sign of Harry. Kitty asked after her father.

'He's gone to work,' said Clara saying anything to quell the child's curiosity and her own despair.

Around lunchtime she heard footsteps. They came from a pair of boots and Harry only wore the one.

'Mrs Sweeping?' called a voice and Clara was at her door in a flash. She knew the man. He used to work with Harry at the stables.

'Where's Harry?'

The visitor said nothing although his face told all. 'I'm sorry, Missus, but Harry's had an accident.'

'Oh, not another one. Is he in the hospital?'

The visitor shook his head. Kitty appeared and grabbed her mother's skirt. 'You're not my Da. Where's my Da?'

The child and her question stopped the man. He needed to rethink his answer. 'It's bad news, Missus. Harry fell in the Thames and he's drowned.'

Clara stifled a scream and picked up Kitty who sensed danger and began to cry. The widow found questions exploding in her head.

The visitor explained. 'Two blokes who drink in the Bermondsey Arms was walking past when he was fished out and they recognized him. I think he's in the mortuary in Whitechapel. I'm sorry, Missus.' He wanted to get out as quick as he could. 'The boss at the stable told me to give you this. It's his unpaid wage.' He handed the coins to Clara who didn't bother counting them. 'I'll be off, Missus.'

He fled; relieved he managed to deliver the news, and wanting desperately to be somewhere, anywhere else.

Clara took her crying daughter inside and closed the door. Her mind spun. She remembered the first time she met Harold Sweeping following her being locked in the coal cellar at Bittering Hall. She pictured their wedding and how he stood by her as she gave birth to another man's child. She could never forget his cries of pain as he suffered from his amputated foot, and how the accident plunged him into a spiral of misery. Now, at least, his torment was over. Her mind raced. *Did he fall into the river? Was he drunk? Did he jump?*

Tragedy happens to many. Clara faced her own. She had no idea how she would explain the situation to her daughter, and her heart groaned as she thought of Jonathon. *What will I say to my boy?*

None of her neighbours were close, many were surly and rude. Poverty and sickness make people angry and bitter. She could confide in Glad the midwife about Harry but no-one else. Clara remembered the money and picked up the coins, counting slowly.

With her modest savings and this extra cash, she had 12 shillings. That would keep the wolf and landlord from the door and put food in their bellies for a while. But should she spend it on a coach ride back to her parents near Norwich? *Are they still alive?*

She decided. 'We're going out, Kitty. Come and get dressed.' The child was excited with no idea they were off to see what happened to the drowned man fished from the Thames, her father.

The morgue in Whitechapel was hardly welcoming. It was a shed in the Workhouse yard. Clara, with daughter in hand, rang the bell.

'Who lives in this house?' asked the little girl.

Clara hushed the child and, with no response, rang again. Eventually the door was opened by a man with a bloodstained apron.

'Yes?' He was busy and hungry.

'I understand my husband may be here.'

'Name?'

'Ah, Sweeping, Harold Sweeping.'

'Wait 'ere.'

Clara smiled at her daughter. She couldn't leave the child alone and hated bringing her to such a place on such an occasion but wanted to discover what happened to Harry. Clara pointed to a group of children playing nearby; anything to distract Kitty.

The man returned with a hessian bag. 'His clothes,' he said.

Clara looked inside and sensed her already cold body freeze. She knew Harry's belongings. 'Can I see him?' she asked.

'You don't wanna, lady, 'e ain't pretty. An' one of 'is feet got chopped off in the water.'

Clara nodded. She learnt everything and nothing.

'Is you claimin' the body? It'll be four an' six.'

Clara's confusion reached its zenith. 'Why would I claim it?' she asked in ignorance.

'So you can bury it of course.'

'And if I don't claim it?'

'Then you'll pay nothin' an' 'e'll get 'imself a pauper's grave. 'e'll likely be one of many in the same 'ole. Wotcha wanna do?'

Her body shook with grief and she saw Kitty begin to cry.

'Thank you, I'll leave it.'

She squeezed her daughter's hand and headed home trying to distract the child as both shed tears. Kitty cried because her Ma cried.

The days dragged and the nights were worse. Driven to despair by Kitty's questions, especially 'Where's Da?', Clara finally sat the girl down and told her about stars in the sky and how Da was now one of those sparkling diamonds up in the heavens.

At first, Kitty was fascinated but her understanding struggled and her missing father's presence, despite his misery, caused her to ask about him coming home.

Could there be a more difficult time for any mother let alone a widow with two children, no income, few savings, her family as good as being on another planet, and of course, no husband?

It seems difficult to believe but life got worse. Jonathon arrived. He hadn't seen his family for two months mainly because his father was so miserable and unfriendly. Still, the blood is thicker than water factor kicked in and the boy walked from Rotherhithe to Bermondsey.

His free Sunday allowed him to leave his employer's home and though steady rain fell, the boy kept walking. Drenched, he called out as he walked down the corridor.

'Da, are you there. It's me, Jonathon.'

Kitty erupted with joy while Clara's heart turned to stone.

Jonathon opened the door to the Sweeping hovel, and Kitty ran to her brother. She hugged him only reaching about halfway up his soot tinged and now soaked body.

'Jonafon,' she cried and he looked down at his sister and then at his mother. She moved to him and kissed his cheek.

'Hello my darling boy. It's lovely to see you. Are you well?'

He nodded and looked around. 'Where's Da?'

Clara struggled. 'He's gone out.'

There was a pause with no-one sure what to say. Kitty helped.

'Da's in the sky. He's a star.'

That broke the ice; smashed it more like. Clara tried to explain the news. 'He's been hurt, Jonathon, and he might not get better.'

The boy of tender years defied his youth and challenged his mother, the mother he loved and would always do so.

'He's dead, isn't he? Da is dead.'

Clara's eyes filled with tears. Kitty looked from brother to mother to brother. She watched as her brother moved to his mother and embraced her, holding her firm as she quietly sobbed. His soot clung to her dress and apron and neither noticed or cared. Kitty went from being excited to being afraid. She didn't know what was happening.

Feeling so much stronger having a man around the house, the room, Clara snapped out of her gloom and fussed making a meal for her children.

'We'd love you to stay tonight, Jonathon, wouldn't we Kitty?'

Baby sister thought it the best idea ever. 'Yes, Jonafon, you can stay and play wiv me and Ma will tell us a story.'

He did stay. He knew Mr Pearce would be angry and worry when he didn't return but once Jonathon explained about his father's death, all would be understood and forgiven.

After Kitty fell asleep, Clara and her boy sat in front of the fire, its glow casting shadows on their faces. She spoke in the softest whisper.

'I need to tell you things, my darling, things you may not understand today or tomorrow, but later when you are older.'

The boy had been working as a sweep for nearly three years. He was well cared for but the dangers of climbing chimneys were ever present. His father suffered a catastrophic injury at work and every day, Jonathon flirted with accidents, breaking bones and death.

'I want you to know your Da was not always sad and angry. Losing his foot changed him. You may not remember but once he was a happy man who loved you with all his heart. He was a special man. He wanted to be your Da even though he ...' She couldn't finish.

Jonathon looked at his mother. 'I don't know what you mean, Ma.'

She couldn't tell him the truth. 'I want you to remember your Da as a good man. He loved you, Jonathon; never, ever forget that.'

He nodded. 'Do you want me to come back here to live?'

His question hurt her, in a good way but still packed a punch. Did such a young child have an understanding about caring for his family? Did he know he was now its patriarch and needed to take his place in caring for his mother and sister?

Clara recovered and explained. 'If things get too hard, I will take Kitty back to my family in Norfolk. For now, if I can get work as a seamstress, it'll keep us together. If you can come to see us on the first Sunday, we'll be thrilled to see you.'

He nodded. 'I wish I could make money and help you, Ma.'

She squeezed his hand in two of hers and tears galloped down her cheeks as the fire faded and the room became as black as the soot in Jonathon's hair.

# Chapter 9

In the morning, Jonathon hugged his mother and sister and left promising to return next month without fail. Kitty waved from the front steps and kept calling to her brother even when he was out of sight. 'Bye, Jonafon, bye.'

It was a fair hike to Rotherhithe that Monday. Traders were busy, beggars too, and housewives shopped while criminals searched for an easy mark. In Rotherhithe Street, one of the longest in London, a man spotted Jonathan who walked planning his speech to Mr Pearce.

'Oi, sonny, oi, over 'ere,' cried the man. Amongst all the other sounds of a busy London, Jonathon paid no attention but did turn his head when the man called again. Jonathon looked, saw the man beckoning to him, hesitated then crossed the road.

'Sir?' asked Master Sweeping.

'You look like you could do with a nice hot drink.'

'Thank you, sir, but I'm late for work and have no money.'

The man appeared shocked. 'You work and have no money? That don't sound right.'

'I'm a sweep, sir, and must hurry as I'm late.'

'Okay but when you're next in these parts, you ask for Bankside Bertie. Everyone knows me. I can put a few pennies your way.'

'Thank you,' said Jonathon and left. The man's voice followed him.

'Don't f'get; Bankside Bertie.'

Mr Pearce's face like thunder changed instantly when Jonathon explained his news.

'I'm sorry, lad. Your father's been sad ever since he lost his foot. How is your mother?'

'I think she has a hard life, Mr Pearce, and I wish I could earn money to help her and my little sister.'

There wasn't much Pearce could say to the boy's remark. The deal was free board and tuition so each sweep could eventually set up on their own with *eventually* being the key word. Meanwhile, slavery and child abuse was in full swing with Jonathon playing a main role.

The boy went back to getting filthy and, at night, lay awake thinking about his parents and particularly his mother. Images of his dead father haunted the boy.

"I want you to remember your Da as a good man. He loved you, Jonathon; never, ever forget that."

The weeks passed and his next Sunday visit drew nigh. Mr Heartless Pearce reminded the boy of his duty.

'Don't forget, lad, you're due back here by nightfall; none of this stopping with your family overnight business, all right?'

Jonathon acquiesced with appropriate humility but hated going to his mother empty-handed. If only he had a few pennies, anything to be able to help her feed and clothe his little sister.

He walked towards Bermondsey pondering his life as a sweep. It had potential but people can't eat or wear potential. Money is needed and now. He saw a fruit stall ahead and searched for the trader. Being overweight he was hard to miss. *I bet he don't have hunger pains,* thought Jonathon. Two women were arguing over the condition of potatoes and the trader grew impatient.

'Look, ladies, they is what they is; take 'em or leave 'em.'

Jonathon was two yards away when the trader lost it. His arguing flared. In a flash the boy grabbed two apples and kept walking. But the trader wasn't born yesterday. He'd battled thieves for years and sprouted eyes in the back of his head. He forgot the spud customers.

'Hey!' he roared and pointed at the boy who quickened his stride.

The trader knew trying to catch the youthful villain was a lost cause so yelled in the hope a citizen would seize the scoundrel. His hope was realised.

Jonathon was seized and a strong arm dragged him into a doorway then through into a warehouse. In shock he looked up and saw the grinning face of Bankside Bertie.

'Well, well, well,' said Bertie. 'If it ain't the penniless chimney sweep. Taken up thievin' 'ave you, lad?' He wagged his finger. 'Naughty, naughty.'

'I'm sorry, sir. I'll return the apples directly.'

Bertie roared with laughter. 'Return 'em? Wotcha wanna go and do that for? Thems is yours, lad. Now, wot's y'name?'

Jonathon recovered a tad. 'Jonathon, sir.'

'Well Jonathon the Sweep, I'm glad to make your acquaintance. Now where is you off to?'

'To see my family, sir. I only have one day a month to visit and they will be most upset if I am late.'

'Okay, here's the deal. I'll show you the back way so you and your apples can go and see your family on the condition you come and 'ave a cuppa with me on your way back this afternoon. Deal?'

Bertie extended his hand. Jonathon nodded. 'Thank you, sir,' he said shaking the strange man's hand.

'This way,' he said and led the boy through the warehouse and into a laneway. 'Where you headin'?'

'Bermondsey, sir.'

'Go down the lane, left then first on y'right.' He pointed at Jonathon. 'An' don't forget our arrangement. Go on, get y'self 'ome.'


Jonathon reached home and his heart raced as he bounced along the corridor to the rear of the slum. He opened the door and two faces beamed.

'Jonafon,' cried Kitty with joy, and Clara hugged the boy. He caused surprise when, from his pockets, he produced the apples.

'A little present,' he said. Kitty squealed and Clara smiled without conviction.

'Thank you but how could you afford them?'

'They were a present, Ma, from a kind old man.'

Clara put them to one side. She would stew them and make custard remembering the apple pies Cook used to make at Bittering Hall when she was but a lowly scullery maid. The peel she would keep for her meal and eat by herself when Kitty was asleep.

The trio sat and chatted. Mother and son went rabbiting. Clara wanted to know about his life as a sweep, and he wanted to know how his family was managing on their own.

'We're doing well,' said Clara before coughing. She recovered. 'I've found work as a seamstress and Kitty has found two new friends further down the street. Kitty prattled on about her friends.

Jonathon looked around the room, his former home, their home now for years. It was in need of repair when they arrived and kept deteriorating. The warmth from the fire fought a losing battle with the chill from the damp, and the wind from the cracks.

'How about I take Kitty to the river to look for coal?' Clara's heart pounded. *My son has become a caring human being but will he be upset thinking about his father and that river?*

Kitty buzzed. Jonathon took her hand and a sack and set off.

Clara took in sewing for which she was paid a pittance. Alone, she lived for her daughter but with her son back in their life, hope became stronger. Her understanding of matters spiritual was basic but she asked God to keep her strong and well so she might care for her children.

They returned with noise aplenty. Kitty called as soon as she entered the property. 'We're home, Ma, and Jonafon found some coal.'

Clara was delighted to see her children together and doubly pleased her coal supply looked so much healthier. She prepared the best luncheon she could and watched as her children enjoyed one another's company as they ate.

'I have to be back before six, Ma,' he said. 'Mr Pearce told me not to be late.'

'Did you get into trouble for staying here overnight?'

'Not when I told him Da died; he understood.'

'What does Da died mean?' asked the youngest Sweeping.

Mother and son looked at one another. Clara tried to explain. 'Remember I said he's gone up to heaven to light the sky at night.'

That thought was still a challenge for the young girl. It sounded believable but Clara knew there would be questions later.

After the meal, Jonathon told stories of his chimney climbing but said nothing about Bankside Bertie. When it was time to leave, Clara and Kitty walked down the corridor with the sweep. On the steps, Jonathon kissed them both promising to return next month. They waved and Kitty called and kept calling.

He waved back and disappeared. Clara pulled her shawl tighter and took Kitty back to their room. That night the fire burned bright although Clara couldn't dislodge the chill from her bones.

Jonathon remembered the way to Bankside Bertie's door. In the busy street, it was easy to avoid the man with the fruit stall. The boy knocked on Bertie's door. It swept open and the gent's face blew up into a smile.

'Jonathon,' he purred, 'it's lovely to see you. Come in, come in.'

They entered a small room inside the warehouse where a kettle whistled as if it had false teeth. A cup of coffee was made and handed to Jonathon.

'Drink up, my friend, and enjoy.'

'Thank you, sir. May I ask what it is?'

'It's coffee, the finest in London.'

The boy hesitated. 'I've never tasted coffee.'

The man appeared shocked. 'Never tasted coffee? Then get stuck in, dear boy. And tuck into this bread and jam and a cake.'

The food was pushed towards Jonathon who found saliva forming as the sight and smell of the refreshments excited his taste buds. He dined well wondering why this man was being so kind.

'I'll be honest with you, Jonathon.'

That sentence represented the modus operandi of such men as Bankside Bertie. Honesty and truth were not so much distant cousins with chaps like Bertie; they were total strangers. He couldn't lie straight in bed. You could tell when he was lying; his lips moved.

'Jonathon, I am a man who believes in equality. Look around London and all you see is inequality. A few people have money, lotsa money, and lotsa people have little or none; nothing. That's *in*equality. Do you understand?'

Jonathon was chewing and sipping. He nodded.

'When you told me you work for no pay, I was incensed. Do you know what incensed means?'

Jonathon shook his head.

'I was angry, Jonathon, no, more than angry, I was furious. Anyone who works must be paid. I wanna help you get paid for doing your work.'

'I get free accommodation and meals, sir, and when I finish my apprenticeship, I'll be able to charge people for cleaning their chimneys.'

'That's if you survive. What if you get injured and can't work? Well?'

The boy didn't answer. He knew of sweeps injured at work.

'How is your family? Do they need any help to buy food? Are they warm at night?' Jonathon certainly knew the answer to those questions. He became seriously attentive. 'Here's a plan. You come here on your next day off and I'll show you how you can make money for your work and help your family. How does that sound?'

He thought. 'I'd like to earn money.'

'Of course you would and so you shall. Now, do we have a deal?'

The boy whispered. 'Yes sir.'

'But there is one important rule.' He paused and went all serious. 'You must tell no-one. Don't tell your employer and don't tell your family. Your employer will try and stop you, and you want to give your family a surprise.' He looked at the boy. 'Agreed?'

Jonathon nodded. This was his lucky day. Bertie stood to show him out and handed the boy another cake.

'Here, stick this in your pocket for later.'

At the door, Jonathon turned to face his benefactor. 'Thank you, sir, I'll return on my next day off.'

Bertie grinned exposing his stained and often picked teeth.

# Chapter 10

The huge house boasted fireplaces on every floor. 'Remember the rule, Jonathon,' said Mr Pearce. 'Tell me.'

'Always start with the top fireplaces and finish with the ones on the ground floor,' replied the young sweep.

'Good lad. Now hop upstairs and get cracking.'

On the top floor, the boy crouched in the fireplace and looked up. At first the chimney was wide but then it grew narrow and quickly so. With his brush in his shoulder bag, Jonathon pushed his back into one side of the chimney then inched his way higher. He didn't fancy getting out of a window and on the roof to tackle the chimney from above. He was scared of heights, the rain made the roof slippery, and it was a long way down to street level. If you fell, hopefully you might miss the railings.

Close to the top, he dragged his brush up above his head, looked at the soot, bowed his head, closed his eyes, took a deep breath then brushed.

Soot rained down and settled in his hair and on his clothes before most of it reached the fireplace. Then something unexpected happened. A lump of soot broke free and struck Jonathon on the top of his skull. The pain hurt but the shock was worse. He panicked enough to lose his position and slipped. He dropped the brush, pushed his back against the chimney, and tried to grab any part of the brickwork to stop or slow his fall.

He slowed his fall but at what cost? He continued to descend but experienced sharp pain. His right ankle hurt like blazes, his head throbbed, and his left hand was bleeding. He reached the hearth and its soot and yelled in agony. His cry brought the boss at speed. Pearce worried. A wounded sweep would cost him money, and worse, if the lad was experienced and couldn't work, a major asset would vanish.

'I told you to always be careful.' Pearce berated the boy on the floor. 'Give me y'hand.'

Jonathon automatically apologised. 'I'm sorry, sir. Something fell on my head and I slipped.'

Pearce helped the boy out of the fireplace. 'Careful,' said the boss wanting as little mess as possible. 'Have you finished this chimney?'

'I think so.' Jonathon saw his bleeding hand. 'I've cut myself, sir.'

Pearce gave it a cursory glance. 'It's a scratch. Now come on, there are two more chimneys on this floor.'

He set off but stopped when Jonathon let out a cry of pain. Pearce turned. 'What now?'

The boy gasped. 'It's my ankle, sir. It hurts a lot.'

Pearce stared at the sweep's bare feet. 'I can't see anything. Here, I'll give you a hand.'

He half dragged Jonathon with the sweep cringing as the pain in his foot screamed. The boy looked at his employer and wanted to cry. The pain was powerful but the prospect of failing to keep his part of the employment bargain crushed his spirit.

'This way,' said Pearce. 'You'll be fine.'

He wasn't fine. His head copped a battering from the lump of soot, and his ankle landed awkwardly against the chimney and in the grate. Forget about the skin scratched from his hand. He limped to the next room.

'Right, young lad, best foot forward and all that,' said Pearce who moved the grate which did nothing for the boy's wellbeing.

Jonathon crouched and looked up; another beast of a chimney. In pain, he began climbing. His hand stung, his head ached and his foot set off explosions of agony whenever he pressed it against the bricks. He didn't know how but he walked the chimney and sent soot tumbling.

It was a day to dread. He heard of boys, even younger than him, who'd fallen and been hurt. One six year-old cracked his skull. One was stuck in a chimney and a second boy was sent up to set him free. Both died, frozen among the soot.

That night, he struggled to clean himself. There was always soot on his clothes, in his ears and through his hair but now he didn't care. He hated his job. He hated not being able to help his Ma and baby sister. In the Pearce basement, he lay on his bed of coal bags, thinking about Bankside Bertie and his offer to help him find paid employment. Whatever it was, it had to be better than his current life. Serving an apprenticeship was sensible, even wise, but if your family is cold and hungry and you're paid nothing, what sort of a life is that? At this rate, his family will suffer and could even die before he might help them financially. He counted the days until the first Sunday of the month.

His war wounds healed slowly. The sprains, scratches and bruises repaired themselves thanks to his youth and general good health. The morning of his free day dawned. He became happy, even excited for the first time in ages. *What is this new experience—happiness?*

'Enjoy your family,' said Pearce, 'and don't be late. It's a busy day tomorrow.'

'Yes, Mr Pearce,' said Jonathon heading off to Bermondsey. There was a stopover before he reached his family. He wondered if Bankside Bertie would remember him let alone their arrangement.

He knocked on the warehouse door and heard a voice. 'Who dares knock at this time in the morning?' The door was flung open and Bertie's face lit up with one of his exploding smiles. 'Jonathon,' he cried and beckoned the boy inside.

'Good morning, sir. I hope you haven't forgotten me.'

'Forgotten you? What nonsense you talk. Why, I've been planning our meeting for weeks.'

Jonathon didn't know if this was true. It sounded wonderful and the hospitality impressed with more coffee and cakes.

Once the refreshments were served, Bertie began his spiel. He had a way with words did this seducer of boys. He chose well. The lads must be young, naive and desperate for money. If their nearest and dearest were suffering, so much the better.

When Jonathon explained his work accident, Bertie ramped up the injustice of the boy's current situation.

'No more, Jonathon, it's time you were rewarded for your labour.'

Bertie again railed against the inequality of life in London. Why should so few have so much? Surely a more even spread of wealth was fair and just.

Jonathon became a convert. All that remained was the job description. Once explained, Jonathon retorted.

'But sir, that's stealing.'

'No, my son, that's adjusting the wealth. It's making sure everyone gets a reasonable share of the world's money.'

Bertie made it personal with many rhetorical questions. 'Do you want your mother and sister to go hungry? Do they deserve a roof over their head? Will the wealthy miss a tiny amount of their riches?'

It was a multi-pronged attack which became a practical class. For the next half hour, Bertie gave the boy a lesson in picking pockets. He told him the targets, the best places to find said targets, and the best methods to do the deed. Bertie saw the boy harboured doubts, and knew he'd been told about basic morality. For Bertie, it was time to establish a new morality.

'Here's the thing, Jonathon,' he said. 'For every wealthy gent who agrees to "donate" their pennies or watch or silk handkerchief or hat or cane, no-one will suffer as a result. No-one will go hungry, sleep in a doorway or have to empty their chamber pot in the street. They certainly won't have to make their own fire or sweep their own chimney. Do you understand?'

Jonathon did indeed. He became a believer. The last bit about sweeping their own chimney nailed it. And when the mention of being paid for his efforts was repeated, Jonathon went from, "This doesn't sound right," to "When do I start?"

They walked in the street with Bertie guiding. 'See those two gents across the road outside the coffee shop?' Jonathon looked. 'Don't stare.' Jonathon concentrated on Bertie who continued.

'The gent with the black hat has a silk handkerchief in his jacket pocket. Which method would best allow you to help that gentleman spread the wealth of Londoners more evenly?'

Jonathon learnt well. 'A distraction behind the man he's talking to.'

'Excellent. Now remember to look disinterested and never make eye contact with the mark. What's the mark?'

'The target person who helps spread the wealth of Londoners.'

'And we only strike when confident. What about the escape?'

'Know your escape route, and only run if you really have to.'

Bertie looked at the boy. Their eyes met. The trainer winked and patted his trainee. 'Brilliant, young man, you'll be a star. Good hunting.' Bertie winked then melted into the crowd.

Jonathon's heart began to race. He looked for a break in the traffic and crossed the road using a horse and cart as cover. He pretended to be interested in the contents behind a shop window while keeping an eye on his target. He wondered how he could distract the gents. Then his luck changed. A child ran across the road in front of a carriage. A parent screamed, the horses reared and everyone turned to see the commotion. Jonathon acted like an old hand. He pinched the handkerchief as its owner fixed his gaze on the near accident, and was away and mingling with the crowd.

The wealthy gent wouldn't discover his silk item was missing for another ten minutes, perhaps longer. Jonathon took the long way home and went to knock on Bertie's door.

'Oi,' said a voice and the pickpocket froze. He turned and saw his grinning boss who was genuinely pleased. The lad was a natural.

At first, Bankside Bertie would encourage his workers through generosity. If they were good, and this boy was very good, his generosity peaked.

'Come 'ere,' he said. Jonathon went to hand over the handkerchief. 'Not now,' snapped Bertie. The boy had much to learn.

They went inside and, with the door shut, Jonathon handed his boss the goods.

'Now I'm a man of me word, Jonathon Sweeping. This is pay for work performed.'

The boy received a shiny shilling. His eyes bulged. A shilling! That was a small fortune. He gasped his thanks. 'Thank you, sir.'

'Off you go and use it well to help your family.' Jonathon hesitated. 'But don't forget to come back 'ere this afternoon.'

All the way home to Bermondsey, Jonathon pondered his position. He'd swapped careers and instantly made money. There was no comparison. Sweep chimneys, get injured and make nothing. Work for Bankside Bertie and earn money, good money.

The idea that theft was wrong, the thought of being caught and appearing before a magistrate and ending up in prison didn't cross his mind. He was immune to the dangers and repercussions of crime.

He so wanted to give his mother the money but what would he say? How would he explain the windfall? As he began lying to himself, he found it easy to lie to her. He would tell her Mr Pearce gave him the money for being such a hard-working sweep.

With his story prepared, he bounced down the corridor, calling. 'Hello Ma, hello Kitty.'

He heard a squeal and the door opened with Kitty in full flight.

'Jonafon,' she bubbled and hugged her brother. He reckoned she was getting smaller. *Why was that?*

'Hello, Sis,' he said, 'where's Ma?'

'Here I am,' said his mother trying to get out of bed. She stood and struggled to stand. Jonathon was at her side in a flash.

'Ma, what's wrong?' He looked at her gaunt face. 'Are you poorly?'

'It's a cold. I can't seem to shake it off.'

Jonathon saw the room was near empty. No fire and no coal sent a chill through his body.

'Right,' he said. 'Mr Pearce gave me money.'

'Money?' said his surprised mother. 'He paid you?'

'Only because I worked so hard and he wanted to thank me for being such a good sweep.' He studied his mother. She didn't seem to distrust him because she was distracted, struggling to breathe.

'I'll pop out, Ma and get a sack of coal.'

'Can I come, Jonafon?' begged his sister. 'Please.'

He smiled. 'Of course,' he said taking her hand. 'We'll be back soon, Ma. You have a lie down.'

She smiled for the first time in a month as her children left. Jonathon grabbed the coal sack and ran away with Kitty. She loved her brother and when he arrived after a month, her happiness spilled over.

He found coal by the river and used his shiny shilling to buy bread, cheese and bacon. Passing a pie shop, he spent the last of his money on an apple pie.

Back home, his mother couldn't control her tears. She tried to thank her son but choked.

'Come on, Ma, you make the meal and I'll light the fire. He did and the room came alive. It was a feast and being hungry every day, Kitty gulped her food. Jonathon studied his mother.

'When I leave, Ma, I'll ask the doctor to come and see you.'

'Nonsense,' protested Clara. 'It's just a cold and I'll be right as rain in no time. Now, tell me all about your sweeping and Mr Pearce.'

He told her all about his old job and nothing about his new one.

It was a strange family gathering. Jonathon's secret remained hidden as did Clara's. Only Kitty spoke the whole truth. When it came time to leave, Jonathon made an announcement.

'Now that Mr Pearce is paying me a few pennies, I can come home more often to give you a hand, Ma.'

'Are you sure?' she asked, alarmed but at the same time thrilled with his news.

He addressed his sister. 'And Kitty, I want you to help Ma if she is poorly. You are getting to be a big girl now.'

The small child knew from his face and the sound of his voice this was serious. She nodded.

'I'll go now,' he said, 'but I'll be back in a week.'

He kissed his mother and in hugging her, touched and sensed her thin and frail body. He took Kitty's hand and asked her to wave to him from the front door.

She was delighted but sad. At the steps, he knelt and looked into her eyes.

'I want you to be kind to Ma, Kitty.' This was serious. 'Help her with the food and the cleaning and the chamber pots. Okay?'

She could but nod. He kissed her, squeezed her tight and promised to return soon. She waved but found calling his name to be tricky. Her throat developed a lump. He waved and disappeared.

'But sir,' said Jonathon back in Bertie's warehouse, 'I must tell my employer I am leaving.'

'Why? All he'll try and do is persuade you to stay. He may even kidnap you.'

That was a worrying thought. Jonathon wasn't sure what kidnap meant but sensed it was dangerous.

'Please,' begged the sweep. 'Let me explain and ...'

'No,' roared the criminal. 'Never explain, never confess. When you work for me, it's all a secret. Tell nobody you work for me. That's what will make you the money. Now come and have some coffee and a cake. Oh, and tomorrow, young man, you are going to the theatre.'

Being kidnapped and going to the theatre were unknown experiences for Jonathon Sweeping. His life changed and markedly so. Coffee, cake and the theatre—whatever next?

After refreshments, Jonathon was taken upstairs. Bertie's warehouse revealed hidden parts. Through a door you didn't know was there, they entered a clean and tidy dormitory empty except for a line of nine small beds.

'Your bed is at the end, Jonathon. The other lads are out doing a bit of wealth distribution. You'll like 'em. Now come and try on these new clothes. You must togger up, my son, and look like the wellfee geezers what will make you rich.'

Bertie led the way towards another hard-to-see door when Jonathon turned and ran.

'Hey!' yelled Bertie and ran after the boy. It wasn't a serious chase as the ageing villain's old bones, the beginnings of gout, and a dodgy heart meant it was a non-event.

Jonathon panicked, turned and called. 'I must say goodbye to my employer.'

'No!' yelled Bertie fearing the boy would be lost to him.

Jonathon fled. He was excited about his new job but inside, he didn't feel right. He wanted the new job particularly after he saw how his mother and sister were in such dire straits. But he knew he must say goodbye to Mr and Mrs Pearce. They gave him a career, a bed and a full belly. To walk away without saying anything was wrong. He didn't know it but the boy was exercising his conscience.

He ran through the warehouse into the street. He panicked when he saw the fruit seller from whom he once stole two apples. Jonathon ducked behind people and a horse and headed for his employer.

Mr Pearce greeted Jonathon. 'Good to see you back on time, young man,' he said. 'How is your family?'

Jonathon had no firm plan. Would he lie? Would he say he'd been offered a job with pay? Would he simply grab his meagre belongings and flee? Mr Pearce gave him the excuse by asking about his family.

'They're poorly, Mr Pearce, and I need to help them.'

Now the employer gave the boy his full attention. 'Oh?'

'I'm sorry, sir, but they need me. I can't be a sweep no more.'

Shock mingled with anger. 'What? You can't leave!'

'You know my Da is dead and my Ma is poorly and my sister is little. Once I help them, I can come back and be a sweep again.'

Mr Pearce struggled. He considered issuing a threat or a carrot by offering to end the apprenticeship sooner thus allowing the boy to earn money. Instead he pushed for answers.

'How can you help them? You have no job and no money.'

'I have no money here, sir. In another job, I could make money.'

'What other job?'

'I'm not sure but I can't allow my mother and sister to starve.'

The employer couldn't argue. He needed this boy especially because he was so damn good. Pearce made excellent money using this child, and losing him meant having to train a new sweep from scratch and who may not be half as good. In desperation, he replied.

'All right, I will pay you tuppence a week and fourpence if you sweep more than 12 chimneys a day.'

Jonathon blinked. He didn't plan to use blackmail or threaten his boss. He simply told the truth and now he was being offered money. But 12 chimneys a day was murder. His body would cop a beating.

Pearce reckoned his offer generous and assumed the boy would not only accept but be grateful. Jonathon showed no response.

'Right, come and have your supper and then to bed. It's an early start in the morning.'

Jonathon did as told with his mind in a whirl. Was working for Bankside Bertie the best way to help his family? Was the promise of money from Mr Pearce better? His mother was proud of him as a sweep. Would she be proud of his work in wealth redistribution? He lay on his bed of coal sacks and tried to sleep. Upstairs in the kitchen, he heard raised voices. He crept out of the cellar and listened.

'Twelve chimneys a day?' asked Mrs Pearce. 'That's impossible.'

'He's young and fit,' replied Pearce, 'and keep your voice down.'

'What if he sweeps ten or eleven? What then?'

'He gets tuppence. I can't afford to feed and clothe the boy, and pay him as well. I'm only paying him to make sure he stays.'

Jonathon crept back to the cellar. The other and younger sweeps slept soundly. He collected his belongings, walked quietly upstairs and out the back door. He would never work for Mr Pearce again.

# Chapter 11

It was late when Jonathon returned to Bertie's warehouse. The man opened the door sans smile. Rudeness flavoured his speech.

'You again? What do you want?'

Jonathon became sick. He turned his back on Mr Pearce to work for the man who believed in sharing the wealth of the world. Now this man seemed hostile, disinterested. If Bertie turned him away, Jonathon would have nothing. Worse, his family would get nothing.

'I'm here to work for you, sir,' he said. 'I've left my job as a sweep.'

Bertie glowed inside but showed no outward pleasure. 'Have you now? And how do I know you're serious an' won't walk out on me again?'

'I give you my word, sir. I'll work as hard as I can and only for you.' The criminal sniffed still not making any commitment. 'Although I would like the opportunity to visit my family if ever they need help.'

Bertie picked his teeth. 'Tell you what I'll do. I'll give you an hour to bring me something valuable. Do that an' I'll consider takin' you back.' He stared at the boy. 'Well?'

'I understand, sir, and thank you. May I leave my bag here?' Bertie nodded. He knew he held all the cards.

Jonathon turned and disappeared into the night. His mind buzzed. Finding something was one thing but was it valuable and could he take it without being caught?

He wandered the streets. In the dark it was hard to see silk handkerchiefs. Many shops were closed. Jonathon kept thinking of the word *valuable*. Then his mind clicked. He knew a house with valuable items; he lived there for years. Mr Pearce owned valuable objects most bought with the money he made sending boys up chimneys. He even sold the soot Jonathon sent to fireplaces.

The boy hurried through the streets. He knew the gardens surrounding Mr Pearce's house. It was pitch black. Crouching in the back yard, Jonathon looked up at the rooms lit by burning candles. He knew what he wanted.

Picking up his weapon, he moved to the side of the house. Outside the darkened sitting room he paused, then heaved. The rock from the garden smashed the window sounding like an explosion. Jonathon set off running to the back door. Raised voices and footsteps sounded within the house.

The former sweep flew into the kitchen and then into the dining room. He knew the two candle stick holders he wanted, grabbed them and ran.

A young servant girl hurried into the kitchen and collided with Jonathon. His speed and her diminutive size meant she was skittled. Jonathon fled. By the time Mr Pearce and his wife left the room with the shattered glass, the thief was well on his way to a certain warehouse. He ran without stopping, the candlesticks hidden inside his shirt.

Puffing but jubilant, he knocked on the warehouse door. It was flung open and Bankside Bertie smiled on the inside.

'So, the hero returns. But he is empty-handed.'

Jonathon stood there gasping for air. He couldn't speak. From under his shirt, he produced his trophies. Stunned, Bertie grabbed the boy, dragged him inside and closed the door.

Now the famous Bankside smile was back on show. 'My boy, my wonderful boy; when I said valuable you 'ave done yourself proud.'

He admired the loot, knew they were silver and worth a small fortune. *This lad must become part of my team.*

'Does this mean you will employ me, sir?'

'Indeed, and when you work for me, young man, you will be well paid.' He put his arm around Jonathon and led him into one of the rooms in his warehouse. 'But first we celebrate.'

Bertie led him to a special room set aside for his team of workers he called his lads-men. Jonathon met the current residents. Three were older and one decidedly younger, aged only six.

'This 'ere is Jonathon, gentlemen,' said Bertie with pride. 'You'll learn a lot from 'im. Tonight 'e brought 'ome ten pounds wurf of goodies.' The announcement shocked the others. 'I'm takin' 'im out on the town to celebrate so say "Good night", gents.'

The four boys spoke as one, 'Good night, Sir.'

Jonathon couldn't believe he was being addressed as Sir. Bertie guided him back downstairs where he handed him a new jacket. Well it was secondhand but definitely a step up in quality for the boy.

'And 'e's a payment for your work tonight.' Jonathon was handed half a crown, money he could only dream about. 'An' that's just for tonight. Keep it safe. Over 'ere.'

Bertie showed Jonathon a secret place behind a chair. A floorboard was lifted and a small box retrieved. Jonathon placed his money therein and admired his new employer all the more.

They headed out into the night. Bertie loved the theatre, a regular haunt for him but a brand new and totally different world for the boy. They entered the Theatre Royal, Drury Lane.

To Jonathon, the auditorium was spectacular. He saw hundreds of people, seated as was he, and above him special and ornate boxes. Before him was a magnificent performing area, and on it, the show itself. The response from people was like nothing Jonathon had ever heard, and the action and reaction pushed his eyes wider than ever. He didn't know where to look.

In a pantomime in the *Commedia dell'arte* style, the performers were serious even dramatic but heavily comedic. The audience laughed and clapped. A few called out in loud voices, even whistled. Bertie joined in. It was a new world and Jonathon gazed in wonder.

His life changed dramatically as he enjoyed money, coffee and cakes, and now the world of the theatre. In a daze, he walked home with the one and only Bankside Bertie.

Exhausted, Jonathon collapsed on his new bed and re-lived the last 24 hours. He fell asleep thinking about the people he saw and the money that now was his.

Bertie wanted him on the job in the morning. After a tasty breakfast, the boss addressed all five of his "team". 'It's a handkerchief day, gentlemen. Look for nothing other than silk. Mr Robbins wants to push his supply to over one thousand, and we must play our part. Yes?'

'Yes,' roared four of the five team members. Jonathon quickly learnt the drill and when Bertie asked the same question again, Jonathon shouted the loudest.

At this time in London, the theft of silk handkerchiefs became so widespread it meant victims didn't bother complaining to the authorities but went direct to this Mr Robbins character, the chief receiver of said stolen items. There, victims would buy back their property dealing directly with the fence. He might handle up to 5,000 stolen silk handkerchiefs in a week. Talk about big business.

Jonathon did well, although not as well as the others who were more experienced. Bertie gave Jonathon a back-hander by giving high praise to the youngest, the six year-old. It was the way Bertie operated, playing one boy off against another.

After luncheon, the thief-trainer handed out cash to each boy according to their haul. Jonathon received less than the others which only made him more determined to do better. He thanked Bertie and made a request.

'May I visit my family, sir?' he asked. 'I'll return directly and be ready for work.'

Bertie liked the boy. He was the only lad who called him sir.

'Two hours,' he said, 'and don't be late coming back.'

Jonathon thanked him and went to the chair which covered the hiding place for his cash. He withdrew the small tin, opened the lid and wanted to vomit. No money. He heard a sound and turned to see Bertie watching.

'That's my insurance, Jonathon, to make sure you know who your employer is, the one who looks after you.'

Jonathon understood, grew a little wiser, and set off for Bermondsey with the pennies he earned from the silk handkerchiefs that morning.

He turned into the street and glowed with happiness. He could help his family. He would look for coal and buy food. He arrived and surprised, saw Kitty sitting on the steps.

'Kitty,' he called and the little girl looked up, a smile flooded across her face. She bounced down the steps and hugged her brother.

'Jonafon,' she said not letting him go.

'Let's go inside and talk to Ma.'

'She's asleep,' said the girl continuing to cling to him.

He unhooked her arms, took her hand and walked down the corridor. The usual sounds of babies crying, raised angry voices and thuds sounded as they headed to the Sweeping suite.

Jonathon knocked and opened the door. His mother lay asleep on the bed. 'Ma, it's me,' he said.

Clara didn't move and Jonathon went to shake her. He died. Her mouth and eyes were wide open, her body was stiff and cold and although but a boy, Jonathon knew a corpse when he saw and touched one.

He didn't have time to grieve or curse. His sole and immediate task was to protect his young sister. He turned and took her outside.

'Let's leave Ma to sleep. We can go and buy a cake.'

Kitty's eyes brightened. Going anywhere with her brother was exciting. Buying a cake was simply the best. He led her through the streets and felt his throat getting tight. He wanted to cry but couldn't. He held Kitty's hand so tight, she complained.

Immediately he softened his grip and knew he'd frightened the girl because when their eyes met, his were awash with tears.

His natural acting skills shone as he switched to happy and carefree and pointed to the pastry shop. 'You come and choose, Kitty.'

In the cake shop, her eyes bulged. After much searching she pointed and Jonathon paid. They were about to leave when Kitty stopped.

'We must buy a cake for Ma.'

Jonathon nodded. 'Of course,' he said and bought another. His remaining funds amounted to one penny.

They walked home and when there, Jonathon told Kitty to sit on the doorstep and eat her cake. 'I'll take this one to Ma.'

Kitty did as told and Jonathon put the cake in his pocket and entered the room. Now he could weep in peace. He knelt beside the bed and tried to speak to his mother.

'I'm sorry I wasn't here, Ma. You are the best mother any boy could have. I love you, Ma, and I'll look after you and take care of Kitty.' With tears splashing down his face, he closed her eyes, tried but failed to close her mouth, and dragged the bedclothes up and over her body. He looked around the room. There was nothing of value. The coal bucket was empty, the fireplace full of soot and ash.

The furniture's value was as firewood. This room was his first home, where he was born and grew up. The cracks in the walls and floorboards were bigger and the cloth stuffed between the window and the wall had weathered with the years.

He looked at the brick fireplace and thought of his horrible life as a sweep. He reckoned having to sweep this chimney had accident, even death, written all over it. One of the bricks was loose. He reached out and tried to move it. The brick came away easily. He looked in the space and saw a piece of cloth. It was a small bag with coins, his mother's life savings. She chose to stay in London rather than return to Norwich as she wanted to be close to both her children. Now she was dead.

Her pitiful savings shrunk leaving only four shillings and seven pence. Jonathon sensed his heart beat faster. He pocketed the money, kissed his mother's forehead through the sheet, and closed the door.

Kitty was enjoying her cake. 'Come on, Kitty,' he said, 'Let's go on an adventure.' She was excited. 'Ma said it's okay.'

The girl trusted her brother implicitly and, holding her cake with one hand, she grasped her brother's hand and together they set off.

'Who's this?' asked Bertie when the Sweeping siblings arrived at his front door.

'This is my sister, sir. May we come in for a little while?'

Bertie dealt with women who he used to coach his lads in robbing females. Little girls though were not his cup of tea.

'Not for long,' said Bertie, and they entered the warehouse. Jonathon took Kitty to a chair and told the girl to sit. He produced the second cake and gave it to her. One cake was a celebration, two a veritable feast. Jonathon asked Bertie to move further into the warehouse.

'What's all this about?' asked the criminal not happy having his rules and routine interrupted. Jonathon told him and received the weakest condolences ever uttered.

'I would like my Ma to be given a proper burial, sir. I am hoping you will know a person who can help.'

Bertie dealt solely in thieving. Receiving and selling stolen goods was his forte, and dealing in stiffs didn't appeal. He shook his head so Jonathon tried begging.

'I can't leave my poor mother to waste away and be eaten by rats. Please sir, is there a person you can recommend?' He paused. 'My mother left me money.'

'How much?' was the automatic reply.

Jonathon hesitated. This man had already removed the money he earned by stealing the Pearce candlesticks. Bertie wouldn't know what a conscience was but a sliver of compassion forced him to give up the name and address of a priest he dealt with when his brother died.

'Thank you,' said Jonathon going to collect his sister.

'Hang on,' protested Bertie. 'Where's the money you owe me?'

'You have it already, sir; your insurance money, remember?'

Kitty took her brother's hand and the pair walked out of the warehouse leaving Bankside Bertie stunned, made worse by the fact he was out-smarted by a child.

As the Sweeping siblings approached their destination, Jonathon grew nervous. They were heading to Rotherhithe where the sweep's former employer lived and from whom he recently carried out a smash and grab burglary.

'Where are we going, Jonafon?' asked Kitty growing weary.

'Won't be long,' he said smiling at the little girl and spoke the truth as they reached St Mary's Church in St Marychurch Street. He knocked on the door of the rector's house.

A priest with the baldest head south of the river looked down at his visitors. Jonathon's discreet request about a burial saw them invited inside. Kitty was entertained by the housekeeper in the kitchen.

In the priest's study, Jonathon began by taking out all the money he possessed. He explained about wanting his recently deceased mother buried then couldn't hold back his tears. The priest picked up all the money and handed it back to Jonathon.

'You will please keep the money. I will have your dear mother collected and brought here to St Mary's. She will be given a Christian funeral and burial in the churchyard and I will conduct the service.'

The boy wept openly, freely, without self-awareness. The pain of losing his mother burnt a hole in his heart. To have kindness thrust upon him was too much. But the kindness overflowed.

Kitty was cared for while Jonathon rode in a horse and cart with a man from the parish. They travelled to Bermondsey and returned with Clara Sweeping well wrapped and secured in the rear.

The gravedigger prepared the site. The children were fortunate because it was relatively new. Soon, the increase in bodies would mean London churchyards overflowed with corpses and later, miasma. Many graves contained up to 20 bodies.

The rector conducted a dignified service. Jonathon attended as did three parishioners. Kitty was kept amused inside the rectory.

After the burial, the priest made polite enquiries. 'Where are you going now? Will you return to your room in Bermondsey?'

Jonathon hated that option. It was a place filled with heartbreaking memories. But going back to Bertie's was far worse.

'You and your sister are welcome to stay the night,' was an offer which caused the boy's heart to sing.

He and Kitty shared a room at the back of the house with Jonathon avoiding saying anything to his sister about their mother. He knew he would have to explain the situation soon but just then he didn't have the heart to share such sadness with the little girl. Kitty's mother was her world. She seemed to accept her father's death but Jonathon knew that describing Ma as a star in the night sky would not work a second time.

Before breakfast, he sat Kitty down and explained.

'We have a new adventure, Kitty. We will go to see Ma's Ma and Da, our grandparents.'

'Why?'

'Because they will be kind and look after us?'

'Why can't Ma look after us?'

'Because she needs a rest.'

There was a pause and then Kitty shocked her brother. 'Is Ma dead?'

He looked at the girl and both their faces spoke volumes. Jonathon didn't need to speak. He opened his arms and Kitty jumped into him hugging as hard as she could. They wept together taking whatever happiness they could find and proving the adage, a trouble shared is a trouble halved.

'Before we go, we must thank the people in this house,' said Jonathon.

'Is Ma going to be a star in the sky tonight?'

He nodded. 'Yes, a big, bright and beautiful star.'

Kitty seemed to accept the fact but then frightened her brother. 'I wish we could say goodbye to Ma.'

He pondered the situation and then decided. 'Let's have breakfast first and don't forget to thank these kind people.'

Kitty showed perfect manners thanking the kind clergyman and his housekeeper. Both wanted the children to stay at least until they could find proper accommodation.

'Thank you, sir,' said Jonathon, 'but we plan to go to our grandparents in Norwich.'

'Norwich?' exclaimed the housekeeper. 'It's more than a hundred miles away.'

'How will you travel?' enquired the worried priest.

'My father used to work for coachmen who drove from London. We'll go and ask them to take us.'

The adults didn't like the situation one bit. Before they could object, Jonathon flattened them.

'My sister and I would like to say goodbye to our mother, sir, if you would allow us.'

The clergyman seemed lost for words. The housekeeper's eyes grew moist. 'Of course,' he said. 'Come and I'll show you her grave.'

Kitty moved to the housekeeper, thanked her and gave her a hug. The elderly woman's tears appeared in no time. Jonathon copied his sister and then the children followed the priest into the churchyard.

He led them to the fresh grave with soil piled high.

Jonathon held Kitty's hand. 'This is where our Ma is resting.'

The young girl stared at the mound. She knelt and patted the soil. 'Goodbye Ma. Have a nice rest.' She looked at her brother. 'I want to go now please, Jonafon.'

He nodded to the clergyman, took his sister's hand and led her out of the churchyard in Churchyard Street.

# Chapter 12

When Jonathon was about as old as Kitty, his father took him to his work place. The boy was both frightened and thrilled to be so close to the magnificent horses which pulled the coaches to and from London. Now, many years later, he tried to remember where his father once worked.

He thought again about returning to Bermondsey to their vacant room. He didn't and would have regretted doing so. New tenants were already ensconced there, and the landlord would never refund the rent Clara paid in advance.

Jonathon asked people in the street about the place where the horses for the coaches were kept and eventually found it. With sister in hand, they entered the yard. They were greeted by horses neighing and snorting, being led in and out of stables with manure dotted liberally on the cobblestones.

'Oi, you children, get out of 'ere,' yelled a man who ran the yard.

'Please, sir,' called Jonathon, 'we want to travel on the Norwich coach.'

The man was having trouble with a horse being frisky, and again gave the visitors short shrift. 'I told you to get out.'

Jonathon yelled. 'Our father used to work here.' That stopped the man and even the horse settled.

'Your father worked 'ere?'

'Yes sir.'

'Wot's 'is name?'

'Mr Harold Sweeping, sir.'

'Harry Sweeping? He's your old man?'

'Yes, sir, and this is my sister.'

The man looked at the children. He remembered the change in Harry Sweeping's life when a horse smashed his foot. 'Wait 'ere,' he said and walked into a building.

Kitty looked at her brother. 'Jonafon, I need to pee.'

He led her around the side of the stables. 'You can go here,' he said and she did. When they returned, the man thought they'd gone then spotted them.

'There you are. Come wiv me.'

They followed him into the building where another man sat behind a desk.

'So you're Harry's kids? Where's y'mother?'

'In the ground, sir.'

'What?'

Kitty helped him. 'She's in the churchyard.'

That settled the matter. 'And you wanna go to Norwich?'

'Our grandfather's the blacksmith in Little Tinker.' Jonathon produced his purse of coins. 'We have money for the coach, sir.'

'Put it away, son.' He addressed the ostler. 'Take 'em to the inn and tell the driver they can ride up top.'

And that was how the orphaned Sweeping siblings were able to leave London and head to Norwich. It was a free ride but what a ride. Naturally they were not inside the coach but on top amongst the baggage. It was tied and they clung to it and one another.

After Bishop's Stortford, the weather gods turned nasty and the children were tossed a sheet which kept them dry with the exception of their feet and heads. Kitty's hair was plastered to her face.

After sleeping in box rooms in inns, and one night behind the bar in a public house, they arrived in Norwich.

They thanked the crew who brought them on their last leg. 'Where are you goin', boy?' asked the coachman.

'Little Tinker, sir. Can you tell us the way?'

'You're not goin' t'walk. It's about five miles.'

'Four,' said the guard. 'Ask old Hoskins at the dairy. You might get 'im to drive you out.'

They found Hoskins and explained their mission.

'Who?' he asked.

'My grandfather, sir, is the blacksmith in Little Tinker.'

'It'll cost ya sixpence,' he said and sniffed. Jonathon took out his purse and opened it but froze when the old man spoke again. 'Each.'

It was an expensive lesson. In future, Jonathon would produce his purse, take out a single coin, and begin with, "It's all I have, sir".

Still they paid nothing to travel from London, so sitting on the cart owned and driven by Mr Hoskins, they set off to meet their grandparents. Clara used to tell Jonathon tales of her family, and the boy now tingled thinking about this first meeting.

In Little Tinker, Hoskins pulled up outside the blacksmith. The children hopped down carrying their few belongings. The cart turned around and headed back to Norwich.

'Come on, Kitty,' said her brother, 'let's meet our family.'

As they approached the forge, they heard the sound of clanging. Having never met their grandparents, Jonathon expected an old man probably with grey hair and whiskers.

The blacksmith sensed someone entered and turned giving the children, particularly Jonathon, a fright. The man was young, well, certainly not old. He smiled.

'Hello, are you lost?'

'We came to see our grandfather the blacksmith.'

The man's face turned serious. 'Fred Sutcliffe?' Jonathon thought the name sounded correct. 'I'm sorry lad, but Fred died, oh, about two year ago.' The children took the news with equanimity; adults dying was a regular experience for them, especially of late.

'Where are you from?' asked the smithy.

'London, sir.'

'London? Well you won't be going back there tonight. Did you say Fred was your grandfather?'

'Yes, sir.'

'Well then your mother must be one of his daughters. I heard she married and went to London. Is she still there?'

'She died, sir,' said Jonathon.

'She's in the church yard,' added Kitty trying to keep up with the conversation.

'I'm sorry,' said the blacksmith. 'You won't know then that your grandmother, Fred's wife, passed away too. But their older daughter, Mrs Cartwright, your Aunt Daisy, lives here in the village. She has five little 'uns so you should pop along and meet y'cousins.'

The children hesitated; so much news and most of it sad. The blacksmith walked out to the street. 'I'll show you her place.' He pointed. 'It's the cottage with the white fence and the garden that looks like a forest.'

Jonathon smiled at the man. 'Thank you, sir, for all your help.

'You're welcome,' he said and watched the siblings as, hand in hand, they walked along the main street, the only street in Little Tinker. There were about twenty cottages, most with speckled brick walls, a thatch roof, and a quaint, small verandah also covered in thatch. You would best describe them as quiet. Behind the cottages were fields and, in the distance, farms with barns and sheds. Animals stopped chewing to observe the strangers who arrived in the village.

The children stopped outside their Aunt Daisy's cottage. It was getting dark and both developed hunger pangs. Their hopes were high. It was a long way to travel to finish sleeping under the stars on an empty stomach. They opened the gate and stood at the front door.

'Will they let us stay?' asked Kitty, never having been to the countryside before and feeling nervous in such a people-free place.

Her brother nodded and used the door knocker. Children's voices sounded. 'There's someone at the door,' called a girl.

'Ma!' yelled another.

'All right,' a woman complained. 'Can't you see I'm busy?'

Footsteps sounded, at least two lots, and the door opened. A girl, about 12 and a boy about 10 stood there staring at the visitors.

The girl was in charge. She sniffed and then put on airs and graces although badly as acting wasn't her strength.

'Yes?' she said, looking down her nose.

'Hello, I'm Jonathon and this is my sister, Kitty.'

Such facts meant nothing to the children in the cottage. 'Why are you here?' asked the girl.

'We are your family,' said Jonathon, and nothing else.

It was a conversation-stopper. The girl turned and yelled back into the house.

'Ma, there are two children here who say they're our family.'

'What?' came from the kitchen.

The shouting from the front door continued. 'They say they're our family.'

Meal preparation stopped and the lady of the house could be heard approaching. 'What nonsense are you talking?' She yanked open the door and stared at the visitors. It took her a moment to respond. This looked serious. 'Who are you and what are you doing here?'

'Hello, Aunt Daisy,' said Jonathon which flattened the woman. 'We're the children of your sister, Clara.'

'Mother of God,' said the mother of five children although her volume was low.

'Our father and mother have died and we came to visit our grandfather but the man in the blacksmith shop said he died.'

'What's your name?' asked Daisy.

'I'm Jonathon Sweeping and this is my sister, Kitty.'

By now Daisy's entire tribe of five arrived, and by squatting and peering through legs or around older siblings and their mother, they stared in wonder at their cousins.

'Sweeping,' said Mary. 'We were on holiday on the coast but I heard about their wedding, rushed and private as it was. And you say Clara and Harry are dead?'

'Our father died last year but our mother died last week.'

Kitty remembered her lines. 'Our Da is a star in the sky and our Ma is in the churchyard in Churchyard Street.'

The words and their delivery were such it was impossible not to believe them. Daisy was forced into a decision.

'You'd better come in.'

This took maneuvering. Mary's five kids needed to back up but didn't want to, not wanting to miss a moment of this major event. The Sweeping children were hardly going to push their way inside.

'Out of the way, Michael,' said his mother and Aunt Daisy shepherded her nephew and niece inside and to the kitchen. 'Sit at the table.'

They did and she went back to her cooking as her tribe gathered and stared. The Sweepings didn't know what to say so stared back.

'All right you lot,' said Daisy continuing to stir the supper, say your names.'

'Margaret,' said the oldest and the others followed in order of age.

There was Michael, Richard, Elizabeth who pronounced her name E-little-bit, and finally Charley who spoke in a loud voice. If you're the youngest and smallest and don't stand up for yourself, you'll be forgotten and miss out on everything.

Aunt Daisy issued orders. 'Margaret, take your cousins to the loft and make sure the bed is made. Then Michael, you take your cousins outside and show them the privy. The rest of you, behave.'

The visitors were led upstairs with those not assigned a task following to watch. This was a major event in the Cartwright home and staring was free.

After the Sweepings came in from a tour of the outside facilities, Mary's husband Desmond arrived home from work. He was a labourer on the biggest farm in the district.

'Da, Da,' cried his three youngest. 'We've got two new children in our family.'

Such a claim sounded nonsensical to the father but his eyes set on the two newcomers and he looked at Daisy.

'So I see,' he said wanting an explanation from his wife.

'They're Clara's young 'uns. She's died and they've come from London to visit their grandparents not knowing the situation.'

Des moved to the children and extended a hand. 'Welcome. What's your name?'

'I'm Jonathon, sir, and this is my sister, Kitty.'

'How do,' he said. 'And you've come from London on your own?'

'Yes sir. My Da worked with the horses that pulled the coaches and the kind drivers looked after us.'

Des shook his head thinking none of his offspring would be able to find their way to Norwich, four miles hence, let alone spend days travelling to London, and on their own.

'Fetch two more plates, Margaret,' said her mother and the Londoners sat down to a wholesome meal.

It was a strange family reunion. The Cartwright children never knew they had cousins, and to have them arrive unannounced only heightened their appeal. Their parents were polite but restrained. They asked a few questions about Clara and Harry and the lives the London children lived. After the meal, all the children were instructed to go to bed.

'Where are your night clothes?' asked Daisy to her nephew and niece. They looked blank. 'I'll send some up for you. Off you go and we'll talk in the morning.'

The Sweepings settled in the room in the loft. It was dark. Footsteps sounded and Margaret arrived holding a burning candle and two nightshirts.

'These are for you,' she said and went to leave. 'Here, you can have this candle.'

'Thank you,' said Jonathon and spoke to his sister. 'Kitty?'

'Thank you very much,' she said trying on the larger nightshirt meant for her brother. Margaret left.

The siblings sorted the night clothes, settled and Jonathon wanted to say things but didn't. 'Goodnight, sister. See you in the morning.'

He blew out the candle and lay in the dark pondering their future. Although only a child, he could read the adults in this house. They did not gush and fuss over their orphaned family members. With their grandparents now stars in the sky or buried in a Norfolk churchyard, the Sweepings were on their last chance for a new home.

Jonathon found it hard to sleep, not so Kitty. He needed the privy so carefully moved the bedclothes and crept downstairs. He heard his aunt and uncle talking in the kitchen. Their voices were low and his bladder and bowel ordered him outside.

He relieved himself then headed back inside. The back door creaked a little and as he closed it, the adult voices grew louder. They were arguing. It was easy to eavesdrop outside the kitchen door.

'We can't feed and clothe two more children,' said Daisy.

'Are we their only relatives?' asked Desmond.

'No idea. I think Harry Sweeping came from up north. No-one would know if he has any family or where they are. Anyway, he's not a blood relative of the boy.'

Des ignored her. 'I can find the boy a job on the Stevenson farm. He can work and live there and he'll be their responsibility.'

'He should be the responsibility of his father.'

'He's dead.' Des forgot the rape incident at Bittering Hall.

'Harry Sweeping's not his father. You remember. Clara was a maid at the Hall and attacked by Lord Rallison's son, Crispin. *He's* the father of the boy.'

In the darkened hallway, the listener shivered. His body turned cold and his mind started spinning. *My father is not my father? What does "my mother was attacked" mean?*

Des shook his head. 'Well we can hardly take him to the Hall and ask His Lordship to care for his own grandson.'

'Why not?' asked Daisy, keen to offload both children.

Des stared at his wife. 'You can't be serious. They'll set the hounds on us.'

Silence settled in the kitchen. Outside the door, Jonathon struggled to understand what he heard. He worried the sound of his beating heart would give him away.

'Well they can't stay here,' said Daisy, 'and the sooner we get rid of them, the better.' More silence before Des agreed.

'Okay, I'll get him a job on the farm. What'll we do with the girl?'

'I'll take her to the workhouse or an orphanage in Norwich.'

Jonathon cringed as mental blows belted his body. Thoughts clashed inside his head. He heard chairs being moved and so hurried upstairs as quietly as possible. He slipped into the loft and under the bedclothes beside his soundly sleeping sister.

They were alone, two orphans in the home of their blood relatives who couldn't wait to get rid of them. Jonathon tried to devise a plan.

If they stayed here, they would be separated and moved. If he ran away, Kitty would be alone and she would have nothing and no-one. If he took Kitty and they ran away together, where would they go and how would they get there?

From the death of his parents, to his horrendous life as a sweep, to his criminal behaviour, to his relatives who shunned him, to the news about his father, with Kitty, they were alone. He made a plan.

# Chapter 13

The Cartwright household slept when Jonathon opened the back door and walked along the only street in Little Tinker. His plan meant leaving his young sister behind and that decision stuck a dagger in his heart. If his plan worked, he would come back and rescue Kitty later and keep her safe forever.

Clouds covered the moon, and a chill wind taunted him as he set off towards Norwich. He reached the blacksmith's building with its only door closed. The boy walked along the side of the building where the house behind the smithy sat in darkness.

Jonathon tried the side door of the building with the forge. It opened. Not much was locked in Little Tinker. He paused then entered and closed it. The shed was pitch black but warm, the fire in the forge still giving off heat. He squinted and discovered a place in a corner. He curled in a ball, wrapped his arms around his body and fell asleep.

'Hello, hello, hello,' said Alfred Lund the blacksmith.

Jonathon was awake in a second. He stood. 'I'm sorry, sir. I wasn't stealing. I needed a place to sleep.'

'What happened to your Aunt's house and where's your sister?'

'Ah, it's a long story and ...'

'Never mind. Come with me.'

The blacksmith, a million times friendlier than Aunt Daisy, led the boy into his house and introduced him to Mrs Lund.

'This is one of the children I told you about, my dear. He's Mrs Cartwright's nephew and needs a hot breakfast.'

Jonathon was treated like royalty whereas up the road all hell broke loose. Kitty woke and couldn't find her brother. She tiptoed downstairs and sent the family into a spin. Cartwright children were sent to look for the missing cousin. Kitty cried and at last her aunt showed a droplet of human kindness by speaking gently to the weeping girl.

Back in the blacksmith's house, Jonathon explained the situation. He related parts of the overheard conversation, shocking the Lunds.

'An orphanage in Norwich!' gasped the wife.

'Stevenson's farm!' hissed her husband. 'You cannot work there. The man's a brute. It's in the middle of nowhere and last year one of his labourers disappeared.'

Jonathon's confusion mounted. 'Could I beg a favour of you, sir?' he asked.

'Of course,' replied the blacksmith.

'Could you please tell my aunt I've gone to find work in Norwich and will return soon to collect my sister?'

The Lunds looked at one another. Their visitor was a boy, strong and sturdy, and speaking sensibly, but still so young.

'Of course I will but what sort of work can you do?'

'I was a sweep in London, sir, and I'm sure there are chimneys in Norwich.'

'And where are your tools?'

Jonathon's shame appeared. His plan was flimsy at best.

'I have a few old rags,' said Mrs Lund and produced them.

Mr Lund went outside calling. 'And I have an old brush I no longer use.'

'Put them in this,' said Mrs Lund handing Jonathon an old bag.

Mr Lund returned and gave the boy the battered brush.

Jonathon's eyes filled with moisture.

'Thank you, sir and madam, and I will return as soon as I've found a place to stay in Norwich. Is there a shortcut to the city, rather than walk on the road?'

The blacksmith led the boy outside. He pointed towards Norwich. You could take a much shorter journey crossing the fields but most of the land hereabouts is owned by Lord Rallison, and he treats trespassers like he treats foxes. Stay well clear, lad.'

Jonathon froze at the mention of His Lordship's name. 'Does he own a big house?'

'He does. Bittering Hall is the biggest stately home in Norfolk.'

Jonathon smiled and offered his hand. 'You have been more than kind, sir, and I won't forget all you have done for me and my sister.'

They shook hands. 'You're welcome, young man, and I'll pop along and tell your aunt and your sister the good news.'

The boy walked along the road to Norwich while the blacksmith went the other way and knocked on the Cartwright cottage door.

'It's Mister Lund,' cried Margaret after she opened the door.

Daisy arrived. 'Good morning,' she said with questions aplenty about his presence.

'I come with a message, Mrs Cartwright. The young lad who called on you yesterday has gone to Norwich to find work.'

The news whacked Daisy with a hard slap. 'What work?'

'And he wants you to know there's no need to take his sister to the orphanage in Norwich as he'll return soon to collect her.'

Daisy fumed. Embarrassment and rage bubbled away causing her to speak without thinking.

'Who does he think he is, the little brat? I've a good mind to tell his sister to run after him.' She looked like she meant it.

Alfred made an instant decision. 'Don't do that, Missus. I'll take the wee girl and look after her until Jonathon returns.'

Daisy's temper exploded. Her plans were overheard and repeated elsewhere, with her heartlessness exposed. Soon the whole village—such as it was—would hear about the evil aunt. She snapped at her firstborn.

'Margaret, fetch your cousin.'

Silence settled on the doorstep with Daisy glaring and fuming while Alfred worked on a pathetic smile. Speaking of pathetic, Kitty appeared. Her eyes were red and her heart broken as she thought the only person she loved had run away and abandoned her. She was pushed at the blacksmith.

'Go with this man and pray your brother keeps his word.'

Daisy slammed the door and Alfred turned on a wonderful smile for little Miss Sweeping. He held out a hand which the girl took in hers.

'Come along, young lady, let's get you some breakfast and then we can talk about your big, brave brother.'

The last part of that sentence sounded wonderful and Kitty met Mrs Dulcie Lund, the childless wife of the village blacksmith.


Jonathon took the road to Norwich and once out of sight of the village, turned into the fields taking the short cut he was advised to avoid. His mind buzzed. His aunt spoke about his mother being attacked by Lord Rallison's son. *What does that mean?* Jonathon wanted answers and Norwich became less important.

The fields gave way to a forest. All he could see were trees. He guessed his direction hoping to stumble upon people, a road or buildings, anything to help him reach this mysterious house and learn the truth about his mother. The comment about trespassers being treated like foxes made him look around. Stepping over fallen branches he kept going. The land was flat until he climbed a small rise. The trees thinned and he stood at the edge of the wood and saw a magnificent house.

Enormous didn't cover it. He'd seen large houses in London but this one had been stretched. Yes it was high but oh so wide. The gardens around the house were massive and immaculate and, in the distance, he could see men working on hedges, lawns and flowers.

From his vantage point, he saw a landau come along the road leading to the house. He'd never seen a carriage like it. It stopped in front of the steps and a lady holding a parasol and wearing a massive hat was helped out and guided up the stairs and into the house.

Jonathon knew he could never go where that lady went. He moved along the wood line, keeping out of sight until the rear of the house was in view. He saw outbuildings including a large stable block. He wasn't to know his father and stepfather both spent time with horses in that building.

Facing the rear of the house, he approached using the various outbuildings as a screen. He turned a corner and startled a young woman. She gave a restrained scream and Jonathon immediately took a step back.

'I'm so sorry, Miss, I didn't mean to startle you. I'm Jonathon, the chimney sweep.'

'Oh,' said the girl, not much older than the visitor. 'I'm Beatrice the scullery maid. Do you want Mrs Beadle?'

Jonathon hardly hesitated. 'Ah, yes please.'

'I'll tell her you're here. Follow me.'

The woman she named was the same housekeeper who welcomed Jonathon's mother and then later advised her to leave and never return. What would Mrs Beadle's reaction be to meeting the child born to the scullery maid she sent away?

The now older housekeeper came into the yard with a quizzical look on her face. 'Chimney sweep? I didn't order a sweep? Who are you?'

'Good day, madam,' said the boy in as humble and respectful manner as possible. I'm Jonathon from Norwich where my master told me to attend Bittering Hall and sweep the chimneys.'

'And who is your master?'

'Mr Pearce, madam. I believe he once swept the chimneys here before moving to London, to Rotherhithe, it was.'

Jonathon sounded convincing despite not knowing the best lies contain a grain of truth. He was helped by the fact that the chimneys at Bittering Hall had not been swept for ages, and Lord Rallison complained about a fire in the breakfast room last week.

'Very well,' she said. 'Come inside and I'll give you instructions.'

With heart pounding, the former London sweep entered the kitchen where his mother once slaved away being bullied from day one. Upstairs in her tiny bedroom was where the chimney sweep was conceived. Of course he knew nothing of such details.

Holding his bag with its brush and rags, Jonathon stood in Mrs Beadle's room. 'If you make even the tiniest mess, I'll have you sent packing without a penny. Do you understand?'

'I do, Missus, but they'll be no mess. And please, what should I do with the soot?'

His question threw her. 'What do you usually do?'

'Mr Pearce always took it away, Missus.'

'Well you can do the same. Now follow me.'

She led him upstairs, then along a hallway and into the breakfast room. It was empty. She stopped at the fireplace. 'You can start here. I'll send Beatrice to give you a hand.'

'Thank you, madam. I'll report to you when the chimney's swept.'

She stared at him, lingering doubts giving her concern. 'No mess,' she said and left.

Jonathon looked around admiring the room and its contents. He saw valuable items on the sideboard and memories of the night he stole candlesticks from his former employer flashed in his mind. He knelt in the fireplace and looked up the chimney. It needed to be swept. He crouched inside the fireplace when the door opened.

'Hello?' called Beatrice not seeing the boy.

Jonathon called back. 'I'm over here.'

She joined him. 'I set the fire but His Lordship went out early so it hasn't been lit this morning.'

'It would help if you could clear it away so I can collect the soot.'

'Of course,' she said and started work. He picked up a portable fireguard to use as a shield once the soot began to fall.

'How long have you worked here?' he asked.

'Only since last Christmas.'

'I know someone who used to work here.'

'Oh? What's his name?'

'It was a lady. She worked as the scullery maid.'

'That's *my* job. I met the last girl, Betty, and she was nice.'

Jonathon thought about his next sentence. 'Her name was Clara.'

Beatrice thought. 'I don't remember anyone mentioning that name. You could ask Mrs Beadle. She's been here forever.'

'Thanks, I will,' he replied, and then prepared to sweep. He placed the guard on the tiles, tied one of the rags over his head, and "walked the chimney".

It seemed an age since he last performed this task and he hadn't missed the work for a second. He reached the soot and brushed. Soot fell. He remembered the smell, the sensation as the horrible material reached out and grabbed you, and the taste, the spit-it-out taste when you breathed in at the wrong time.

After a few minutes he heard voices. Mrs Beadle entered to inspect the work. 'Sweep up any soot, Beatrice.'

'Yes, Mrs Beadle.' The housekeeper examined the scene and, satisfied, began to leave. 'Oh Mrs Beadle, do you remember a scullery maid called Clara?'

The housekeeper froze, her mouth resembling a fish on a market stall. She gasped, 'What did you say?'

Jonathon heard the words and stopped work to listen.

Beatrice chatted away. 'The sweep said he knew a lady who worked here called Clara.'

'The sweep?' whispered the housekeeper. Her mind exploded. She definitely remembered a scullery maid called Clara, the sixteen year-old girl raped in her bedroom by the son of the Lord of the Manor.

But how could this boy know her? He wouldn't have been born when Clara was sent packing.

Then the penny dropped. *He is her son!*

She didn't know that of course and was never going to ask. She panicked. If this boy is Clara's son and makes a fuss, the Marquess will explode and his son, the Earl, will seek a simple resolution—kill the bastard and bury the evidence.

'Stay here,' she said to Beatrice, 'and come and tell me the moment the sweep comes down the chimney.'

She left, the maid stood confused and Jonathon resumed sweeping but with an accelerating heartbeat.

Over her thirty years of service, the housekeeper normally solved every crisis, but this had her worried with the potential to become a scandal of tragic proportions. The only person in the house she trusted was Lady Rallison. The housekeeper set off in a hurry.

She found the Marchioness in the conservatory, asked if she might speak with her with neither woman knowing the son and heir, the villain himself, Earl Crispin, was within earshot, smoking in the garden.

'I'm terribly worried, my Lady,' said Mrs Beadle telling the story.

Crispin heard each word and quietly took off. He crashed into the breakfast room scaring the daylights out of the scullery maid.

'Out,' he bellowed and Beatrice fled in fear. Crispin bent by the fireplace and called. 'You, sweep, stop what you're doing.' Jonathon stopped. 'Come here now.' Outside, Beatrice heard the threats.

Jonathon hesitated. The tone of the man's voice screamed danger and the boy stayed still. 'I haven't finished, sir.'

'Why are you asking about a scullery maid called Clara?'

More hesitation from Jonathon. 'She was my mother, sir.'

'Was?'

'She died, sir, in London.'

'So why are you here?'

'I was told she was attacked, sir, and want to find out what happened.'

'Who told you that?'

Jonathon worried he might put others in the same predicament he now faced. He lied. 'Several people told me, sir.'

Crispin raged. This insignificant, working-class brat might spread lies about his, Crispin's faultless behaviour. He wanted his hands on the brat, his own flesh and blood.

'Come here, now.' This was his final demand. Jonathon reckoned the best course of action was to stay put and sweep. He sent soot flying as Crispin poked his head in the fireplace and looked up.

He screamed as the soot landed. 'I'll fix you, Master Sweep.'

He grabbed the grate with the prepared fire material and placed it back in the fireplace. He lit the paper and soon the flames crackled. Jonathon panicked. It was time to descend. Coal was heaped on the flames and now the ascending smoke turned black.

Jonathon coughed. The smoke made him cry. The heat greeted his feet. He couldn't stay put. It was climb down and be burnt, and goodness knows what else, or climb skywards.

Beatrice burst into the conservatory. A shocked Mrs Beadle was about to reprimand the maid who, distressed, blurted her news.

'Oh, Mrs Beadle, come quickly, I think Earl Crispin is attacking the sweep.' This was a cat-landing-amongst-the-pigeons moment.

The housekeeper took off for the breakfast room with Beatrice in tow as the woman with the parasol, the one who arrived in the landau, entered the conservatory.

'What on earth is happening?' she asked her mother-in-law.

The former Lady Catherine Denbigh-Wallace married way below her station when she wed Crispin the Cad. Financially it was a good match but in terms of class, compassion and elegance, a disaster. Her father couldn't pay his debts. She was beautiful. It was a trade of social status and wealth, a marriage made in the City. Crispin won a stunning bride and Catherine's father's debts were paid. The loser was Lady Catherine who won an horrific husband.

Lady Rallison explained the situation which failed to surprise Catherine. She knew her husband's past would disgrace the worst criminal. Drunk as a Lord suited Crispin to a tee.

'I'll see if I can help,' she said and left the conservatory. As she approached the breakfast room, voices clattered down the hall.

Crispin shouted to the sweep and to Mrs Beadle. She begged Crispin to cease his attack on the boy. Catherine headed upstairs.

Meanwhile, driven by fear, Jonathon climbed as fast as he could up the large and tall chimney. His skill as a sweep helped him this far but as he neared the top, the smoke continued to chase him. He looked up and died. It was as he expected. Pots sat atop the chimney. There was no way he could escape. It was fall and be killed or climb down, be burnt and, like his mother, attacked. Jonathon had no idea the man who raped his mother was the man who now attacked him and was in fact his father.

At the top he saw daylight. Pushing hard against the walls of the chimney, he reached up and used the brush to break, crack or topple one of the pots. He held the brush by the bristles and the sharp pain never registered as smoke and heat hammered his slim body. It was useless. In desperation he pushed against the wall heading down while moving his feet up. His feet were above his head. He kicked.

Hallelujah. One of the pots moved, not much but enough to encourage him to try again. He did and the mortar between the top bricks failed to hold the baked clay. A crack appeared. His desperation drove him hard and the next kick saw a pot prove the theory of gravity. It smashed against the tiles on the roof, shattered and fell. Fortunately no-one below copped the debris.

Jonathon climbed to the top. The air was glorious, the sunshine divine but his problem became worse.

He could escape from the chimney but to where? The strong Welsh slate lay on a steep incline. To climb onto the roof would be tricky; to slip and slide would be fatal. He could hear the brute below continuing his threats. How could the sweep escape?

Someone spoke. A dormer window opened and a woman's voice called. 'Over here.' Lady Catherine's head appeared and she beckoned and called again.

Jonathon's options were the lady's offer or death. He dropped his bag and brush scaring the life out of Crispin then stepped onto the tiles and their angle made him slip. He lay flat on his front, digging fingers and shoes into any gap which might give him traction.

Once level with the open window, he would need to go below it to gain entry to the house. He began sliding across the roof. The space between the bottom of the window and the gutter of the roof was only about six feet. Moving sideways was scary; moving downwards terrifying. He moved as fast as a tired snail. The woman spoke words of encouragement. Floating out of the chimney, she and the boy heard threats from her husband.

Jonathon reached the window and faced his problem. He needed to squeeze under it before he could try to enter. Now he must move down, towards the edge of the roof. One slip and gravity would do for him what it did for the chimney pot.

'You can do it, young man,' said Lady Catherine. Jonathon chose not to speak. Down the roof he moved, his heart using the tiles as the surface of a drum. Once his head was below the open window, he inched upwards. But what could he grasp to go higher?

With a soot-covered rag wrapped around his head and a blackened face, he looked like a strange creature from a black lagoon. Higher he inched. The woman leant as far as she could, her hand extended. He could see it and prepared to extend his hand to grasp hers. Then as he went to lunge, he slipped. Panic.

She stifled a scream and he saw his sister's face staring at him. To desert her as he did was bad enough. To fall off a roof and die without saying goodbye, and leaving her with their horrible aunt was cruel and unforgiveable.

As he started to slide off the roof, his head copped a whack. It hurt being hit by the sinker on the end of a fishing rod stored in the room. Jonathon grabbed the end of the rod and looked up. The other end was held by the lady from the landau minus her hat. She gripped her end with both hands. In her glorious, high-fashion outfit, she looked incongruous. Her face offered encouragement. Then she spoke.

'You can do it.'

The sweep placed one hand over another and dragged himself up the roof. His rescuer reached out and grabbed his hair. With a handful, she yanked and he fell into the top-floor room.

'Thank you, madam,' he croaked and tears formed rivulets on his soot-covered cheeks. She stood back trying to avoid her expensive clothes being seriously stained, well, even minutely stained.

'Don't make a sound. I'll lock the door and return when it's safe.'

She left and Jonathon looked around. He was in a small room used for storing materials. A bath or even a basin and water would have been perfect but who cares, he was safe.

# Chapter 14

Kitty enjoyed meeting Mrs Lund the blacksmith's wife, and loved a proper breakfast. Using discreet language and whispers, Alfred told his wife about the treatment the Sweeping siblings received from their aunt up the road. Dulcie was saddened and determined to give the child much love and comfort.

Despite her tender years, Kitty sensed she was safe in this new environment. She longed for her brother but when told he was away finding a new home for her, she perked up no end. After an hour in the blacksmith's home, the residents and their visitor were getting on like the fire in the blacksmith's forge. Was this a marriage made in heaven?

Not far away, Jonathon grew restless in his hideaway. He tried the door and found it locked. He wondered if that was to keep him in or others out. He thought he heard raised voices and knew he would be the topic of conversation.

Minutes passed although the boy had no idea of time. He dozed then snapped awake when he heard a sound. The door opened and the lady who saved his life entered. He stood in a hurry.

'Put these on,' she said handing him a coat and a hat. Both were too big but Jonathon didn't hesitate. 'Come with me,' she said and stepped out of the room. She pointed. 'When I give you the signal, go down those stairs. Don't stop for anyone. Run. Do you understand?'

Jonathon nodded but asked a question. 'What signal, madam?'

She crossed to the window where his life was saved. 'Come here.' She pointed. 'I will be in the landau when it's parked down there. I will look up to this window. Watch and be ready. See me and fly.' She headed to the door, turned and tossed him a key. 'Lock the door after I leave and keep watch at the window.'

She closed the door. He hurried to lock it then watched from the window. He saw nothing but heard footsteps, loud and angry voices.

'The chimney pot came crashing down, my Lord. He must have climbed out onto the roof.'

'That's bloody obvious so where is he now?' snarled Crispin.

The door handle rattled and Jonathon panicked.

'It's locked. Where's the key.' The underling didn't know. 'Find it and if you can't, bring me an axe.' Footsteps faded. 'And hurry!'

Jonathon had been through many frightening experiences. To describe this one, he needed a word stronger than terrifying. He ran to the window and looked out. He saw nothing, no landau in sight, and even if he did, with the enemy at the door, his escape was over.

The boy again surveyed the room. Not much to see. There was nowhere to hide. He heard shouting.

'I have a key, sir.'

That was it. Jonathon fell back on his life as a sweep.

He heard the key in the lock. It proved tricky and swearing began. Then the key worked and the door was flung open. Crispin stepped in and stared at the near empty room. The sweep was not there. This provoked even more swearing.

'There's another room down the corridor, my Lord.'

The men disappeared. Jonathon breathed again. He balanced on the door frame pressing himself flat against the wall. As he moved, soot broke free and drifted to the floor. He ignored it, dropped as silently as possible and hurried to the window.

He saw the landau and didn't wait for a signal. He flew out the door and down the stairs. As he reached the ground floor, Mrs Beadle entered the hallway and nearly died. A boy with a black face, oversized coat and hat bounded past her and into the kitchen. The cook and maids dropped whatever they were holding. The back door groaned on its hinges.

Lady Catherine saw the boy running. She yelled to the driver. 'Go!'

Upstairs, the underling with Earl Rallison looked out of a window and saw the fleeing escapee. He screamed to the aristocrat. Crispin raced to look, swore yet again and took off.

Jonathon leapt at the moving landau. He clung to its side and clambered over and into the vehicle.

'Lie down,' screamed Lady Catherine and to the driver, 'Faster!'

There was only one driveway into Bittering Hall. The landau set a steady clip. Crispin ran to the stables, grabbed an unsaddled horse, leapt on its back and whipped it hard. The horse could easily outrun the four-wheeler.

The road to Norwich was a good half mile away and Catherine knew she would likely fail. She looked behind and saw a horseman, her husband, starting after them. She bent and spoke to the sweep.

The chase grew faster. The landau took a broad right turn and Catherine shouted, 'Now.' On it drove with the chasing horseman gaining by the second. Catherine looked to one side and saw her glowering husband. He shouted and gesticulated.

'Pull over!'

The driver did as ordered and the rider dismounted. He was pretty close to frothing at the mouth.

'What the hell do you think you're doing, woman?' He didn't restrict his uncouth behaviour to those below stairs and glared at his wife. He couldn't see his quarry. Ah, but there was a blanket on the floor covering something. Crispin opened the door, leant in and ripped away the blanket. He stared at a box beside his wife's feet and that's when the frothing of the mouth began.

A quarter of mile behind them, Jonathon stumbled into the woods. They were part of the estate and provided great cover for any escapee. Lady Catherine gave the boy instructions, and once the landau entered the bend in the road and was momentarily out of sight to her galloping husband, Jonathon leapt into the bracken at the side of the road. His ankle hurt, his shoulder clipped a tree stump but he survived, and scrambled into the woods. He clasped two coins his rescuer gave him once he settled in the landau.

'Go to Norwich and then flee to London,' she said. 'You are never going to be safe in this county. Go and God speed.'

Finding the coach to London was relatively simple for Jonathon. With cash in his pocket, he could have bought an inside seat but knew how to scrimp and save. Rescuing his sister troubled him but he couldn't if he was dead.

He stayed out of sight, washing his face and hands at a pump behind a public house. Food would have been nice but he knew a certain gentleman would be looking for him. Only when the coach prepared to depart did he come out of hiding and climb atop the vehicle. Next stop London.

A week later, Bankside Bertie spat. His blood boiled as he addressed his cohort of criminals. He trained them, gave each lad the benefit of his wisdom, and paid them when they brought home the bacon. Not today he didn't.

'It ain't good enough,' he growled. 'Three silk handkerchiefs from five boys is pathetic. What is it?' His rhetorical question meant their repeating the word pathetic was pathetic.

The young thieves sat in silence. Their lack of success meant the boss yelled at them, cut their suppers, and paid them next to nothing.

'So what's going on?' demanded the boss.

'We've got competition, Bertie.'

He fumed. 'Of course you've got competition. Life is a competition. Work harder and smarter.'

'That boy who left is damn good,' said another of Bertie's gang.

Bertie's eyebrows flew skywards. 'What boy? Who are you talkin' about?'

'The one who nicked them candlesticks.'

Bertie came alive. 'Jonathon, the kid who was a sweep?'

The others nodded. 'I saw him nick a gold watch today and the geezer had no idea it was took,' added another in the gang.

Bertie stroked his grizzled beard. He wished he'd kept Jonathon Sweeping, and now regretted stealing the boy's wages with an excuse of insurance money.

'Okay, listen. I want two of youse to tell Sweeping 'e's welcome back any time he likes. Tell 'im I'll give 'im the best deal any finance equalizer ever earned in the whole of London.' The others scowled. They were to recruit a boy who would make more than them.

Bertie sensed anger. 'An' any boy who persuades Sweepin' to come back t'work, gets a guinea.' They gasped. 'You 'eard me, a guinea.'

That put a smile on certain faces.

Incentive drove the boys to pinch more items, more expensive items, and when they could earn 21 shillings just for talking a fellow pickpocket to work for Bertie, well, let's go and find 'im.

A couple reckoned they could offer Jonathon money for him to come home. How about five bob to come home? I mean, 16 bob for the persuader was a damn good deal in anyone's book.

Back in London, Jonathon returned to his family's old address in Bermondsey. He found waste building material and made a fourth wall in the space above the laundry. With straw on the floor, he created a perfect hideaway. Well, perfect's an exaggeration. Yes it was rent free but being in close proximity to the privy meant deep breathing was out. His new coat was a godsend but he knew come winter he wouldn't so much freeze as die. He found a new hiding place for his cash and set about executing his plan.

Stealing was his forte. What he needed was a fence who paid a fair rate. He found one in old Miser Ryan. People said he was a Jew but Miser was a Mick, a Pádraig from Donegal.

'Bring me more of dis stuff, me darlin' and I'll make you rich,' he said when Jonathon showed him the pocket watch. 'Pity you left the chain.'

So Jonathon stuck to his routine. Steal well, sell well, hide his fortune well, and prepare to rescue his little sister. He didn't know Kitty moved her address in Little Tinker and now resided with the blacksmith and his wife. The child hadn't been loved so much since her mother died, and the childless, middle-aged couple doted on the new arrival. Aunt Daisy fumed.

It was a grand day for robbing. Jonathon learnt how to observe without being seen. No wonder Bankside wanted him back as the boy was good at being bad. He saw his mark, in this instance an elderly gent in a beautiful town coat. Jonathon strolled towards the victim. He paused, prepared to strike when, without warning, a hand landed on his shoulder. He froze then turned.

'Hello me old mucker,' said a boy he knew from Bertie's stable.

'Go away,' hissed Jonathon, 'I'm working.'

A second boy appeared, accosting Jonathon from behind. The duo had agreed to work as one to persuade Jonathon to return. They manhandled him to an alley and made their generous offer.

Jonathon looked at one then the other. 'You can tell Bertie I wouldn't work for him for all the jewels in the Tower. He robbed me and he's what proves the saying, there's no honour among thieves. Now leave me alone.'

He glared at them and walked away. The two boys looked worried.

'What'll we tell Bertie?' asked one.

The other shrugged. 'Whatever we say, 'e ain't gonna be 'appy.'

They were wrong. Bertie wasn't unhappy, he was furious. Nobody turns down Bankside Bertie. He hatched a plan to deal with Jonathon Sweeping.

It was a lovely day for a hanging. Execution mornings pulled a crowd. The scaffold in the street outside Newgate prison was erected during the night. Those in the jail waiting for the noose heard the carpenters. But strangely, if you interviewed many of the prisoners awaiting execution, many weren't upset.

'I've 'ad a good life,' said one.

'Nah, nuffin scares me,' said another.

You could put these relaxed comments down to life in a city with a million plus people where starvation, infant mortality and open sewers were rife and created a certain atmosphere. It was a sort of alive-last-night-dead-in-the-morning type of city.

The threat of hanging for stealing your daily food ration didn't cut the mustard. I'm hungry, I steal. I get caught. I die.

Jonathon Sweeping developed a different motivation. Oh he needed grub but having seen his parents die, his employers abuse and defraud him, his aunt give him the cold shoulder, and some toff try to murder him, he wanted to make sure his kid sister received a half decent start in life, and it was what now drove him to steal.

He knew the crowd could be big at Newgate, as many as 100,000. He knew the wealthy would be there and distracted as the wretches did their infamous sailors' hornpipe on the gallows. It was the perfect scenario to pilfer silk handkerchiefs, watches, purses and whatever else he spied.

At this time in London, Sir Robert Peel pondered the possibility of setting up a police force. He wanted men in uniform with a baton, handcuffs and a rattle; yes, a rattle. At present, in London and elsewhere in the country, there were constables, and other men known as night watchmen. Both groups were employed to prevent crime. The night watchmen, as per their job title, went on patrol at night. The constables wandered the streets mainly by day looking to nab any ne'er-do-wells.

Despite his youth, Jonathon developed two finely-honed skills. He could find and filch saleable items and, more importantly, do so without being caught. On his own, he was a successful crime machine.

Alas all good things, good for the thief that is, come to an end. Jonathon spotted three well-heeled gents downing beer as they watched the spectacle of criminals being executed. For Jonathon, these men were easy pickings.

He was about to claim his first trophy for the day when, out of nowhere, whack. Betrayal reared its ugly head.

The enraged and slighted Bankside Bertie sought revenge on Jonathon Sweeping. *No boy turns me down and gets away with it.*

Bertie paid his boys to find the sweep, and certain constables to do the business.

Bertie's boys pointed out young Master Sweeping. The constables took their time. They watched, waited and approached with care. Jonathon made his strike and was nabbed.

'Gotcha,' cried one constable and the mobile crime spree died.

Jonathon struggled against two men. Their grip was rock solid and the lad was marched away. His cash supply remained hidden, his sister lived in blissful ignorance, and Jonathon's life would never be the same again.

When Bertie heard the news about Jonathon's arrest, he smiled exposing his few remaining rotten teeth.

# Chapter 15

There was a time in Britain when children were not treated as criminals. If a cheeky youngster went scrumping, he might cop a clip over the ear by a farmer or parent. When they existed, calling a constable to deal with youthful miscreants rarely happened.

But times changed and as crimes increased in seriousness, often due to poverty, authority figures jumped on board. The assizes, courts across the country, began dealing with young criminals.

And once young offenders attended court, punishments changed. Forget a ticking off or that proverbial clip over the ear. Now the children were sent to a reformatory where whipping youngsters was definitely part of the curriculum.

From there it was a slippery slope. More children committed more crimes and more children ended up before a magistrate, and then before a judge and jury who often found the little blighters guilty, meaning these young criminals finished up in jails built for adults.

Jonathon Sweeping was dragged from the riotous crowd fixated on the executions. The constables led him through the streets of London with the boy having no say in the matter.

They reached a respectable house in a respectable street with a row of elegant townhouses either side. They climbed the few front steps where one constable rang the bell. A servant appeared.

This was a private house and the residence of magistrate, Mr Charles Drake. Part of his job was to interview criminals—the word *alleged* was not required at this time—and decide if there was sufficient evidence to have the lawbreaker brought before a court. Being in London, that court was located in a street called Old Bailey.

Jonathon was marched into the study. Mr Drake, a God-fearing man, sat behind his desk. A male secretary stood behind and to one side of his master ready to notate actions and attend to any request.

'This boy was caught in the act of stealing a silk handkerchief, sir,' said the first constable. 'We witnessed the act. The boy has a reputation for thieving in different parts of London.'

Mr Drake looked at Jonathon who struggled to understand the last hour of his topsy-turvy life. From roaming free and making a good living, he was standing before a serious-looking man in a posh London house being accused of stealing. He didn't know the term but in short, they had him bang to rights.

'What have you to say?' asked the magistrate.

Jonathon hesitated wondering if speaking would help or hinder his case. 'Good day, sir.'

'How old are you?'

'I think I'm eleven, sir.'

'You think? Don't you know?'

'Not rightly, sir, no.'

'Where do you live?' asked the magistrate.

'In Bermondsey, sir.'

'What address?'

The boy shook his head. 'I don't know the name or number, sir but I can take you there.'

'Can you read and write?'

'No, sir. I've never been to school.'

'Where are your parents?'

'They're dead, sir.'

'Do you have any family?'

'A sister, sir.'

'Does she live with you?'

'No, sir.'

'How old is she?'

'I think she's five, sir.'

The magistrate pondered, hoping to find an excuse to have the boy avoid jail. He failed. 'You will be brought to the Old Bailey and in the meantime, you will reside in Newgate Prison. Take him away.'

Newgate was a shocker; overcrowded, cold and with rations of bread and water. Babies lived there because their mothers were locked up. Prisoners with money bribed guards for food and wine. For the right price you could even enjoy conjugal visits. One chap on a long stretch married twice and sired ten nippers. Ten!

Newgate Prison became the residence of one Jonathon Sweeping. He had good cause to feel shattered. Not many children finished up here. He rubbed shoulders with murderers, monsters and madmen. His hidden stash of cash was outside the walls of the prison, probably lost forever, and he could now do nothing to help his little sister.

Lawyers were not common at trials in the early part of the 19th century, and a child without money or family attracted nobody. Juries heard several cases in succession, and would stay in the court to quickly reach a decision. Trials often ran for only a few minutes.

Jonathon didn't have to travel far for his appearance in court. The Old Bailey was next door to Newgate Prison.

He was manhandled into the dock. All around him were strangers. The lawyers wore clothes he'd never seen before. The judge sported an enormous wig, balanced spectacles on the tip of his nose, and spoke with a whisky and tobacco flavoured voice.

Jonathon thought he had no chance in his case. He was right but couldn't imagine the witnesses who appeared for the prosecution.

The constables caught him red-handed and said so. That would have been more than enough for any jury to find the boy guilty. But the prosecution decided to use a sledgehammer to crack a nut.

'The prosecution calls Mr Clarrie Pearce, m'lud.'

Jonathon stared in amazement and then fear as his former chimney sweep employer entered the witness-box. *Why is he here?* Jonathon's stomach lurched when he remembered the candlesticks. *But how did he know about my case?*

Bankside Bertie proved himself beneath contempt. He it was who received the items stolen by Jonathon, and who went to Pearce saying nothing about the fence's role in the theft but ratted on the boy. The chimney sweep boss delighted in giving evidence against the sweep who ran away only to return and steal his property.

The jury didn't need this extra evidence. The accused was guilty beyond doubt. But what this extra evidence did was turn the judge from displeased to furious. Jonathon faced the man in the wig.

'Jonathon Sweeping, you have been found guilty of the theft of a silk handkerchief and a pair of silver candlesticks. Many villains who have come before me have been sentenced to death.'

Jonathon's body became cold. He didn't shiver but it seemed as if ice was coursing through his veins.

'However, because of your age I'm prepared to show mercy. You are sentenced to transportation for seven years. Take him down.'

In 1776, the Americans created the Declaration of Independence, and the parliament in London passed the *Hulk Act*. The two events were related. Britain could no longer use her former colonies in America as a dumping ground for criminals, and English jails became so overcrowded, temporary prisons were rushed into service.

These temporary prisons were old ships including retired naval vessels. They were anchored in the Thames and elsewhere around the country. The ships or hulks became unseaworthy, floating jails, and Jonathon Sweeping moved from Newgate to the former *HMS Honourable* which settled in the Thames off Woolwich.

If Newgate Prison was a hell hole, the hulks were worse. Boys like Jonathon were treated as adults. Bashings for misdemeanors, which included not moving out of the way of a guard fast enough, were handed out daily. Hulks were known as "hell on water".

Spending money on prisoners was, and arguably never has been, a priority for governments as evidenced by private contractors being given the concession to run the hulks for profit. Being in it for the money, the food provided was scant and often inedible.

Once a prisoner inspected the latest food delivery, considered it disgusting, which it was, and tipped the lot into the Thames. His fellow prisoners went hungry, and the food critic copped the cat. If it'd been the feline type, they may well have eaten it.

Jonathon sat in the boat being rowed across the stinking river. Living in Bermondsey with its leaking or nonexistent sewers, he helped create the condition of this murky cesspit flowing through London.

Stripped of masts, sails and rigging, and decorated in obnoxious slime, the hulk loomed large in the river. As they rowed closer, the stench of sewage and slime slapped their faces. Climbing the stairs, the convicts gathered on deck to be addressed by the man in charge.

'Listen good,' he growled. 'You lot is 'ere because you're criminals. You'll stay 'ere till there's a ship to take you to the uvva side of the world. You do as you is told or else. An' if you try any funny business, you'll be cryin' for your muvva. You fink you're tough, well you'll need to be after you see what we've got in store for you.'

He glared at the prisoners. Even the toughest ones worried. Jonathon thought he was in a nightmare. He was.

'Now get below,' bellowed the man in charge.

This hulk had been a warship with various levels below deck. Stripped of its weapons, the vessel sat anchored in the Thames. The hundreds of prisoners went below deck where every third or fourth man was struck by a guard using a ponderous stick. Why? Because he could.

Jonathon escaped the blows and joined grown men, tough, foul-mouthed criminals cursing in the cramped space.

A guard yelled. 'Every man will strip and then wash using the water in those tubs. Throw your clothes over there. When you've cleaned your filthy bodies, put on these uniforms. Now do it!'

Jonathon trembled. He'd worn the same clothes forever. He couldn't remember when he last took a bath. Naked, he stood between burly grown men who muttered oaths and splashed cold water on their hairy, scarred and dirt-encrusted bodies.

The uniforms were of a coarse material with a shirt-like top and trousers in the colour of bland. It was one size fits all. Jonathon looked comical and quickly rolled up his trouser bottoms and sleeves.

'Right,' shouted the guard, 'answer your names.' A list was called and the prisoners gave cursory even spiteful replies. Guards looked at these men noting the troublemakers.

Jonathon responded to his name by saying, 'Sir'. Many looked at him. He sounded young and certainly looked it.

Roll call over, the order was given, 'Pick up them irons and get below.'

They were already below deck but with four levels overall, down another set of stairs they went. "Them irons" consisted of a short chain with two circular pieces at either end. These manacles went on wrists or ankles, sometimes both. If around ankles, it meant the prisoners could only take short steps. You never forgot the sound.

In their "dormitory" on the next level down they found hammocks in rows. Crude best described the facilities. The smell of rotting wood mingled with the stench of sewage. This was their bedroom.

A blanket was tossed in each hammock. Ordered to find a place, the men picked a spot. Jonathon moved to one but was pushed aside. He finished up at the end and in strife. He struggled to place irons around his ankles. The shoes supplied were too big. For a thin lad, walking became a chore. Forget running.

Once they were settled, guards checked their irons were secure.

Ventilation in this space well below deck didn't exist. The stagnant air was foul and sanitation broke every rule. What rules?

'Right,' said the guard. 'Rest up because in an hour you'll start work.' The men groaned. 'An' you'll keep workin' till there's a ship available to transport you to New South Wales.' The guards left.

A man beside Jonathon spoke quietly to the boy. 'You did the right thing before when you treated the guard with respect.' Jonathon looked at the man who owned a kind face and smiling eyes. He wasn't old and the boy wondered about the crime he committed.

'My name's Geoffrey,' he said, 'and I'm waiting to be transported to New South Wales.'

'I'm Jonathon and I have the same sentence.'

'Fourteen years?' asked the man, shocked at the sentence.

'No, I was sentenced to only seven.'

'Good for you. Actually I was sentenced to death but my lawyer applied for the Benefit of Clergy or the Ecclesiastical Defence.' He showed his thumb with a branding mark. 'I can only apply once.'

To Jonathon, the man might have been speaking Chinese. Geoffrey realised the boy was lost so tried to explain.

'It's an ancient law which allowed religious men to escape the death penalty. Then it was applied to non-religious men like me but only if you could read a passage from the Bible.

Still Jonathon looked bewildered. 'I can't read,' he said and Geoffrey gave a weak smile.

'How's your hammock?' he asked, changing the subject.

The guard was correct when he said they'd start work in an hour. 'On y'feet,' he bellowed and the prisoners stood making all manner of clanging sounds.

As they shuffled out of the putrid boudoir and up the stairs to the deck, Jonathon asked Geoffrey about this work they were to do.

'It's ashore, lad, is all I know, and you should be excused. You're too young. I'll speak to the guard.'

Jonathon clasped his arm. 'No, please don't.' They looked at one another. Before either spoke, a guard smashed Geoffrey's shoulder with a stick. 'No talkin'.' These guards were unemployable elsewhere, sadists, the dregs of society; ruffians who enjoyed causing pain and having unrestricted power made their cruelty more intense.

Up on deck went the convicts. Steps lined the outside of the hulk but still climbing down to the small boats was tricky. They were rowed ashore and lined up on the bank of the Thames.

In this part of London, one of the problems with the river was silting. The prisoners were there to dredge the Thames or to shore up its crumbling banks. It was backbreaking work and carried out in full view of anyone passing. You could add humiliation to the crosses these men (and a boy) were forced to bear.

Safety standards didn't exist. Falling timber broke bones, caused amputations and death. Take me back to Newgate.

As a sweep, Jonathon's work experience involved physical, muscle-stretching work. His sweeping work did him a favour. Now he was out in the open air and, given a choice, he much preferred mud to soot.

It was not a good idea to stop work. Guards were there to crack the whip—literally. When the day's shift ended, the prisoners were returned to their floating hotel, their bodies battered, their stomachs grumbling.

This is when the amount and quality of food became important. Just when their bodies needed nourishing food, none was provided. Even the drinking water, essential for survival, was suspect. In the fetid air of their sleeping quarters, disease gathered ready to strike.

Jonathon lay in his hammock listening to the sounds. Men cursed, farted, belched and snored. If a prisoner moved, his chain rattled. The boy wondered. *How long must I live in this floating hell?*

It got worse. His sleep was shattered when a convict screamed. A rat ran across a prisoner who reacted waking not only everyone aboard the hulk but half of Woolwich. How nice; rats for company.

But this was now his life. Days turned into weeks where he ate the terrible food, worked like a navvy dredging the river, and daily lived with the crude language and filthy habits of men, many of whom were habitual criminals.

Being able to talk to Geoffrey became the one saving grace. They discovered one another's family history, and what they did to end up on the hulk and this intimacy brought them closer together. Despite their age difference, they became kindred spirits.

Geoffrey, once a professional man, fell foul of the law in matters financial.

The friendship between the young and older man proved decisive one night when Jonathon was shaken in the wee small hours. 'Hey, son, I'm feelin' cold. Come an' sleep in my bed.'

One of the vilest prisoners decided to acquire Jonathon for some sexual pleasure. The boy knew nothing of the specifics but believed the man was pure evil and wanted nothing to do with him.

'Go away,' he hissed drawing his feet away from the man's grasp.

The brute was having none of that and tried to remove the boy's bedding. 'Come 'ere,' he growled.

The voices and chain rattling woke convicts who complained. Jonathon continued to resist driving the attacker to greater fury. He snatched hold of the boy's blanket pulling it back. Now Jonathon panicked. He was in a room full of men and horribly alone. On his back, he pulled himself into a foetal position. Still the man came closer. In the darkness, Jonathon made out the brute's slobbering face. As it loomed large, Jonathon lashed out with both feet. His hardened heels smashed into the brute's face re-arranging his nose.

The unholy scream woke the entire group. Many complained but their ruckus was nothing to the ferocious roar of the attacker. To his smashed nose, he copped something metallic on the side of his head.

Guards arrived with lanterns and the attacker was dragged away. 'Take him to the sick bay,' snapped a guard, and the thug departed. 'Get to sleep the lot of you or it's no rations and a floggin' for you all.'

In the darkness, silence eventually returned.

'You all right, Mr Sweeping?' whispered Geoffrey.

'Thank you, Mr Shipp, I am,' replied the boy. 'Was that your chain I saw flying through the night?'

'Yes, I got the idea from someone else.'

Both convicts smiled as they settled down to sleep hoping the rats stayed away. The growing friendship between the boy and the man grew even stronger.

# Chapter 16

As their friendship grew, time on the hulk seemed less arduous. On board, having a midday meal of bread and broth, the older prisoner suggested he could help the lad. 'I've been thinking, Jonathon. How about I teach you to read?'

The former sweep's eyes and mouth reacted. His mind struggled to comprehend the offer. 'Learn to read?' he gasped. 'You mean I could read a letter?'

'And a book and a newspaper.' The surprises continued. 'And once you can read, the next step is to be able to write.'

It was all too much for the boy. Tears welled. He struggled to express his thoughts. 'Do you think I could do those things?'

'I don't think you can, I know you can. You must work hard and it will take many lessons but perseverance will win the day.'

Sadness swamped the boy. 'I have no money, sir. I can't pay you.'

Geoffrey scoffed. 'Did I ask for money?' Jonathon shook his head. 'You could pay me in kind.' Jonathon didn't understand. 'You could teach me how to sweep chimneys.'

A grinning Geoffrey looked at Jonathon who understood and laughed so loud he attracted the attention of a guard. Prisoners were not allowed to be happy.

And so that night, in the darkness, Geoffrey started by explaining the vowels found in English, and Jonathon Sweeping went to sleep, not counting sheep, but reciting the vowel letters, *a, e, i, o, u.*

There will always be prisoners who plan to escape. Jail is not for them. The hulks provided a different and unique opportunity. In prisons like Newgate, at best you were let out of your cell. Here, on the Thames, every day you were allowed out of jail and into London; well at least onto the river bank.

Thomas Whittaker and Benjamin Flowers were habitual criminals with no morals and no shame. They didn't fancy a voyage to the end of the world, and they certainly didn't fancy living a day longer on a disease-ridden, hell-on-Earth prison hulk. They planned two tasks—an escape and a robbery—the latter to net them a king's ransom.

They kept their plan secret; one never knew if there were two-legged rats on board. But the budding escapees needed a third partner, and one with specific talents; namely climbing.

The escape plan was simple. Get a convict up on deck and with the guards asleep or in a certain part of the ship, unbolt the hatch above the stairs to the lower levels. Of course removing one's chains was essential as you won't get far with clanging metal bracelets around your ankles.

The convicts faced two problems. How to remove their chains and how to recruit a new member, preferably small of stature. The men could obtain a file from a friend as they worked ashore but far more difficult would be persuading a child to join their team.

Now both Whittaker and Flowers didn't even know social graces existed so persuading a young lad who'd been attacked by one of the prisoners, and bullied by others, would be a task way too difficult for the escapees. Besides, they even looked like desperadoes.

Simply asking the lad to escape had risk written all over it. One simple question could jeopardize the whole scheme. Could the boy be trusted? Would he report them to the guards?

They noticed how Jonathon and Geoffrey were pals. They decided to get at the boy through his mate.

On dredging duty one morning, Whittaker arranged to be working near Geoffrey and struck up a conversation. Geoffrey suspected something as Whittaker speaking to him, even in a civil way, was suspicious. After fake pleasantries, Whittaker got down to business.

'Me and m'mate, we seen how you've been helpin' the boy. It must be hard for a small child to be on a hulk with all these rough blokes. We'd like to do a favour for 'im too.'

This offer came out of the blue and Geoffrey whipped his defences into position. 'Oh?' he asked. 'What did you have in mind?'

Whittaker stayed calm. 'We could teach him how to tie knots, and sharpen knives, oh, and a bit of boxing; we could help him learn how to defend himself against bullies.'

Geoffrey hesitated. His reading lessons were going well, slowly, but well. Self-defence skills were one trick Geoffrey could never pass to his young friend.

'Let me think about it,' he said and Whittaker, wisely, left it at that. He'd planted the seed and knew moving slowly was the way to go.

That night, after their reading lesson, Geoffrey raised the subject of additional tuition. Jonathon's eyes expanded.

'*More* lessons? You are too kind, sir,' he said.

'How does boxing, learning how to fight sound?'

Jonathon's eyes gleamed in the dark. He remembered the bullying from Bankside's bullies and wished he knew how to defend himself. He had courage but few skills. He was a swing-and-miss man. If he learnt to box, it would do a world of good for his self-confidence.

'Do you know how to box, Mr Shipp?'

Geoffrey chuckled. 'Good lord, no. But there are prisoners who do, and I think they could be persuaded to give you lessons, but only if you're interested mind.'

Jonathon bubbled. 'Oh I'm interested, sir. And please, do try and persuade them to teach me how to box.'

The boy slept, not repeating words he learnt to recognize but dreaming of right hooks, jabs and uppercuts.


Geoffrey moved along the bank of the Thames until he was close to Whittaker. 'I spoke to the boy about your offer of boxing lessons,' he said.

Whittaker scowled and hushed the man. 'Quiet, you fool. If the guards hear us, they'll whip me *and* the boy.'

Geoffrey winced but noticed the nearest guard was far away.

'This is me mate, Flowers,' said Whittaker introducing his partner in crime. The two men nodded. 'We have to do this away from the guards. There's a place at the end of the ship where the guards never go. We can sneak down there at night and teach the lad how to be a prizefighter.'

Flowers grinned and Geoffrey sensed a chill. 'I'll come too,' said the reading tutor. He wanted the boy to be safe and trusted these men about as far as he could throw them.

'Okay,' said Whittaker. 'Tell the lad we start tonight.'

Having mixed feelings, Geoffrey moved away and resumed work. He knew the boy was keen and if these men were genuine, here was a wonderful opportunity for the lad. Being able to defend oneself in this wicked world and, who knows, in the unknown world once they were transported, could be as valuable as being able to read and write.

Over their evening meal, Geoffrey told Jonathon about the new classes. The boy's eyes sparkled, his heart raced, and he even forgot about the tasteless broth with fragments of ancient and unknown so-called meat he was consuming.

The guards were upstairs. Quietness ruled. Convicts walking to the stern of the ship meant their chains were lifted and carried. Jonathon was introduced to his new teachers and called them Sir or Mr Flowers and Mr Whittaker.

Geoffrey stayed in the background and Jonathon purred as, in the darkened lower deck, the lessons began. Whittaker instructed.

'It's no good bein' able to hit your enemy, son, if he can hit you back. Learn to defend. Stand like this and raise your fists like so.'

Jonathon copied his teacher. When Whittaker threw punches which he pulled, the student learnt how to block and duck and evade. All the time he kept his feet still, not only to maintain a strong balance but because chains on a wooden floor make one heck of a noise.

All went well and Whittaker called a halt not wanting to stress the lad. The move impressed Geoffrey who began to doubt his suspicions of the two men. They retired and, in their hammocks, Geoffrey and Jonathon discussed the lesson in whispers.

'I feel much better, sir,' said the lad. 'I think I can master boxing and it should serve me well whenever I need it.'

'Will you use it to start a fight?'

The question stopped Jonathon in his tracks. 'Do you mean will I change from being a pickpocket to being a robber with violence?'

Geoffrey tingled with pride. He was not only teaching the boy to read but now to think about life and morality, about right and wrong.

'Remember, a boxer who can read is a far better person than an illiterate fighter.' Jonathon pondered the comment unsure about the word illiterate. 'Good night, *Mister* Sweeping.'

'Good night Mr Shipp.'

The daily routines continued. Growling, vicious guards beat prisoners, with several being carted off to the sick bay and dying.

Concern about the health and wellbeing of the prisoners was never a priority. New convicts were ten a penny. Having them die became good news for the government. Men were rowed ashore to work and then back to the hulk at night. On a particular ship, after the evening meal, one convict learnt to read and to box.

The excitement Jonathon experienced at learning another skill meant Geoffrey believed the boy was safe on his own in the darkened below-deck spaces. The youth went alone to his self-defence lessons.

He'd come back sweating, boasting of new moves he'd learnt. Life for Geoffrey and Jonathon, despite the appalling conditions, was better. What neither suspected was the plan being hatched by the hardened criminals, Whittaker and Flowers.

At the next lesson, Whittaker asked Jonathon about his life away from the hulk. Baby sister Kitty was mentioned as was her possible loneliness, and Jonathon's pain at not being able to help the little girl.

Eureka! The would-be escapees found the key to the boy's heart. The criminals now used familial love as their lever of persuasion. Again they didn't rush. When they did broach the subject, it was all in terms of a family reunion, about their family members who needed help—a lie. If all three escaped, they could save their loved ones.

'But this is the most important thing, Jonathon,' said Whittaker. 'If you tell a soul, we'll fail and you won't be able to save little Kitty. Do you understand?'

Jonathon understood. He was locked in emotionally. The right or wrong of an escape and the consequences if they were caught faded. Kitty dominated his thinking.

As he lay in bed whispering to Geoffrey, he thought he should tell his friend about the massive news. But the words of his other teachers made him stay silent. Geoffrey remained ignorant of the real reason those men taught the boy to box.

They chose Jonathon because of his size. To get out of the hold, a convict needed to get up on deck and unlock the bolt of the hatch. Their hulk, a retired war ship, once carried 74 guns, 35 on each side and two each at the bow and stern. The guns were long gone but the openings were still in place; boarded up but still intact.

'All you have to do, young man,' said Flowers, 'is break open one of these gun placement openings, climb up the side and, on the deck, undo the bolt so the hatch can be opened.'

'Can you do that, Jonathon?' asked Whittaker.

The boy nodded. 'I can climb chimneys, gentlemen, so the side of a ship should be no problem.'

'Good lad,' said his cohorts reckoning they were on a winner.

'But wearing these chains is a real problem,' objected Jonathon.

'What chains?' asked Flowers with his revolting grin.

Whittaker produced a file he collected thanks to his brother who hid the tool ashore ready for collection. Jonathon's eyes popped.

'Are you ready?' asked Whittaker, staring at the former sweep.

Jonathon's heart started to run then to sprint. He nodded and Whittaker went to work with the file. The noise it made was a worry, not so much from a nosy guard, but rather a nosy prisoner. If anyone thought there was an escape about to happen, they'd definitely want to be part of it.

If Geoffrey knew what was happening, he'd be out of his hammock in a flash trying to save his young friend.

The first bracelet opened. In the darkness, Jonathon waggled a free leg. The filing continued. His other bracelet opened and the boy stood with exposed ankles. On the floor lay a chain with its two opened irons. Jonathon Sweeping was free.

# Chapter 17

The file did its job. All three prisoners stood in the dark, their ankles unshackled. Mind you, being unchained meant nothing while still below deck in the hulk.

'Right lad,' said Whittaker, 'you get to the level where the guns used to be, and as quiet as you can, knock out the board blocking an opening and start climbing. You know the rest.'

Jonathon hesitated. The others worried. Was he getting cold feet?

'What's wrong?' asked Flowers edging towards a threat.

'What do we do once we get ashore?'

The men sighed with relief. They'd said nothing about their plans being sure it would stop the youth from continuing.

'We get ready to visit our families,' said Whittaker.

That sounded good but the boy wanted details. 'Do we stay together and work as a team or …'

'Always, my son,' said Whittaker. 'We're a team now and forever. We'll both help you find little Kitty. Now, off you go and God speed.'

Neither man ever gave God a thought. Their morality was no morality. They wanted their freedom and the right to rob. Right now they could even taste the Bank of England £50 notes, and fresh air, fine food and wine. Quietly, they crept back to their dormitory, chain free, to wait, listen, and prepare to tip-toe up the stairs to the washroom, then up to the soon-to-be unlocked hatch.

Jonathon crept to the deck where cannons used to sit, waiting to fire round, chain and grape shot at England's enemies.

The space was as dark as a chimney at midnight. Jonathon was to find a weak covering. He started and kicked with the heel of his shoe. The sound made a crack. Would this attract the guards up on deck? He removed his shoes and socks and swapped them over with the socks on the outside. His next kick sounded softer. The covering moved a little. He lay on his back and used both feet. Bang! The covering disappeared into the Thames.

Jonathon froze. He heard the splash and waited for a response from either prisoners or guards. Silence.

Fixing his shoe and sock situation, he poked out his head. It rained in a gentle way, and the river slapped the hulk. The space to exit was big enough for the cannon to poke out its mouth and for a chimney sweep to depart the vessel.

Half out, he looked up. The side of the ship, painted with slime by a drunken artist, meant climbing would be tricky. One slip and he'd drown. Jonathon thought of his father. He drowned in this very river.

Out of the opening he found places for his fingers so stood with his feet in the space he created. Then he climbed.

The rain didn't help and the slime proved hazardous but step by step he headed up. Close to the top he waited and listened. He thought he could hear muffled voices but the guards were not silly, getting out of the rain. Besides, the convicts were locked below deck.

The boy grasped the side of the ship and slid over onto the deck. He crouched. The hatch he needed to open was close. Creeping along the deck, he reached it and slowly drew back the bolt. It squeaked. He froze. No movement from anyone. Still the rain fell.

With the bolt drawn back, he went to lift the hatch and nearly died. It rose as if by magic. Two desperate criminals gave it a shove.

'Well done, lad,' said Whittaker and held the hatch for Flowers.

'Yeah, brilliant, my son,' said the other climbing out.

The hatch was lowered, the bolt put back in position and the three, led by Whittaker, moved silently towards the steps attached to the side of the hulk. The boat they wanted was moored against the ship.

'You go first and hold the boat,' said Whittaker, and Jonathon was helped over the side. Climbing down the steps in the dark was tricky. He made it and stood in the wobbling rowing boat.

Jonathon held it steady against the hull. The men climbed down with Jonathon gasping when both slipped but clung on—just.

They reached the boat and fell on board.

'Untie the rope,' hissed Whittaker and another of the men's lessons paid off as Jonathon knew exactly what to do. Each criminal grabbed an oar and they rowed downstream then across the Thames.

The mud banks were a trap. They pulled in beside a small jetty, climbed out, tossed the oars in the river, and shoved the boat into the current. It drifted away into the night.

'This way,' said Whittaker, climbing the steps to the street above. Jonathon was last but kept up. His heart and mind raced, and he found it hard to believe he was free and finally able to help his sister.

He said nothing to his fellow escapees about his other goal; to return to Bermondsey and grab his hidden cash.

Before he could say anything, a man appeared out of the shadows, embraced Whittaker and greeted Flowers. Whittaker turned to Jonathon.

'This is me brother, Jake.' The brother shook hands with the boy then ignored him.

'Come on,' said Jake, 'we're all set.'

The trio of men set off and Jonathon scampered to catch up. They knew where they were going; along dark, narrow streets where the rain continued to wash the cobbles. What could the boy say?

Walking away from the river, they stopped near a main road. Jake explained. 'I've unlocked the rear door. Upstairs, the office and safe are both locked. I've timed the watchman and he comes by every half hour. We'll have to be quick. When he passes, we go.'

Jonathon knew something, no everything was wrong. These men weren't talking about their families. They didn't tell him anything about a locked office, a safe and a watchman.

He reckoned they were about to commit a robbery. No, he knew they were. Picking pockets and one smash and grab were familiar to Jonathon; he definitely knew about stealing. But this sounded different. He decided to ask but Jake spoke first.

'There's the watchman.' The men pressed against the wall of a factory while watching the main road. A watchman appeared. He was supposed to check doors and windows but the rain became heavy and he fancied being home. He walked away.

'Right,' said Jake, 'let's go.'

Flowers and Jake hurried along the side street. Whittaker turned to Jonathon. 'You stop here, son. If the watchman comes back, you shout and run away, distract him like. Okay?' Jonathon said nowt. 'Good lad,' said the criminal and went after the others.

For Jonathon, life became a mess. Not long ago he learnt to read, taught by a kind man when both were prisoners on a hulk. Then he learnt to tie knots and how to box. Now he was a lookout for a gang of robbers in a rainy London street at midnight. What could he do? What should he do? Well, for starters, get out of the rain.

He sheltered in a doorway trying to think about his sister and his hidden stash of cash in Bermondsey. A man and a woman came along. They argued. Jonathon didn't understand the details but they were negotiating the price, 3d, for an intimate activity. It would have been of no consequence to the boy until the couple chose his doorway for their transaction. The preliminaries began when the boy moved.

The woman screamed and loud she was too. The man cursed and went to strike the child. Thank goodness for boxing lessons as Jonathon ducked and punched the overweight gentleman in the solar plexus. He staggered into the street and, as his trousers were level with his knees, he tottered and tumbled into the gutter.

'The woman lost it. 'Murder!' she shrieked. 'Help, I'm being murdered!'

This was a lie and gross exaggeration but Jonathon failed miserably in his one task as a lookout. The man in the gutter wanted his money back. The woman feared for her life and said so, and windows began to rise and open. Sleepy, angry residents joined in the loud voice activity suggesting those outside should be quiet. Certain adjectives were repeated ad nauseum and Jonathon knew them all from his time in the hulk.

He wasn't in a safe place and decided to scarper. He ran but only far enough to observe the activity. Eventually it settled. The courting couple called it a draw, and the disgruntled neighbours retired.

Jonathon crept back to his former position, the now vacant doorway. Out of the rain, he watched.

In the still, dark night, the action exploded. His three compatriots climbed over a fence, and dropped to the ground carrying bags. The trio was unaware of an approaching watchman. Jonathon failed the lookout test. The watchman saw the three thieves.

'Hey!' he cried and ran towards the men. Naturally, this put the wind up the burglars but reckoning three to one was a fair fight, they stopped and turned on the official. Poor beggar, he didn't stand a chance against desperate villains.

Blows and more blows landed on the watchman. He went down and a gratuitous final kick to his head kept him there. The trio ran towards Jonathon who stepped out of the doorway.

'Come on,' cried Whittaker as the trio raced away not caring to see what Jonathon was doing.

He looked at the disappearing men and then back at the fallen watchman. Jonathon didn't know why but he took off—to the watchman. He knelt beside the man who groaned. In the darkness, Jonathon could see blood on the man's face. The boy spoke.

'Please rest, sir, and I will fetch help.'

'Don't leave me, please don't leave me,' he begged.

Jonathon was in a bind. He stayed and yelled. 'Help! Somebody help!'

He tried to comfort the watchman and leant over his face to shield him from the rain. From out of the darkness another watchman came running. He knelt beside his colleague.

'It's all right, Stan, I'm here, I'll get help.'

'Could I do that, sir?' asked the boy.

The fit watchman nodded and gave directions. Jonathon set off. He found the office and spread the news. People left the boy alone.

He was confused. *Where do I go?* He wandered into the street. He didn't know where he was. He wished he was back on board the hulk. He wandered off feeling sad even despairing. Two men came towards him. One shouted.

'There's the boy I saw him bending over the watchman.'

People rushed at Jonathon. Two watchmen grabbed him and marched back to their building with young Sweeping under arrest.

Being accused of the theft was bad enough. Being accused of attacking the watchman was shocking. Surely the watchman who sent him to summon help would speak out in Jonathon's defence. But being distressed, the man said nothing. His friend, the watchman who was attacked, lay dead.

Now the authorities wanted information. 'Who were the men who attacked our colleague? Tell us their names.'

Jonathon reckoned playing dumb was his best move.

'What were you doing late at night in that street?' asked his interrogators. The boy struggled. 'Tell us your name and address.'

Pressure rained down on Jonathon. He surrendered and came clean. He wasn't involved in any theft. He didn't attack the watchman, he tried to save the man's life. Jonathon's only crime was to escape from custody. No-one believed him.

The next day, the boy was brought to court in the Old Bailey. At least the man in a wig and the others in their uniforms were not so intimidating but the charge was. Murder meant the death penalty.

The charges were read. Escaping from custody. Burglary. Attacking a watchman. Murder. Naturally the jury took no time to find the prisoner guilty.

'How old is the boy?' asked the judge.

No-one knew.

'And he escaped from a hulk while awaiting transportation?'

'Yes, m'lud. He was sentenced to transportation for seven years.'

His Honour addressed the prisoner. 'You have been found guilty of escaping from custody. That alone requires me to increase your transportation sentence from seven to fourteen years. The robbery of such a large amount of cash makes matters worse, and I understand you have not cooperated or revealed the names of your accomplices; a further black mark against your name. But when your crimes include the act of murder, I am left with no choice. Of all the 222 crimes punishable by death, murder is the most serious. Before I pronounce sentence, have you anything to say, boy?'

Jonathon panicked. He knew about the death penalty. He used to pick pockets outside Newgate Prison while men were hanged. Now it was his turn. He remembered his talks with Geoffrey and in desperation blurted a request. 'Sir, may I ask for the ecclesiastical defence?'

The courtroom fell silent. The shock from the words uttered by a child they all assumed to be illiterate stopped the court. Even the judge was momentarily lost for words.

The prosecutor spoke. 'I think he means the Benefit of Clergy defence, my Lord.'

'Is that still a Law?' asked the judge.

A hubbub began with lawyers discussing the situation and two speaking quietly to the judge.

'Give him the Bible,' said the man with the big wig. A court official took the book into the dock. 'Have him read the 51st Psalm.

With the opened Bible placed in front of him, Jonathon looked at the text. His reading lessons took forever. Learning in darkness, by moonlight and, if lucky, with a candle, Geoffrey explained vowels and diphthongs always encouraging his student to sound the word in his mind before speaking.

The courtroom hushed. Jonathon wasn't trying to milk the moment but he did as his brain focused on the words in front of him.

'Begin,' said a booming voice from the bench.

Jonathon spoke in a soft and steady manner pronouncing each word separately. Words of more than one syllable were pronounced separately so *mercy* became *mer-cy*. He spoke.

'Have mer-cy up-on me, O God, acc-or-ding to thy lov-ing kind-ness: acc-or-ding un-to the mul-ti-tude of thy ten-der mer-cies blot out my trans-gress-ions.'

You could hear a wig rustle. Onlookers' mouths opened and stayed open. The boy could read.

'Enough,' cried the judge and slammed his gavel on his bench. 'I sentence you to fourteen years transportation to New South Wales. Take him down.'

An official spoke to the judge who reacted. 'Wait! Bring him back.'

The prisoner was returned to the dock to face the music. Jonathon's heart sank. His request for mercy was to be denied. No judge would allow an escaped convict who committed murder to be shown mercy. He'd heard of the practice of a judge placing a cap, a piece of black cloth, on his head before proclaiming, "You will be taken to a place of execution and be hanged by the neck until dead." There was no cap.

'There is a ship sailing tomorrow. I sentence you to fourteen years in Van Diemen's Land. Take him down.'

Jonathon escaped the scaffold. His sentence was doubled and his destination moved south.

Young Master Sweeping never returned to the hulk, never retrieved his life savings behind a brick above the laundry near the privy in Bermondsey, and never said goodbye to his sister Kitty.

Instead he became a prisoner on a convict ship sailing for the other side of the world.

# Chapter 18

By the time she was 22, Dimity Carlisle looked exquisitely beautiful with femininity and natural innocence in abundance. She led a sheltered life in a respectable home, but jumped the tracks to start a new career which involved sex. Did it ever?

She went on to make a great deal of money entertaining gentlemen although calling her clients gentlemen was debatable. Most were married, and climbed the stairs to Dimity's rooms in Berkeley Square because they were sex addicts and could never persuade their wives to do what Dimity did. Her specialty involved sex with strangulation.

In the early years of the 19th century, London offered a wide range of carnal delights or dangers, as one often came with the other. For the same price, a chap might get off and pop off all at the same time.

In the London slums, for a pittance, a quick thrust for lust could be had in doorways and dark alleys. But Dimity knew none of that. She offered danger and fantasy with class. It was none of your canal-path quickies for her. Her furniture was upmarket, the carpets plush and the candles sensuous.

Her new career happened by accident. Dimity's father died leaving his wife and two daughters their cottage in Slough, and a modest annual endowment. The older sister was blind and Dimity's mother, a caring and kind soul, was poorly and needed help. She relied on her able-bodied daughter to run the house for Dimity's mother and sister.

Such a task troubled Dimity, not because she was cruel or lacked charity but because she wanted to live life. Staying home caring for relatives with weekly trips to the grocer and church on Sundays for the rest of her life didn't appeal. She dreamt of travel and being wooed by a wealthy and dashing chap, and so being stuck at home began to frustrate her.

One day, her mother asked Dimity to visit the family solicitor in London on a matter regarding her father's estate. Talk about lucky. Dimity was given the day off but never dreamt of the opportunity the trip would produce.

The solicitor, Cuthbert Golightly, was an odd fellow. He belonged to a small circle of professional, well-to-do males who fancied sexual activities with beautiful young women. Each member was sworn to secrecy and used code words to inform other members when an "opportunity" became available. Miss Dimity Carlisle was considered one such opportunity, and a glorious one to boot.

With the legal matters resolved, the quietly bubbling Mr Golightly invited Miss Carlisle to take tea. Having impeccable manners and the best fine bone china in Lincoln's Inn, of course Dimity accepted. A day out in London was super, and being charmed by a wealthy and attentive gentleman held all manner of possibilities.

Obviously Dimity didn't know Cuthbert adored young females and, in particular, their flesh. His secret desires were well hidden as the two sipped and chatted. Dimity swam in flattery.

Mr Golightly reckoned Dimity was perfect for this unnamed club of well-off professional and mostly married chaps. He wanted her to perform activities to titillate each member's member.

Cuthbert threw all his charm Dimity's way and persuaded her to dine with him. He sent a note by courier to Mrs Carlisle, on the legal firm's letterhead of course, assuring the dear lady her daughter would be delivered to Slough safe and sound that evening.

She was delivered safely and on time but not before agreeing to attend a garden party at a stately home where she could stay the night; an upmarket weekend in the country.

Mrs Carlisle overflowed with reservations but finally agreed and, on the day, the coach arrived in Slough and away to the country went the excited and excitable Dimity.

To cut a long story short, Miss Carlisle fell into the well-planned trap and, having been seduced by a lothario hired for the occasion, agreed to entertain gentleman of a certain class, all for a fee of course.

Club members paid for a live-in maid at Slough, and Dimity's mother and sister were told of Dimity's new job—secretarial work in Lincoln's Inn—with her accommodation being full board provided by the respectable widow, Mrs Genevieve Loughborough, who worshipped every Sunday in the beautiful and ancient Temple Church. All lies.

And so from humble beginnings, Dimity established the art of seduction in rooms upstairs in Cuthbert's swanky dwelling in Berkeley Square. She proved a hit. Club members nearly came to blows to obtain a booking, and Dimity's bank balance grew at an alarming rate.

She discovered a technique by accident. An Old Wykehamist placed an untied bowtie around his neck and requested Dimity to tighten same as his pleasure reached its zenith. With refinement, she became surprisingly good at the routine, and so offered expertise in erotic asphyxiation.

It's believed the practice began when ne'er-do-wells being hanged, became aroused. Some even remained so after death. Whether deeper coffins were required for the stiffs is unknown.

By day Dimity explored the smart establishments in Oxford and Bond Streets, and by night explored the fantasies of posh chaps. Once a fortnight she would travel to Slough to visit her family where tall tales were the order of the day. Dimity explained how she fetched tea for the solicitors and attended Holy Communion on the Sabbath. Mrs Carlisle remained in blissful ignorance and Dimity in blissful bliss.

Club members held meetings in a private room at their club, Brooks's in St James's Street. They boasted of their cavorting with Miss Carlisle upstairs in Golightly's Berkeley Square abode. One fellow would claim his pleasure was the best ever, only to be mocked by two or more wealthy fellow adulterers.

Sex and cash dominated their lives. One offered to pay 500 guineas to any chap who might have sex with Dimity in a hot air balloon high above Piccadilly. Lovely lads.

Dimity did well because her rapid understanding of the male psyche taught her to add something strange and exotic. Her initial bread and butter menu was replaced with her deluxe special, erotic asphyxiation. Put simply it involved the client, the male deriving sexual pleasure, receiving a dangerous side order of strangulation.

For this to work, Dimity needed new skills. Helping the gentleman to ejaculate as he was being strangled required excellent timing and a fair amount of brute strength; not often found in a young woman.

She found the simplest way was to attach a silk noose to a door handle, have the client lie on the floor with the noose around his neck, so while she attended to the downstairs, upstairs the weight of the man's body tightened the noose. The two actions came together to produce exquisite pleasure for one and financial delight for the other.

Word soon spread. 'My God, have you tried Dimity's strangulation sex?' The recent converts raved. Soon many a chap in fashionable London wanted the stroke and suffocate special.

Now it should come as no surprise to learn that one night, the trick didn't work, or rather did, too well. The client was a wealthy civil servant with the ear of the Prime Minister. A pillar of the Church of England, and married with two sons at Eton, Sir Nigel Bottomley enjoyed having his bottomley nigeled. Having heard other chaps rave about Dimity's sex and strangulation routine, Sir Nigel was up for it. So, on with the prayer meeting.

Once the fun began, the pleasure kept building. Dimity reckoned she'd finally perfected the routine. When Sir Nigel climaxed, his cry of pleasure was heard two floors below.

Dimity smiled at her superior service servicing another happy customer. Sir Nigel too smiled and kept smiling. In fact he never stopped smiling. The grin froze because the poor bugger was dead.

Oh dear.

This was the first time Dimity suffered any regrets at having embarked upon her new career. No guilt or remorse ever crossed her mind, until now. Now despair jumped the queue as she couldn't open the door for her client to depart—he blocked it—nor would he provide a generous tip and tippy-toe downstairs off home to his loving wife. Dimity was in a jam.

She despaired, saw the immediate end of her career, and felt the terrifying fear of disposing of a stiff. And not just any stiff but that of a prominent public official and member of London's high society. Oh dear indeed.

She sat on an expensive Georgian chair and wracked her brains. Sir Nigel was useless, saying nothing, just lying there grinning.

She reckoned the man who first recruited her to the deadly game, Cuthbert Golightly, should be her first port of call. Because of his age and inability to be ready to set off when the starter's flag dropped, the solicitor did not actually participate in her erotic asphyxiation activities. However, he took enormous pleasure in hearing intimate details of Dimity's latest performances; from his chums, yes, but especially from Dimity.

She girded her loins, powdered her face, heaved the stiff off the door handle, went downstairs and knocked on Cuthbert's door.

He opened it with great excitement wanting to hear intimate details about Sir Nigel Bottomley's bottom and beyond. She entered his ornate sitting room and shattered his expectations.

'He's dead?' gasped Cuthbert. Dimity nodded. 'But how? Are you sure?' He put his head in his hands. 'But he *can't* be dead,' he moaned. He was. 'What are we going to do?'

That was not what Dimity wanted to hear. She perspired but Cuthbert's distress overwhelmed him. He collapsed. She was the sensible one and demanded a solution. He gave her the address of one of her clients, and told her to explain all to this gentleman. Apparently he knew dubious characters; a handy benefit for aristocrats who wanted a problem to disappear.

The address wasn't far and Dimity followed instructions. 'Under no circumstances approach the front door. Go to the rear and tell the housekeeper you have a message from the club secretary.'

She did all that and found herself being shown into a sumptuous office in a seriously wealthy part of London. The gent's face didn't seem familiar but then Dimity didn't spend a lot of time staring at faces. Perhaps if he dropped his pantaloons she might remember him.

She explained the situation and was told to return to Berkeley Square directly and say nothing. Everything would be taken care of.

Half an hour later, in her rooms, she heard footsteps. Cuthbert knocked and with him were two men dressed as undertakers.

Sir Nigel, still smiling—what an advertisement for Dimity's services that was—found himself wrapped in a dark cloth and carried off to God knows where.

Cuthbert looked at Dimity, speaking quietly but with a firm and serious tone. 'This never happened.'

He left and Dimity worried. She couldn't leave, couldn't sleep and wished she was home in sleepy Slough. Hearing muted voices she crept out and headed downstairs hardly daring to breathe. She knew the one creaky step and stepped over it. Close to Cuthbert's study, she strained to hear.

The voices were familiar—Cuthbert and the gentleman she called on an hour ago. What she heard chilled her to the bone.

'Can we trust her?' asked the visitor.

'I think so,' said Cuthbert.

'You *think* so?' he asked with exasperation in his voice.

'She's fine, she won't say anything.'

'Did she kill him?'

Cuthbert gasped at the audacity of the suggestion and Dimity froze with fear.

'No! Of course not. Well, not on purpose. Why would she ruin her money-making career?'

The visitor seemed unconvinced. 'The plan is simple. Sir Nigel is being delivered to hospital where he'll die of a heart attack. But the woman is a liability. She has to disappear.'

Cuthbert gripped his hands. 'You ... you don't mean kill her?'

Dimity heard her stomach ring the fire bell.

'Stop being so melodramatic, Golightly. There are plenty more fillies in the stable. Keep her here and I'll arrange for a trip to the Thames.'

Dimity heard footsteps and hit the stairs at record speed. She cleared the squeaky step and flew into her room closing the door and turning the key. Her nightmare accelerated.

*They're going to kill me!*

How could she think straight in this horrific situation? Many ideas popped into her head but one dominated—flee. She grabbed a bag and placed any small items of value and particularly her cash therein. She listened at the door, took a final look around the room, unlocked the door to her business empire, stepped onto the landing, locked the door and pinched the key. She was out the back door and walking quickly when Cuthbert crept upstairs to be sure she was inside. When she failed to respond, he used his own key and entered, found her gone, and his nightmare produced suicidal thoughts.

When two hardened criminals arrived, he feared they would murder him instead of the intended victim. They didn't but reported to their employer who issued one simple command. Kill the woman.

The woman in question headed into central London and entered an upmarket hotel where she sat in a corner nursing a gin. She was too well-dressed to be a woman of the street. Her heart couldn't, wouldn't stop thumping. She kept trying to think of a way out of her mess.

If she went to the authorities, and told the truth, the establishment would flatten her story with her body thrown in for good measure. If she went home to Slough, the killers would find her in no time. She had no friends of substance and believed her life was over.

She looked so sad, a woman approached and asked if she wanted company. Dimity meekly nodded and was never more miserable.

'Penny for them, darling,' said the woman.

Dimity said nothing at first then found herself spilling her tale of woe; no names of course. 'So whatever I do, I'm dead.'

'Not necessarily,' said her new pal, her sister-in-arms.

Dimity couldn't believe there was a way out. 'What do you mean?'

'Emigrate,' said the woman and finished her drink.

Dimity was speechless then wanted details. 'Emigrate?'

'Dear old England has colonies all over the world. Pick one you fancy, hop aboard the next ship and sail away.'

It made sense. 'But it could take weeks or months before a ship sails. While I'm waiting, the killers will slit my throat.'

'Then hide somewhere safe until departure. And sail for free.'

This was too much for Dimity. Somewhere safe and free, right now, was incomprehensible. 'I don't understand.'

'You could buy a ticket but while you're waiting for the next ship, you're right, you could be killed. However, if you get caught breaking the law, you'll be put in prison, and when the next convict ship sails, you'll be on board emigrating for nothing.'

These facts added to Dimity's confusion. 'I still don't understand.'

'I know a woman who hated her life so started a fire, was arrested and sent to New South Wales. You need to commit a minor crime— you don't wanna be hanged—and make sure you're caught.'

Dimity shook her head. The idea sounded preposterous but possible. Besides, what were her alternatives?

'Find a watchman, then pinch something where the owner makes a fuss and has the watchman come running guaranteeing you'll be locked up. Mind you, if they shove you on the next ship leaving England, you won't be able to pick and choose your favourite colony.'

Dimity drained her glass, took 125 pounds from her purse and handed it to the woman who looked aghast. 'Don't be stupid,' she said.

'I want this money given to my mother who is poorly and my sister who is blind.' The woman froze. 'Tell them Dimity has gone overseas, nothing else, and she will write one day.'

'I'm not sure,' mumbled the stunned woman.

Dimity took out her best necklace. It came from an exclusive London jeweller. 'This is for your trouble. Please don't let me down. You helped me. I'll help you.' She wrote the Slough address and gave it to the woman who remained speechless.

Dimity stood, kissed the shocked and speechless woman, and left.

Soon she spotted a watchman doing his rounds, and on the other side of the street a dandy strolling with his wife or mistress. Dimity approached the gent from behind, knocked his hat to the ground, grabbed a silk handkerchief, and "accidentally" ran in the direction of the watchman.

The victim yelled, his companion likewise, and the watchman swooped on the thief who, of course, didn't want to escape.

She finished in a cell far from the clutches of the killers. Up before the judge, Dimity nearly died. Despite his wig, monocle and fancy dressing gown, she recognized His Lordship. He wore somewhat less when last they met. He was one of her seriously satisfied customers. Would he recognize her? And if he did, would his exciting encounter in Berkeley Square encourage him to set her free and thus able to be stroked and strangled in the future? If he did, she could be murdered.

Dimity kept her bonnet over her forehead, spoke with a West Country accent and naturally gave a false name. With fingers crossed, she got lucky—twice.

The judge gave her seven years transportation and, as it happened, a female convict ship sailed that week and Dimity Carlisle, now Miss Annie Smith, set sail for Van Diemen's Land.

She may have found a few relatives. Of the approximately 160,000 convicts transported to Australia, 603 were named John Smith.

# The Journey

## Chapter 19

id anyone think it cruel to place unattended children on ships and send them half way round the world as punishment for stealing food because they were hungry? Many child convicts were cut off from their family forever. Of course people objected to what they considered inhumane treatment but authorities were simply following the law.

In Britain, legislation to protect animals came into being about seventy years *before* legislation to protect children.

The time taken for the first few convict ships from England to New South Wales took many months; the First Fleet almost a year. Over time the journey became quicker. When Jonathon Sweeping sailed for the new settlement of Hobart Town on the estuary of the Derwent River in Van Diemen's Land, the journey took a little over five months; about 150 nights at sea.

After his second appearance at the Old Bailey, Jonathon spent the night in a cell before boarding the ship *Indomitable* moored on the Thames. He was about to start the longest journey of his life. His misery plumbed new depths. Or did it?

Having been bullied, abused and betrayed so often during his short life, despair at this latest injustice lost its sting. Perhaps he was born to suffer, perhaps he developed a glass-half-full strain of optimism. Perhaps he was a fighter.

He thought about his friend Geoffrey from their days on the hulk. He thought about his sister Kitty and hoped she was safe, well and happy. He thought about the savings he left behind in Bermondsey, and his dead parents, and then the grandparents he never met.

Looking back gave little comfort. He decided to look ahead, plan for the future, and make something of his life wherever he landed.

He stood on the main deck of the *Indomitable* with hundreds of male convicts, the ship's crew, the free passengers and soldiers.

There were several British regiments which sailed to Australia acting as guards on convict ships. A few soldiers were married with children meaning there were females and youngsters aboard. On the *Indomitable*, one soldier's wife was expecting.

The ship's captain, Dickenson Nutter, well-named, was a short, ugly man with a large boil on his nose. Jonathon disliked him from the start and wasn't alone. The skipper addressed the ship's company.

'Most of you are making your first voyage. Not me. I've sailed from Africa to the Americas many times with a cargo not unlike you lot. That's right, slavers. The difference with you lot is I've been paid *before* we sail. I've already got me money. So if any of you convicts happen to die or accidentally fall overboard, it's no skin off my nose.'

It was easy to hate or fear Captain Nutter. The convicts knew the voyage would take months. They knew floggings would be freely applied, and rations would never be generous. Smiling convicts were a rare breed. Captain Nutter continued.

'Let there be no misunderstanding, you will be treated as the convicts you are. The courts found you guilty and your punishment is transportation to His Majesty's colony in Van Diemen's Land.

'Anyone who breaks my strict rules will be punished with floggings carried out before the full ship's company. The soldiers will report to me any refusals, tardiness and crimes. Step out of line and you will suffer.' His glare took in every convict. 'Now, weather permitting, we sail on the next tide.'

Captain Nutter handed control to another man, few knew. The free passengers and families of the marines returned to their quarters. The convicts awaited instructions.

A young man stood next to Jonathon. He was a bit older and a bit bigger. He introduced himself.

'I'm Peter Rowe.'

'Jonathon Sweeping.'

'Thank God we've found a fair and friendly captain.' Jonathon stared at Peter who paused then made a sarcastic face. 'I'm joking.'

Jonathon perked up and liked his new companion.

'The captain's not important,' said another convict on the other side of Jonathon. He was an older man, about 40, and wore the marks of someone who'd worked hard and suffered much. 'The man stood up there now is the one who'll control our lives on this God-forsaken tub.'

The younger convicts looked at the man the captain deferred to. He was as tall as the captain was short.

'He's the surgeon,' said the convict. 'He looks after us.'

As only the convicts and soldiers remained, the surgeon took control. His voice barely carried.

'My name is Forster, and I'm the ship's surgeon. You are my responsibility. Your health, food, activities, and accommodation are all matters over which I have control. If you follow my instructions, your life on this voyage will be bearable. However, one of my responsibilities is to report any acts of defiance to the captain. I can help you or become your worst enemy. You choose. We know cleanliness is next to Godliness so before we sail, let us begin as we intend to proceed. Gentlemen, it's bath time.'

The surgeon walked down the steps to the deck as the soldiers herded the convicts below. As they were shoved together, Jonathon spoke to Peter.

'He seems a reasonable man.'

'Yes well sitting here in the Thames, every man is reasonable. Let's see how he behaves at sea in a gale.'

Jonathon knew all about living on a ship even if the hulk barely moved. The bathing routine here was pretty much the same. Below deck, watched by soldiers, the convicts were told to strip, use the soap and water, and get scrubbing. Jonathon and Peter did so while others were not keen. When a soldier poked a reluctant convict with a rifle butt and mentioned the word flogging, everyone washed harder.

'And your hair,' yelled a soldier, meaning the lice already settled on convict scalps copped a nice old touch up.

Washing over, new clothes were issued. The surgeon appeared. 'And your uniforms are to be washed too,' he said. 'You'll be told when and where to do your laundry. If you're sick or injured, report to a soldier who will report to me. I may put you on the sick list. If you're malingering, you'll regret it. Now I'm going up on deck and you will be called for an interview two at a time.

Up on deck, he opened his diary, and convicts joined him where he checked their details—first and last names, age, height, identifying marks if any, crime and sentence.

Jonathon and Peter found themselves standing before the surgeon. He looked at Jonathon. 'You were sent to the Old Bailey twice,' he said. 'Stealing I can understand but surely a boy is incapable of such a crime as murder.'

'I am innocent, sir. I never killed nobody.'

The surgeon tried teaching. 'Anybody, you say, I never killed anybody.'

Jonathon squinted not understanding the correction. 'Yes, sir.'

'Let me tell you, Sweeping, almost every convict I meet claims he is innocent.' The boy knew the truth but the book said otherwise.

'It says here you're sentenced to 7 years for murder.'

Jonathon knew it to be 7 for stealing and another 7 for murder. A clerical error had halved his sentence. 'The book must be right, sir.'

Unsure, the surgeon looked at the young convict. 'Now I intend to hold classes during the voyage. It's a chance for young convicts, to learn to read and write. I hope you'll both take this opportunity.'

'I definitely will, sir,' said Peter with enthusiasm.

Jonathon showed no enthusiasm and Dr Forster quizzed him.

'And what about you, Sweeping? Are you interested?'

'I can already read and write, sir.'

He shocked the surgeon and Peter. Forster stared at the boy. 'Really?'

'That's the second time today, sir, you haven't believed me.'

Forster was not used to a convict questioning his behaviour and more so when the convict was a child. He showed his diary to Jonathon, and pointed to the name of the convict who happened to be the one standing beside him. 'Read that.'

Jonathon used the method taught by Geoffrey. 'Pe-ter Lons-dale.'

'That's me,' said Peter, impressed.

The surgeon was equally impressed. 'What about counting?

Jonathon shook his head. 'I know the names of the coins, sir, and their value but need help in counting their total worth.'

'Then by the time you reach Van Diemen's Land, young man, you will be able to add and subtract like a bookkeeper.'

The young convicts exchanged glances and both managed to smile.

Their interview ended because Captain Nutter gave the order to cast off. The first officer bellowed a command. The hawsers were released, and the unfurled sails began to flutter then fill. The ship drifted from the wharf. The flag on the stern stirred and the tide gave the *Indomitable* a helping hand. The voyage began.

Convicts stood along the side of the ship. Families were few as most convicts departed unknown and unloved. What families?

The river widened, the Foulness mud flats faded from view, and the English Channel was all one could see. They were on their way to Van Diemen's Land.

Jonathon spent the last few months aboard a ship although this time life was different. The hulk stank. Human waste, no ventilation and full-blown slime decorated the vessel. Sea-sickness didn't exist but disease ran around looking for convicts to infect.

Here, Jonathon was still stuck below decks with fellow convicts and guards but this time the ship moved. At first the movement was negligible but once the open ocean surrounded the vessel, sea-sickness jumped aboard.

Below deck, he and his fellow inmates were fed at long tables and slept, not in hammocks, but on rows of wooden beds.

Everything was wooden which is why men were threatened with death if they ever lit a candle anywhere at any time, and especially below deck. The tar used to help waterproof the vessel was flammable, and the quickest way to end the journey was to have the ship catch fire.

After an hour or two at sea, meal time was announced and the convicts were keen to read the menu; not that many could read and not that there was ever a menu. Choice would be a fine thing and none arrived. The secret to long voyages was to have living food as in chickens, or salted food which could remain edible after weeks, even months at sea. One easy-to-make biscuit was called hardtack; flour, water and salt.

They set like stone which is why they were known as teeth breakers. Mind you, convicts in the early 19th century sported choppers with more holes than an ant's nest and, as if on cue, one convict screamed in pain as he bit into a biscuit and lost half a molar.

Food was the major issue with the convicts, quickly followed by boredom. On the hulks, men were taken ashore to work at back-breaking tasks. Here they were stuck in a cramped space below deck, trying to avoid disease and sea-sickness and dying from boredom.

Jonathon and his new mate, Peter, survived the first day and their meals and retired. The rules at first were strict. Convicts would wear irons until they were deemed safe to be released.

'What do they think we're gunna do?' asked one surly convict. 'Jump overboard and swim home?'

Groans and foul language comments bounced around the hold.

'Sleep well,' whispered Peter to Jonathon.

'You too,' he replied and they tried to sleep. Both knew there could be more than a hundred nights like this and the thought scared them. Both drifted to sleep only to be rudely woken by a convict screaming.

'Ahhh,' he yelled, 'something bit me.' He screamed again and louder.

The ruckus meant everyone was awake. Many impolitely requested the yelling convict to shut his gob and go to sleep. The language used would never be heard in a chapel.

Instead of doing as asked, the screamer was joined by a second convict who went one better.

'It's a feckin' rat!' he exploded. 'It's crawled up me feckin' leg!'

Well did that ignite a bun fight! The word rat terrified the convicts, and because the pitch darkness made it impossible to see the vermin, the fear exploded.

Jonathon pulled himself into a ball and tugged the excuse of a blanket tight. Who didn't hate rats? The two complainants kept swearing and kicking, a soldier stumbled down the stairs holding a lantern, and the first night at sea included a mini riot.

Word soon reached the captain and surgeon. Both were woken although the sounds from below deck woke everyone.

'It's only a damn rat,' moaned the captain. 'What do they want, silk sheets and a chamber pot with painted roses?'

'Rats eat our food, sir,' said the surgeon, 'and spread disease.'

The captain wanted another brandy and sleep. 'Have their chains removed,' he ordered, 'and tell them to stop that bloody racket.'

Removing the chains helped the convicts settle but the thought of rats running about set many to hate the authorities more and to ponder how they might respond. Thoughts of mutiny began.

Next morning after a breakfast of burgoo, a cheap porridge, the convicts were allowed up on deck. The weather was fine and heading south, the ship behaved. Miles away on the port side, the French coast stared back. The surgeon studied his charges and knew the convicts must avoid disease and especially boredom.

He called for their attention. 'I want you men involved in activities.' They showed no interest. 'We start with a spot of dancing.'

You could sense the instant objection. Even though many of the convicts came from rural areas where community dancing was common, being on a ship in the middle of the ocean being transported to what seemed like another planet, dancing was their least preferred option. Strangling the skipper and throwing soldiers overboard had far more appeal.

No-one showed the slightest interest in dancing and the surgeon's idea was like a mainsail in a dead calm. As the medical man implored the convicts, on the poop deck the observing captain bellowed.

'Mr Forster, a word if you please, sir.'

The surgeon couldn't refuse. He climbed the steps for his dressing down in private. Mind you, the captain treated everyone with the same lack of respect. The convicts drifted apart with many walking to the sides of the ship to gaze at the sea. Most had never left dry land until this voyage.

'Did I hear you asking the men to dance?' asked the captain knowing full well the answer.

'I want to avoid the men becoming bored, Captain.'

'Have you joined the wrong ship, sir? These men are convicts. They are being punished, not going on a sea voyage for their health.'

'Yes Captain, but if they become restless, their behaviour may become an issue, and I'm sure you want as little trouble as possible.'

'They won't become restless, sir, if they are kept busy.' He turned to the sergeant of the soldiers. 'Have the convicts scrub the deck.'

And so the would-be dancers became the live-in cleaners.

# Chapter 20

A pattern emerged. Sleep below deck with the rats. Dine below decks on teeth breakers, porridge and an evening stew containing mysterious solid bits. Become seasick and bored. Hate the captain and the soldiers. Find new issues to complain about.

The convicts were given bread at luncheon and, as with the rats, one convict let fly in a fit of rage.

'What's this?' he cried and spat his food on the table. He pointed.

'It's a weevil,' said the convict beside him.

'*Two* weevils,' shouted the offended diner and slammed his fist on the table attempting to murder the damn insects. They fled under fire from fists and then, on the floor, from stamping feet.

Anger ran through convict veins. The surgeon wanted them to dance, the captain ordered them to work, and now the inedible food was full of bugs. And even worse, they'd barely left port.

Several convicts were thinking they'd crack long before they reached their destination.

Still muttering amongst themselves, after lunch they were called up on deck to again be addressed by the surgeon.

'This is a long voyage and I want to offer all of you the opportunity to better yourselves. There will be tuition in reading and writing. Later this afternoon, the chaplain, Reverend Wood and I will begin classes. I hope to see many of you there.'

He left and the convicts settled in groups around the deck. The sea behaved with the ship making good progress. Jonathon was in a small group. An older convict, Smithers, criticized the surgeon.

'First 'e wants us to dance and now 'e says we should be goin' to school. The man's mad.'

'He's only trying to help us,' said Peter.

'Don't you encourage him,' snapped Smithers intimidating Peter.

Jonathon spoke up to help his friend. 'I once saw people dancing.'

'We've all seen people dance,' scoffed Smithers.

'This was on stage in a theatre.'

That stopped the conversation. 'On the stage?' asked Smithers. 'When was you ever in a theatre?'

'In London, I went to the Theatre Royal, Drury Lane and saw people on stage singing and dancing.'

His answers intrigued the others. A few joined the group.

'I don't believe you,' said Smithers. 'You're a child with no money. How'd you get in?'

'A man called Bankside Bertie took me. He wanted me to work for him.'

'Steal for him more like,' said another convict.

'I would have worked for him but he cheated me and then told my employer I was a thief.' Jonathon chose not to tell the whole story.

The others were angry. One senior convict, Freeman, badly named, snarled. 'You mean he grassed you up.'

Jonathon nodded. 'He did, out of spite.' Many growled.

Freeman fumed. 'Any man who is a grass is the lowest of the low. If I come across a grass, I'll strangle 'im with me bare 'ands.'

The way he spoke, the sound of his voice, and the fact he spat as he threatened, left those within earshot in no doubt he meant it. Jonathon and Peter both made a private promise to never ever grass.


During the night, locked below deck and worried about rats, terrible sounds were heard. The usual cries of 'Shut up' sounded from many beds but the awful groaning continued.

A convict next to the groaning man yelled for the others to be quiet. 'Look, he's sick, give him a break will you?'

A couple of convicts tried to comfort the ailing man. One touched him and recoiled. 'Jesus, he's hot,' he cried.

'It's the plague,' gasped another who knew nothing.

Panic spread—like the plague. Convicts scrambled away from the groaning man. The complaints faded when a rat decided to liven up the party. Everyone was aware of the rodents and when one ran up a convict's leg, he managed to tell the entire ship about it.

Pandemonium erupted. This would normally have the soldiers arrive in force and threaten the convicts with serious harm unless they behaved forthwith but the soldiers didn't arrive.

They were distracted by Thor, the God of Thunder. He began warming up his vocal cords and the world received the message. The lightning flashed, Thor roared, the wind screamed, and the waves let their hair down, but not the crew. In the stormy darkness they were sent aloft to shorten sail, too late as it happened, and the ship started to buck.

The build-up in movement gave even the rats something to think about. Men who'd avoided being seasick, joined the upset-stomach club.

Despite no longer wearing chains, convicts struggled with their balance. Heads banged against wooden beds, a chorus of curses competed with the gathering storm, and anyone with even a skerrick of religious faith, rediscovered their ability to pray. It was as if Blaise Pascal was below deck taking bets.

Jonathon resumed his foetal position routine. He whispered to Peter who ignored him. A whisper was non-existent and even a shout struggled.

Jonathon hated living in the hulk on the Thames but right now, in a heartbeat, would happily swap this ship for that rotten, slimy wreck. And speaking of heartbeats, his beat to quarters.

A storm at sea can be frightening. A storm at sea at night is terrifying. You can't see what terrors are heading your way. The helmsman is being whipped with spray and blinding rain. The officer on the watch is gripping anything tied down and shouting, in vain, for the helmsman to keep her into the wind.

Massive seas swamp the deck and anything loose vanishes.

Of course unborn babies have no consideration for their mother, and choose to enter this world at the most inconvenient of times. As the storm raged, the surgeon and clergyman and the pregnant woman's sister were in a tiny cabin delivering a wee girl. Her mother's screams were drowned out in the storm, and the new-born's bawling was the sweetest sound amid the cacophony all around.

The baby was held tight against her mother's breast with celebrations on hold. The prospect of a brutal death is frightening but when you hold another's life in your hands and see no hope of rescue or survival, fear mocks you. The prayers of the priest were sincere but even the man of the cloth reckoned Jonah would never survive this maelstrom. It was rough and wild out there, and if the mother became sea-sick, she would be unable to produce milk. Tragically, hundreds of babies perished on such voyages.

Being a hundred yards from land was the same as being a hundred miles from land. The ship could capsize with all living creatures aboard lost in minutes, even seconds.

The convicts were painfully aware they were trapped in their mess. At this time in history, many sailors never bothered to learn to swim. If they went down in seas like this, how would being a swimmer help? Convicts never expected to go to sea and most couldn't swim a stroke.

If a mighty crash sounded and the sea flooded in, that would at least give a few seconds warning and a chance to pray or curse the Almighty. But something far worse began to happen; a leak or leaks.

A torrent would mean a quick death whereas a slow but increasing leak was the cruel path to extinction.

'Water,' screamed a convict feeling drips land on his head. Others suffered the same experience.

Their ship was of average size, about 350 tons, with a square stern and three masts; a reliable workhorse. But sailing cargo across the Channel and down to the Mediterranean was about her ideal route. Of course the Bay of Biscay could challenge any ship, but sailing the Atlantic and then the ferocious Southern Ocean put this average convict ship under serious pressure. She was a cork in the ocean.

The hull from Hull struggled to repel boarders. Thank goodness the shipwrights knew their craft. If the *Indomitable* survived it would be no thanks to Captain Nutter who, in his cabin, drank himself into a stupor. The ship lurched, dropped and rose and fell, again and again.

Below deck, convicts screamed their frustration. A hatch opened and spray flooded in. More screams. A saturated soldier came down the steps to tell them to stay calm. More fool him. The convicts grabbed a blanket and began to feel the sides of the vessel. Finding a leak, they pressed their blanket against the hull hoping like hell their efforts would not be in vain. They battled for almost an hour and survived as, thanks to Thor feeling tired, the storm ran out of steam. The ship resumed its normal movements and from below deck, a cheer was heard as convicts rejoiced in being spared.

The mother with the infant still cried but this time tears of joy. She was lucky. The baby suckled well.

As dawn broke, the captain, still able to hold his liquor, came out on deck. The first officer sent the crew up the rigging to set the sails. It was obvious the storm had damaged the ship. They were too late in getting in the sails.

The best sailors can sense a storm from various natural phenomena—a drop in temperature, an increase in wind speed and the sky at sunset. The captain missed all the warnings. Depending on the size of the vessel, it can take an age to get all the sails in. With not all securely tied, parts of the sails were shredded. This spelt danger for the remainder of the voyage and would add days even weeks to the length of the trip.

'We'll need to head to Rio, sir,' said the first officer. 'Repairing those sails is a priority.'

The captain sniffed. He wanted the quickest journey to Van Diemen's Land enabling him to refill his ship and thus increase his pay. Before he could say anything, a hatch opened and convicts came up on deck. His fury erupted.

Ten minutes earlier, the surgeon went below deck to check on his charges after the storm. 'Good morning,' he called. 'Are we all safe and well?'

The convicts grumbled. A few being genuinely pleased to have survived, told the medical man they were well. But Jonathon added a note of alarm.

'There's a man down there, sir, who is poorly.'

The surgeon moved to the convict, the one who made all manner of noise before the storm. Now he barely uttered a sound. A quick examination alarmed the surgeon.

'I want you all to stay away from this man.' He pointed. 'You two, move to another bed.'

'What other bed?' one asked. 'This hotel's fully booked.'

The surgeon called to the soldiers who came below deck. 'Take this man to the sick bay. Carry him in a blanket. Do not touch him.'

This command made the soldiers nervous and the convicts distraught. They moved as far as possible as fast as possible.

'No wait,' called the surgeon. 'Get all the convicts up on deck.' The soldiers hesitated, unleashing serious and unusual anger from the doctor. 'Now!' he bellowed. 'Move!'

The convicts wanted to get away from their sick fellow-traveller and the chance to breathe fresh air pushed them up the stairs.

The captain, having seen the damage to his ship, was in no mood to deal with the human cargo he hated on a good day. Seeing the convicts spilling onto the deck, his anger matched that of the surgeon below.

'What is the meaning of this? Who said these men were allowed on deck?' bellowed Nutter.

The surgeon appeared, pushed past convicts and spoke to the person supposedly running the ship.

'I did, Captain.' He moved to one side. 'A word in private if you please.' The still furious Captain strode to the surgeon and froze when he heard one word.

'Typhus?' he gasped. 'Are you certain?'

'I've seen it spread like wildfire, which is why I ordered the convicts up on deck and away from the patient.'

What could the skipper say? 'Is he dead?'

'Not yet but I fear for his chances.'

Without hesitation, the order was given. 'Pronounce him dead and get him overboard.'

The surgeon stalled. He needed a second to process the command.

Nutter fumed. 'You said he was as good as dead. Let's prevent the typhus spreading.'

The surgeon looked hard at the Captain. 'I'll see to my patient,' he said and went below.

The captain glared at the convicts most of whom glared back. 'Give these men a job to do,' he bellowed.

Soldiers looked at one another. One spoke. 'Right you men, you can scrub the deck or dance. What'll it be?'

Two seconds was all it took. Men began to clap. A few began to sing in time to the rhythm, and then half a dozen convicts hopped about with grins they hadn't shown for years. More convicts danced.

The look on Captain Nutter's face was priceless. Boiling blood makes you look strange or, in his case, more strange.

# Chapter 21

Rio de Janerio was a regular port of call for many convict ships en route to the Great South Land. The eleven ships of the First Fleet all called at the South American harbour. Captain Nutter had no choice. His torn sails and damaged rigging needed repair. He changed course.

Below deck, the sick patient died. The surgeon wrote in his diary. *Convict Percy Fellowes died of typhus and was buried at sea. Thank God there seems to be no spread of the disease. Men are showing signs of scurvy so supplies at Rio will be essential.*

The already angry captain became furious when a crew member made a report.

'What, in the hold?'

'Yes, Captain,' said the seaman. The food supply door was forced, food's been taken and we found candle wax on the floor.'

Captain Nutter exploded. 'Candle wax!'

Up on deck, the convicts huddled together. It was another bloody dressing down from the same bloody captain.

He gave them both barrels over the break-in, the theft and the use of a candle, expressly forbidden below deck.

'I'll give the convicts responsible a chance to come forward. I'll reduce your flogging from a hundred to fifty lashes. If you don't confess, every man, *every* man will get half rations for the remainder of the voyage.'

Jonathon stood in the front and could see the bulging veins in the captain's neck. Spittle sailed through the air. The theft of food and the disobedience was a personal affront to his leadership. Talk about crime and punishment. Unless and until the perpetrator was flogged, the captain's honour would remain besmirched.

'Step forward the man who did this.' No-one moved.

Jonathon found himself shaking despite having no knowledge of the crime.

'This is your last chance. I will make it my duty to find the culprit and until I do, every man jack of you will suffer.' He said each word with emphasis. 'Step forward now!' No-one moved.

The sails flapped and the waves slapped the side of the ship as it groaned and creaked. The sun shone as fear and despair spread amongst the convicts.

Jonathon wondered if more than one convict was responsible. He wondered if anyone knew the guilty party but refused to grass. He wondered what months of half rations would do to him and, more importantly, to those who harboured desires and dreams of rebellion.

'Very well, be it on your own head.' He gave orders to the officer in charge of the soldiers. 'All convicts to remain below on half rations.'

The officer ordered his soldiers and the fuming convicts were shepherded to their mess.

That night, as the odd rat ran across a terrified body, and stomachs begged for sustenance, certain convicts spoke in hushed tones. Jonathon lay on his bed hearing most of what was said.

'Of course we can escape at Rio. That'll be our chance.'

'Not if we're locked in here.'

'We need someone to break out and open the hatch.'

Jonathon's mind exploded. It was a repeat of his previous venture when he led the escape from the hulk. He refused to even think about repeating that routine and said nothing of his hulk adventure.

'The ship needs sail and rigging repairs,' said a convict with sailing experience. 'There'll be none of this drop anchor in the harbour routine. We'll be tied up fast beside a wharf.'

'I'd prefer the harbour,' said the only convict who could swim.

'Well harbour or wharf makes no difference if we can't get off this damn ship.'

One convict was interested but worried. 'So what happens if we do escape? Where do we go? How do we survive? Can any of us speak their lingo? We'll be penniless in a foreign country.'

That stopped the mutiny talk. They turned in with a few continuing to belly ache about their belly ache, and how they were planning to kill the captain.

Next morning their half rations appeared with the convicts mixing hunger with anger. Jonathon and Peter looked at one another and at their pathetic breakfast.

'Surely this won't continue the whole voyage,' said Peter.

'Well if you confess to the theft, I promise I'll share my full rations with you,' replied his new young friend.

Such gallows humour was all they had left.

But life soon became too serious even for gallows humour. During the night, a convict died and the men either side of the corpse said nothing. Instead they stepped forward to collect the half rations for their comrade. It had come to that. Don't report a dead convict because his food could keep you alive.

The surgeon worried. He believed locking up convicts below deck and half starving them was morally wrong and dangerous. With an obligation to see the convicts healthy in mind and body, he discussed the situation with the Reverend Wood, the ship's chaplain, and together they approached the captain.

'I've made my decision,' barked Nutter. 'If the man responsible confesses, I'll change the rations.'

The surgeon tried a different tack, appealing to the mariner's sense of history.

'So, Captain, are you going to be the first naval officer in history to refuse to acknowledge the crossing of the equator?'

The captain baulked. He hadn't expected such a comment and didn't want to tarnish his reputation; not that anyone admired the man.

'What do you mean?' he asked knowing full well the situation.

'We're close to the equator, sir, and the custom of inviting King Neptune and Davy Jones to greet newcomers must be honoured.'

The clergyman reckoned the practice bordered on idolatry but starving the convicts and keeping them below deck with no recreation was anathema to his Christian beliefs.

Begrudgingly, the captain muttered a reply. 'I may make an exception when the time comes.' Then he pointed at the visitors. 'But if there's even a hint of a mutiny, you'll be responsible.'

'Thank you, Captain,' said both men and left before he could change his mind.

The word was passed to the soldiers and the crew, and once they knew, the convicts knew. Most celebrated if only because they would get out of their hell hole.

'What's the equator ceremony?' asked Jonathon. Peter shrugged.

'I think the equator is a line around the middle of the Earth and when you cross it, we'll pass from the top half to the bottom half.'

Peter's attempted explanation intrigued Jonathon. On the hulk, Geoffrey once showed him a map of the world but they studied a flat book making it hard to imagine a globe.

The next day, after breakfast of half rations, the prisoners were brought up on deck. They were ushered into groups either side of the main deck where a large tub of water sat waiting. Everyone on board attended with the settlers, women and children in their own space, and crew members and soldiers likewise. The captain sat in his cabin.

Whoosh! A loud laugh erupted and Jonathon and the others turned to see why.

A member of the crew, a long-serving sailor, strode onto the deck wearing a long shroud-like cloth, a straggly wig that had seen better days, a Viking helmet, and carrying a three-pronged spear. Here was King Neptune.

Despite the crude disguise, everyone knew him and joined in the banter and laughter. The surgeon and clergyman relaxed, feeling relieved to see people enjoying life as the ship ploughed ahead.

King Neptune sat on a high-backed chair, and beside him, sat another sailor in disguise calling himself Davy Jones.

The ceremony began. Crew members and soldiers, who'd never crossed the equator, were brought forward one at a time and questioned by King Neptune. He would confer in private with Davy Jones, and the inevitable result saw the virgin traveller tossed into the tub of sea water much to the ship's company's amusement.

The convicts laughed and especially enjoyed seeing those they disliked—even hated—get the treatment, and the rougher the better.

With the ceremony over, the convicts were sent below, and boredom and anger again began to bubble away. At least the event brought a bit of relief with many discussing it.

At night it was back to their chains, bedding, half rations and rats.

Not long after dawn, the convicts came alive when they heard a cry of 'Land ho!' from the lookout. At last, a possibility of freedom.

'We must be close to Rio,' said Jonathon and he and Peter enjoyed the fact they'd reached land, the first country they'd seen up close other than the land of their birth.

As they tried to make their meagre breakfast last longer, above deck, the clergyman and the surgeon again went to the captain to discuss the situation.

'If you continue to keep the convicts in these prison-like conditions, sir, you risk driving them to despair,' said the Reverend Wood. 'These men have souls, Captain, and it is my responsibility to care for them.'

The captain scoffed. The surgeon spoke.

'There's already one case of typhus. If disease breaks out, keeping the convicts in a confined space could see the disease spread to the crew and military. Do you want that on your conscience, sir?'

More disinterest from Nutter. He'd grown to hate his work. His alcohol addiction made it worse. He threw his conscience overboard long ago, and all he lacked was the courage to kill himself. Mind you, he was doing that slowly with his liver fighting a losing battle.

'Good day, gentlemen, I have a ship to repair.'

The priest and surgeon left, angry and frustrated. Both determined to write reports on the savage treatment of convicts, although such reports would not be read for months, if at all.

Actually their entreaties worked although the captain was too proud to admit same. The convicts looked up in surprise when the hatch opened and a soldier appeared.

'Right you lot, strap on your ankle bracelets.' The convicts fumed. Why now? Why when they were locked below deck? This was cruelty writ large. Men complained and a few refused to obey although their attitude changed instantly when the soldier spoke again.

'And once you're dressed proper like, you can come up on deck.'

Chains were snapped on ankles and men jostled to get out. Jonathon and Peter were pushed and pulled as men scrambled up the steps. The sun was out, the breeze friendly and the fresh sea air tasted glorious. It filled lungs with enthusiasm.

'And let the crew do their job,' roared the soldier.

The convicts understood the situation. Here they were, closing in on land and a chance to escape. Wearing leg irons made such an adventure nigh on impossible. Still, being on deck was great and seeing land, superb.

Jonathon pushed his way through the mob to look at another country. They were in the harbour of San Juan with ships all around, tied up, and beyond the wharves stood buildings of all shapes and sizes. People were everywhere. Being busy, they ignored the new ship.

Small boats paddled alongside with people offering fruit and nuts and various gifts. They called in broken English.

If only they knew. These convicts didn't have two farthings between them. Soldiers hustled the convicts to one part of the ship as the captain and an officer came through, climbed onto a gangway and went ashore. The convicts were kept well away from such an exit.

The excitement and relief enjoyed by the convicts was only the beginning. The officer in charge of the soldiers addressed the men.

'Provided you continue to behave, you will be allowed to come back on deck.' The convicts cheered. 'And again, depending on your behaviour, you will be restored to full rations.'

The cheer this time was longer and louder. Peter grabbed Jonathon and the young men danced, if you could call it that, and smiled for the first time in ages.

The convicts planning to escape were relieved to be up on deck and back on full rations but these men retained their anger. They remained dead keen on their escape.

The surgeon and clergyman were thrilled to see the convicts on deck, and the pleasure enjoyed by Forster and Wood increased when supplies of fresh fruit and vegetables came aboard.

Fresh food tasted superb and if this situation continued, life might not be so bad after all.

As the sails and rigging were repaired, every convict was offered lime or lemon juice. The danger of scurvy faded although the trip was far from over. First, the southern tip of Africa beckoned and then the real test would begin; the wilds of the Southern Ocean with those monstrous Roaring Forties lay ahead. Prepare for 6,000 miles of brutal, constant gales.

# **Chapter 22**

With repairs complete and new supplies aboard, they set sail for southern Africa. As the ship crossed the Atlantic, the Reverend Wood and surgeon Forster spent time alone discussing life, history and the British Empire.

'I assume you share my objection to slavery,' said the clergyman.

'Of course,' replied the surgeon, 'and I was shocked to hear the Captain admit to being a slaver.'

'We Europeans have been at the forefront of slavery for centuries where indigenous people are regarded as sub-human.'

'I've often wondered why we behave like so,' said Forster.

'The obvious reason is profit; because there's money in slavery.'

'And it works because guns are more powerful than spears.'

The priest had inside knowledge. 'My missionary contacts tell me the indigenous people around Cape Town have suffered for centuries, been driven from their land, forced into slavery, and if they rebelled, were tortured and killed.'

The surgeon shook his head. 'It's the evil side of human nature.'

The clergyman continued. 'And as if slavery itself wasn't cruel enough, we Europeans dispensed injustice calling it justice.'

The surgeon shook his head. 'How did we allow that to happen?'

'When the indigenous people around Cape Town protested against European invasion, we responded by hanging rebels, breaking bones or horrendously, cutting the Achilles tendon of the locals creating cripples in perpetual agony.'

'No,' protested Forster, 'that can't be true.'

'It *is* true,' said Wood. 'I know missionaries who saw it with their own eyes.'

The surgeon knew how excruciating an injury to that part of the body would be. Cutting the large rope-like tendon which connects calf muscles to bone would be devastating. He shook his head. 'It's hard to believe such cruelty. I am ashamed.' He paused. 'Do you think we'll find any such behaviour in Van Diemen's Land?'

'I'm hoping not,' said the priest. 'Surely we've left barbarity behind. We must have respect for everyone regardless of race. After all, we're the people with a parliament making slavery illegal.'

To many seafarers, the harbour at Cape Town on the southern tip of Africa is the best deep-water harbour in the world. And to top off its facilities, there is the magnificent backdrop.

Table Mountain, so-called because its long flat peak looks like a table, adds status and majestic beauty to the waterfront landscape.

The *Indomitable* enjoyed an incident-free journey across the Atlantic and reached the African coast early one morning. By the time the ship reached Cape Town, the convicts had eaten their breakfast and were on deck to see the sights. Jonathon and Peter were struck by the mountains and particularly the one with the table top.

'Wouldn't it be great if we could go ashore,' said the former sweep.

'Chance'd be a fine thing,' replied Peter with his friend not understanding the expression.

Away from the boys, three older convicts, the would-be escapees, were deep in a sotto voce discussion.

'This is our best chance,' said Taylor, the convict with one eye.

'Our *only* chance,' replied Metcalf, the convict missing half an ear.

'With a barrel, we could float ashore,' added Walters, the convict with no visible missing parts but few working brain cells.

The trio wanted to escape because it was in their nature to do so, and being habitual criminals they hated being imprisoned. In Rio, they wore chains on deck, so escape proved impossible. Now, in their last port before Van Diemen's Land, it was Cape Town or bust. The locals spoke their language. The convicts could survive here.

Taylor's escape plan was simple. It meant pretending to be sick, being sent to the ship's hospital, and making a break from there. 'I'll claim my dead eye is giving me hell and is infecting my good eye. I'm going blind.'

'I like it,' said Walters.

'I'll stagger around like I can't see, and the surgeon won't worry about me escapin'. He'll think I'm goin' blind.'

'How does that help us?' asked a still skeptical Metcalf.'

'I'll ask to see me best pals before I go completely blind.'

'I like it,' said Walters again, approving anything.

Taylor had another plan. 'Or we could just walk off the ship.' The others scoffed. 'We bribe a crew member to get us new clothes. We change, hide on the deck till it's dark, and then go ashore for a spot of leave.'

'Brilliant,' gasped Walters.

'What do we use for the bribe?' asked Metcalf. 'How much cash are you hiding under your pillow?' All three were penniless.

Each idea hit a brick wall. So when a blinder came from the least intelligent member of the trio, jaws dropped. Talk about "out of the mouth of babes and thick convicts", Walters hit the jackpot.

'Why don't we set the ship on fire?'

The others looked at Walters and then themselves. Setting fire to the ship while it was tied up in port had panic and mass escape to burn but the hint of genius lurked in the idea.

Of course the others wanted to know how and where to start the blaze, and what would happen to the escapees if they remained trapped below deck, but the idea sprouted wings.

Once the *Indomitable* was tied up beside the wharf, the convicts were allowed up on deck. The gangway was heavily guarded. Anyone thinking of diving overboard didn't. Crew members and soldiers watched the convicts, and being shot in the water didn't appeal. Besides, were there not marine creatures called sharks in these temperate climes? Having your torso crunched didn't appeal.

In their small group, convicts Taylor, Metcalf and Walters waited. Their arson plan was set. That night, when the alarm sounded and the fire raged, their escape would not even be noticed. These three men would never reach Van Diemen's Land.

The stay in Cape Town was short. No need for repairs, simply take on supplies and sail away on the morning tide.

This meant the escapees couldn't afford to wait. Unless they struck tonight, the *Indomitable* would sail with them on board.

After their evening meal, a few convicts wanted to spend time on deck to watch the lights of Cape Town. 'Come on Sergeant,' they pleaded, 'one more hour.'

The soldiers relented and this decision gave the escapees their chance. As most of the convicts gathered on deck to watch Cape Town by night, the daring trio prepared their arson assault.

A crew member spotted the captain and first officer returning and the convicts were ushered below post-haste.

They settled for the night with the trio of rebels gathered in a corner, whispering and watching.

'We wait till they're all abed,' said Taylor. 'The panic will be much greater if everyone's asleep.'

Their heartbeats built in speed and volume. They were taking a huge risk. If the fire spread quickly and the hatch was not unlocked in time or at all, they were setting themselves up to be burnt alive.

Taylor went over the plan. 'It all depends on the screaming. We need to make it so loud the whole ship starts to panic.'

'Have you checked the flame?' asked Metcalf.

'It's out of sight and burning bright,' replied Taylor, referring to the lantern they'd stolen and hidden below deck. 'Now get some sleep and I'll wake you when it's time to go.'

They tiptoed away and bedded down. Sleep became tricky.

The slapping of the water on the hull lulled the convicts to sleep. Taylor woke, he'd only dozed. He rolled off his bedding and moved in the dark. He shook Metcalf who responded maintaining the silence.

His job was to wake Walters who was not only asleep but snoring. Metcalf placed a hand on the sleeping convict's mouth. He woke in a start and went to yell. A hand over his mouth killed the sound but it was enough to wake the convict in the next bed.

Jonathon Sweeping opened his eyes and saw two, then three men creeping towards the bow of the boat.

Heading off to pee happened constantly. But three men having a pee together in the dead of night seemed strange. Jonathon peered into the darkness.

The trio planned and prepared well. The stolen lantern was the key. With the candle alight inside the covered and hidden lantern, all they needed was flammable material. They stole and hid fat from the galley, plus old rope and old rags from parts of the ship, and hid them below.

When ocean-going ships encountered a storm, the cooking fire in the galley was killed. In a wooden ship, the risk of fire was too great.

Jonathon could see three body shapes but not what they were doing. He heard someone peeing, two people peeing then whispers. He thought about getting up to explore but thought better of it. If they were stealing food and he poked his nose in, three men would do for him. Even with boxing skills, a fight in the dark screamed danger.

He snuggled under his blanket and tried to sleep. Then he gasped in fright. He saw a light, a flash, a flame—fire! He didn't need to yell because the three men who came towards him did enough yelling to wake the ship and half of Cape Town.

Jonathon leapt off his bed, grabbed his blanket and headed forward. Convicts woke and panicked. They saw the flames and couldn't miss the shouts and screams. They ran up the steps to smash their fists on the hatch.

As Jonathon moved towards the flames, the three men who started it, hurtled towards him, collided and knocked him flying. He whacked his head on a beam, and lay on the floor in a daze. The flames licked higher.

The tar to waterproof the hull gave the fire a boost. It spread. The screaming and fist banging from convicts exploded. Death became a real possibility for these rats trapped below deck. The rats with tails headed for the ropes holding the ship against the wharf.

Jonathon pushed himself up, ran towards the fire and saw the homemade chamber pot recently topped up with urine. He grabbed the pot and hurled its contents at the fire. The hiss from the piss seemed to ignite the flames but gave off a shower of steam or was it smoke? Jonathon grabbed his blanket and threw it at the flames. He stamped on the blanket with his feet. He was dancing!

The hatch opened and soldiers and crew members poured in as convicts fought to climb out. The screaming from all parties faded as people turned towards the bow of the ship and saw the flames decrease and die.

Panic over.

Roused from his bed, the captain appeared badly dressed and more worried about his disturbed sleep than the loss of his ship. He stumbled below deck. Soldiers pushed convicts aside leaving a path for their commander. An officer raised a lantern exposing the scene of the fire.

On the floor, clutching his singed blanket, Jonathon looked up at the fuming captain.

'Trying to burn my ship are you, son? You sniveling God-forsaken urchin, I'll flog you m'self.'

The captain bent to grab the boy when an old convict pushed forward. 'No!' he yelled and startled everyone, even the skipper. 'He didn't light the fire, he put it out.'

Jonathon couldn't stop the tears. He barely knew the convict but wanted to stand and shake the man's hand.

It didn't take the captain long to try and find the arsonist. He pointed at Jonathon. 'So, if you were so close, you must have seen the man who started it. Tell me his name or I will flog you anyway.'

The company stared. In the hold of the vessel, in the darkness with only two flickering lanterns to shed light, all eyes settled on Jonathon Sweeping.

'It was dark, sir. I couldn't see any faces.'

Without realizing, Jonathon became a hero twice over. He saved the ship from destruction, and convicts being injured or killed, and he refused to become a grass. Everyone appreciated his heroism and even the arsonists, although furious their escape was foiled, appreciated the young lad's code of honour—never, ever grass.

There was no sleep that night. The convicts were clapped in irons, two soldiers spent the night in the hold, the captain drank himself to sleep, and Jonathon shivered on his bed with his blackened blanket stinking of pee.

The captain failed to discover the mutinous arsonists on his ship and frankly, didn't care. He was on the last leg of his voyage and, it could be argued, the last leg of his life.

The *Indomitable* sailed due east. Pushing it along were the Roaring Forties; the tailwind to end all tailwinds.

They're formed when air from the Equator heads towards the South Pole. Windbreaks such as mountains and forests can weaken strong winds but the vast Southern Ocean is a little short on windbreaks. The *Indomitable* sailed into the ocean from hell.

The convicts were allowed on deck during daylight hours. Few were interested and remained below shivering and seasick. Mind you, with the Roaring Forties on song, anyone out for a stroll on the deck would never wear a hat. Often you needed to tie down your head.

Jonathon and Peter took the opportunity of going above and heeded advice from the surgeon and several soldiers. Hold on tight to anything. The young convicts wore every piece of clothing they could find. The spray from the sea and the rain gave you a soaking to never forget. This was a time for feeling alone in the world.

'Where is the nearest land?' yelled Jonathon.

'The Moon,' shouted Peter, his wit finding its mark.

The young convicts slipped to the side of the ship, and held tight to the rigging. Nearly all the sails were in use. As the vessel dropped into a trough, the wind disappeared and the lower sails fell flat. Then up the next sea mountain climbed the *Indomitable* causing the sails to puff out their chests.

It was the middle of the day but you couldn't see far; no horizon and no sunshine. If it were possible for the sky to be bland, it was bland.

A marine artist, with easel and canvas nailed, glued and screwed to the vessel would only require three colours in their palette—grey, grey and grey.

The ocean resembled a giant bowl of mud. Of course there were peaks and troughs—just ask those on board—but it sat there, challenging ships and the occasional albatross to a fight. The ocean always won.

The colour blue was drained from the sea and the mass of grey water looked like a giant chocolate cake with rivers of cream drizzled along its top.

Five minutes was enough for anyone to be up on deck unless they were sailing the ship. Apart from the danger of being blown away, your hands, ears and face were numb with the cold. Imagine this on a day when the storms came out to play.

Jonathon and Peter slipped and slid and fell en route to the hatch. When they opened it to go below, howls of rage erupted from convicts trying to stay dry while huddled beneath a blanket for a skerrick of warmth.

The temperature of the sea pushed the temperature below deck to freezing. The cold seeped through the hull. Don't touch it!

Anyone prone to seasickness vomited anything they'd eaten in the last few weeks. Life on the ocean wave was constantly described in lurid, foul terms, and for these men, it was true. Every convict swore to never go to sea again.

Probably the worst aspect of this part of the journey was its monotony. The wind seldom dropped below gale force and it blew night and day. Would it ever end?

And the ship was often on an angle meaning not only did it rise and fall but standing and remaining upright became a skill. Moving from bed to chamber pot and back to bed became an obstacle course. Some couldn't be bothered and relieved themselves where they were.

And such was the life for Jonathon Sweeping and the rest of the convicts, crew, passengers and militia on board the *Indomitable* as they sailed to reach the ancient island, Van Diemen's Land.

The Dutch explorer, Abel Tasman, gave the island its name in honour of his fellow countryman, Fred Van Diemen.

# Chapter 23

As the child convict landed in Van Diemen's Land, back in England, in Northamtonshire, the county of spires and squires, a Church of England vicar faced a problem. The Reverend Andrew McFarlane's blossoming career was blighted when his father, a solicitor from Cheltenham, found himself up before the assizes on a charge of embezzlement. What an embarrassment and source of shame for his family. Well, for one particular member of said family.

Andrew, a bachelor and only child, shared the vicarage with his mother, a fusspot. Andrew bore his father's predicament stoically whereas his mother died of shame. 'We must move,' she declared.

'Mother, you're over-reacting. Besides, we've done nothing wrong.'

Matilda McFarlane exploded. 'Nothing wrong? Your father is a thief. He's paraded before the world as a member of the criminal class which is even worse than the working class. How can I ever show my face in public again?'

'He hasn't been found guilty yet.'

'We must change our name.'

'No, certainly not.' Andrew fought valiantly but struggled.

'And you must find a new parish as far from here as possible. You can become a missionary in a remote archipelago.'

Andrew's mother often turned over-reacting into an art form but her latest response took the biscuit. 'Now Mother, I can't see you living in a grass hut and drinking tea with a witch doctor.'

She hated his mocking and failure to understand her distress.

'You must make an appointment to see the Bishop.'

Andrew despaired. 'Mother.'

'And if you won't, I will. Fancy treating your poor, ailing mother in such a disrespectful fashion, and you, a so-called man of God?'

She fell into a fit of coughs and sobs. All his pastoral skills would never console the devastated mater. He knew there would be no peace until he took action. He capitulated.

'I see your predicament, Andrew,' said his bishop. 'Not a good look for the Church. I think your mother may be right.'

Andrew winced. His mother and bishop were peas in a pod. They worried about what people might think, and would do anything to prevent the name of the Church or rather *their* name being tarnished.

'With your permission, Your Grace, I am prepared to move, and being single makes such a move relatively simple although I do have an obligation to care for my mother.'

'Indeed but tell me, why is it you haven't married? Remember St Paul's letter to the Ephesians; "For this reason a man will leave his father and mother and be united to his wife, and the two will become one flesh".' He paused. 'Well?'

Andrew clenched his fists. 'Speaking frankly, Your Grace, finding a suitable wife has proved difficult; the main stumbling block being my mother. Any future spouse must prove acceptable to you know who.'

The bishop mused. 'Of course, I take your point.'

'Mother prefers to move far from my current parish; to a quiet village with parishioners of good standing and of a certain class.'

'Ah, you mean ladies with the right type of bonnet.'

'Indeed but the problem remains, Your Grace. If we settle in a far-flung parish, and news of my father's troubles reach local ears, the same problem will rear its ugly head, and then what will I do?'

His Grace was tempted to ask, "Have you considered matricide?" but knew his weird sense of humour was often misunderstood.

The bishop made a steeple with his fingers and posed another shocking question. 'Have you considered the other side of the world?

Andrew gulped. Talk about out of the blue. 'Pardon?'

'The colony of New South Wales has need of clergymen.'

Andrew mimed the words. All the way home, he dreaded his mother's reaction; surely she will explode. Surely she'll take the suggestion as an insult to her intelligence and good character. But no, her explosive outburst never eventuated. Of course she complained, such being her default reaction but her brain devoured the prospect. She thought.

*Nobody in Sydney will have even heard of me. I shall declare myself a widow and once more be able to show my face in public. What is the weather like in New South Wales?*

Matilda announced her decision. 'New South Wales is satisfactory. See to it at once,' she ordered. Andrew needed a brandy.

With a letter of recommendation from his bishop, Andrew and his sainted Mama prepared to leave (some might say flee) England, to set sail for the relatively new colony of New South Wales.

Mrs McFarlane could hardly boast about her destination.

'I'm leaving because my husband is a criminal. I'm going to a new settlement founded as a dumping ground for criminals.' No, instead she opted for a nuanced description.

'I'm going to New South Wales where my son has been promoted to bring civilization to the savages.' There now, honour is satisfied.

So a posting was secured for the Reverend Andrew McFarlane in the far-flung British colony. Mr McFarlane Senior was convicted and goaled in the West Country. For his wife and son, all that remained was to identify their ship and its sailing date. They waited. Everything went well with the preparation until the vicar's mother suffered a terrible thought. She screamed. Andrew heard the cry from his study and hurried to the parlour.

'Mother?' he asked fearing the worst.

'We can't go to New South Wales,' she groaned.

He knew she'd find an excuse. 'Why? What's happened?'

'They send criminals there. Your father might be on our ship.'

'True, but it would be a remarkable coincidence.'

'Coincidences happen,' she growled.

'I'll investigate,' he said and did and found his father in the Gloucester City Gaol. The pater's former professional status helped him avoid transportation.

His mother greeted the news with a smidgeon of relief. 'Are you certain?' she asked.

'I am, Mother, and now we know where my father is living, would you like to accompany me on a final visit to see him before we sail?'

She didn't need to speak as her horrified face screamed her reply.

Without telling his mother, Andrew did visit his father and their sad farewell brought tears to the older man's eyes.

So, with their passage booked, the Reverend Andrew McFarlane and his mother, Matilda, set sail Down Under.

# A New Life

## Chapter 24

Once upon a time, Van Diemen's Land was part of what is now known as mainland Australia. But when the last Ice Age ended, oceans rose and lands disappeared beneath the waves. One newly formed island, later called Van Diemen's Land and later still Tasmania, meant the people living there could no longer walk north to the large continent.

The British settled in New South Wales in 1788. Sydney was born. A decade or so later, the French, then an enemy of Britain, were spotted loitering with intent. They had form. La Perouse in Sydney was named after the French navigator, Lapérouse who arrived in Botany Bay only hours after Captain Arthur Phillip and the First Fleet. As a consolation prize, would the French claim Van Diemen's Land as a Louis XVI colony? Not on your Nelly Duff.

The British rounded up some of Sydney's worst convicts, and sent them south. In the early 19th century, Hobart Town was born.

Here could be found plenty of work for convict slaves, gifts of free land for settlers, and a potential black eye for any nosy Frenchman.

But long before any Europeans settled in Van Diemen's Land, others arrived. The aborigines set up camp tens of thousands of years before Abel Tasman, Antoine Bruni d'Entrecasteaux or Captain James Cook.

We can easily trace the history of European settlement on the island but it is difficult, if not impossible, to trace much of the history of the original inhabitants. The Europeans destroyed so many aboriginal sites.

Jonathon Sweeping arrived in Van Diemen's Land as the Europeans moved from tents to dwellings as Hobart Town was born.

Governor Macquarie arrived from Sydney, cracked the whip and had locals designing townscapes and constructing roads and private and public buildings. The convicts, the slaves, did the donkey work. Some were transported from New South Wales but many, like Jonathon Sweeping, were sent direct from England.

Major prisons at Port Arthur for men, Point Puer for boys, and the Cascades Female Factory for women would soon be built. But when the convicts from the *Indomitable* first landed on colonial soil, they were locked up in the solitary Hobart goal on the corner of Murray and Macquarie Streets.

No distinction was made with young and old lumped in together and put to work as manual labourers.

Jonathon and Peter formed a team. They were given clothes, shoes and utensils. Their sleeping accommodation was about the same as on board ship although without the constant motion, the weevils and rats. Replacing the insects and rodents were two creatures desperate to build a friendship with the new arrivals—mosquitoes and flies.

Hobart Town in winter was a lot like England with its cold and rain. The mountain overlooking the settlement often sported a good dusting of snow. It was named after the famous General Wellington.

Come the warmer months, the heat pushed out your sweat and the flies wouldn't leave you alone during the day, while at night, mosquitoes whined above then dive-bombed as you tried to sleep, before enjoying a wee dram of your blood.

This was the pattern of life for Jonathon and Peter; building roads with a pick and shovel. Luckily for them, this tiring work didn't last.

The free settlers on their gifted land needed help, and a scheme using indentured labourers began. It was the Rotherhithe chimney sweep arrangement only in Van Diemen's Land.

Convicts worked on a farm receiving full board but no pay. At the end of their contract, usually 7 years, provided they kept their nose clean, they'd be free. The alternative was to keep working on the roads or government buildings, again for no pay, and return to goal and prison food at night.

When the opportunity arose, Jonathon and Peter couldn't believe their luck. They sat by the side of the road discussing the deal.

'This is marvellous,' said Peter. 'We'll work on a farm in glorious sunshine and sleep in a proper bed without a guard in sight.'

Jonathon was less enthusiastic. He remembered his previous indentured servant experience sweeping chimneys in London.

'It's a risk,' he said and Peter reacted.

'A risk? How? Anything must be better than this.'

'What if we get a cruel farmer? He could flog us and who would protect us? No-one. If we run away, where would we go? How would we survive? Could you survive in this bush?'

Peter argued. 'But why would a farmer who gets our labour for nothing, treat us badly? He'd be cutting off his nose to spite his face.'

Jonathon pondered. He hated living in the goal where convicts swore and fought and, with grog, turned into monsters.

'You're right, Mr Lonsdale; anything has to be better than this. Let's see if we can get posted together.'

Peter grinned, his English teeth and gums hating the hot sunlight. 'Good idea, Mr Sweeping. Who do we see?'

They went to the soldier in charge of the road gang and asked for directions. He sent them to the government man in charge of turning slave convicts into slave labourers.

'Smart move, lads,' he said. 'Now tell me your names.'

After he'd finished taking their details, Jonathon and Peter exchanged glances and Jonathon sensed an obligation to bell the cat.

'Excuse me, sir, but could we be indentured together?'

The official smirked. 'What, so you can rob the farmer and run away together? Not a chance.'

The young convicts copped a slap in the face. They knew they would work hard. They knew they wanted to do the right thing and the official saw their disappointment.

'All right, I'll try and get you placed on nearby farms.'

A shiver ran up the spines of the young men. They spoke together. 'Thank you, sir.'

'Now get back to work before I change me mind.'

Jonathon and Peter ran to the road gang, and the soldier in charge worried. He'd never seen a convict hurry back to work.

The farms the boys were appointed to were miles apart but nearby because "next door" here meant you were neighbours albeit miles apart. Settlers were greedy and land plentiful. No free settler ever asked for a small holding. The bigger their land gift, the more sheep and cattle they could run. The more livestock they owned, the bigger their income.

'Sweeping,' cried the official and Jonathon moved to the desk in the office. 'This is Mr Rawlings. You're indentured to him.'

Jonathon looked at the farmer who was about 40, wiry and sunburnt. Jonathon sensed unease but spoke with respect.

'Good day, sir,' he said, tugging his forelock. The farmer nodded.

'He'll do,' he said and made his mark on the contract.

The official looked at Jonathon. 'Put your mark there, son,' he said holding out the quill. Jonathon stepped forward and took the quill.

'My mark, sir?' he asked.

'Yes, write an X,' he said, making a sign with his hand in the air.

'If you like, I can write my name,' said the former sweep, and his comment produced a sudden hush in the room.

'You can write?' asked the official in disbelief.

'And read too, sir,' added Jonathon without boasting.

The farmer worried. He wanted a simple servant, one who followed orders and didn't think. Anyone who could read and write might be smarter than him; *was* smarter than him.

'Who taught you?' asked Rawlings.

'Another convict taught me, sir.

'Another convict?'

'Yes, when we were on a hulk on the Thames in London.'

The farmer hesitated. 'If you don't want him,' said the official, 'I'll give him to someone else.'

Rawlings looked at Jonathon. 'Sign the contract,' he said and watched as his new labourer carefully transcribed his name. 'This way,' he said and walked from the room.

As Jonathon left he looked at Peter. Both wore bitter sweet smiles.

'Good luck,' they both whispered.

In the street, the farmer climbed onto a basic cart with one horse. This was not the coach and four he took to and from London, or the gorgeous landau in which he escaped from Bittering Hall.

'I'll say this once, son,' said Rawlings. 'You work hard, and stay away from my wife, and I'll see you right. You work slow or even think about makin' eyes at my missus and I'll flog you. Run away and I'll hunt you down like I would them black bastards. Understand?'

Jonathon thought he was listening to a certain chimney sweep employer called Pearce, and a groomer of child thieves called Bankside Bertie. 'Yes sir,' he replied as he climbed on the cart.

*These men are everywhere.*

# Chapter 25

When Jonathon set off for his new life as a farm labourer-cum-slave for one Henry Rawlings, the Reverend Robert Knopwood went about his business in Hobart Town working as a Church of England priest and part-time magistrate.

You could never describe Knopwood as your average, ordinary vicar. He came from old money, gambled badly, never married, and travelled widely and well. His life story was remarkable.

To enable the new-born to suckle, his mother first removed the silver spoon from wee Bobby's gob. His old man's considerable wealth was bequeathed to the boy.

Growing up in Norfolk, the wealthy young Knopwood went gambling with the Prince Regent set and blew the lot. Whether as penance or following a Damascene type event, he graduated from Cambridge and took holy orders, as did a fellow student by the name of Patrick Bronte. Both were admitted as impecunious students.

The Reverend Knopwood then decided to see the world so joined the Royal Navy, and in time became chaplain on the vessel *Matilda* sailing to the new colony in New South Wales. From there he went to Port Phillip, conducted the first service at Sorrento, and when that expedition failed, the party sailed south to Hobart Town.

As a priest, he landed for good in the British settlement in Van Diemen's Land.

His former sprawling estate in Norfolk with its grand house and hundreds of candles, didn't exactly match the tent and candle, singular, he acquired in this beautiful but brutal penal settlement.

But now, for Bobby, Hobart became home. The Governor granted him land, where a house, Cottage Green at Battery Point was built, and his days of living under canvas ended. The vicar took on other duties including that of the local magistrate where he dispensed justice with a heavy heart. There sat the kindly vicar ordering floggings.

Coming from a landed gentry background with riding to hounds a fixture, the Reverend Knopwood would often be seen on a charger doing his rounds of the parish. Wearing a top hat and riding his trusty steed, Bobby rode out to visit fellow Europeans and preach the gospel to all and sundry.

He had little trouble rounding up a congregation because, in its early days, those running the penal colony were big on church attendance and made sure the convicts—male and female—swallowed their solid dose of religion.

The vicar enjoyed a tipple, and he and the then Governor would visit one another to enjoy fine food and lively conversation washed down with an excellent vintage. By the time George Arthur won the top job, the tea-drinking Governor and the priest were at odds.

Subsequent generations would become grateful to Knopwood because the clergyman became a poor man's Samuel Pepys and, in-between parish duties, growing vegetables from seeds he obtained from afar, fishing, and performing magisterial duties, Robert kept a diary. It survived and gave pleasure and information to anyone wanting to know more of the British settlement in Van Diemen's Land from the early 1800s.

He would never have known how his scribblings about life in the colony would be read, nay devoured, by those interested in history centuries after his passing.

Alas his health caused problems, and in time he wrote to Governor Macquarie in Sydney asking if he might retire and enjoy a pension. His request was granted and Bobby Knopwood ended his days in solitude. He died in 1838.

As Jonathon Sweeping and his new boss headed out of Hobart to the Rawlings' farm, the Reverend Knopwood sat at his desk in his cottage penning observations he made on the day's activities. His fishing exploits featured often. However, there was no mention of the youthful convict, Jonathon Sweeping.

It took a good part of the day to reach the farm given to Henry Rawlings, not because it was a vast distance from Hobart but because the roads, tracks more like, were crude, and solid, regular rainfall made travel tricky.

Conversation between owner and worker was limited. Several times Rawlings spoke the following; 'Get down and push,' or 'Get down and lead the horse.'

The journey produced a few firsts for Jonathon. A mob of kangaroos, grazing in the bush, interrupted their luncheon to stare at the cart and the humans who were white, not walking and without spears. The boy had heard of kangaroos but this was his first sighting.

'This is my place,' said Rawlings as the track became the driveway—not the right word—leading to the homestead—again, not the right word—built by the farmer as the residence on his property, on his gift of land. Like many settlers, Rawlings was given 100 acres, tools and livestock and told to get on with it.

"Basic" best described the house, cottage more like. Colonial Regency it wasn't. Rawlings, like other settlers, made use of clay, timber and stone on or near his property. In this case, the delicate box-like building sat in a clearing with the virgin bush all around.

The door at the front of the house opened and two small children burst out running towards the cart. The horse stopped without being asked, and a dog appeared from the side of the building. The children called to Rawlings.

'Father,' called a girl about six. A boy, a year or two younger pushed past his sister to be first to greet his old man. The dog kept its distance.

Rawlings dropped down and hugged his children, ignoring the visitor who remained on the cart. A woman appeared and kissed her husband. As the farmer continued to ignore Jonathon, his wife asked.

'Is this the new farmhand?'

Rawlings looked back and addressed the slave. 'Get down.' Jonathon did so but kept his distance. 'This is my wife, Elsie, Mrs Rawlings to you. And these are my children, (*my* not *our* children), Alice and Willie.

'Hello,' said Elsie and smiled with kindness. The children were slightly awe-struck and said nothing. 'Say hello, children,' to which the offspring murmured a greeting. Jonathon nodded.

'Get the supplies from the cart,' said Rawlings, 'and take 'em 'round the back.' Jonathon looked at the sacks of flour and the boxes of various items. His seven-year stretch of work began.

The family headed inside and Jonathon picked up a heavy sack and set off. It was autumn in this part of the world and Jonathon longed for an extra layer of clothes. He looked at the bush. He heard sheep and then birds he'd never heard or seen before. He was hungry and wanted to pee. He struggled along the side of the cottage and went to turn when a large man crashed into him. The sack hit the ground.

'Oi, watch it,' snapped the man who easily picked up the sack and placed it by the back door. It opened and the boss appeared.

'This is me brother, Lennie,' said Rawlings. 'You'll be working with him. He'll show you where you'll stay.'

Lennie was bigger than his older brother, grew whiskers which helped hide his ugly face, and wore clothes not washed since Christmas, the one before last. He said nothing but slouched his way along the side of the cottage to the cart. Jonathon followed. Lennie took the other sack leaving the boxes to the boy. All the supplies were placed by the back door.

Jonathon surveyed the cleared space at the back. You couldn't call it a yard because there were no fences.

There were two outbuildings which appeared to have been designed and built by a drunk. The smaller shed stood apart. The first building produced sounds and smells with pigs and chickens residing therein.

'In here,' said Lennie and headed to the second building. It offered an earthen floor, no ceiling, cracks created to welcome winds, and two straw-filled areas, sleeping for the use of. A solitary window had never been opened.

'You're over there,' were Lennie's welcoming words. What could Jonathon say? He couldn't ask where he could put his possessions because apart from a battered hat, he owned nothing but the clothes he wore.

He turned brave and asked a question. 'Where's the privy, please?'

Lennie laughed. Like his face, his laugh was ugly. He gestured with a huge movement. 'Try the bush, stupid, or if you fancy a spider up y'arse, the outhouse is over there.'

Jonathon turned and looked out of the opening. The door was a piece of filthy material tied back during the day. There stood the world outside. He thought. *It's a lot like London. You pee anywhere.*

A hand grabbed the back of his neck. It hurt. Lennie's breath frightened the flies. 'Now you listen good, sonny. You do what I tells you or I'll kick y'feckin' head off y'feckin' shoulders. All right?'

Jonathon tried nodding but couldn't so muttered, 'Yes, sir.'

Lennie shoved him forward causing him to stumble. The thug moved to give the boy a kick but stopped when Elsie's voice sounded from the back of the house.

'Tea's ready.'

Lennie glared at his workmate and headed indoors. A fair way behind, Jonathon followed. Memories of London surfaced although the curious dog gave him a welcome. Jonathon patted the dog and it wagged its tail for the first time in ages.

To Jonathon, the kitchen looked like the family room in Bermondsey; no bed but a simple table with a fireplace against the wall and ill-matching, homemade chairs. The children were on the floor to one side. Lennie pulled up a chair and sat. Elsie pointed.

'You sit there. What's your name?'

'Jonathon, Miss, er, Ma'am.' He sat. 'Thank you.'

'You can call me Elsie,' she said and placed a mug of tea in front of him. 'Do you have sugar?'

'Yes please.'

'No he don't,' snapped Henry cutting costs and objecting to the polite discourse. 'Stop fussing, woman, he's a convict for God's sake.'

Elsie ignored her husband, put a plate with a piece of bread and homemade jam in front of the boy. 'Help yourself, Jonathon.'

He did. Being in the middle of the bush on the other side of the world was unusual. Being abused by bullies happened before, and being hungry was a regular occurrence. So a lot was familiar. He gave the bread and tea a fearful thrashing. There were no seconds.

'Come with me,' said Henry, and Jonathon followed his new boss out the back door. Lennie followed like a soldier guarding a convict. The dog tagged along behind the new arrival.

They walked through the bush until they came to a clearing. The English might call it a field. Simple fencing meant a flock of sheep was confined in a paddock.

'I need to clear more land, build more fences and breed more sheep,' said Henry pointing into the distance. 'If you want your freedom, son, you're going to have to earn it.'

'I'll do my best, Mr Rawlings.'

Henry looked at him not convinced a convict so young would be able to do the work needed. 'Have a wander round. There's a river beyond this paddock.' He pointed. 'And that hill gives you a view of all my land. Be back before dark.'

The brothers turned and walked away. The dog waited. Jonathon tapped his thigh and gave a soft whistle. Without hesitation, the dog padded to his new friend.

'What's your name?' The dog wasn't sure having only ever been called 'Get here', 'Get Out' or 'Shut up'. Jonathan spoke to the animal. 'I reckon I'm lucky to have met you. How about I call you Lucky?' The dog smiled.

Lennie asked his brother if leaving the convict alone was a wise move. Henry grunted. 'Where's he gunna go? Manchester?'

The sheep ignored Jonathon. He and Lucky walked through the paddock, went beyond the fence and reached the river. It was about ten yards wide and so clear you could see the bottom. *Are there fish here?* He followed the river admiring the massive trees. Felling them would be one hell of a job. But then what happens once the trees are felled?

He looked up at the hill. It was a cloudy afternoon but he thought he'd head in that direction. There were no tracks and the bush was thick and hard to tackle. The thought of getting lost scared him. *If they think I've run away, the farmer said he'd hunt me down.*

Forget the hill. He retraced his steps and relaxed a tad when he heard a sheep bleat. He set off with head down to see where to step when whoosh!, someone or thing leapt out of the bush and knocked him flat. Were they hunting for him already? Lucky barked.

Jonathon stood and saw a kangaroo bound away into the bush.

Welcome to Van Diemen's Land, son; just don't mess with the locals. Oh, and we were here before you and your lot.

# Chapter 26

Life for Jonathon on the Rawlings' farm was tough. Fortunately the indentured convict came from a background of grinding poverty, cruel and vindictive employers, hellish living conditions, and a voyage with hardened criminals, inquisitive rats and pesky weevils. Anything the family Rawlings threw his way would be met with seasoned resistance. Young Sweeping was used to tough.

Elsie was lovely and her kids great. Henry struggled in this new land, and his brother hated everyone and everything.

Sleeping in the same "room" as Lennie was awful. He was like many young males, and even not-so-young men, who were desperate for sex but faced a dearth of partners. The female population, at least in the European community, was way out of balance. There were far fewer females around and, unlike big English cities like London, brothels were few and far between with nary a one in the bush.

Lennie knew about black women in Van Diemen's Land. He heard about settlers and sealers capturing black females, some who were still children, and keeping them for their own use. He didn't think about any pain this might cause the captured females, or the distress it caused their families. Lennie was good at thinking about himself.

At night, he bemoaned his plight with Jonathon wishing he'd shut up. Having lived in prisons and mixed with men of dubious or even no morals, Jonathon developed an understanding of sex. The young farmhand knew a little of Lennie's complaints.

And first-hand experience came Jonathon's way when the brothers started their latest round of sheep breeding. The ram and ewe were introduced and told to get on with it. Talk about learning on the job. It wasn't long before Henry didn't need to explain anything. The boy was a quick learner and better still, a good worker.

Lennie was the fly in the ointment. He managed to make rot-gut liquor and at night, in his cups, would threaten the boy. The only thing that saved Jonathon was Lennie's fear of his brother. The farmhand was a precious resource to be worked like a slave and fed as little as possible. But if the boy copped an injury which stopped him working, Lennie would face the wrath of the boss.

Jonathon's best friend was the dog. Lucky was a working animal with the children forbidden from playing with it. Lennie abused the animal so it was natural it took a shine to Jonathon who gave Lucky crusts and other titbits whenever he could—always secretly of course.

At night, Lucky would wait until Lennie fell asleep and snoring before the dog crept in and hopped on the straw at Jonathon's feet.

As his stay on the farm continued, Jonathon became genuinely friendly with the children. This pleased Elsie who appreciated her children having a person to talk to and even play with.

Henry watched this blossoming relationship noting the farmhand was growing into a young man while his wife grew to enjoy his company more and more.

One evening during their meal, Jonathon asked if the children would go to school.

Elsie laughed with sadness. 'What school?' she asked. 'The nearest is in Hobart Town and how would they get there?'

'If you like, I could teach them to read,' he said and the room fell silent. Henry knew Jonathan signed his name on their contract but didn't consider he would be able to teach reading.

Elsie was overjoyed and her happiness ignited her children's faces. They could go to school in their home.

'Oh yes please, Ma,' cried Alice.

Little brother Willie trembled with excitement. 'Can I learn to read?' he pleaded.

'That sounds wonderful,' said Elsie. 'What do you say, Henry?'

'We haven't got no books. How can you teach without them?'

Jonathon pushed his proposal. 'We can write on bark using clay for ink. And when you next go into town, sir, you could buy paper and ink. I'm sure the hens could spare us a pen or two.'

Henry wanted to object but the ideas from the convict and the response from his family flattened his opposition. He grunted.

'Let's start,' said the teacher and sat on the floor in front of the children. Every eye settled on the former sweep. 'Say after me,' he said in a slow and deliberate way. 'The cat sat on the mat.'

The children were fired up and repeated the sentence with ease. He used simple sayings, repeating them over and over. The students were in raptures, their mother thrilled, their father quietly impressed but their uncle fumed, left and got drunk.

And so bit by bit, Jonathon Sweeping became a part of the family Rawlings. Lennie's hatred grew more intense, Elsie and the children grew to love the farmhand, and even Henry admitted, the young man worked well and brought joy to his children.

Jonathon did as promised and used pieces of bark from the trees in the bush around the cottage. He mixed clay from the river bank with water and made a paste as a substitute for chalk or ink, writing with his index finger. Before long the children could read certain words. Their progress brought tears to Elsie's eyes.

After one lesson and the children were sent to bed, Elsie thanked Jonathon, moved to him and gave him a hug. He was embarrassed, she grateful. Lennie opened the back door and saw the embrace, and friendly kiss his sister-in-law planted on the farmhand's cheek.

Jonathon stepped back, said goodnight and left. He walked past Lennie who glared at him and then at his sister-in-law.

'Tea, Lennie?' she asked with nothing to hide.

'Where's Henry?' he replied then heard him coming to the cottage carrying wood for the fireplace. 'I want a word with you,' said Lennie and walked outside.

'What's up?' said Henry to his wife. She shrugged and went back to kneading dough for tomorrow's bread. Henry joined his brother outside.

'I seen your wife kissing the convict.' Lennie refused to use the farmhand's name. He was "the convict".

Henry tensed, his blood boiled. 'Keep y'voice down.'

From his bed, Jonathon heard snippets of the conversation.

'I warned you about him. He's old enough, he ain't got a woman and now he fancies Elsie.'

Henry sniffed. He wanted to say, "Just like you," but didn't. 'Leave it to me. I'll sort it.' The husband went inside and the brother entered his dump of a bedchamber. Jonathon barely breathed. Lennie moved to his own bed, said nothing then cleared his throat and spat. Spittle landed close to Jonathon's bed.

They were asleep when a scream filled the night air. Lennie, Jonathon and Lucky were awake and out of bed. Lucky disappeared. Lennie snapped. 'Stay there.' He left and Jonathon crept to the opening of their shed and listened.

Raised voices came from inside the cottage. They became louder. Children cried. Then it was silent and dark. The night sounds of the bush were strange yet comforting but humans yelling and screaming, they were the seriously scary sounds.

Lennie came out of the cottage and Jonathon scurried back to his bed. When Lennie arrived, the young man decided to speak.

'Is everything all right?'

Lennie repeated his spitting routine.

Next morning, Jonathon was reluctant to enter the cottage for his breakfast. When he did, the children were absent, in their bedroom and quiet. Elsie put a mug of tea and toast and jam on the table in front of the farmhand. He wanted to look at her but sensed Henry and Lennie were staring at him. He ate in silence, stood to leave and as he did, glanced at Elsie. Her left cheek was swollen and bruised. She averted her face.

'I'll check on the lambs,' said Jonathon and left. As he set off, a sound made him stop. A man on a horse rode towards the cottage. He waved and Jonathon waved back. They drifted together.

'Good day, young man,' said the rider.

'Good day, sir,' said Jonathon and held the horse allowing the rider to dismount. He held out a hand.

'I'm the Reverend Knopwood and you, I believe, are Jonathon Sweeping, the indentured convict.'

Jonathon didn't get a chance to reply as Henry and Lennie arrived and took over the conversation. They both knew the visitor and invited him into the house.

'See to the lambs,' said Henry, and Jonathon started but stopped when the clergyman spoke.

'Oh, I'd like a word with the young man too. I need to make a report on his progress.'

What could Henry say? All four entered the cottage.

Look who's here,' said Henry to Elsie, and Knopwood reacted.

'Oh dear, what happened to you, Mrs Rawlings?' he asked looking at Elsie's bruised face.

Henry answered for his wife. 'She bumped into a door in the dark. Go and lie down, Elsie.'

She defied her husband. 'Thank you, I'm all right.' She stared at the cleric wanting him to see her bruise. 'Tea, Mr Knopwood?'

Naturally he accepted and three male adults sat at the table while the wife and farmhand hovered. Henry gave news of his farm and family and, when prompted, reported on the convict doing a satisfactory job.

His wife interrupted. 'Oh he's more than satisfactory, Henry. Tell the Reverend how he's teaching the children to read.'

The brothers fumed as Elsie took advantage of the visitor's presence. The cleric reacted.

'Teaching the children to read? How on Earth ...?' He turned to Jonathon. 'How does a young convict know how to read? And how do you teach in this setting?'

Jonathon was under a spotlight. He explained, dominating the meeting. Elsie passed the tea and biscuits as the budding teacher described his history in the hulk, and his progress and plans for the children's continuing education.

'What would help, sir,' said Jonathon, 'is paper for the children to learn to write as well.'

Without hesitation, Knopwood opened his saddle bag and withdrew his diary. From the end of the book he removed a few pages and handed them to Jonathon.

'Here, start with these and I'll see what I can find in Hobart Town.'

They all stared with Jonathon stunned.

'Thank you, sir. I'm sure the children will be delighted.'

'And where *are* the children?' asked Knopwood. 'They are not poorly I hope.'

'Fetch them,' said Henry to his wife in a low-key threat. The look he gave her reinforced what he said last night during his cowardly display of domestic violence.

Many settlers in parts of the colonies lived in isolated places. If a settler's wife died, some widowers took the lack of a woman badly. If drought, flood or fire damaged or destroyed their crops and livestock, depression and desperation drove some men to violence. The nearest neighbour might be days away. Women became victims with no help or comfort, and worse, nowhere to go.

Knopwood walked in on the harsh reality of one pioneer family battling to survive. Here he found good and bad. The convict was a triumph of a person rising above adversity and becoming a kind and useful member of society. The wife suffered from her husband's ignorance, jealousy and rage.

The children entered the room unsure of how to behave. Their father intimidated them and their loving mother stood subdued.

'There you are,' smiled the cleric. 'It's Alice and Willie, yes?'

The children perked up a tad with Willie cracking a smidgeon of a smile.

'A little birdie told me there are two children here who can read. Is that true?' Two heads nodded. 'So who will go first to show me what you know?' Both children became keen. They loved their new skill and wanted to tell the world about it. Alice's hand shot up. 'Alice, tell me one thing you have learnt.'

The girl spoke without hesitation although there was a slight pause between each word. 'The cat sat on the mat.'

Willie jumped in desperate to speak. 'I know the cat sat on the mat,' he said speaking more fluently than big sister.

'Ah, but can you *read* the words?' said the cleric opening a page of his diary. He wrote three words in large print using a pencil, the type of which had only been invented in the last 20 years. He turned the page to the children. 'Now, Alice, please read these words.'

'mat, sat, cat,' said the girl with her mother and teacher delighted. Willie began to blub. Why was he left out? He wasn't.

'Now, Willie, please read the word when I point to it.'

Knopwood pointed at the words but not in the order in which they appeared. Without hesitation, Willie named each word correctly.

'Well done,' exclaimed the clergyman and Jonathon and Elsie clapped in a muted way. The child beamed. Henry experienced a mixture of pride and shame. Lennie fumed.

The visit was timely and successful. Jonathon was dismissed with an order to check on the lambs.

'Thank you, Jonathon,' called the cleric. 'I'm glad to see you doing so well, and I'll find those teaching materials for you.'

'Thank you, sir,' said the convict who left, and none of the Rawlings' clan added a word of praise, Elsie being too scared to do so.

When the cleric left, Jonathon was far from the cottage checking on the new lambs. Naturally Lucky followed waiting for a command from his favourite and beloved master.

The lambs Jonathon helped deliver were special and he gave them names. Telling Henry and Lennie of this routine would never happen. Giving animals names—are you mad?

Thinking and worrying about Elsie and her bruise, Jonathon decided to walk as far from the property as he could. If they looked for him, he could always say he went looking for lost sheep.

On his first day with the family, Henry told Jonathon to walk to the river and then to the hill, away to the north. He didn't climb the hill then but now decided to do so.

'Come here, Lucky, here boy.'

Van Diemen's Land reminded Jonathon of those parts of rural England he saw as a child. He saw greenery, trees, miles of countryside with rivers and creeks in abundance. Climbing the hill proved tricky, not because it was steep but because trees, saplings, ferns and other plants thrived. Lucky took it all in his stride.

The vegetation thinned as they reached the top. The summit was fairly flat and they walked along a ridge then stopped to admire the view. Jonathon wanted a drink and reckoned Lucky did too.

He surveyed the land on the other side of the hill. More of the same as far as the eye could see. Then he spotted smoke rising slowly from a clearing. It was a long way off but his heart kick-started when he saw people. Distance made it impossible to see faces but what he could see were people with black skin and not many clothes.

He'd seen people with coloured skin in England, and then on his travels in Rio de Janerio and Cape Town. But these were the first dark-skinned people he saw in Van Diemen's Land.

The sun increased his thirst. 'Come on, Lucky, let's go and find that river.' They did and both enjoyed a long and satisfying drink.

# **Chapter 27**

If Mrs Matilda McFarlane, mother of the Reverend Andrew McFarlane, had even the slightest notion of the size of her cabin on the ship *Rose,* and the length of the voyage, the size of the waves, and the dress sense of most of her fellow passengers, she would never have agreed to leave England. The woman, whose first response automatically became a complaint, was stuck. The ship sailed and she had nowhere to go, well, apart from out on deck.

'Can we turn back?' she asked her son on the first day.

'No, mother we can't. Please get used to the situation and remember we have several months of sailing.

'Months!' It was fit-of-the-vapors time and Andrew went to chat to the captain, crew, soldiers, convicts, anyone, even the ocean.

Getting no sympathy, Matilda lived in her cabin, and her son enjoyed the happiest months of his life.

Suffice to say the ship arrived safely in Port Jackson and the ship's company disembarked. Matilda wore her finest outfit selecting black to advertise the fact, the possible lie, she was a widow.

'You may suggest the fact, Mother, but please do not state you are a widow. Your husband, so far as we know, is very much alive.'

They climbed into a carriage which hardly suited madam's desired status, and made their way into the city. As a new clergyman in Sydney, Andrew was afforded a fine residence although hardly possessing grandeur. Inside, Mrs McFarlane ran her fingers along surfaces raising her eyebrows in disgust.

Despite her outward disappointment, excitement bubbled away inside. Her husband's scandal lay dead and buried on the other side of the world. She was the mother of the new vicar, and would soon make her mark socially in a new town in a new colony.

Andrew had any number of people to meet and a church to inspect. He too became excited, particularly upon spying the number of young women in colourful dresses and bonnets who walked freely in the streets. He was not the twin of Lennie Rawlings in Van Diemen's Land but nevertheless Andrew's loneliness haunted him.

He wanted a wife—did he ever?—and he needed a wife and being in a new country, set a goal to find a wife and to hell with what his mother said.

Sydney was the oldest of the European settlements in the land originally called New Holland but now being referred to as Australia. The settlement spread from the shores of Port Jackson along the coast and into the hinterland, and when the McFarlanes arrived about 30 years after the settlement began, progress was in full swing.

Over supper, Matilda basked in a warm glow as she envisaged a bright future for herself and her son.

'There are well-to-do families from the old country, Andrew. Two women called this afternoon when you were out; excellent breeding, outstanding families from Buckinghamshire. I found it easy to explain my dressing in black and they expressed their sympathies understanding my status as a widow.'

Andrew fumed quietly. 'You do realise, Mother, that having announced your marital status, you may be subject to a marriage proposal.' Matilda blanched and even more so when her son added the following, '*several* marriage proposals.' She hadn't thought of that possibility.

He caused the matriarch to cease speaking, a rare feat in itself.

The son changed topics. 'The present church is basic but there are plans afoot to build a new and more substantial one. I met a brilliant architect today called Greenway who showed me his design for a church to be called St James.'

'Why would an architect come to the other side of the world?'

'He's a convict, mother, convicted of forgery and sentenced to ...'

'Forgery?' hissed Matilda. She was about to mention her husband's fraud when the maid came in to clear away the teacups. Silence reigned.

When Andrew took his first service, the church was packed with many wanting to inspect the new vicar. Matilda sat near the front fanning herself in an attempt to imitate a peacock in full display.

After the service, she became miffed when most of the congregation pressed the flesh with her son. Alarming for Matilda were the number of young women who wished to greet the clergyman. Word quickly spread regarding Andrew's bachelor status.

He once worried he might never find a suitable wife. Now he worried about being spoilt for choice.

Over luncheon, he mentioned this fact, and his mother sounded the alarm. 'You have no idea of the background of these persons, Andrew. They may even have a convict in their family.'

'As do we,' he replied, and she wanted to throw something.

Life proceeded in a smooth fashion. Matilda luxuriated in pleasure when ladies of Sydney society called upon her. Andrew became a minor hit with the locals, and several spinsters of the parish wished he would pay more attention to them.

Governor Lachlan Macquarie invited the McFarlanes to Government House and all was well with the world.

Andrew took great interest in preparations for the building of the new church using Mr Greenway's design. The only thing missing in Andrew's life was sex. If he could pluck up the courage to begin courting the prettiest young woman in his congregation, and his mother would keep her nose out, a whole new chapter of his life might begin.

Andrew told his mother about Miss Letitia Cornwall, and with the said lady's family history discreetly investigated, Mother was satisfied. She didn't approve mind, but agreed to allow the courtship to proceed. Her opposition revolved solely around losing control of her son to a daughter-in-law. But she hated procrastination.

'And for heaven's sake, Andrew,' she complained, 'don't dither. If you're going to do it, do it.'

Andrew wasn't sure what "it" was and did dither. When it came to romance and courtship, Andrew reverted to type because the poor chap lacked courage. His virginal life meant women were easy to relate to so long as intimacy remained under lock and key. However, gradually, the clergyman made progress. He told his mother he and Miss Cornwall had "an understanding".

'Whatever does that mean?' she asked putting even more pressure on the frustrated man.

He struggled but built up the courage to ask for Letitia's hand. He even asked the Almighty for strength and wisdom. He thought about asking his mother for advice on how to go about it before realizing that would be the worst mistake he or anyone could ever make.

Tonight was the night. He would call on his beloved's father to seek his permission to ask to marry Mr Cornwall's daughter. With a new church and vicarage on the horizon, the Reverend Andrew McFarlane would be able to offer his bride a style of living and status to keep everyone happy.

Andrew's blood pressure, heartbeat and sweat glands were busy tending towards being out of control. This further worried the vicar. He headed home to change, determined to tell his mother nothing until the proposal was made and, of course, accepted.

His heart burst with pride as he arrived. In a second it crashed to Earth, caught fire and burnt to a crisp. His mother exploded.

Matilda was beside herself with a mixture of fear, rage and panic. Andrew knew this was the end of his best attempt, possibly his only attempt to find a wife. At the final hurdle, he fell with his horse landing on top of him. Worse, this display by his mother reached new depths.

'Please, Mother,' he begged, 'you gave me your blessing, you even encouraged me to get on with it. Now kindly stop this outrageous behaviour.'

She ignored him. He worried like never before. He'd more or less surrendered, again, so why the blood-curdling reaction from Mama.

'Mother, are you ill?'

'I'm dying.'

Not enough information. 'What's happened?'

'The Honourable Langford Beaumaris,' was all she said.

Andrew knew the name, vaguely. 'What about him?'

Matilda looked ready to collapse. She gasped. 'He's here.'

More head shaking from Andrew. 'And?'

'He's here in New South Wales. He's a grazier out in the Brown Mountains.' She meant the Blue Mountains. 'But he comes into Sydney. He's here in this city; *here!*'

Andrew struggled to understand. 'But why is he so important?'

She looked at her son unable to believe he could be so stupid. She spoke slowly in a flat voice with a touch of evil.

'He knew your father.'

The penny dropped and Andrew knew it was not only his marriage prospects that were gone for good. His current position and life in New South Wales were now in jeopardy.

His mother stood and moved remarkably well for a woman of her age and condition. Stiff joints had long been her closest friend. 'We have to move. I don't want to but it's back to England we must go. When is the next ship?'

'Mother,' sighed a groaning Andrew.

She ignored him. 'Or India or the Americas. Yes, the Americas. It's such a big country.'

Andrew swallowed some gumption. 'I'm sorry, Mother, but I'm not moving.' She seethed but he carried on. 'Who cares if this man knew father?'

'Who cares?' she hissed. 'I care. Me. I do. The respectable people of Sydney must never know I married a convict.'

The last word took its time in leaving Matilda's mouth. It left a sour, bitter taste on her tongue.

Andrew tried reason. Poor fool. 'What if you never meet this gentleman? What if he knows nothing of father's past?' Then Andrew found an idea. 'What if you make sure everyone *knows* you're a widow?'

The wind in Matilda's sails disappeared. They went limp as she sat and pushed a handkerchief to her mouth. Andrew pushed harder.

'If everyone believes you really *are* a widow, who will care about your late husband?'

She knew his idea might work but admitting to anything other than her misery was too hard. She moaned.

'I wish I were dead.'

The months rolled by and Jonathon worked hard for the Rawlings, taught their children, and learnt about raising sheep in Van Diemen's Land. Touring the colony, a shearer called and gave the men a lesson in shearing. Selling lambs made money but with the mills in England screaming for fine wool, the brothers Rawlings were told about the merino.

'You'll make a quid from growing the best wool in the world,' said the shearer. 'People buyin' merino sheep in New South Wales are doing very nicely.'

So the farm began to prosper and the boy began to grow. Moving from cramped chimneys in filthy, polluted London to the fresh open air and sunshine on a farm in Van Diemen's Land helped the boy become a strapping youth. His healthy physique made him a first-class farmhand and Henry worried. The time would come when Jonathon Sweeping would be free.

After the fracas on the night before the Reverend Knopwood appeared, a fragile peace settled on the domestic front although Lennie seemed only a small step away from an explosion. He was clearly frustrated telling Jonathon often about his need for a woman.

The routine in the outdoor shed was set in stone. Lamenting his lot, Lennie would fall asleep after which Lucky would scamper in and jump on Jonathon's bed joining his master for a well-earned rest.

This routine changed dramatically one night when Lennie was not around. It was dark and Jonathon worried. Where is Lennie? Should his absence be reported to his brother?

Jonathon decided he was not his master's brother's keeper so went to bed and called Lucky inside. The two settled down and were sound asleep when Lucky came alive.

His movement woke Jonathon but even without the dog he would have been disturbed by the noise. Lennie was cursing and his heavy footsteps told the world of his arrival.

Before he turned in, Jonathon lit a lantern in case Lennie arrived drunk and tripped in the dark. The boor arrived complete with swearing and his large shape filled the doorway. He was not alone.

'Get in,' snarled Lennie and a young, black female was thrust into the shed where she fell on the straw-covered earthen floor.

'Lennie,' said Jonathon wanting to know what was happening and, at the same time, issuing a warning to be careful.

'Shut up,' snapped Lennie and took a step towards his co-worker. Lucky was having none of that and growled. Lennie chose discretion over brutality and moved to the girl.

Jonathon reckoned she was young, a year or two younger than him. Her eyes radiated fear. The man who dragged her to this place was twice her weight, more, and angry to boot.

Lennie bent, grabbed her, dragging her to her feet. He propelled her to his bed and shoved. She sprawled on the blankets.

'Stay!' he demanded and pointed. 'Stay there.'

Her terror increased. Lennie ripped off his shirt and dropped his trousers. He was forced to stop disrobing when he copped a mighty slap on his bare back. He spun around frothing at the mouth.

He was angry at being hit, and furious about having his plan of coitus interrupted. This was his big moment, his opportunity to finally be able to have sex with someone other than himself.

Jonathon spread his legs as per the routine he learnt in boxing lessons below deck on the prison hulk.

'You can't do this,' said the younger man. 'You have to let her go.' He stood facing his semi-naked enemy. The girl couldn't escape but nor could Lennie continue with his fantasy.

Naturally the chances of Lennie agreeing to Jonathon's demands were less than the fires of hell being put out in a snow storm.

'You're dead, convict,' spat Lennie. 'You've been askin' for this ever since you got 'ere, you miserable little shit. Say goodbye, convict.'

Lennie threw a punch which might have killed the younger man. He swayed back, the fist missed, and Lennie overbalanced.

Lucky joined the fray as an opponent of Lennie. His bark was as good as his bite.

With Lennie off balance and distracted by the dog, Jonathon used the ungentlemanly tactic of kicking his opponent's genitals. In Lennie's case, this area was currently in a state of high excitement having been told to "stand ready" by Lennie's overexcited brain. In such a heightened condition, a bony shin giving a chap's privates a decent smack meant Lennie's pain mushroomed into the agony zone. He dropped to his knees, tears in his eyes. He wanted to speak but found an obstacle, exquisite pain, blocking his ability to go verbal.

Jonathon stepped around Lennie, took the wrist of the frightened girl and spoke. 'Come on, let's go.'

She was unsure but sensed anything with the second white man was better than anything with her captor. She hurried out of the hut and ran with Jonathon towards the sheep in the first paddock. Lucky didn't need an invitation to join the party.

The trio disappeared into the night as Henry, wearing a nightshirt, came out of the back door and headed to the groaning sounds.

'What the hell's going on? Where's Jonathon?'

Lennie started his baloney. 'Blacks attacked me and kidnapped the convict.'

'Aborigines? They attack in the day. What happened?'

Lennie's pain lingered. Each tiny movement, even breathing, ramped up his suffering.

'I don't know. It was all so sudden. It might have been a trick. He said there were aborigines and when I went to help him, he kicked me in the nuts and took off.'

'He attacked you?' Henry seriously doubted his brother's tale. 'But why? He's been here for years.' Henry stared at his suffering brother. 'I tell you, if he's run off, he's blown his chance of freedom.'

The farmer reckoned they should try and rescue Jonathon but Lennie was adamant. 'There were too many of them and they'll spear you as quick as look at you.'

Henry accepted Lennie's advice. When the husband and father went inside and told Elsie and the children, there was much weeping.

'But will Jonathon be all right?' asked Alice.

'Will he come back?' asked Willie.

Henry gave vague answers about Jonathon possibly coming back. Elsie looked at Henry whose face told her the farmhand was lost.

To her and the children, Jonathon was part of the family. The children had learnt to read and write thanks to the indentured convict. His work as a labourer, shepherd and shearer was invaluable.

Jonathon knew this part of the bush and led the girl at a good clip. Her lean body and rude good health meant she had no trouble keeping up. He wouldn't let go of her wrist. As they slowed to cross a creek, he looked and her eyes seemed less scared. In fact the terror she once exhibited was no more. Lucky was never more excited.

When Jonathon reckoned they were safe from Lennie, he stopped. He released the girl's wrist. Would she run? Would she disappear into the bush to never be seen again?

She stood still and looked at her rescuer. They spoke different languages so said nothing. The moonlight allowed them to see each other's face. Jonathon became uncomfortable as the girl was partly naked. He gestured to the bush.

'Go home,' he said. She remained. 'Go home,' he repeated and, as if understanding his words, she walked away. After a few yards, she stopped and looked back. He watched her hoping she would leave.

She continued to walk away then repeated her stop-and-look-back routine. Now she was about 15 yards away and beckoned to him. Off she went again. Jonathon knew Lennie would lie about their fight. He paused then set off following the girl. Lucky came too.

The girl's bare feet made no difference to her gait or speed. Jonathon's hardened feet were okay but less nimble. He worried as they headed towards the unknown. Behind him was the wrath of the man who hated him before their bust-up, and who now would want to shoot him on sight. Jonathon's predicament made him shake.

The sounds of the bush meant nothing to the Englishman but his dog lived on another plane. As he walked beside Jonathon, Lucky growled. Softly he gave a warning, increasing his master's fear.

A yell from a human put the fear of God into Jonathon as people, all males, appeared out of the darkness. He was surrounded.

The moon was bright but the dense bush acted as a shade. Lucky barked and kept barking as Jonathon was grabbed by each arm and, in the darkness, saw a spear, a long, beautifully-made weapon with a sharp and lethal tip raised and pointed at his chest.

He yelled but his sound was drowned by another. The girl he rescued let fly with a ferocious cry which stopped the attackers in their tracks. Lucky continued to jump and bark but even he fell back.

The girl spoke quickly in her language, words her ancestors first spoke thousands of years ago. The men with the spears looked at

Jonathon. One stepped forward and spoke directly to the white fella. Jonathon understood nothing and everything. They thanked him for saving their woman and invited him to join them for a meal.

In the time Jonathon had lived in Van Diemen's Land, he never saw a black man or woman up close. From a distance, yes, but now he was in the midst of a whole group of aboriginals.

They reached a camp site with a fire and huts. Those escorting Jonathon explained to the others in the camp what happened. The others showed great emotion at the return of their family member. She was mobbed.

One man, an Elder, pointed to a fallen log and with sign language, Jonathon understood and sat with Lucky beside him.

They all sat and ate. A woman handed Jonathon his first meal of kangaroo, fresh from the hot coals in the fire. He saw the others watching him. He half smiled then took a bite.

Different, yes, but tasty. He took a bigger bite and saw a row of black faces displaying white teeth as they grinned. He broke off a piece of the food and indicated Lucky. More grins from his hosts and so he fed the dog who scoffed the food and looked for more.

An aborigine approached with a bone from the recently killed kangaroo and placed it in front of the dog. Lucky reckoned he should come here more often. The locals laughed.

The meal over, Jonathon needed to know how to leave and discover basic directions to find his way home. With no knowledge of the language, he reckoned his lucky streak might have run its course.

As he stood thinking about what to do next, the girl he rescued approached and took hold of his wrist as he did with her. Their eyes did the talking. She led him to one of the huts and pointed. He was uncertain and hesitated. She pointed again and urged him forward.

He knelt and crawled inside finding something soft. Possum skins lay on the ground. He made himself comfortable. No sooner had he settled than Lucky squeezed his way inside, tail wagging and face grinning with a bone between his teeth.

This was where he slept back home. This was where he would sleep tonight. And they did; the dog and its master.

Jonathon and Lucky woke to the sounds of the bush. There were animal sounds on the farm but these were different. Here were birds that'd been nesting in these forests, possibly for millennia.

Jonathon crawled out and saw many aboriginals; the first time he could clearly see them. Plenty of sunshine made for excellent viewing.

They were slim, strong and smiling. The young girl greeted him and patted Lucky. Their different clothing proved a challenge for him. They seemed to have no problem with *his* garments.

Jonathon worried about last night. Attacking Lennie and fleeing was risky but he did what he believed was right. Thinking about his action made him feel proud and quietly happy.

Breakfast was a wooden bowl with fleshy leaves and small purple fruit. Aborigines here had enjoyed pigface forever. It was a fruit, a plant they both ate and used as medicine. For Jonathon it was new but filling. He would certainly eat it again, and as it was obviously growing locally, he wondered if the Europeans even knew it existed.

Lucky discovered a water pot and emptied it. He cocked his leg on a log and Jonathon wished to do the same. He moved into the bush and worried the aborigines might think he was running away.

Behind a mighty gum, he peed and the relief brought pleasure. He led his dog back to the camp.

During the night, he decided. He would never return to the farm. He would run away and go to Hobart Town and ask the Governor or magistrate or even the vicar, Mr Knopwood, if his indenture could be ended making him a free man or at least changed to another farm. *But where is Hobart Town?*

He tried to explain his need for directions with pointing and saying Hobart Town. Jonathon assumed they knew of the settlement. He pointed again and received no response. Then the girl he rescued stepped forward and took his hand. She smiled and set off, gently tugging the visitor leading him away from the camp.

Lucky wagged his tail as the party set off with Jonathon looking back to see the aborigines all watching him, the girl and the dog. His first encounter with the people, who were here ages before the Europeans, was good. No, better than good. He wondered how it would end.

# Chapter 29

Jonathon knew little of the land beyond the Rawlings' farm. He once investigated the river and the hill in the distance but to him, the bush was the bush. The girl stopped holding his hand and moved smoothly through the countryside. As they travelled, he needed to change stride, duck and, at times, leap while she barely missed a beat. Even Lucky faced a few obstacles and needed to spring and swerve.

As he grew older, Jonathon began to look at older females in a new way. He found them interesting and when not watching where to put his feet, he studied the aboriginal girl from behind. He remembered Lennie dragging her into their hut and began to imagine what Lennie would have done to the girl. The group kept moving.

When the girl led him to her camp last night, apart from intermittent moonlight, Jonathon had no idea where they were or going. Now, in the daylight, he recognized nothing. Was this the way they travelled last night? He was lost. The girl didn't hesitate.

They seemed to walk for ages before the girl stopped and pointed. Jonathon caught up with her and looked. In broken scrub he saw sheep, lots of them. He hoped to see settlements with farmers and then the town of Hobart but if the farms and town were nearby, they were hidden. All he could see was the bush and the sheep.

The girl faced him and spoke. He understood not a word but sensed she was leaving. She hadn't understood his request to be taken to the European settlement but had instead accidentally done him a huge favour. She delivered him to a settlement. But whose?

The girl smiled, bent to pat Lucky then skipped away into the bush. Jonathon looked at the dog with a wagging tail.

The sheep were 100 yards away and doing what sheep do, grazing.

'Come on, old boy,' said the master and headed towards the sheep.

They didn't look up when the newcomers appeared although a few took note of the dog. He was their boss. Jonathon moved closer and examined a few. He gasped. They sported a mark used by Henry to identify his flock.

'These are our sheep,' said Jonathon looking around. He saw only bush. There were no fences or buildings, not even smoke from a kitchen or a fire used when clearing land.

'Let's go exploring.' Jonathon headed beyond the sheep until he came to a river. It looked like the one at the rear of his farm but it was too wide and deep for the sheep to cross. He headed south along the bank, turned a bend and saw it.

Rocks were placed in the river on a bend near where a tree fell in the water. This formed a small weir-like structure where the current slowed creating a ford or crossing point. The river here was narrow. This must have been how the sheep reached their position. But how did they reach beyond the fence on the Rawlings' farm?

Back to the sheep went Jonathon with Lucky in tow. When they reached the flock, the dog needed only one instruction. Jonathon headed back to the ford with Lucky rounding up the sheep.

At the crossing point, Jonathon urged the sheep forward with Lucky bringing up the rear. They headed in the same direction and stopped when they heard voices.

The brothers were shouting and good manners were absent.

'You were supposed to check that part of the fence last week,' yelled Henry as the brothers came crashing through the bush.

'I did,' screamed Lennie returning fire.

Jonathon waited. They were obviously looking for their sheep but moving further away. The young man yelled. 'Hey! Over here.'

The other voices and bush bashing stopped. The occasional stunning bird song bounced around the valley led by a Dusky Robin.

'Hello?' called Henry, curious and relieved.

'Over here,' replied Jonathon and the brothers changed course.

When they burst through the bush and saw the farmhand, his dog and the flock of sheep, both men were momentarily speechless.

Lennie was quick to react. 'It's him,' he pointed at Jonathon. 'I told you he stole our sheep.'

'Shut up,' snapped Henry. 'Where were they?' he asked Jonathon.

'There's a sort of ford back there and they must have walked across the river. They were grazing on the other side so Lucky and I brought them back.'

Lennie fumed and Henry breathed easier.

'Thanks, Jonathon. But what happened to you last night?'

Ah, the burning question. Lennie's concocted and implausible scenario about an aborigine attack, and Jonathon using it to make an escape awaited contradiction. Jonathon paused then offered the minimum defence.

'I went for a walk and got lost.'

He chose not to elaborate thinking what Lennie might do if he told the truth, and how being a grass was a person he never wanted to be.

When the flock, the dog and three males arrived back at the farm, Elsie and the children ran towards them full of joy, so much so the sheep panicked and scattered.

'Stop, you're scaring the sheep,' yelled Henry, and the greetings were muted.

Lennie boiled inside. His new concubine was rescued by the brat of a convict who then proceeded to cause him massive aches and pains still throbbing the next day. To make matters worse, the family members from the cottage went solely to Jonathon with welcoming hugs and kisses.

To have him find and return the flock with not a single sheep missing only added to Lennie's internal rage. He was like a powder keg on a slow burn. Give him an opportunity to punish Sweeping, and Lennie was ready and willing to execute.

That night, there was a feast for their evening meal. Not exactly the fatted calf for the prodigal son's return but along those lines. It was agreed Lennie checked the fence but later, a mob of kangaroos must have crashed through allowing the sheep to go wandering. The mood was upbeat until Lennie stood.

'I'm not well,' he grunted, speaking the truth, and left.

The mood in the cottage bounced around but with Lennie gone, it buzzed. The children were growing fast and their understanding of how adults behaved kept expanding. They sensed conflict. But the mood changed dramatically when Elsie asked a question. 'Tell me Jonathon, when does your contract end?'

That threw him and Henry. 'I'm not sure. What year is it now?'

'What's a contract?' asked Alice genuinely interested.

Her father explained. 'After he arrived from England, Jonathon came to work here. He signed a piece of paper, a contract, which says he can live and work here but after a few years, he can leave and work on another farm.'

The children were upset.

'But you should stay here, Jonathon,' implored Willie. 'You're the best teacher we've ever had.'

'He's the *only* teacher we've ever had,' replied his sister and everyone smiled.

'When my time is up, we'll see,' said Jonathon, standing. 'I've had a long walk today and need to sleep. Goodnight to you all.'

'Goodnight,' chorused the family who continued to talk about the farmhand after he left.

Lucky waited until his master left the cottage and trotted to him. Jonathon worried. He was about to be alone with Lennie and after what happened the previous night, this could quickly become an explosive situation. Would Lennie take his revenge? Would he attack Jonathon when the farmhand fell asleep?

The former sweep approached the shed and heard snoring. Lennie was asleep so the farmhand and his dog entered quietly and bedded down. It was hard to sleep knowing the madman in the other bed might go crazy. But it was hard to stay awake after last night and today. Knowing Lucky would bark if Lennie threatened, Jonathon fell asleep.

He woke refreshed and looked around. Lennie was missing. Lucky looked up. Obviously nothing dangerous happened during the night. They ventured out, ate breakfast and began work. The day passed without major incident. Lennie kept quiet although Jonathon sensed he was angry; not surprising because Lennie was permanently angry.

*He must be furious to not only lose the girl he kidnapped but because I beat him in a fight. That must really sting.*

They went to the cottage for their midday meal and Lennie was late arriving. With lunch over, Jonathon couldn't see Lucky so went searching for the dog. He called and got no response. Now he panicked.

He reached the sheep and called again and heard a whimpering sound. Jonathon ran through the sheep and the animals scattered allowing the dog to be seen. His master called to him.

Lucky tried to stand but couldn't. Jonathon rushed to the animal and knelt. The dog's eyes told him the bad news—*I'm hurt, Master, I'm in pain.*

Jonathon saw Lucky's back right leg was limp. He tried to lift the animal, to help him stand. He could but only on three legs. Jonathon gently touched the injured leg and the dog yelped.

'Sorry, boy,' he said, 'sorry.'

Jonathon sat on the ground and embraced his best friend. This was the worst possible news. He'd watched his father drink himself to death. He found his mother dead in their hovel of a home, and he abandoned his young sister. Lucky was the first friend he ever made once he became an indentured convict, and their friendship grew stronger every day for five, or was it six years?

They worked together, shared food and adventures, and Lucky always slept at the end of Jonathon's bed. Now the animal couldn't even walk, let alone run.

Ignoring the tears welling in his eyes and avoiding the injured leg, Jonathon picked up Lucky and set off back to the cottage. The animal looked at his master and spoke with his eyes. Gratitude stared back. He knew he was being cared for.

Through the paddock and into the cleared space at the back of the cottage they went and were spotted by the children. They ran to Jonathon, their cries attracting the three adults.

'What's happened?' asked Henry as Jonathon put the dog on the ground.

'He's hurt his leg,' exclaimed Willie, pointing.

Alice knelt to stroke the dog.

Jonathon spoke not caring about his wet cheeks. 'I found him with the sheep. He can't walk and if he tries, he's in serious pain.'

'How did it happen?' asked Elsie, worried as much for Jonathon as the dog.

Henry shook his head. 'Could have got it caught in the fence or been trampled by the sheep or even been attacked by one of those crazy kangaroos.'

Lennie sniffed. 'Might 'ave been one of them aborigines.' The others looked at him in disbelief. 'They're savages, I've seem 'em.'

Henry spoke quietly. 'Put him in your hut, out of the sun and leave a bowl of water. We'll see how he is tonight.'

What else could Jonathon do? Helped by the children, he carried Lucky to the shed and placed him on the ground beside their bed. Alice appeared with a bowl of water.

'Here's his water.'

'Thanks Alice. If you could pop in and check on him this afternoon that would be grand.'

'I will,' said Willie who by now was a worker on the farm with Jonathon.

'We both will,' said big sister.

Their mother arrived with some of the mutton she was to cook for tonight's main meal. She handed it to Jonathon, didn't say a word, gave him a caring smile and left.

'Come on, Alice,' she called and they left. Henry, Lennie and Willie returned to work.

Alone, the convict lay down beside his dog, their faces close together. 'Have a rest, old boy. I'll do your work this afternoon.' Their eyes met. The young man placed the mutton beside the dog, leant in and kissed his head then stood and walked out not wanting to look back.


It was a hard day's work, felling trees and collecting undergrowth, building a bonfire and setting it alight. The more land Henry cleared, the more sheep he could own. The three men and a boy laboured without talking. The sun was sinking and Henry called it a day.

They made sure the fire was out and headed back to the cottage. Still the conversation didn't happen. Back at the cottage, the others followed Jonathon into the hut. Lucky's tail flicked but he made no attempt to get up. The mutton lay untouched. Jonathon's tears flowed as he knelt beside the animal.

Henry stood above the pair with Lennie lurking in the background and Willie's heart beginning to ache. Henry called a spade a spade.

'The dog's in pain, son. You can't let him go on like he is.'

Jonathon looked up and, with tears and saliva interrupting his words, he asked the hardest question ever. 'You want me to kill him? Is that what you're saying?'

'It's been the way on the land forever, son. Back home in England, every decent farmer has compassion for his animals. If a horse, cow, sheep and even a dog goes lame, the kindest thing is have the animal put down and as soon as possible.'

'No,' spat Jonathon, literally as spittle chased his cry.

'There's no pain, son. The animal feels no pain it's so quick. I can do it for you. I promise the dog won't feel a thing.'

The worst part for Jonathon was knowing his boss was right. He looked up and his gaze went from Henry to Lennie who smirked and then the penny dropped. Jonathon understood. Lennie's revenge was the worst possible. He didn't touch the young man who stole his woman and whipped him in a fight. No, he attacked the thing his enemy loved the most. He crippled his dog.

The roar from Jonathon scared everyone including Lucky and even Elsie and Alice in the cottage. Jonathon leapt at Lennie thrusting his hands around the man's throat. Lennie was shocked and struggled to fight back. He was being choked.

Henry grabbed Jonathon pulling him back and shoving him away.

'Stop! You don't know what happened. The dog may have been injured by a wild animal. Now stay there!' He looked at his brother. 'Get out.' Lennie left and Henry knelt to collect the dog.

'Leave him,' said Jonathon. He paused. 'I'll do it.'

Henry stepped back. Slowly Jonathon moved to the dog and, cradling him in his arms, picked up Lucky and headed into the bush.

It was getting dark and when he stopped it was dark. He placed the dog on the ground then realised he didn't know how he would actually end the animal's life. That compounded his misery.

He ran back to the cottage to collect a knife. He stumbled in the darkness, entered the kitchen, grabbed a knife and fled. Elsie and the children watched in silence. All three cried and joined in a group hug.

Jonathon stumbled through the bush not being able to perform what he knew had to be done. He was about fifty yards from Lucky when a loud bang echoed through the bush. Jonathon sprinted.

He reached Lucky and Henry, and in the gloom saw the lifeless body of his best pal.

'I wanted to save you the worst part,' said Henry. 'He didn't see the gun or feel a thing.' Jonathon couldn't speak. 'You might like to bury him by the river,' he said handing the former convict the spade.

And that's what Jonathon Sweeping did. He made a speech, a farewell to his best friend then made a decision; a major decision. It would change his life forever.

After burying Lucky, he returned to the cottage and walked into his shed holding the shovel. In the gloom, Lennie, lying on his bed recoiled in fear.

'No, please,' he gasped, a pathetic sight of a grown man being terrified by a young man ten years his junior.

Jonathon threw down the shovel, snatched his blankets and went to the cottage. Henry and Elsie came into the kitchen to see the farmhand making a bed in front of the fire.

'If it's all right, I'll sleep here tonight,' he said.

'Of course,' said Henry.

'I'll fetch you a pillow,' said Elsie and did.

In the morning, the family came out early and discovered the teacher and farmhand asleep.

<h1 align="center">Chapter 30</h1>

Dimity Carlisle fell on her feet. In London, she escaped death by going to prison. Her luck continued with her stay behind bars being short as the *Lady Caroline* sailed for Van Diemen's Land that week.

The ship carried 124 female convicts, a small group of soldiers, a dozen free settlers and crew. It was a good voyage; no-one died, most avoided being sea-sick, and fights between convicts were few and short-lived.

The ship's surgeon took a genuine interest in his patients, and provided good care whenever any of the women became ill with such conditions as scabies, ringworm and scurvy.

Dimity, now Annie Smith, suffered bad dreams. She fled without saying goodbye to her mother and sister. She hoped they received the money she asked a stranger to deliver. She wondered if those men who wanted to murder her would blacken her name and have her blamed for the death of her prosperous client, and worse, if they would attack her innocent mother and sister in an act of revenge.

Then she worried less realizing the toff's demise would never be linked to a lady of the night, even one so glamorous in such a fashionable abode. Aristocrats abhor scandal.

As the ship crossed the Equator and everyone went through the pantomime celebrations, and then drew ever closer to a new country, she began to wonder about her future. How long would she be in prison? When she was set free, what would she do? *What can I do?*

'Yes, sir, I'm highly trained in prostitution specializing in erotic asphyxiation. Would my services be required here in this colony?'

On board, she made friends with a few women and with so much time on their hands, they shared their life stories. Not Annie. She concocted dull tales so as not to attract attention. 'I was a lady's maid in a fancy part of London, got treated like dirt so pinched one of m'lady's silk scarves, and paid for me sins with a free ticket to Van Diemen's Land.' The others laughed. For Annie, this transportation lark was a chance to start afresh.

'Wotcha gunna do, Annie?' she was asked.

'Scrub floors, dust shelves and empty chamber pots,' she said which sounded like the future role for many of the convicts.

'Not me,' said one of Annie's pals. 'I'm going to marry a rich farmer and have more kids than he has sheep.'

That comment produced howls of laughter and helped pass the time of day. Good and not-so-good weather sent them scooting along and, after months at sea, all were pleased when told they would be in Van Diemen's Land tomorrow.

'What's it like, Captain?' cried one woman. 'I heard it's a land of wild animals and even wilder savages.'

'You'll find out soon enough, all of you. Keep your nose clean and work hard and who knows, it might be the making of you.'

The convicts chatted and nattered late into the night, excited they would soon be off this damn ship and in a land of adventure.


When the Reverend Andrew McFarlane first arrived in Sydney, life soon became reasonable for his mother and first-class for him. The climate and clean air appealed, progress of the city's development was on show, and his sermons were much appreciated by the many parishioners. Better still, a new church was to be built and the future looked rosy.

When you add the fact that the enchanting Miss Letitia Cornwall with her sparkling eyes and bewitching nose was open to his entreaties, then life was most definitely wonderful.

But that was before a new disaster struck. When his mother discovered a minor aristocrat from England, who *may* have known Andrew's father back in the old country, and was now living a good day's journey from Sydney, Andrew's happiness vanished.

Mrs McFarlane insisted on moving. Having travelled half way round the world to avoid the shame of gossip about her husband's criminal conviction, the whole journey now seemed a waste of time.

Andrew tried reasoning, begging, mildly threatening and even suggesting prayer, but having totally failed to convince the mater, he fell into a trough of despair. He wallowed in sadness.

He thought he'd found paradise here on Earth with Letitia his angel. Now the romance was off and he must move—again.

The Governor, Lachlan Macquarie, worked tirelessly to develop the colony in Sydney and the regions beyond. Andrew paid him a visit and asked for help. Andrew's excuse had to be a lie. He could never reveal the truth; his mother needs to live elsewhere to avoid being recognised as the wife of a common criminal.

'I'm rather keen on doing missionary work, sir,' said Andrew. 'Would you happen to know of any areas where I might best serve God and His Majesty's government?'

Macquarie had recently returned from an island to the south and spoke warmly of the place.

'I can, indeed, sir. Van Diemen's Land is crying out for young men of faith and determination. How does Hobart Town sound?'

Andrew sighed with relief. The journey was relatively short, his mother would no longer need smelling salts, and he could but hope another angel might reside in Hobart enabling him to take a wife.

His mother willingly agreed to move and as soon as possible.

'I will remain indoors until the ship is ready to sail.' She did.

Ships regularly plied their way between Sydney and Hobart Town and soon Andrew and his mother were back on board heading for another British colony. They arrived safely. In Hobart Town, the Reverend Knopwood welcomed a fellow cleric, and as the resident clergyman lived in Rokeby, and spent his days visiting his well-spread flock and maintaining his diary, having a new chap preach in his stead was ideal for both vicars.

The Governor of Van Diemen's Land welcomed Andrew and his mother, making a fuss over the widow—as she called herself—and a new chapter in the McFarlane expedition began.

When the *Lady Caroline* docked at Hobart Town, the female convicts were the last to leave the ship. The surgeon and captain both gave the women a stern speech on keeping out of trouble, working hard and taking this opportunity to make a fresh start.

'You'll find one of the requirements of your new life is to attend church every Sunday,' said the captain.

Under their breath, most of the convicts groaned.

'You'll be housed together or in small groups until a domestic role can be arranged. If that doesn't appeal, we can always find you accommodation in a cell.'

And so Annie Smith, the former Dimity Carlisle, spent her first week in a new town in a new colony. Before long she moved to a Hobart house as the domestic servant-cum-nanny of a well-to-do merchant, Mr Alexander Pike. Come Sunday, she accompanied her new employer, his wife and their children to church.

The vicar too was new; his name, Andrew McFarlane.

Sitting in a pew towards the front of the church—the wealthy and important took the better seats—meant Annie scored a good look at the vicar. She thought him pleasant on the eye and liked the sound of his voice. Like many females, she fancied a man in uniform.

At service's end, the congregation filed out greeting the vicar in the porch. Being new to Hobart, Andrew found it difficult to learn and remember names. Mr Pike had made a point of calling on the new cleric and so his name was one Andrew recalled.

'Excellent sermon, Mr McFarlane,' said Pike and Andrew graciously accepted the compliment. 'This is my family, my wife and my children.'

'How do you do, Mrs Pike,' he smiled at the group and especially at the attractive woman standing behind the children.

'Oh, and this is the children's nanny, Annie Smith,' said Pike and chuckled at his poetic masterpiece.

'How do you do, Miss Smith,' smiled Andrew and found another reason to like his new posting in Van Diemen's Land. He addressed the patriarch. 'I'm inviting my parishioners to take tea and would be delighted sir, if you and your family could attend the vicarage this afternoon at three.'

Pike succeeded in business by putting himself about in social circles. He accepted with pleasure.

Over lunch, Andrew reminded his mother about the social activity of having parishioners visit to better get to know one another. Unsurprisingly, Matilda complained.

'I thought it was the vicar's job to visit the sick and the poor.'

'You're right again, Mother,' he sighed, and used his serviette to disguise his frustration.

He excused himself and retired to his study. Poring over a newspaper, the *Hobart Town Gazette*, he hoped to learn more of the settlement and its inhabitants. Reports of a clash between settlers and local indigenous people distressed him. Apparently several aborigines were killed. He dared not discuss such matters with his mother knowing it would be a new reason for her to consider moving.

He wondered how far it was to the Americas, and then found himself thinking about a young woman he met in church that morning. The name, Miss Annie Smith, settled in his mind.

His thinking ramped up when his parishioners arrived. Mother was introduced and once all were seated, Matilda held court.

'My son has travelled all the way from England to serve the people of this colony,' she said. 'I hope the people of Hobart Town appreciate the great sacrifice he has made.'

Andrew suffered from the disease of *Mother's Embarrassment* and tried to change the topic. He focused on Mrs Pike.

'How are your children progressing with their schooling, madam?'

He was good was Andrew. Asking a mother about her children never failed to get the proud parent off and running. After Mrs Pike's explanation and boasting—all mothers are convinced their offspring are special—Andrew added to his popularity.

'I'm always available and happy to provide extra tuition if necessary. Being able to read and write is so important.'

'Oh thank you, Mr McFarlane, that is most generous and kind.' She turned to her husband. 'Isn't it dear?'

'Most generous indeed.'

Having dealt with the family, Andrew switched his focus to their employee. 'And Miss Smith, how do you find living in Hobart Town?'

Annie used her humble persona. 'It's charming, sir,' she said. 'And Mr and Mrs Pike and the children have made me most welcome.'

Matilda, the dragoness, held her fire but now attacked. 'So what did you do in England, Miss Smith?' Andrew failed his Christian faith pondering thoughts of matricide. The Pikes were fascinated not knowing any intimate details of their nanny's past.

'I was a nanny, madam, as I am today.'

Her lie was a straightforward reply delivered without irony or malice. It failed to satisfy Matilda so she probed in a seemingly polite manner with rudeness straining to decorate her language.

'Was this with a respectable family like Mr and Mrs Pike?'

The focus on Annie became intense. She'd been circumspect with the truth when first she met the Pikes. In fact, she lied. There was a shortage of capable females in Hobart Town—actually any females—and as Annie presented well, and didn't look like a murderess, she was hired. Now a new investigation began. Everyone wanted details. Being a million miles from her previous life, Annie decided to lie and used real people she once knew; intimately as it happens.

'I worked for families, madam, all within London.' Not true.

This was not good enough for Matilda. She persisted.

'I know many respectable families in London. Perhaps you were employed by one or more of my friends.' Andrew's fists clenched.

It was a leading question, probing without subtlety, and Andrew wanted to tell his mother to be quiet, and change the subject. He was about to do so when the nanny spoke.

She decided to call on her past life. Mentioning the names of her previous clients in Berkeley Square could backfire spectacularly. But she gambled. Would the snobbish woman know the toffs? If she did, would she write to them? Annie took the punt.

'Do you know Sir John and Lady Fitzwilliam of Belgravia, madam?' Matilda paled. It was rare for the vicar's mother to be struck dumb. Her eyes widened and Annie piled on the pressure. 'Perhaps you are acquainted with the Marquis of Bedford in his London address around the corner from St James' Palace?' Matilda joined the Mute Society. 'My last employer was Lord Fledgling-Harcourt of Old Brompton Road in the Royal Borough. Do you know his Lordship?'

This was not a close run thing. In racing parlance, Annie streeted the field and left her fellow rider, namely Mrs Matilda McFarlane, flat on her face in the mud after the first hurdle. She, the matron wearing mud, looked for a hole in the carpet.

Thrilled to see his mother browbeaten, Andrew jumped in. 'I'm hoping to arrange a fete for next month and I do hope I can involve the Pike family.'

They were all keen, especially the children who reckoned the vicar was a gentleman they really wanted to stay in Hobart Town. Their nanny was thinking exactly the same thing.

# Chapter 31

Embarrassed to be found by the children as he slept on the kitchen floor, Jonathon packed up his bedding quickly and gave Elsie the pillow. She sent the children out to collect the eggs and feed the hens and pigs.

'How did you sleep?' asked Elsie.

'Okay,' he replied, lying. I'll go and wash.' He headed for the door.

'And don't forget to shave,' she called and he half-grinned feeling the stubble struggling to grow on his face.

He passed Henry and Lennie coming back from checking on the sheep. They looked angry. 'We're missing two sheep,' snapped Henry.

Jonathon stared at Lennie who averted his gaze. Henry looked at Jonathon. 'Did you hear anything last night?'

'No sir, and I'd like a word about another matter please.'

Tension appeared and all three sensed a serious subject in the wind. 'After breakfast,' said Henry and led his brother inside.

Jonathon's nerves came out to play. Events of the last couple of days pushed him to think about leaving. With the death of Lucky, and its likely cause, he wanted a resolution. He washed and tried to remove his fledgling whiskers with more pain than success. He went inside and joined the others for breakfast.

'You've scratched yourself, Jonathon,' said Alice, concerned about his wellbeing and never intending to embarrass him.

'Alice,' said her mother. 'It's rude to make personal comments about people.' Alice became sad and Jonathon gave her a wink and a smile which vanished when Elsie approached offering him a wet cloth to wipe his face. Now he really *was* embarrassed.

Henry cut to the chase. 'What did you want to talk about, son?'

'My contract, sir; do you know when it ends?'

Henry didn't like the question. He never raised the topic wanting the boy, now a young man, to stay forever. He was a damn good worker, educated his children and got paid nothing.

'I'm not sure,' said the settler.

'There's a copy in the trunk at the end of our bed,' said Elsie. 'I'll fetch it if you like.'

What could her husband say? She disappeared. Willie finished his boiled egg. 'Is you going to leave, Jonathon?'

'You say *are* you going to leave,' corrected big sister who looked at her favourite teacher. 'Are you, Jonathon?'

He paused and was grateful when Elsie returned. 'Here it is.'

She handed it to her husband who studied it pretending to be able to read. He gave up and handed it to the farmhand.

'You read it.'

Jonathon studied the document. 'It says seven years from when I arrived. What's the date today?' Nobody spoke. Nobody knew.

Elsie made a suggestion. 'Last Christmas it was 1820.'

Jonathon counted silently. 'Next year in March it will be seven years.'

He said nothing more. No-one spoke. No-one wanted to speak. Then the most unexpected voice was heard. Lennie the dog basher spoke.

'If 'e wants to go early, let 'im go.'

That set pulses racing. Henry looked at the convict.

'Is that what you want?'

Without trying to build the tension, Jonathon paused and held their attention. 'Yes please,' is all he said.

The children and Elsie groaned and looked miserable.

Henry spoke. 'How about next time I'm going into town, you come with me and we'll see the official in charge of these matters? If they give you this ticket-of-leave or whatever it's called, you can pack y'bags and go whenever and wherever you want.'

Jonathon purred with pleasure. 'Thank you, sir, I appreciate your kindness.'

Lennie too liked the possible move but everyone else, and for different reasons, hated the thought.

It was a fortnight before Henry needed to go into town. Elsie and the children stood there watching Jonathon throw his meagre belongings on the cart. As they were set to leave, the young man moved to the waiting mother and her growing children, and hugged all three. Lennie hid.

Elsie clung to the hope that Jonathon would return but the children were desolate. They were sure they would never see their friend and teacher again. They loved him. Alice cried freely and even Willie found it hard to call out so big was the lump in his throat. They kept watching and waving until the cart was out of sight.

Henry said little on the journey. When they arrived in town, he dropped Jonathon outside the official's office, went to collect supplies, and said he would return soon.

Inside, Jonathon explained his situation. The official found the contract and told him there were many more months still to run. Despondent, Jonathon went outside and sat by a water trough.

A well-dressed man came along and stopped to chat.

'Good day to you, sir. Are you well?' asked the stranger.

Jonathon stood. 'Thank you, sir, I am.'

'My name is Andrew McFarlane. I'm the vicar here in Hobart Town. I don't think we've met.'

Andrew held out his hand which Jonathon shook. 'I'm Jonathon Sweeping sir, an indentured convict working for Mr Henry Rawlings.'

'I see, and may I ask how long before you'll become a free man?'

Jonathon's heartbeat kicked. 'I was hoping to be free today but alas it will not be until next year.'

'Well if there's anything I can do to help, please ask.'

Jonathon's mind came alive. 'Do you happen to know the Reverend Knopwood, sir?'

'I do indeed. I've taken over most of his duties here in town.'

'He knows me and I think he might speak on my behalf.'

'Well let me have your name and address and I'll write to him.' Andrew fumbled in his pockets to find his notebook and took down Jonathon's details. He'd finished when Henry arrived with a cart full of supplies.

Jonathon introduced the vicar. They discussed the young man's situation and all three went to the office. The official paid respect to the two older men and especially as one was a man of the cloth.

'Well you can petition the Governor for an early release but you would need the approval of your employer and a reference from a leading member of the community.'

By the time the trio left the office, a petition was prepared with the approval of Henry Rawlings, and a reference pending from the Reverend Robert Knopwood. Jonathon buzzed with excitement.

Henry made a decision. 'I'm sorry to see you go young man but I'm willing to shake hands here and now. What do you say?'

Jonathon choked. He shook his employer's hand with all the strength he could muster. 'Thank you, Mr Rawlings. You've taught me a great deal, and I'll never forget the kindness you and your family have shown to me for all these years.'

'Well I'll be off. Come and see us if you're ever out our way.'

'I will, I certainly will. And please say goodbye to your family.'

Henry climbed on the cart and urged the horse on giving Jonathon a simple nod of his head.

The vicar saw it all. 'Congratulations Jonathon Sweeping,' said Andrew. 'Now, I have a spare room in the vicarage and I insist you stay there as my guest until you find your next job. I warn you, sir, I won't take no for an answer.'

Jonathon couldn't speak. Everything happened in such a rush. With luck, he would soon be a free man and until he found a new job, his accommodation and meals were settled.

Matilda rarely smiled and when introduced to the new guest, her words were simple. She ignored Jonathon and addressed her son.

'How long is he staying?'

Andrew smiled. 'For as long as the Lord requires.' He led Jonathon through to the rear of the vicarage. 'This is your room, young man. I see you haven't a great deal of luggage.' He had nothing. 'I have a collection of clothes in the shed in the back garden. Let's go and see what's there.'

Aladdin's Cave it wasn't but Jonathon acquired two shirts, a half decent pair of boots, and a hat to ward off the hot Hobart sun.

Andrew had no intention of leaving the boy to sit around doing nothing while they waited for a response to the petition.

'We're planning a fete to raise funds for the church, and I would be most grateful if you could help with the preparation.'

'I'll do all I can, sir.'

'Good man,' said the cleric and showed Jonathon the raw materials and explained the work required. Jonathon began building stalls for the fete. Andrew was delighted and even more so when interrupted by the arrival of the former Dimity Carlisle.

'Miss Smith, how lovely to see you again. This is Mr Sweeping.'

The couple greeted one another and both men immediately relieved Annie of the two parcels she was carrying.

'Mrs Pike asked me to deliver these items for the jumble sale.'

'How kind of her and how kind you are to deliver them. I could have called to collect them,' said Andrew finding his pulse becoming active. 'Now let me offer you some refreshment.' He indicated inside.

Jonathon wanted to repay the generosity shown to him. 'I'll keep working, sir, and place these goods in the shed.'

Andrew appreciated his new friend and house guest stepping back thus giving the suitor a free run. He guided Annie indoors. With guest seated, he went to find his mother who showed no interest.

'She's a convict, Andrew. Why on Earth would you entertain her?'

'Thank you, Mother. I'll give her your best.'

He left and fumbled his way around the kitchen when Annie appeared. 'May I help?'

'Oh would you?' said the cleric who watched and admired the woman who caught his eye in church. Having a confrontational mother and no other female for company, he longed for feminine companionship and, if possible and far more importantly, a wife.

The more Annie worked to prepare tea and biscuits, the more Andrew's heart, mind and particularly his loins began to gather themselves and start to sing.

The couple sat alone in the sitting room and enjoyed each other's company. He couldn't stop thanking and complimenting her and Annie lapped it up. He threw caution to the wind.

'May I escort you back to the Pike residence, Miss Smith?'

'Thank you, sir, you're most kind.'

'If there is any service I can provide, Miss Smith, please do ask.'

Andrew hoped he wasn't trying too hard. They left via the front door with the cleric walking on the street side of his visitor. If any carts splashed mud or water, he would be there to prevent any damage to the lady's attire. People watched them but Andrew didn't notice. His eyes were elsewhere.

They reached the Pike residence with Andrew keen, almost desperate to tell Annie of his interest in her. He forced himself not to stare at and admire her shapely body, not the result of any corset.

'I hope to see you in church on Sunday, Miss Smith.'

'I shall be there, sir, and listen attentively to another of your most interesting sermons.' He opened the gate and she passed through. 'Good day to you, Mr McFarlane.'

'Au revoir, Miss Smith,' he said smiling with hope in his heart.

He walked home and people noticed a smile never left his face.

Robert Knopford called at the vicarage having received a note from Andrew. Meeting Jonathon again gave great pleasure to the two men. The clergyman transcribed a reference for the young man which was effusive and sincere. This was duly delivered as part of the petition and within a week, the Governor granted Mr Sweeping his freedom.

Jonathon stood in Andrew's study and read the document.

## TICKET OF LEAVE

No. *21/124*                    Date *17 August 1821*
Name *Jonathon Sweeping*
Ship *Indomitable*
Master *Nutter*

The now free man's gratitude knew no bounds. 'I can't believe it,' he said more than once.

Andrew made him even more proud. 'Jonathon, you are a fine example of a person being able to overcome his past and make a new life in a new country.'

'Thank you, sir.'

'But your task is incomplete. Now you must find a new job with a wage, and make your way in the world. What do you have in mind?'

'Working the land is all I want to do, sir. I'd like to be my own master, a farmer, and provide for my family and others.'

'Your family?

The young convict hesitated. 'It's my dream, sir, and as far as I know, even former convicts are allowed to dream.'

Now free, Jonathon resided in Van Diemen's Land, knew a lot about sheep, once met friendly aborigines, and was now looking for work. He could read and write but knew next to nothing about history.

He had no idea the aborigines in Van Diemen's Land arrived tens of thousands of years ago. When Londinium was but a glint in the eye of Gaius Julius Caesar, various tribes of aborigines were catching fish in the river at the end of what would become the Rawlings' farm.

When Adam and Eve were chatting with the greengrocer in the Garden of Eden, various tribes of aborigines were dining on kangaroo and pigface at the base of what would be named Mt Wellington.

Jonathon knew none of these facts and nor did the people running the penal colony of Van Diemen's Land. Yes, they knew the natives were there but of their history they knew less than nothing.

They were fairly certain the original inhabitants hadn't published any novels, built any tall ships or made use of corsets to shrink a woman's waist and highlight her cleavage.

But of aboriginal culture, diet, art, storytelling, ceremonies, family structure, medicine, longevity and more, the Europeans knew nowt.

Jonathon Sweeping was one of the few Europeans who had enjoyed meaningful and peaceful contact with the locals albeit short-lived.

As far as we know, Europeans landed in Van Diemen's Land in the early 1600s. Some of these explorers made contact with the locals but it was not until the British set up a penal colony in 1803, that Europeans put down roots and serious contact began. For serious, read deadly.

A decade after Hobart Town was established, Jonathon Sweeping arrived as a convict; the same Jonathon Sweeping who now was free.

But as marvellous as being free was, the big question remained—what next? He spoke with Andrew McFarlane and sensed guilt about accepting his hospitality without doing much in return. Jonathon helped with the church fete, weeded the clergyman's garden and was as polite as possible to the elderly Mrs McFarlane.

When the Reverend Knopwood called not long after Jonathon received his ticket-of-leave, the three men rejoiced at the news.

'So you want to be a farmer on your own land, Mr Sweeping,' said Knopwood. 'Well jolly good luck to you, young man.'

'Thank you, sir,' said Jonathon.

'But you should know there has been trouble in parts of this island and not far from here in Hobart Town.' The others looked at Knopwood. 'Stories are told of serious clashes with the aborigines.

'What have you heard?' asked McFarlane.

Knopwood looked grim. 'Killings have occurred on both sides. I've heard about Europeans stealing aboriginal women for their own pleasure with the blacks wanting revenge and killing whites. I visit settlers whose sheep have taken over traditional aboriginal land meaning farms have been raided by aborigines stealing flour, tobacco and blankets.'

Jonathon absorbed all this. He remembered the time he spent the night with aborigines.

'And you say they're killing one another?' asked McFarlane who'd spent little time outside Hobart Town. Knopwood nodded. 'But Jonathon is hoping to move inland. Surely that's too dangerous.'

'I agree but if he wants a job, I may have a solution. Two of my parishioners are struggling. Arnold Walker runs sheep on his land but his wife, Vera is poorly. They have no children and need help.'

The hairs on the back of Jonathan's neck came alive. He asked in hope. 'Would Mr Walker welcome someone to work on his farm?'

'Indeed,' said Knopwood. 'A good worker may well save his farm.'

'But he would have to be paid a proper wage,' added McFarlane. 'He's been as good as a slave working here for six years.'

'Of course he must be paid. As any working man, he deserves the basic right of a fair day's pay for a fair day's work.'

Jonathon held his breath.

'And you could have the inside running, sir. Work hard and you might have first refusal to buy the farm when the Walkers retire.'

'Buy the farm?' asked a puzzled young man. 'I'm sorry, Mr Knopwood, but how could I ever afford it?'

McFarlane challenged his fellow cleric. 'Are you sure about that, sir? If a farmer is given land, is he legally entitled to sell it?'

Knopwood paused. 'You might be correct, but Mr Sweeping, this is an opportunity for you to make your mark. What say ye, sir?'

Jonathon's face said it all. He beamed. 'I cannot thank you enough, gentlemen, for all your kindness. I am indebted to you both.'

The two clerics looked at Jonathon. They saw his excitement mixed with a tinge of concern.

'I can visit the Walkers and see if they support the idea,' said Knopwood. 'I take it you'd want me to do that.'

'How kind of you, sir, but perhaps I could come with you and introduce myself to the couple. If they want my help, I could start work immediately and no longer be a burden on Mr McFarlane.'

Knopwood smiled and McFarlane clapped.

'Brilliant,' he cried and slapped his young friend on the back.


That night, Jonathon lay on his bed in the small room at the rear of the vicarage and pondered his possible new life. He could find a job he loved, be paid for it, and start work tomorrow. It sounded wonderful. But would the couple want him? Were they kind or cruel? His mind raced as another new adventure beckoned.


Arnold and Vera Walker once lived in a tied cottage on a large estate in Cambridgeshire. Their small home came with the job where Arnold worked on the farm and Vera helped in the landowner's residence assisting the cook on big occasions. Their wages were poor but with free accommodation and access to farm produce, they lived a humble, comfortable life. They wanted children but Vera failed to conceive.

When the Industrial Revolution brought machinery to farms and elsewhere, many rural workers, including Arnold and Vera, were out of a job. Faced with moving to a big city and living in an overcrowded and polluted slum, they took the chance to leave the Mother Country and try their luck in a new colony.

They sailed to Van Diemen's Land on a convict ship in cramped quarters although far better than those in chains. The authorities in Hobart Town wanted people to open up the land and welcomed Arnold and Vera with a generous gift of land.

The authorities were able to make such gifts because no-one in Hobart, or elsewhere in Australia, raised the issue of previous ownership. The thinking of many Europeans was, "What's yours is mine, and what's mine is mine alone." They regarded the aborigines as having no claim to the land, and vast swathes of the country were freely bestowed on fellow whites.

Despite being middle-aged, Arnold and Vera made a good fist of their property. Their cottage was crude, their fencing basic and their income miserly for many years. Over time, they established a thriving vegetable patch and apple orchard, ate fresh eggs, and even tried kangaroo. In time, their flock of sheep began to dwindle.

One morning, a group of aborigines came through the bush and Arnold saw them and panicked. 'Hey!' he called and they stopped. His old and seldom-fired musket was in the cottage, and the aborigines carried spears and other weapons. If they attacked, he had no hope. His greatest fear was for the safety of Vera.

Opening his arms and moving slowly, he approached the intruders. In the early years of European settlement, conversations between white and black people were rare. Few could speak the other's language and even if a settler did learn the local language, it probably was different from the language of another group of aborigines in the next valley or a few miles in another direction. There were different tribes of aborigines in Van Diemen's Land.

Arnold moved to the shed where his hens lived, grabbed an old blanket and approached the aborigines. He offered it.

'Blanket, for you,' he said.

The leader hesitated then accepted the gift. A stalemate ensued and Arnold wondered if he should offer them flour or other items. He moved but stopped when the aborigines turned and disappeared into the bush. He wiped his brow and headed to the cottage.

He reckoned it was a time to be grateful but panicked when he found Vera on the floor. She'd witnessed the visitors arriving, believed Arnold would be speared, and collapsed.

He struggled getting her into a chair. Water containing salt all the way from Epsom was swallowed under protest. Arnold made the supper although food was the last thing on their minds.

All this happened a few weeks before Jonathon became free. The Walkers discussed their situation. If they gave up farming and went into town, what would they do? Did Hobart Town have the English equivalent of the poorhouse? Should they go back to the old country and fall on the mercy of family? It could be months, even years before they reached England. Arnold dreaded staying here and dying first. He could bury Vera but she would have no-one to deal with his corpse.

They decided to stay put for now and hoped the aborigines would stay away. When the Reverend Knopwood called on his rounds, they gave him chapter and verse. He prayed for them and promised to make enquiries about accommodation in town for the elderly.

A few weeks later, the clergyman returned with a young man riding a borrowed horse. Knopwood had no news about Hobart Town accommodation but delivered something much better.

'Good day to you, Mr and Mrs Walker,' cried Mr Knopwood. 'May I introduce a friend of mine, Mr Jonathon Sweeping?'

Jonathon met the Walkers and the older couple took an instant shine to the young man. He came across as genuine, humble and caring. When they heard he wanted farm employment, the settlers came alive. They were desperate for help. Vera's health took an instant turn for the better. An offer of a job was made on the spot and accepted without Jonathon even inspecting the property. All that remained was to find suitable sleeping accommodation for the vicar and his friend in the Walkers' chicken shed overnight.

The wheel turned for young Sweeping and he began to wonder if at last, he might make a go of things in this new land.


Back in Hobart Town, Andrew McFarlane scratched his head trying to imagine a way he might find himself in the company of Miss Annie Smith. He couldn't stop thinking about her.

She reciprocated although with less outward enthusiasm. Her London lifestyle would never be resumed in this colony. She didn't want it to resume. But the thought of marrying a clergyman intrigued her. Marriage was not a situation she actively considered back in London or when sailing the oceans of the world. Survival became her primary goal. But having put down roots, she pondered becoming a wife. *But to a vicar? Do they like sex? Is it even allowed for a priest?*

Andrew worried. Convincing Annie to marry him became his immediate challenge. Persuading his mother to give the couple her blessing meant a lot. But by far his greatest concern concerned intimacy. Would he be able to perform in the conjugal bed?

He possessed no prior hands-on experience in matters carnal. Being the husband, the head of the household, he must lead. If Annie became his wife, she would look to him for guidance. As a humble domestic in London, she would have no experience in the world of intimacy. The pressure would be on the man to guide. Could he cut the mustard?

Of course he had no idea his intended led a spectacular life in Berkeley Square, and was way ahead of him in "becoming one".

But first things first, he needed to win the heart of Miss Smith. He needed to take action. Simply waiting for something to happen would result in even more frustration. An idea arrived and Andrew took off for a building in Hobart Town. He entered and asked to see the proprietor. Mr Pike arrived.

'Mr McFarlane, good day to you, sir.'

'Good day, Mr Pike. Please forgive this intrusion but I'm hoping you can help support a new project of mine.'

'Of course,' said Pike. 'How can I help?'

'I have decided to conduct a Sunday School class for the children of Hobart Town, and I am hoping you and your good lady will allow your dear children to attend.'

'But of course, sir, and what a splendid idea. When will you start?'

'This Sunday at 10 am.'

'I shall inform the children tonight and have their nanny, Miss Smith, attend to help keep them in order. Is that satisfactory?'

'More than satisfactory,' said Andrew feeling his chest swell and his undergarments itch. Using the firmest of handshakes, he shook hands with the father of four.

Andrew's next idea involved convincing Miss Smith he held nothing but the purest of intentions in winning her hand. And to substantiate his claim, he would fall back on scripture. All the way home he kept thinking of the verse, "He who finds a wife finds a good thing and obtains favour from the Lord."

God ordained marriage and never was Andrew so keen to please his creator.

# Chapter 33

Hobart Town expanded and so too did the farms in Van Diemen's Land. More settlers arrived, more land grants were made, and more incursions into the bush began.

For Europeans, there was no problem about taking possession. To the incomers, the aborigines were at best simple peasants, and at worst, wild savages. Not for a moment were they considered landowners.

Europeans developed laws to resolve disputes with title deeds, wills with codicils, and courts with judges in wigs. In England, the locals knew who owned what. In Van Diemen's Land, the Europeans failed to find any aboriginal solicitors with a shingle outside their office in the Main Street of the Huon Valley. There were no documents listing boundaries of properties. The white people made a simple assumption. No-one owns the land. I'm not stealing it. Finders keepers, thank you very much, I'll be having some of that.

For the Europeans, holding a flag-raising ceremony and claiming possession of the land for the British Empire was the legal equivalent of buying property. Simple. To take possession, you took possession. It was part of the, "What's yours is mine," philosophy. And to the "superior" Europeans, of course it was all legal. Besides, the original inhabitants didn't even have a word for land.

Sorry. What was that? The aborigines have no word for land? Are you serious?

Had the Europeans studied Aboriginal dialects, they would have discovered the original inhabitants used about 20 words meaning "country," and believed the land was of supreme importance. Their controlled use of fire was one brilliant way they protected the environment. They managed the land for tens of thousands of years living well on the plants and animals thriving on Van Diemen's Land.

And their attachment to the land was far deeper than survival. To the aborigine, the land is integral to their culture, a spiritual place, a source of their history, and the location of their life beyond Earth. Their Dreamtime explains the creation of the world.

The early Europeans knew nothing of aboriginal culture and many treated the natives as less of a human or certainly as inferior to the white man. And this belief in superiority and the occupation of what was sacred land led to conflicts, and from these came skirmishes which became deadly, got out of hand and led to war.

Sealers were attracted to the waters of Van Diemen's Land with seal skin and oil being prized products. On land, the marine creatures were easy to kill. With a plentiful supply of seals to plunder, the men involved would come ashore and make camp.

In hindsight, the sealers were as thick as two Eucalyptus regnans. Killing seals indiscriminately, including mothers and pups, meant the number of mammals collapsed and within a generation or two, the men wiped out their own industry. The same applied to the whalers who were hunting before the settlement at Hobart Town began. They harpooned themselves in the foot by wiping out the whales.

The sealers then wiped out many aborigines. Whether the aborigines approached the sealers out of curiosity or the sealers went inland looking for water, is not important. The two groups met. Male sealers fancied female company and tempted them with gifts or, if that didn't work, kidnapped them; an extension of the "what's yours is mine" philosophy.

Language skills were poor or non-existent and misunderstandings thrived. Some men have always been prone to anger and rage if they believe their status or honour is challenged. If "your woman" has defied you or been stolen, reactions can be extreme. They were.

Spearing sealers and shooting aborigines happened. A single death became multiple deaths. Tit for tat killings turned into all-out, planned atrocities, and murder thrived.

Encounters defied belief as in the tragic Cape Grim massacre.

Having firearms gave the Europeans a mighty advantage. Knowing the authorities might never hear about a slaughter, attackers held little fear of being caught. One murderous atrocity was reported to the Governor—two years after the event.

Because Van Diemen's Land was sparsely populated, appalling violence took place unreported, and women and children were as much in the firing line as adult males.

The situation was a ticking time bomb. Newly arrived Europeans built enterprises on land occupied by aborigines forever. Negotiation? What negotiation?

When newspapers reported atrocities, the aborigines were the enemy, the ones in the wrong. And still the bloodshed continued.

With settlers accepting grants of land, clearing it, erecting fences and bringing in animals never before seen on the island, the locals found themselves forbidden from accessing what had been their traditional land for generations, millennia.

The aborigines wanted to hunt and travel where they always roamed. The settler demanded no trespassers. Someone threw the first spear or fired the first musket and revenge killings exploded.

The settlers fired two types of bullets. One was metal and from a gun, the other was a disease carried by a person. Diseases imported with Europeans meant many aborigines suffered and died without ever being struck by a bullet.

And this activity, these deadly clashes between aborigines and Europeans, had been bubbling away by the time Jonathon Sweeping took up working for the Walkers on a property about 30 miles north-west of Hobart Town.

His partnership with the couple was a marriage made in Heaven. They needed and wanted him and likewise, he needed and wanted them. Jonathon built himself a room at the back of the chicken shed and settled in. Vera was a brilliant old-fashioned cook who knew how to make omelettes with vegetables and ham, and bake bread the smell of which started your saliva jogging.

On his first day, Jonathon explored the farm with Arnold, and found his head filling with ideas and plans to create new things and of ways to do current things better. The farmer's heart filled with happiness. He lacked the imagination and the determination to succeed, and delighted in being a helper to his new employee.

The three would chat late into the night telling each other the story of their lives with Jonathon keeping the Walkers fascinated. The young man's arrival proved to be the best thing for everyone.

Back in Hobart Town, the tale of true love between Mr McFarlane and Miss Smith, the former Dimity Carlisle, moved inexorably towards its climax. Having thought of a way to be alone with the lady in question, Andrew decided to plight his troth.

After Sunday School one morning, he asked Annie if she would care to walk out with him next Saturday. He suggested a stroll along the River Derwent. She accepted with pleasure and all week the vicar counted the days and then the hours before their meeting.

He made the dreadful mistake of telling his mother of the event and, of course, she looked horrified. Her disquiet was a combination of Annie's convict past, and Matilda's lack of an excuse to move yet again. If Andrew married, the mother would slip down the pecking order and lose her ability to manipulate her son.

The day of the stroll dawned fine and sunny. The birds sounded chirpy, and the wattle seemed more golden. Spring as well as love was in the air. By noon, the blue sky invited a number of clouds to tag along and by the time Andrew reached the Pike abode, overcast best described the heavens.

Mr and Mrs Pike had long known the vicar was keen on their nanny, as had the entire congregation, and the Pikes enthusiastically agreed to Miss Smith having a free afternoon.

Andrew arrived and was ushered inside. The children were wondering why the vicar stood there and didn't sit to drink tea. Annie made her entrance. She didn't require much of an effort to "dress up" as her natural beauty placed her in the radiant category.

She smiled. 'Good afternoon, Mr McFarlane.'

His heart exploded. 'Good afternoon, Miss Smith.'

And then a loud silence stepped into the room. The Pikes were unsure what to say. The courting couple used up their full catalogue of sentences, and so it was left to one of the children to break the ice.

'Are you going to marry, Miss Smith?' asked the inquisitive daughter, old enough to have an inkling of what was happening but innocent enough to realise she was causing embarrassment.

Mrs Pike ushered the children from the room and Mr Pike led the couple to the front door.

'No need to hurry back, Miss Smith. We'll keep the little devils locked in the wood shed till you return.'

His desperate attempt at humour helped the couple smile before moving into the garden and off on their private but public outing.

Andrew hoped his shaking would not be obvious. Annie struggled to believe her situation.

His nerves began to fade and he made small talk until they reached the river. He desperately wanted to tell her he loved her. She was happy to say the same but thought it might be wrong to speak first. So the weather, the church and the weather again it was.

They sat on a bench beside the river and Andrew wanted to speak. God looked down in despair. Damn it, man, faint heart never won fair lady.

He turned to Annie, took her left hand in both of his then froze. The overcast sky turned spoilsport and sent down serious droplets as a prelude to the main event. They hurried to a nearby Eucalyptus globulus where its branches did a good, although imperfect job.

Annie struggled to open Mrs Pike's parasol.

'Allow me, Miss Smith,' said Andrew and demonstrated his brute strength. He so wanted to protect her.

Alas the rain increased and the parasol did its job for Annie although Andrew copped the odd droplet.

'Oh, Mr McFarlane, you are getting wet. Please share my parasol.'

Hallelujah! The suitor was handed a gift from the Almighty who sent down the rain. He gave His servant the prod to get cracking. This was the Big Man upstairs giving Andrew his blessing and backing.

'Oh thank you, Miss Smith,' he said and moved so close to her, their bodies touched. Their eyes met, their pulses danced and then he did it. He bent and kissed her so softly she thought he missed her lips but, at the same time, a shudder of excitement flooded her body. This was nothing like the excitement she experienced assisting wealthy gentlemen in a certain upstairs room in Berkeley Square. This was much, much better.

The ice was broken. 'Oh Annie,' he said, dumping convention. 'I have longed to kiss you ever since we met.' He was up and running.

He shocked and pleased her. 'Then why have you taken so long?'

He answered a question with a question. 'May I kiss you again?'

She was about to say yes when he did kiss her again—he was on a roll—and this time the lighter touch was replaced by something stronger and magnificently passionate. He stayed in the kissing position as the downpour increased, and neither took any notice of the rain, the river or the rabbits. A whale in the Derwent set off a water spout as the best local alternative to a 21 gun salute. The romance became official.

When the damp clergyman arrived home, flushed and with heart aflutter, his mother observed and worried. The battle was lost and now, certainly the war.

'How are you, Mother?' he asked in the sweetest and most sincere way possible. She grumbled a reply. 'I need to write a letter. Do excuse me,' he said slipping away to his study.

> *My dear Knopwood*
> *Greetings in the name of the Lord.*
> *I have a favour to ask. Will you kindly conduct a marriage service here in Hobart Town on the first Saturday in October? The banns will have been read.*
> *I know I agreed to conduct such services but this is a rather special marriage—my own.*
> *The bride-to-be is Miss Annie Smith, nanny to the Pike children, and my very able Sunday School assistant.*
> *I look forward to your next visit.*
> *Yours in Christ*
> *Andrew McFarlane*

One thing was certain; Andrew would never show this epistle to the mater.

# Chapter 34

The colony in Van Diemen's Land continued to boom. More settlers, more land grants, more convicts, more pardoned convicts, and more occupation of land, previously the domain of the aborigines for tens of thousands of years.

Conflicts were on the rise. Europeans drove off aborigines or kidnapped their women. Aborigines launched raids on farms stealing goods. Tempers flared. Wounding and killing became commonplace, and lawless best described many areas of the island.

An added ingredient to this explosive mix was the bushranger. Not wearing metal armour and storming banks, these renegade Europeans who were often escaped convicts, robbed settlers, sealers, even explorers—anyone they fancied.

It was a dangerous time for Jonathon Sweeping to start a new career as a paid farmhand on the Walker property.

He rounded up sheep on the back paddock one morning when he heard a crashing sound coming from the bush. The Walker's dog, Smokey, barked with fervor, sensing danger to the sheep, his new master and even himself.

The flock scattered as Jonathon moved to get a better look. Behind the back fence, a horse burst out of the bush, threw his front legs in the air as the fence loomed large.

There were two riders although the second, head bowed, appeared ill or wounded and ready to fall. Jonathon ran towards them, hopped over the fence and held a bridle as he patting the sweating and scared horse. The rider's face shouted fear.

'Thanks,' said a young man with a Yorkshire accent. 'Can you help us? My mate's been wounded.'

'Of course,' said Jonathon and led both horses back towards the cottage. They reached the chicken shed and Mr and Mrs Walker came out looking distressed.

'These men have been attacked,' said Jonathon who helped the rider dismount.

'I'll get water,' said Mrs Walker.

'My friend's wounded,' said the rider as he, Arnold and Jonathon reached up and lowered the second man to the ground. He lay on the grass as Vera bathed his head, wiping blood from his face and neck.

Jonathon recoiled in shock. 'Peter!' he exclaimed, looking at Peter Lonsdale, his friend and fellow-convict on their voyage to Van Diemen's Land.

Like Jonathon, Peter Lonsdale worked on a farm in the colony although still as an indentured convict. He worked on a large property with several other convicts.

In all the years since they parted in Hobart Town, the boys, now young men, never saw or heard from one another. Although in a bad way, Peter recognized his former friend and raised a weary hand.

Jonathon took control. 'Let's get him in the shed.' They carried him inside placing him on Jonathon's bed. The rider grabbed Jonathon's arm and beckoned. They went outside.

'Do you know Peter?'

Jonathon nodded. 'From years ago. What happened?'

'It was a surprise attack by blacks. They came at us with spears. Two of our men were killed and Peter copped blows with a club.'

'We'll look after him.'

'Can you?'

'Of course,' said Jonathon.

'I need to get back and help the others.'

'Did the aborigines keep fighting?

'Yes, that's why I left. They may have murdered the others.' He mounted his horse. 'Be on your guard,' he said and pulled the horse's head and rode away.

Back in Jonathon's hidey-hole, Arnold and Vera fussed over Peter. He looked terrible but again raised a hand to acknowledge his long lost friend.

'Mr and Mrs Walker, let me have a word with him. Peter and I knew each other years ago when we first came to Van Diemen's Land. I'll come and get you later.'

The settlers left and Jonathon moved a box and sat. 'Well,' he said, 'this is a surprise. I never see you for years and then, out of nowhere; you appear with your head in a new shape.'

Peter wanted to smile but it hurt. 'Sorry,' he whispered.

'What can I get you; food, water, tea?'

'Nothing, thanks. I just need to rest.'

They looked at one another remembering the times they spent sailing a few of the seven seas. Jonathon chose to chat.

'Your mate said you were attacked by aborigines.'

Peter struggled to nod. He was in pain and thinking about the attack made it worse.

'Bastards, they're filthy, rotten savages. My God, Jon, I saw a mate with a spear driven into his chest and sticking out the other side. The screaming was worse than any of those floggings we saw on the ship.'

Jonathon saw his friend's distress and gently touched his arm. 'Take it easy. You're safe now and you can stay here until you're fit and well.'

Those words helped Peter settle but he kept re-living the incident. 'I was repairing a saddle when they exploded out of the bush. I looked up and saw my mate, a young convict who only arrived in Van Diemen's Land a year ago, cop this huge spear right here.' He indicated his chest and tears welled in his eyes. He pushed himself up. 'I'll never forget the look on his face. He tried to cry out but couldn't. He froze in fear. If only I had a musket.'

He fell back on the bed and wept, an arm across his face. Jonathon saw hopelessness before him and said nothing.


While this terrible event took place, many miles away in Hobart Town, a wedding service began. Matilda McFarlane tried subtle ways to delay her son's nuptials but failed. Her son became a new man. His heart worked overtime as he stood at the front of the church with his fellow cleric beside him, ready to begin.

Annie Smith looked a picture. Her breathtaking natural beauty shone. Giving her away was her about-to-be former employer Mr Pike, and his daughters became flower girls. Mrs Pike dressed her daughters but spent much more time on the bride's outfit, a lovely dress where her sleeves were puffed and the decoration, particularly on the hem, was detailed and exquisite. The trim on her bodice pointed down drawing attention to her slim waist. Her bonnet looked enchanting and she carried a posy of native clematis, a fragrant white flower picked by the parishioner who decorated the church every Sunday.

As Annie walked down the aisle on the arm of Mr Pike, the overflowing congregation stared and kept staring. At the altar, Andrew beamed and saw no-one other than his bride.

The night before, when he and Robert Knopwood shared a glass of wine before retiring, Andrew pondered the possibility of asking advice from his fellow cleric on matters intimate.

He'd never seen his bride in any state of undress and wondered about the etiquette, the ritual in preparing for the bridal bed.

Then a thought struck him. Reverend Knopwood, a confirmed bachelor, was probably as ignorant of such matters as was he. Tomorrow night Andrew would "Cry God for Harry, England, and Saint George!" and take the plunge.


The service went smoothly. Andrew's preaching voice lost its usual projection until a glance from the celebrant got the groom going and his enthusiastic, "I will", produced a smile from many onlookers.

His mother, seated in the front pew, and still dressed in black as the widow pining for her deceased, or rather locked-up husband, suffered in silence.

'But where will I sleep?' she whined in the weeks prior to the wedding. 'You cannot expect me to use the second bedroom.'

'It will have new curtains, Mother, and a rug all the way from India. You won't recognize the place.'

He grinned and won another battle within the ongoing war.

The night before the wedding, bride and groom thought of family. Andrew wondered if his father was still alive and in prison. Annie thought of her mother and sister and how proud they would be to see her happily married and to a clergyman. Both bride and groom suffered from what would become known as the tyranny of distance.


Speeches after the ceremony were short and witty, and the couple was sent off in a flower-bedecked cart to travel 100 yards to spend their wedding night in the best hotel in Hobart Town.

Andrew's worries seemed to reach a climax. Would he be able to perform the duties of a husband, and would such a performance win the approval of his beloved. If only he knew.

Annie's two outstanding qualities on this night were her performance as an innocent young woman, and her ability to manipulate the besotted groom into performing in such a way he thought he was in charge.

In short, Andrew came to grips and gropes with the full meaning of Ephesians 1:2 and "they shall become one".


Peter Lonsdale took a day to recover. Jonathon made up another bed in the shed leaving Peter to have Jonathon's bed. Mrs Walker made a wholesome meal and everyone treated him with kid gloves.

Next morning, the two friends went walking in the paddocks of the Walker farm. They strolled and Jonathon wanted to discover more about the battle.

'I don't want to upset you, Peter, but I admit I'm shocked to hear the natives could be so brutal and attack without provocation.'

'They were brutal all right.'

They continued strolling with Jonathon pushing for more details. 'My experience with the blacks is nothing like yours. I once spent a night in one of their camps.'

Peter's face contorted. 'You what? Are you mad? They're savages.'

'These ones fed me, gave me and my dog a hut, and then showed me the way back home.'

'Were the men carrying spears and clubs?'

'Most of the time I was with a young girl.'

This rocked Peter. 'You were alone with a girl?' Jonathon nodded. 'Was she naked?'

Jonathon shrugged. 'Not completely.'

'And you didn't kiss her or make love?'

Jonathon knew he'd looked at her a certain way but nothing romantic or sexual happened. 'No,' he said.

Peter stopped and looked sheepish. 'That's why they attacked us.'

Jonathon didn't understand. 'Sorry?'

'The blacks attacked us because we took their girls and women and made love to them.'

Shock gripped Jonathon. 'What do you mean?'

Peter gawped. 'You don't know what making love means?'

'No, what do you mean by "we took their girls and women"?'

Peter shrugged. 'We stole them, kidnapped them; we grabbed them when they were alone collecting food. They screamed and fought but we overpowered them and took them back to our farm.'

'You overpowered them?'

'They were screaming and fighting to get away so we had to hit them.' Jonathon couldn't speak. Peter saw his friend disapproved. 'Oh come on, do you know how many white females there are in Van Diemen's Land?' Jonathon shook his head in disgust. 'It's about 10 men to every 3 women—10 to 3. That's why we took the black girls.'

The birds kept singing in the bush but neither human spoke.

'Did your mate who was speared take a black girl?'

Peter couldn't look into his friend's eyes. 'We all did.'

The sentences were interrupted by pauses. 'Then he got what he deserved,' said Jonathon and turned and headed back to the farmhouse. Unhappy, Peter ran after him.

'Jonathon, they're savages. They can't read or write. They live in grass huts. They walk around killing kangaroos. They slaughter our sheep for God's sake.'

He looked at his friend. 'Do they steal our women? Do they have guns and fire indiscriminately into our homes at night? Do they drive us off our land; their land?'

Peter didn't answer, didn't want to answer, and followed Jonathon back to the farmhouse about ten paces behind.

# Chapter 35

The Walkers knew something was wrong. Peter packed up and left without any fanfare. The old folk said nothing but noticed Jonathon became quiet, morose even, and hoped he would not leave their employ. Without young Sweeping, this farm would have been abandoned by now.

Many of the ideas Jonathon introduced bore fruit. He tried cross-breeding his sheep and produced a better fleece. His lambs were healthy and strong. He added more poultry and the fruit and vegetables kept Mrs Walker's larder filled to overflowing.

After the evening meal, Jonathon retired and was in the yard with Smokey admiring the stars in an inky black sky when he heard a fearful cry. Both man and dog ran to the house. They burst in and headed to the bedroom. Mrs Walker was in bed.

'No, no, no,' sobbed Arnold.

Jonathon was beside him in a flash. Mrs Walker looked terrible. One side of her face was contorted and she gasped for breath.

'Let me help, Mr Walker,' said Jonathon gently moving the old man. 'Come on, Mrs Walker, let's make you comfortable.'

He tried moving the pillow to give her more elevation. It made little difference. He thought she was dying but not why. The blood supply to her brain struggled to flow normally causing her paralysis. The terror she experienced induced panic in the poor woman and she found it difficult to breathe.

'Fetch some water, please,' said Jonathon if only to get the despairing man out of the room and away from the tragic situation.

It became a vale of tears through which the living must pass. Here lay a seriously ill elderly woman, medical help a whole day's journey away, a dark night, and no knowledge of what to do. This was an ideal opportunity for prayer although Jonathon wasn't big on religion.

The water arrived and Jonathon tried to have Vera take a sip. She couldn't operate her lips. The water splashed on her face and onto the bed. It was as if she wanted to say, "I'm dying, can't you see I'm dying?" Arnold looked ready to collapse. Jonathon took control making it up on the spot.

'I'll sit here and hold Mrs Walker's hand, sir, and you get back into bed. Smokey and I will keep watch and we'll wake you if we need you.'

How could the husband argue? Helpless he was. The farmhand, a brilliant worker, now became a caring and thoughtful family member.

Arnold did as advised. In the gloom, Jonathon looked at his patient, her piercing eyes begging for help, even an explanation. He smiled at her and when her eyes closed, he blew out the candle.

The sound of the couple's strained breathing dominated the silence. Smokey lay on the floor and didn't help the situation by snoring, and again Jonathon thought about prayer.

He remembered other cruel times like this. First with his father, the one who adopted and cared for him, and having lost a foot and his inability to earn money and support his family, spent his final months lying in bed drinking himself to death. His dear mother, having been raped by a sadistic monster, spent her final months, or was it years, suffering an incurable lung disease having worked long hours in the cramped hat factory.

Now the older couple who took him in, struggled with health issues, were without help, and any assistance was miles away.

Jonathon thought of the misery the local black girls and women endured having been kidnapped and raped by Peter and his mates. And then, amidst his depression, Mrs Walker shuddered, gasped for even a tiny amount of air and died.

He tried to find her pulse and found nothing. He chose to let Mr Walker sleep. Bad news can wait.

When Mr Walker woke, Jonathon, who slept fitfully on the floor, was up and awake. In the early morning light, the old man turned to check on his wife. Jonathon had lifted the bedclothes up and over her face. The two men looked at one another.

'I'm sorry, Mr Walker. Your wife died peacefully in the night. It was quick and I'm sure she was never in pain or distress.'

He wasn't sure of that at all but wanted to lessen his employer's grief. He remembered how his first boss explained the death of his beloved dog, Lucky. "He never felt a thing."

Arnold struggled to get out of bed, looked again at the shape of his wife of several decades, and went outside to pee. Jonathon looked at Smokey.

'You go, old chap, I'll hang on till Mr Arnold returns.' The dog looked uncertain. 'Outside, go.' Smokey departed.

Jonathon took a peek under the bedclothes to check on Mrs Walker. He'd closed her eyes during the night and despite the odd shape of the left side of her face, she did look at peace. He wanted to give the widower the chance to make decisions about the body.

Mr Walker returned and seemed to have steeled himself.

'I don't want to cart her into Hobart Town. I'd rather we bury her here. What do you reckon, son?'

Arthur continued to call Jonathon, son, as if he were family.

'What do you think Mrs Walker would want?' asked Jonathon.

Arnold stopped. He was grieving but when he thought again, he knew his wife would like a proper funeral and a Christian burial.

'You're right, again,' he said. 'Can I ask you to wrap her in something ...' He looked around.

'Leave everything to me, sir. It'll be an honour to care for your dear wife.' Jonathon started to move out of the bedroom. 'Come on, let's have some breakfast.'

It was the first meal Jonathon ate in the Walker cottage not prepared by Vera. Jonathon cooked eggs and made tea. Mrs Walker's latest bread baking with her homemade jam made for a great physical start to the day.

They finished and Jonathon sensed Arnold wanted him to lead. He did. 'Why don't you check on the animals and I'll prepare Mrs Walker for the trip to town.'

Arnold nodded but didn't stand. Jonathon hesitated wondering why the old man hadn't moved.

'Are you okay, Mr Walker?'

'I want to tell you something.' Jonathon sat. The tension in the room got busy. 'Mrs Walker and I decided we want to give you the farm.'

It took a while for the words to sink into Jonathon's brain. He heard them clearly but found them shocking and dramatic. He finally managed to speak.

'That's very kind, Mr Walker,' wasn't a great response but understandable due to the magnitude and meaning of the offer.

Arnold raised a hand as if to fend off a negative response from the farm worker.

'Vera and I discussed this over many nights and agreed it was the best thing to do and also,' he hesitated,' the one thing we *wanted* to do. Before you came our way, we were ready to give up. Vera's been poorly for a while, and I can't do the hard work anymore. Since you arrived, the place has gone ahead like wildfire. We both want the farm to prosper, and you're the best person to make it happen. So please don't insult my dear wife's memory and refuse.' He hesitated again. 'There, I've said what needed to be said.'

'I wouldn't dream of insulting Mrs Walker or your good self, sir.' He stood, moved to the old man and extended his hand. Arnold stood to shake Jonathon's hand but instead pulled him close and embraced the young man.

A man of few words, Mr Walker exposed his feelings as his hug lingered. He broke free and wouldn't make eye contact. 'I'll see to the animals,' he said and left.

Jonathon couldn't stop tears forming in his eyes. His mind raced. *Do I now own my own farm? Has the chimney sweep from Bermondsey come up in the world? Is the boy from the hulk on the Thames now a landowner in the colony of Van Diemen's Land?*

He found a clean bedsheet and wrapped Mrs Walker well, tying the ends with old, clean rope. He went outside to the cart and cleared a space in the back. He found an old tarpaulin, folded it and placed it on the cart. He added two solid branches.

He waited by the back door for Arnold to return. The old man arrived and this time made eye contact with his farmhand and spoke.

'After we finish giving Vera the dignified funeral she deserves, I want to visit the people who handle the colony's business and have it put in writing that you are the new owner of the farm.'

Jonathon nodded. 'Thank you, sir. I really am grateful.'

They carefully carried the body to the cart and placed it parallel to the sides. Arnold looked uncertain until Jonathon climbed onto the vehicle and opened the tarpaulin to cover the corpse. Then the branches were placed either side to give the body the security and, if needed, the waterproofing required for the bumpy and possibly wet journey. The widower nodded his approval.

'I'll drive, sir,' said Jonathon and the old man climbed onto the seat. Jonathon ran back to check the chickens were secure and the gate to the paddock was fastened. He made sure the fire in the kitchen was dead then closed the back door. There were no locks; they're for keeping out honest people.

Smokey bounded alongside and waited for an order. Jonathon took the reins then patted his knee and the dog jumped up and sat beside him. There was more room in the back but Jonathon reckoned Mrs Walker should ride alone for this trip.

The funeral cortege set off for Hobart Town.

It took the best part of the day and their first port of call was the vicarage. Jonathon knocked on the door. The place seemed quiet and he wondered if the vicar was at home.

Footsteps sounded and the door opened about half way. Jonathon swallowed. Before him stood a young woman he thought the prettiest girl he'd ever seen.

'Hello, is Mr McFarlane at home?'

'May I ask your business?' she replied in a polite manner.

'He knows me. I'm Jonathon Sweeping and I've come about a funeral.'

'But the date of the funeral has not been set,' said the girl.

The visitor hesitated. 'No, I'd like to set a date ... if that is satisfactory.'

The girl paused. 'I think there's been a misunderstanding.'

Before Jonathon could speak, he heard a familiar voice. 'Who is it, Cate?' The door opened fully and Andrew McFarlane appeared. 'Jonathon,' he said throwing him a smile.

'Good day, Mr McFarlane. I'm sorry to disturb you, sir, but we've had much sadness on the farm. Mrs Walker has died.'

'Oh I am so sorry. Please come in. This is Cate our new maid.'

'Hello,' said Jonathon filing the girl's name in the best part of his memory bank.

'Hello,' she said, 'and I'm sorry I was rude to you before.'

McFarlane looked disappointed and Jonathon doubly so.

'You were not rude,' he said. 'I should have explained better.'

'I thought you were referring to another funeral,' she replied.

'Oh I see,' said the vicar understanding. 'You were not to know, Jonathon, we too have suffered a death in the family. My dear mother passed away in her sleep two days ago.'

Jonathon winced. 'Sir, please forgive me, I didn't know.'

'Of course not, how could you? Now come away in and tell me what you need.'

They sat in his study and Jonathon explained about Mrs Walker being in the cart in the street.

'It's all right, she's well wrapped and Mr Walker is with her.'

'Well I suggest you head to the undertaker, Mr Bridekirk in Murray Street. He's also a cabinetmaker and his coffins are first-class. We can have a small service tomorrow.'

'That would be wonderful. Mr Walker is not well and I want to get him back to the farm as soon as possible.'

'As you wish. Come back and see me once you have Mrs Walker safely settled with the undertaker.'

They opened the door and a woman appeared. This was the second beautiful woman Jonathon met that day.

'My dear, you haven't met Jonathon Sweeping. Jonathon this is my wife.'

'Hello Mr Sweeping.' She offered her hand.

'How do you do, Mrs McFarlane? I'm very sorry for your loss.'

She thanked him and Andrew led him to the front door. 'I'll see you soon,' said the vicar. Jonathon left and boarded the cart.

They found the undertaker and his polite and sensitive handling of Mrs Walker's body gave both farmers a sense of peace. There were papers to complete and sign.

Back on the cart, Jonathon patted Smokey and looked at Arnold. 'How are you bearing up, sir?' He nodded not wanting to talk. His grief began to grow stronger. 'All we need is a bed for the night then we'll be ready for the funeral in the morning.'

There was more nodding from the widower.

'Mr McFarlane wants us to pop back and fix a time for the service.'

They headed to the vicarage. Smokey was up for a chat but none of the humans said anything. Outside the McFarlane house, Arnold finally spoke.

'You go in, son. I'll trust you to fix things proper like.

Jonathon understood. 'Won't be long,' he said and pointed at Smokey. 'Stay.'

The front door was opened by Cate and Jonathon copped a tingle down his spine. 'Hello again,' he said.

'Hello,' she replied and Jonathon entered and stood there holding his cap. 'I'll let Mr McFarlane know you're here.'

'No need,' said the vicar approaching. 'How did you get on with Mr Bridekirk?'

'Very well, and he said he would wait till he hears from you.'

'Of course. Now where are you and Mr Walker staying tonight?'

'We haven't decided but we'll find a hotel.'

'Nonsense, one or more of our parishioners will be only too happy to put you up.' He called. 'Annie, are you there?'

His wife appeared. 'Yes my dear?'

'Who could put up our two travellers tonight?'

'The Pikes have a spare room since we pinched Cate but Mrs Hodgson has plenty of room.'

'Of course, Mrs Hodgson. Let's go, young man, I'll come with you.'

They left and the vicar hopped in the back and gave directions.

Mrs Hodgson was a widow with much compassion for Mr Walker. She was delighted to have company and with bedrooms to spare the farmers were set for the night. Jonathon mentioned the dog.

'Oh I love dogs,' she said. 'Does he like stew?'

The welcome was warmer than warm. Jonathon walked out to the cart to collect their belongings and offered to drive the vicar home.

'No need, the walk will do me good.' At the cart, Andrew asked a favour. 'Can you pop over later tonight after your supper?'

'Of course,' said Jonathon.

'I know little about the Walkers and it would be nice to have a few personal tales about Mrs Walker to mention at the funeral. Come over once the old folks have retired.'

After Mrs Hodgson's superb supper, Jonathon walked to the vicarage and tapped lightly on the door. Annie opened it. 'Come in,' she said. 'Andrew's expecting you.' Smokey was told to wait.

The vicar again welcomed the young man and asked questions to help in writing the eulogy. When they were finished, the subject switched to Jonathon.

'So how are you getting on out there on the Walker farm?'

'All was fine until poor Mrs Walker died in her sleep.'

The vicar smiled. 'We share a tragedy, Mr Sweeping. My dear mother passed on in her sleep. It's always a good way to greet your Maker. Do you agree?'

'I've never been one for religion, sir. Most of my life has been about hardship, slavery, sickness and death. But lately I've wondered why God doesn't do more to help those in need.'

'Oh, and why lately, if I may ask?'

'I met two men from a nearby farm and discovered they kidnapped young aboriginal women and attacked them. Why does God allow that?'

The cleric pursed his lips. 'I wish I knew, and I too have heard terrible stories of violence between settlers and natives. I've spoken to the Governor. He seems genuinely conflicted trying to develop the colony but respect the locals. If the Governor has a plan, it's certainly not working.'

'I wish him luck,' said Jonathon.

'So will you return to the farm after Mrs Walker's funeral?'

Jonathon hesitated causing the vicar to worry.

'Is something wrong?'

Jonathon told him about inheriting the farm.

'But how wonderful. You'll be a landowner, a free man and your own boss. All you need now is a wife and a family.' He smiled then whispered. 'I've recently married, Jonathon, and I must tell you marrying a woman you love is the best thing any man can do. Find yourself the right wife and you will become the happiest man in Van Diemen's Land.'

'After you, sir?'

'But of course,' he said and they laughed as Andrew walked his guest to the door. 'I'll see you in church, Mr Sweeping, and congratulations on your windfall.'

'Good night, sir,' he said and walked back to Mrs Hodgson's home with Smokey by his side.

# Chapter 36

Vera's funeral was as she would have wanted; religious, simple and with as few people as possible. No fuss was a catch cry for Mrs Walker. Thanks to Jonathon, the Reverend McFarlane was able to say kind, personal and touching stories about the woman who lived with her husband and animals and their employee alone in the bush. Arnold showed little emotion but inside he experienced a torrent of love and sadness. Jonathon walked with him and sat beside him throughout.

The dozen mourners, rustled up by the vicar, gathered in the small hall beside the church for a cup of tea. Jonathon found himself alone when the former Dimity Carlisle approached. 'I understand you've been a big help to Mr Walker and his dear wife.'

'To be fair, Mrs McFarlane, it is they who've been a big help to me.'

'My husband tells me you are the new owner of the Walker farm.' He shrugged. 'So, we reformed convicts *are* able to make good.' She stared at him then put a finger to her lips.

He wasn't sure how to react. The *reformed convicts* phrase took a second or three to register. They were interrupted by the McFarlane maid offering a plate of biscuits.

'Thank you, Cate,' said Annie.

'Thank you, Miss,' said Jonathon trying not to stare at the pretty young woman who drifted away. Annie observed Jonathon's reaction.

'Are you returning to the farm after the burial?'

'We are. It takes a few hours and I'd like to be back before dark.'

'I wish you well as your own master.'

He thanked her as Mr Walker and the vicar approached.

'It's time to move, young man. If you and Mr Walker will go to the cemetery I'll meet you and the undertaker there.

They left with the other mourners smiling and wishing them well. Pleased to see his masters, Smokey remained on the cart.

Jonathon kept an eye on his passenger who remained quiet, and Jonathon reckoned the burial might be the toughest part of the day.

It was short and simple. Mr Walker dropped a handful of soil on the basic coffin and stood looking into the grave. He stood alone with his thoughts. After an appropriate time, Jonathon took Arnold's arm which brought him back to reality. They walked to the cart with the gravedigger already shovelling.

The two farmers shook hands with Andrew who wished them well and left. Arnold turned to Jonathon and seemed like his old self.

'We need supplies and I have to visit the government office.'

They climbed onto the cart with Smokey in the back this time. He enjoyed a grand time with the widow Hodgson slipping him a lamb shank for his tea and a bowl of oats and bacon for breakfast.

They bought supplies and then stopped outside the government office.

'You come with me,' said Arnold.

'Stay,' said Jonathon and Smokey settled.

In the office, a clerk approached. 'Yes gentlemen, how can I help?'

'My name's Walker and was granted land here in 1811. This is the document.' He produced a piece of folded paper. Jonathon looked on, open-mouthed.

The clerk looked at the paper. 'What do you want?'

'I want my name removed from this document and the name Jonathon Sweeping put in its place.'

The clerk shook his head. 'I can't do that.'

'Why not?'

'I have no authority to alter a government document.'

Arnold pointed at his employee. 'This is Jonathon Sweeping. He has been my employee ever since he received his ticket-of-leave. I know this man and he knows my farm. I want it to continue under his ownership.'

'I understand,' said the clerk, 'but what you are asking is not for me to grant. You will need to write to the Land Commissioners.'

'And how long will that take?' The clerk shrugged. 'Well will you make a note on your files to say I have attended this office and made the request I've just mentioned?' The clerk hesitated. 'Oh come on, man, attaching a note to a file can't be illegal.' The clerk reluctantly produced pen and paper. 'I'm not long for this world, and I don't want any Tom, Dick or Harry taking my farm because he can. Let the

record show I want the Walker farm to belong to Jonathon Sweeping.
Is that clear?'

Jonathan whispered wanting his boss to be polite. 'Please ... sir.'

The clerk scribbled while the visitors waited. When he finished,
the clerk looked up. 'It's done.'

'Show me,' said Arnold almost threatening.

'Please,' whispered Jonathon.

Arnold grunted. 'Please,' he said.

The clerk showed his work. Arnold looked at Jonathon. 'Happy?'

Jonathon gave a forced smile and mouthed, 'Thank you.'

They left with Jonathon wondering if the clerk would destroy the
note the moment they drove away. They did drive away with Smokey
pleased to be back with his masters one of whom was now,
unofficially, the new boss of the Walker Farm.


Not many miles from Jonathon's new home, a group of Europeans
gathered in a shed. They'd all been granted property in and around
the Derwent River Valley, a beautiful part of Van Diemen's Land, and
a piece of magnificent bushland where the Mouheneener people lived
for thousands of years.

The white settlers were angry as their lives were being interrupted
by marauding aborigines. They stole provisions, killed sheep,
damaged fences and even attacked fellow Europeans.

'I've had enough,' snarled a farmer. 'It's my damn property. Back
home, trespassers would be arrested and taken to the assizes. Where
are the soldiers when you need them? What does this Governor do to
help?'

Others murmured their support.

'I'm not waiting for no soldiers. I'm goin' hunting blacks—tonight!'

More support from angry farmers with new voices being heard.

'They're savages. The sooner we drive 'em out the better.'

'They're not all savages,' interrupted one farmer whose comment
stopped the murmuring. 'Some of their women are damn fine.'

A few laughed and one scoffed. 'Would you walk down the main
street of Hobart Town with a black woman on your arm?'

'I don't take 'em to town, I take 'em to bed.'

A huge response erupted. None would refuse a black woman.

The first farmer took over. 'I know where a mob of blacks camp. I say we go there and give 'em a serve of shot. Who's with me?'

Most of them yelled their support. A cautious farmer worried.

'What about their spears? They can kill from nearly forty yards.'

'We attack at night. No warning. We creep up and open fire.'

No-one objected. They agreed on where and when to meet.

That night, in the Derwent River Valley, by a pristine stream, a mob of aborigines went about their lives as they'd done for millennia. The men talked about their favourite hunting ground being taken over by white men, about sheep replacing kangaroos, and about black women being attacked, stolen and raped, even murdered. They talked about their lifestyle being destroyed with the original inhabitants having no say in the matter.

They finished eating and prepared to retire to their huts. A fire lit their faces. The night sounds of the bush were universal although Van Diemen's Land had unique creatures. Suddenly nocturnal animals panicked as, without warning, the air exploded. Weapons using gunpowder flung metal into the camp.

Who chose where the metal would strike? Human beings, including women and children, fell to the ground. Some died instantly. Some were nicked and others carried metal in their bodies suffering horrific and never-ending pain.

Their screams filled the valley. The still night became the perfect sounding board for the sounds of a massacre. A few male aborigines tried to find their spears. Many of the males were dead or injured. In the darkness, the cowardly attackers fled.

No artist or writer was present to record and describe the event. Tales would be told but not for years if at all. In Hobart Town, soldiers, officials, townsfolk, and the Governor slept soundly unaware of the carnage.

Escaping into the night, the killers took pride in their work. Not a skerrick of bravery was required by the assassins but self-belief in their superiority, and a sense of entitlement warmed the cockles of their hearts; their strange, evil hearts. It was a skirmish to start a war.

# Chapter 37

Smokey, Arnold and Jonathon returned to the farm. With the old-fashioned cook no longer in residence, domestic chores provided a challenge. The farm continued with Arnold growing old and Jonathon growing strong. Both men often thought about the future without ever discussing it.

They were in the paddock mustering sheep when a rider appeared.

'Hello,' called the Reverend Robert Knopwood. The men waved, left the sheep then walked to the visitor.

He hopped down from his steed. 'Greetings gentlemen. I was passing and thought I'd call in. I stopped by the house but couldn't find Mrs Walker.'

His query was met with silence until Jonathon answered because the widower couldn't say the words.

'Mrs Walker died, sir. A month or so ago now and she's buried in Hobart Town cemetery.'

Knopwood's face turned ashen. He dropped the reins and shook Arnold's hand with two of his. 'My dear sir, I am so sorry. Please accept my deepest condolences.' Arnold nodded but still found it tricky to speak.

Again Jonathon took over. 'We've learnt how to boil a kettle, Mr Knopwood, and we bake a mean loaf of bread. We'd be pleased if you could join us.'

Of course he accepted and they settled in the kitchen.

'I've moved to a cottage out in Rokeby and don't get into Hobart much these days. But I still see the farmers in the area and I did hear a terrible tale. Do you know about it?'

They didn't and he explained the massacre at the aboriginal camp.

The vicar's calm demeanour and lack of flowery words gave the scene a chilling sensation. Killing and maiming people, including women and children, at night when they had little or no chance to flee or defend themselves, sounded monstrous.

'I don't wish to alarm you gentlemen, but I fear for the settlement here in Van Diemen's Land. The hatred between black and white men is growing and that massacre may not be the last. I pray I'm wrong.'

They chatted a while longer before Jonathon walked the vicar out to the horse. 'I'm worried about Mr Walker, young man, he looks poorly and depressed—not a good combination.'

'I agree,' said Jonathon, 'but what can I do?'

'Persuade him to move to Hobart. He can be looked after and there is the hospital if he needs medical care.'

Jonathon nodded. 'I'll try but I don't like my chances.'

'There are people in Hobart who would be happy to care for him. There's a widow, Mrs Hodgson, a Christian and a wonderful cook.'

Jonathon sparkled. 'We stayed with her when Mrs Walker died.'

The vicar mounted his horse. 'Take care of yourself, young man. God bless.' He rode away. Jonathon and Smokey watched him with the young man thinking about Mr Walker.

Thoughts danced inside Jonathon's brain. *Will he think I'm trying to get rid of him? Will he think I find him a hindrance on the farm?*

Arnold potted in the kitchen but turned when Jonathon entered. 'We need to talk, son,' he said and sat. Worried, Jonathon joined him. 'I know this may come as a shock but let me finish.' He paused. 'I need to move into Hobart Town, permanently.'

Jonathon's shock turned him dumb. Arnold raised a hand.

'Now please don't argue with me. I've given it some thought. I ain't getting any younger, if I fall over or hurt meself, I'll be an even bigger burden on you. And after what the vicar told us about these black and white killings, I don't fancy ending me days at the end of a spear. If it turns out like the vicar reckons, we'll be dead in our beds and the animals will eat us before anyone finds out.'

Jonathon found his voice. 'If that's what you want, Mr Walker, I'll support you all I can.'

'Good, it's settled.' He stood. 'Okay, let's get back to the sheep.'

'But where will you live?' The question stopped him.

'I reckon the widow, Mrs Hodgson, might take me in. I'll pay her.'

'Of course,' said Jonathon, trying to hide a smile.

As they headed out to work, the farmer spoke. 'I'll pack me case tonight and you can drive me into town in the morning.'

*Goodness, he _is_ serious.*

The trip to town was unusual. Arnold was hardly a chatterbox but now he spoke freely. He talked about his childhood growing up in Lincolnshire, how he met Vera, their married life in Cambridgeshire, and their trip to Van Diemen's Land. Did growing old mean you hark back to times of yore? Jonathon moved to assure him.

'I'll still be coming into town for supplies, and with fleece and eggs to sell, Mr Walker, and I'll make a point of dropping in to see you.'

The old man's affection for his former employee grew stronger. Jonathon was the son he never had. No words were uttered by the old farmer who grasped Jonathon's arm and squeezed it. On cue, Smokey barked as if to add his best wishes to the senior master.

Jonathon's concern about Mrs Hodgson not wanting or being able to take in Mr Walker was dashed in a flash. Her smile answered all questions. They sat in her kitchen drinking tea and devouring the best scones, jam and cream in Hobart Town as she fussed about her new tenant's wants and wishes.

It was impossible to say who was happier. Arnold enjoyed relief and pleasure and Mrs Hodgson purred.

Jonathon left, bought supplies, and called at the Government office dealing with land grants. The clerk remembered him.

'It's been approved,' he said. Jonathon couldn't speak. 'You are now the landowner of the farm previously owned by Mr Walker. Here's the title document.' He showed Jonathon. 'I'll read it for you.'

'Thanks,' smiled Jonathon. 'I'll read it myself.'

He skipped back to the cart and told Smokey the great news. He wanted to share it with someone and called on the Reverend McFarlane. The door was opened by Cate the maid. To him, her smile seemed brighter than a room full of candles.

'Hello, Mr Sweeping. It's lovely to see you again.'

The former sweep was swept off his feet and suffered a speech impediment. 'Hello ... Miss. I was passing and wondered if Mr McFarlane is at home.'

'He's out but should be here directly. You're welcome to come in and wait.'

What was happening? The lad who could climb chimneys, box bullies, breed and shear sheep, and steal candlesticks, now acted strange. He became timid.

'I don't want to be a nuisance.'

'The kettle's boiled,' was all she said and by throwing in another of her smiles, Jonathon found himself floating through the door and into the hallway. 'Come through to the kitchen,' she said and his floating journey continued.

She made tea while he tried not to stare.

'How is Mr Walker getting on since his wife died?'

Jonathon welcomed the new topic and explained today's events.

'That sounds wonderful. How kind you are to persuade the old man to make such a move.'

'Well I didn't really ...'

'How do you take your tea, Mr Sweeping?'

He was about to explain when the front door opened and the vicar and his wife arrived. Their surprise and delight filled the kitchen.

Before Jonathon could explain his visit to Hobart Town, the pretty maid did it for him. He would never describe her as pretty. To him she was undoubtedly beautiful.

'Mr Sweeping has been exceptionally kind in caring for Mr Walker.'

The McFarlanes loved hearing the tale, and this meeting gave everyone a fillip especially when Jonathon produced the title deed announcing his new farm ownership.

'Wonderful news, young man' said the vicar. 'All power to you.'

Jonathon received a second fillip being invited to call when next in Hobart Town.

On the cart with Smokey beside him, they headed back to the Walker Farm henceforth to be known as the Sweeping Farm.


As Jonathon headed home, two separate meetings were taking place. The first in Hobart Town saw a deputation of settlers call on the Governor of the Colony, Lieutenant-Colonel Sir George Arthur.

'It's ridiculous, sir,' said the self-appointed leader of the settlers. 'The blacks have no respect for our property, any property. We know they're savages because they have no respect for the law.' Others agreed. 'We need soldiers in the area now to drive them off our land.'

More agreement from his colleagues left the Governor in no doubt. He knew the settlers were the backbone of the colony. A prosperous town like Hobart was nothing if the land beyond was not farmed and able to provide food for the growing population.

'Gentlemen, I understand your predicament.'

'Do you, sir?' snapped the leader. 'How would you fancy a mob of violent black savages bursting through your front door aiming a spear at your heart?' He snarled. 'Well?'

'It's not as simple as me giving an order and everything being fixed. I haven't enough soldiers to cover all your properties. It's a vast land and as you know, the natives know every square inch of it.'

'I warn you, sir, unless you take decisive action, the blacks will kill not just settlers but our women and children. And when that happens, and your masters in Westminster hear about it, your name will be mud. You sir, will have blood on your hands.'

The other settlers gave strong support to their leader. Fighting words loaded with threats bounced around the room. Governor Arthur wanted to plead, argue, even discuss the matter further but his audience stormed out. He faced a problem which, if it exploded, would leave him with more than a flesh wound.

The second meeting was held in the bush not far from Hobart Town between men of the Paredarerme people, the largest indigenous tribe in Van Diemen's Land. Word spread of the recent night attack on the aboriginal camp.

That murderous attack with aboriginal people being killed in cold blood sent anger waves through the indigenous community. Women and children being casualties stoked the anger. And being unable to help the wounded became a permanent and traumatic reminder of black suffering. How could they remove metal from bodies? How could they help loved ones crying, screaming and in constant pain?

How could they hunt on their land when it was occupied by strangers and their sheep? How could they travel when many of their tribe carried wounds caused by the guns fired by white men?

There was no choice. Revenge must happen. It would not be taken at night but now, in broad daylight. With spears and clubs they set off through the bush heading for the nearest farm.

# Chapter 38

For the first time in his life, Jonathon Sweeping was alone. As a child in London, as a sweep, on a hulk or ship at sea, and as a convict in Van Diemen's Land, he lived with others. Not now. There were chickens, a horse, a flock of sheep, and Smokey but no fellow humans, white or black. Mind you, the surrounding bush was full of native animals.

The dog was always with him, and both slept on the only bed in the cottage. This was the first time the young man enjoyed a proper bed since ... well, since ever.

He missed the Walkers, and kept thinking about his future. Living alone had its drawbacks. Loneliness jabbed his mind. He grew hungry for companionship. He could move back to Hobart Town, get a job and have friends. Or he could get married, if anyone would have him. That would solve all his problems in one fell swoop. He'd have a companion and be able to give all his love to someone who loved him.

As he worked around the farm, he found his head filling with images of the McFarlane maid, Cate. How could he find out if she was walking out with a marine or government official or the son of a prosperous businessman? What excuse could he invent to go and see her again? Who could he ask about her marital prospects?

He knew there were far more males than females in Hobart Town and when a female was young, single and beautiful, well, how long is the queue of suitors? And anyway, he'd be way down the line.

Days drifted by and shearing sheep took time. He knew the man who bought the fleece was due any time and so kept his wool safely inside the shed ready to go. Then the man arrived but on horseback.

'Where's the old man?' he asked.

Jonathon explained then asked his own question. 'Where's your cart?'

'Sorry, it's in dry dock. I'll be back next week. If you want your money sooner, you could take your fleece yourself. There's a ship sailing on Friday and I've heard the demand for good fleece, and especially merino, is going to be sky high.'

The wool buyer stopped for a meal then left. Jonathon decided to take his wool clip to town. He could be paid there and then, would be able to call on the McFarlane residence, and hopefully visit a certain female employee.

In the morning he loaded the cart, double-checked the animals were secure, and called Smokey up onto the seat. Off they went with hopes high.

The cart moved steadily for a short distance until the horse began to slow. A gentle slap of the reins and a word of encouragement did nothing for the beast. Jonathon ordered a stop and examined the horse. Horror of horrors, it appeared to be lame.

It wasn't a cart stuck in the mud or losing a wheel. This problem shouted trouble. No horse meant no journey to town. The next ship would sail this week meaning no quick income. But those problems could wait. First, the animal needed help.

They'd only come about 100 yards. Jonathon couldn't find a stone or other foreign object in the animal's hooves. It stood without reacting. Jonathon untied the beast and led it forward. Without the full cart to pull, it walked better. Strange.

Leaving the precious cargo, he led the horse back home with Smokey following. Jonathon set the horse free in its paddock, collected a tarpaulin and rope and set off.

The cart still had its load. He stretched the tarp on the ground, tossed every fleece on the tarp then pulled one end over the wool and tied the two ends of the tarp. Now came the fun part.

He placed the rope over his shoulder and started walking back to the farm. The track was reasonably level but wool is heavy. He covered about fifty yards then stopped for a rest. Smokey hadn't played this game before and watched awaiting commands.

None came and the dragging resumed. It took a bucket of sweat and a sore shoulder before they reached the shed. It was restocked with the wool, and man and canine staggered into the cottage where both enjoyed a drink.

The water in the streams and rivers in Van Diemen's Land was crystal clear, slaked any thirst and was free. It washed your insides.

Jonathon checked the horse and weighed his options. The first, do nothing, didn't appeal. Walk to Hobart to get help sounded reasonable. Walk to a nearby farm to borrow a healthy horse won.

Rather than leave all the wool behind, he rolled up a fleece, tied it to his back, explained his plan to Smokey and set off.

The nearest farm would take a couple of hours by the track so he opted to head through the bush. Mr Walker taught him a few navigation skills using the sun, and he knew the river near the rear of his farm went close to the next farm. He was right.

It was over an hour later when he saw smoke drifting skywards from the chimney in the farmhouse. He moved through the bush with Smokey excited to have reached a new settlement. Both man and hound experienced relief when another dog began to bark. It appeared giving warning to stay clear. It saw Smokey, stopped barking and the two dogs ran to one another for the customary sniff and greet.

Jonathon scanned the paddocks looking for the workers but saw no-one. He headed to the house when the local dog went back to being angry. It barked furiously but not at Jonathon or Smokey.

They were confused. Jonathon called. 'Hello. Anyone home?'

No voices, only more barking from one agitated dog as it spun around and around as it jumped. Jonathon followed the canine towards a shed. The silence, apart from the dog, caused the hairs on the back of Jonathon's neck to lose control.

He entered the shed and froze. Two male bodies lay on the ground. There was a spear buried in the back of each corpse. The dogs barked. Jonathon checked the bodies. Both men were dead.

He moved quickly, the dogs following. He bounded onto the verandah and in through the open back door.

'No!' he screamed kneeling beside the body of a woman, surely the farmer's wife. The back of her skull was a bloody mess. The tragedy overwhelmed Jonathon but worse was to come. In the main bedroom, on the floor, lay the lifeless body of a child; a girl about five. She lay face down with her lovely brown hair dyed red. Jonathon wept.

The dogs were distressed and Jonathon bereft. Were the attackers still nearby? Would they kill him? Through tears, he stumbled outside and scanned the paddocks. Sheep grazed oblivious to the carnage with not a human in sight.

His mind and heart fought one another. What do I do? He looked at the dogs who wanted instructions. He raised a hand to calm them.

He spoke in a soft voice. They caught the mood and settled and that's when he heard the sound.

What was it? He turned and went inside, stopped and listened. He heard it again. It wasn't a cry or scream but it sounded human. He followed the sound to the larder. The sound grew louder. Food was all he could see. He went to the flour box and lifted the lid and stared at the smiling face of a baby. The infant cooed. That was the sound he heard.

Surrounded by two excited dogs, with great care Jonathon lifted the child from its temporary cradle, in truth its hiding place.

The mother, hearing the screams from the men and seeing the natives, grabbed her baby and put it in the closest hiding place she could find. As she ran to save her daughter, a club smashed her skull. She died, never knowing one of her children survived.

It took time to pat most of the flour from the baby's clothes and hair. It was a boy and the wee lad waved his arms as babies do meaning a fine cloud of flour decorated the child giving him a ghost-like appearance. Jonathon placed the baby in the middle of the bed.

It was a sunny day in Van Diemen's Land, a fine day for a massacre. The ones which occurred in the night were terrifying with guns exploding and victims not seeing the pieces of metal before they ripped into bodies. But it's different for the victims in daylight although not in terms of suffering. In daylight you can see your enemy's face, they're up close. You can see his spear and club, and you can hear his screams and cries of vengeance.

Jonathon faced many a tricky decision in his short life but this was beyond tricky. What the hell could he do, should he do? He decided. He put the baby on the floor then placed the bodies of the mother and daughter on the main bed, covered them with a blanket and closed the door. In the shed he removed the spears from the two men and placed their bodies side by side then closed the shed.

He went into the paddock, called the grazing horse and added its saddle and bridle, tethering it outside the shed.

Back inside the house, he searched and found a homemade cane basket. He lined the basket with one towel and formed a pillow from another. He lifted the baby and placed the infant in the basket. Using rope, he made a noose which went over his shoulder and around the handles on the basket, allowing the baby to reside in the homemade papoose which rested against Jonathon's chest.

Unlike his own horse, this animal was young and fit. With difficulty, Jonathon stood on a stump and mounted the animal. Looking down he saw Smokey all excited. The other dog looked confused. Jonathon spoke kindly to the canines.

'Come on, boys, let's go.'

The local dog was a she, and intelligent, and the two dogs trotted after the horse as it headed towards the track to Hobart Town.

Calling the dogs, speaking softly to the baby, and working hard to keep the horse at a steady but gentle gait, this unusual travelling group grew closer to the main settlement on Van Diemen's Land.

Jonathon knew his first priority was the infant. The people he knew would and could help were Mr and Mrs Andrew McFarlane.

He reined in the horse and saw Mrs McFarlane in the garden picking flowers.

'Hello,' he called.

She looked up and smiled. 'Mr Sweeping, how lovely to see you. Andrew and Cate will be delighted.'

*Cate will be delighted?* thought Jonathon. 'Might I ask you to give me a hand please?' he called and she opened the gate and moved to the horse.

'Have you brought more stray dogs to Hobart Town?'

'No, madam, but something rather special.'

He slipped the noose over his head and holding the basket with a firm grip, lowered it towards her. Naturally her eyes were drawn to the contents.

'Oh my lord!' she exclaimed and held the basket with care.

Jonathon dismounted, tethered his horse to the front fence, and allowed the dogs to follow him into the garden then shut the gate telling the canines to wait.

She carried the basket inside calling, 'Andrew, Cate, come quickly.'

Jonathon followed and the attention the others might have paid to him was switched to the contents of the basket.

Annie lifted the child out and held it as the baby began to cry.

'He needs a feed, Mrs McFarlane. I've given it a little water but nothing else,' said the visitor.

Annie handed the baby to Cate and hurried to the kitchen. Jonathon looked at the young woman and couldn't control his heartbeat.

The vicar was more than curious. 'Young man, you never cease to amaze me. You are now a father?'

'May I speak to you in private, sir.' He turned to Cate. 'If you don't mind, Miss.'

'Of course not,' said Cate and left with the baby.

Andrew led Jonathon to his study where the young man explained the tragic tale. The vicar couldn't speak and only shook his head. Then he looked into Jonathon's eyes.

'You are a hero, Jonathon Sweeping, one of God's angels. You have saved the life of a child and on behalf of his family, I thank you.'

He moved to Jonathon and embraced him. Jonathon needed those words and that embrace. What he discovered this morning seared a mark on his soul. Those were images he might never forget. Now, kindness and love helped ease the pain. He broke free.

'If I may, sir, the horse and dogs need a drink. I'll be back as soon as I can.'

He went outside and attended to his animals. They appreciated him as much as he them.

When he returned, the baby was in a crib being gently rocked by the maid, the one with the dancing curls and wearing a pretty dress which decorated what Jonathon described as an entrancing body.

Both women turned to Jonathon. They'd been told a less violent version of events. Annie copied her husband and hugged the young hero. He didn't mind her hug, it felt good, no fantastic.

He smiled and looked humble hoping the third adult in the room would catch the hugging habit.

Caring for the child, Cate stayed seated but spoke. 'Thank you, Mr Sweeping. You've done a wonderful thing today and I hope you are well rewarded.'

He muttered his thanks then excused himself. 'I need to report the matter to officials. Will it be all right to leave my dogs in your yard?'

'Of course,' said McFarlane and led him out.

Annie called. 'Come and see us before you go.'

His heart skipped a beat as he climbed onto the saddle and left.

The soldier in the office was bored and not in the mood for time wasters. He changed in an instant when Jonathon spoke.

'I wish to report a massacre.'

The more the story unfolded, the more the officer's quill wobbled. He wanted to ask questions but Jonathon kept talking. Finally the young farmer finished.

'I have a question, sir?'

'*You* have a question. I have a hundred. Go on, what's yours?'

'May I keep the horse, just to get home?'

'As far as I'm concerned, you can keep the horse forever. After what you did today, son, it's the least you should receive.' He called a senior officer who entered and like the first soldier, listened with incredulity.

He snarled. 'Bloody blacks; the sooner we kill the lot of them the better.' He looked at Jonathon. 'And the baby's being cared for by the Reverend McFarlane and his wife?'

'Yes sir.'

'Haven't they got a maid called Cate Ramsay?'

Jonathon hesitated. 'I think that's her name, sir.'

'A couple of my men have their eye on her. Pretty as a picture I hear and well worth a kiss or three.'

Jonathon froze. Military men were discussing the girl he couldn't stop thinking about; and with disrespect. *How dare they!*

The fact she was a she gave Cate tremendous value but being pretty and single was an added bonus for sex-starved males in Hobart Town. The gender imbalance in Van Diemen's Land was stark. For every female convict sent to the island, four male convicts landed.

Jonathon signed a document declaring the details of the massacre were true. He rode to the home of Mrs Hodgson, still smarting from the words the men used in discussing Cate.

The widow and the widower Walker were thrilled to see him. He lied about his visit stating the need for supplies. He said nothing about the massacre, stayed for a cup of tea and those world's best scones then chose to leave. Arnold followed him out to the street.

He admired the new horse. 'Hey, what's happened to Clive? And how could you afford a beauty like this?'

'Clive's been limping a bit so I borrowed this one.'

Arnold laughed. 'Oh don't go falling for his sore leg routine. Was he pulling the cart?' Jonathon nodded. 'That's his trick. Give him a full cart and he goes lame. It's all an act but only on an outward journey. On a homeward journey, he's fine. And you can tell him I told you.'

Arnold held out his hand and they shook with a firm grip. 'It's lovely to see you, my boy. Drop in any time. Good luck.'

Jonathon waved as he turned the corner then, when Arnold went inside, did an about turn and headed for the vicarage.

In the back yard he was greeted by two happy hounds. Annie opened the door and welcomed him inside. Cate Ramsay, the objective of sex-hungry soldiers, sat with the baby in her arms. She smiled when Jonathon returned.

'The knight in shining armour returns,' she said.

Without thinking he spoke. 'You'd make a wonderful mother, Miss Ramsay.'

She tried to smile but was shocked by the frankness of the compliment and the fact that he spoke her name.

'I'll fetch Andrew,' said Annie and disappeared.

Jonathon didn't know why, especially for someone naturally shy, but he spoke without thinking.

'Would you like to keep the baby?' he asked bumping up her shock. These were personal questions and the last one carried such importance.

She hesitated. 'He's lovely and if there are no relatives, yes, I would although as Mrs McFarlane is with child, I don't think it would be possible.'

He struggled taking time to comprehend the 'with child' part. She sensed his confusion and, being a caring soul, let it ride.

'Of course if you were married, Mr Sweeping, you and your wife would have a strong claim to young Moses.'

'Moses? Is that his name?'

She smiled. 'Mr McFarlane said the baby in the Bible was hidden to avoid being killed and thought the name Moses appropriate.'

Jonathon continued his lack of understanding but survived further embarrassment when the vicar arrived.

'And how did the authorities react to your tale?' he asked.

'Quite well, sir, although I fear they have revenge on their minds.'

'And what did they say about Moses, our new family member?'
Everyone clung to the answer, being desperate to hear.

'I told them the infant was being well cared for in this house, sir, and I can see it is exactly the case.' The others were pleased. 'I guess you will receive a visit in the next day or so.'

There were more polite smiles with nobody beaming. The tragedy shocked them all. They wanted Jonathon to stay but his traumatic day and animals at home pushed him to leave.

'I must be going, sir,' he said. 'Thank you for caring for the animals and, thank you Miss Ramsay for being such a good mother.'

He left with the vicar as the two females looked at one another. Annie folded towels for Moses.

'I think that young man has taken a shine to you, young Cate.'

She said nothing, struggled to control her excitement, and turned her attention to the new man in her life.

# Chapter 39

Once Jonathon reported the massacre at the farm where baby Moses was rescued, the news spread. Governor Arthur heard about it from the soldiers who rode to the farm and investigated. With the heated exchange he suffered from angry settlers fresh in his mind, this latest carnage rattled the top man.

Even the press jumped in publishing their opinion. The aborigines were as good as cursed. Their behaviour was beyond the pale. The settlers were law-abiding and entitled to protect their property and family. The savages acted like savages. These attacks from the blacks must be stopped—permanently.

The Governor made public statements condemning the violence and urging Europeans to take heart.

At the massacre site, the bodies were given a Christian burial and a new family appointed to take over the farm.

This was a highly-sought after property but several settlers, keen to make a start, developed cold feet once they discovered its history. Eventually one family settled there giving Jonathon a new neighbour albeit several miles away.

He made his way home taking the dogs in turns. The dog he collected he named Ash because it went with Smokey. Jonathon's education didn't stretch to knowledge of the legend of Phoenix. One dog would sit on the horse for a while, and then be lowered while the other took a turn. He named the new horse Queenie.

Eventually he arrived at the Sweeping property, saw his travelling companions were fed and watered then checked on the other animals. The hens worked overtime and eggs were good for a week.

Clive, the reluctant horse, grazed in his paddock with sheep. He refused to make eye contact with Jonathon, worried his go-slow trick may have been rumbled but he took a long hard look at Queenie.

Back in Hobart Town, Jonathon's comment about a visit from the authorities came true as an official and soldier arrived at the vicarage.

The vicar was out visiting parishioners so Mrs McFarlane and Cate entertained the visitors.

'How is the baby, madam?' asked the official.

'He's well. Mr Sweeping undoubtedly saved his life, and Miss Ramsay is taking excellent care of the child.'

'There are no relatives here on Van Diemen's Land so we're not sure which family will adopt the lad.' He looked at Cate. 'What about you, Miss? Are you interested?'

The soldier jumped in. 'She's not married. It would have to be a married couple.'

'Is that true, Miss?'

'Yes sir, I'm not married.'

Her answer seemed to disqualify the saddened maid until her employer jumped in.

'But she is walking out with a gentleman,' said Annie. Her statement stuck a pin in the soldier and a massive spike in Cate's pulse. She looked at Annie with eyes impersonating organ stops.

The official thought out loud. 'Are you willing and able to look after the child for the time being?'

'Yes,' said Annie in a determined voice.

The official grunted. 'Well I'll write a report and come back soon. If there's any change in your marital status, Miss, please notify the office. Good day, ladies.'

They left, the soldier grinding his teeth because he now knew the maid was a corker and damn, she's walking out with some lucky so-and-so. The women stared at one another in silence.

Moses cooed as if to say, "If it's all right with you, I'd rather be here."

'Mrs McFarlane, what on Earth made you say that?'

'Well it's the truth.'

'But we're not walking out.'

'Cate, if Mr Sweeping lived in Hobart, you would be. Is that true?'

Cate hesitated. 'Perhaps.'

'Now listen to me my girl. Men have what they call man to man conversations, and we're about to have the same only this is woman to woman. What we say here and now is never to be repeated. Okay?' Cate nodded. 'Say it.'

'Okay.'

Annie pulled her chair close to Cate and Moses. 'In another life, I met a number of gentlemen, and learnt a lot about the male sex. What you see in Jonathon Sweeping is what you get. He is a kind, loving and sensitive man who treats people and animals with respect.

'If you want to remain here and be our maid and help with my baby and any others to come, you are most welcome to stay. But if you want a family of your own, you have the chance to start with Moses, and then have another child of your own but only with a husband. I know Mr Sweeping is besotted with you. The question is, do you feel the same about him?'

Cate licked her lips. This conversation scared her.

'I do like him.'

'Does he make your heart beat faster?'

'Yes.'

'My experience is that opportunities don't often come your way but if they do, sitting around waiting for something to happen gets you nothing and nowhere. How about I get a message to Mr Sweeping and give you the chance to accept his offer to start walking out?'

'But he hasn't made an offer and he lives in the bush?'

'I've told you waiting for something to happen gets you nothing and nowhere. Do you want me to get a message to Jonathon?'

Cate pursed her lips and squeezed Moses a little harder.

'Yes please.'


In bed beside her husband, the former Dimity Carlisle explained her plan. 'Is my wonderful wife now a matchmaker?' he asked.

She squeezed him in a way she learnt in Berkeley Square all those years ago.

'We're relying on you, vicar,' she purred.

'But that means we'll need a new maid,' he protested in mock dismay as the squeezing continued. The plan was agreed.


Two days later, Andrew prepared to visit his parishioners. He kissed his wife and little Moses being fed by a doting maid.

'I'll be home in time for dinner, ladies. Hopefully I'll have pleasing news. Goodbye.'

He left and Cate's curiosity piqued. Annie shrugged off her query about Mr McFarlane's current journey. 'Oh he's visiting a wealthy new arrival he hopes will contribute to another stained glass window in the church.' Annie was experienced in telling fible-fable tales.

Andrew's visit was to the home of his predecessor, the Reverend Robert Knopwood. Bobby loved his out-of-town residence. It gave him a chance to fully appreciate the beautiful bush in Van Diemen's Land. As a bachelor he could write his journals, go fishing and visit friends.

One tragic event gave him the opportunity to start an immediate family. Knopwood adopted an orphan girl, Betsey Mack. Knopwood paid for her education, although some of it was not unlike the schooling given to one Jane Eyre, and, over the years, the clergyman took much pleasure in watching the girl grow and blossom. Tragically, as a grown woman, Betsey died giving birth to a daughter and when Knopwood died, the daughter and her older brother were the sole beneficiaries of Knopwood's estate.

So when Andrew McFarlane tethered his horse and found Robert in his rear garden, the visiting vicar used a lever, a trigger point to persuade the diarist to join the matchmaking quest. The visitor saw an opening for his Moses mission.

'How is your adopted daughter, Robert?'

The question gave Knopwood the chance to wax lyrical about his favourite child.

'That's wonderful,' replied McFarlane. 'Annie will be thrilled to hear your news.' He paused.

'And?' asked Knopwood. 'Your sentence sounds incomplete.'

He told the story of little Moses, the maid and her would-be beau.' Knopwood adored the tale but when McFarlane identified the beau as one Jonathon Sweeping, the retired vicar came alive.

'Oh how marvellous. I have so much admiration for that young man. What can I do to make this work?'

They chatted for an age, and shared a meal before Andrew set sail for Hobart Town bursting to tell the news to the women in his home.

It took the Reverend Knopwood a couple of days to set off for the Sweeping farm. Strangely, butterflies got busy in his stomach as he approached the cottage. Playing the role of matchmaker was all new to him, and being a bachelor, he was ill-equipped to advise anyone about marriage.

Two barking dogs announced the arrival of company and Jonathon's face lit up when he spotted the visitor. It was around midday and luncheon was served.

The longer they chatted, the more nervous the cleric became. Why? He was an older man, experienced in conducting marriages, and only needed to make a simple suggestion to perform his role in the matchmaking scheme.

But the vicar hesitated. Why not broach the subject? Time moved on and the vicar's departure drew nigh. In a panic, the visitor decided to blurt out the fact a young lady in Hobart Town would love to receive a proposal. As Knopwood cleared his throat to speak, Jonathon spoke.

'Sir, may I ask you a personal question?'

Mightily relieved, Knopwood replied. 'Of course; how can I help?'

'In your work, you must have married many couples.'

Knopwood nodded and wanted to smile. 'Yes, I have.'

'Can you give me some guidance?'

'Certainly; what would you like to know?'

'How should I go about proposing marriage to a young woman I've fallen in love with?'

Knopwood's relief was so powerful, he wanted to cry. 'Fallen in love you say? But how wondrous.'

Jonathon waited for him to continue. 'And?'

'Oh, guidance, yes, well I would call upon her with the largest bunch of flowers I could find, and with a ring; a ring is essential. And then I would give her the ring, no, the flowers first, and after she thanks you; she will certainly thank you, I would say, Miss Ramsay will you do me the honour of ...'

Jonathon gasped in shock. 'You know her name?'

Knopwood blew it and knew it. 'Pardon?' He looked and sounded guilty.

'You said Miss Ramsay. How do you know her name?'

He struggled. 'You must have told me.'

'I haven't told anyone.'

Knopwood cracked. 'Oh it's no use, Jonathon. Mrs McFarlane worries you'll take too long to tell Miss Ramsay how you feel about her, and Cate might accept an offer from one of the soldiers in Hobart Town. Mrs McFarlane asked Mr McFarlane to have me encourage you to, well, get a move on.'

Jonathon's grin became as wide as his hat. 'Thank you, sir,' he said shaking the cleric's hand. 'You've given me the best advice in the world.'

They parted on the friendliest of terms. Waving goodbye to his visitor, Jonathon couldn't contain his happiness. He began to dance in the yard confusing then exciting the dogs.

Next morning he placed Clive between the shafts. 'It's your turn old man,' said Jonathon, and with an empty tray, Clive did as told.

The dogs hopped in the back with Jonathon going back inside to check his hair and shaving, conducted in Mrs Walker's old mirror.

The horse and cart made good time but stopped whenever pretty flowers were spotted. Jonathon hopped down and picked wattle, ferns, lilies and more placing them in the back and warning the dogs to stay clear.

Close to Hobart Town, he used twine to tie the flowers as best he could. He worried about a ring knowing nothing about jewellery or the finer points of a wedding.

He pulled up outside Mrs Hodgson's house where she and Mr Walker were thrilled to see him. When he explained the purpose of his visit, his marriage proposal, the old folk sparkled.

Arnold grasped his "son's" arm. 'That's wonderful news, my boy. Vera would be delighted. Now, have you got the ring?'

Jonathon groaned. 'I'm not sure what to get or where. Can you advise me please?'

'Get nothing,' said Mrs Hodgson. She hopped up and fossicked in a drawer. 'Here,' she said producing a small box. 'This was my mother's engagement ring. I have no-one to give it to. Now I do.'

She placed it on the table and Jonathon was speechless. 'I can't take this, Mrs Hodgson.'

'Of course you can. Now stop dithering and get on your horse and tell the girl you love her. Go on, shoo.'

Tears welled in his eyes. He left feeling elated and nervous. Now people knew about his proposal. How could he face them if Cate said no? He pulled up outside the vicarage.

The dogs were told to be on their best behaviour. He picked up the biggest bunch of flowers ever seen in Hobart Town, opened the gate and knocked on the McFarlane front door. He wasn't shaking. He was trembling. Crash, bang, crash pounded his heart.

The door opened and there stood Annie McFarlane.

'Mr Sweeping,' she exclaimed seeing the flowers and excited her plan appeared to be in its final phase.

'Please come in.'

He hesitated. She worried. 'I'd like to speak to Miss Ramsay, please, if she's at home.'

Annie controlled her euphoria. 'She is. I'll fetch her.'

The matchmaker disappeared and the wait for the suitor proved excruciating. Footsteps sounded. Dainty footsteps could mean only one thing. Cate appeared.

'Hello, Miss Ramsay,' he said wishing he wasn't so formal.

'Mr Sweeping, this is a nice surprise.'

It was his cue and all the rehearsing at home and en route kicked in. He held out the huge floral display. 'I've brought these for you.'

She gasped. 'Oh, thank you so much. They're beautiful.'

It was now or never; it was time to execute the plan. 'And I would like to give you something else.' He fumbled in his pocket for a small object. Two hearts raced as one.

'Miss Ramsay, I mean Cate, please will you marry me?'

He opened the tiny box revealing the ancient but elegant engagement ring. Her eyes filled with tears.

She said nothing. It didn't matter, he knew. Despite the massive bouquet, he took her left hand and slipped the ring on her finger; a perfect fit.

She looked at the ring then at him. 'Yes, Jonathon, I would love to marry you.'

This was another tricky part for him. He bent his head and she understood. They kissed in a featherweight encounter. She smelt clean and fresh and lovely.

She dropped the flowers, and reached up and placed her hands around his neck. They kissed again and this time the timid approach was replaced with one more enthusiastic; much more enthusiastic. His arms went around her back and the romantic embrace sealed the mission accomplished.

As if on cue, Smokey and Ash barked, although not to herald their master gaining a mistress but because a local stray cocked his leg on the cart and the two dogs wanted it gone; the other dog that is.

Everything happened in a rush. The McFarlanes were cock-a-hoop with the news, Annie celebrated with care due to her expanding abdomen, and Jonathan remembered he had supplies to collect.

When he placed them in the cart, Clive didn't complain. It *was* true, a load on the homeward journey would be carried.

Back at the vicarage, the newly-engaged couple strolled in the garden. Nervous, Cate raised an issue which troubled her.

'There's one thing I need to tell you, Jonathon.' He swallowed fearing bad news. 'I have a younger brother, James. I feel responsible for him as we have no other family. I wonder if he might be able to ...'

She didn't get to finish her question. 'Will he sleep in a shed and work hard?' asked Jonathon.

Cate found another reason to love her fiancé and hugged him so hard it hurt. The future brother-in-law was 15 and still finding his feet in the colonies. The best thing to happen to the young lad took place when he moved to the Sweeping Farm and got his hands dirty.

Next Sunday, Andrew McFarlane read the banns for the first time. The Governor approved the adoption of Moses by the future Mr and Mrs Sweeping, and several folk looked through their wardrobe for something special to wear. A Hobart Town wedding didn't happen every day.

# Chapter 40

The wedding proved delightful. James gave away his sister who drew gasps when she entered the church. Pretty as a picture hardly did her justice. Annie became her matron of honour, Bobby Knopwood the best man and Andrew McFarlane conducted the service.

Apart from the whispering amongst the guests with hard of hearing Arnold replying to Mrs Hodgson by saying, 'What's that?' or, 'Pardon?', the biggest noise came from Moses and new-born Hannah, Annie having given birth only a month before Cate and Jonathon's big day. Andrew revelled in fatherhood.

The honeymoon shaped as being unusual as the baby and brother-in-law came too. When they arrived in their bush hideaway, the dogs struggled to contain their excitement especially as James fell in love with them. Cate saw her new abode and relished the chance to make it their home.

In the weeks before the ceremony, Annie toyed with the idea of giving Cate a few tips on entertaining her husband in matters intimate. She wanted to help without revealing the unusual part of her previous life. In the end she decided to whisper good luck and left the two lovebirds to enjoy their own trial and error adventure. Apparently such a method has worked for one or two other couples down the millennia.

Moses fell on his feet literally and metaphorically. He was crawling by the time he arrived in the bush and needed constant watching. Jonathon built a fire guard to keep the wee boy from the stove.

The new husband got to know his wife and her family history. Back in England, Cate's parents died and their only uncle, who didn't want the responsibility of caring for his late brother's children, suggested they join a cousin of his as free settlers in the colonies. They travelled on a female convict ship whose surgeon took it upon himself to protect the beautiful young Cate from any randy males.

He chose the wrong sibling. It was a hundred plus female convicts who had their eye on young James. One night near the equator he needed to be rescued, and James would later dine out on his eye-watering encounter and go on to embellish the tale in years to come.

Jonathon taught his brother-in-law a number of farming skills dealing with sheep and horses. Both learnt on the job when they bought a pregnant sow and soon dealt with a litter of pigs.

The shed was extended and James shared a comfortable spot with Smokey and Ash. His sister made the curtains.

Firearm training was new to the teenager and Jonathon gave wise and serious instruction. The family discussed the stories of bloodshed between settlers and aborigines with Jonathon working hard not to frighten his wife. He insisted the rifle was to be kept hidden but accessible at all times. He spoke privately to James about a plan of action if he was away and any aboriginals approached.

Months went by and life was never dull. Their farm provided a solid living and the Sweeping family grew in love and happiness. It grew even more when Cate wandered to the sheep paddock with Moses, carrying water for the men.

'Thank you, wife,' he said slaking his thirst. He went to shout to James.

'Don't call him yet,' she said and he worried.

'What's wrong?'

'Nothing's wrong but I think Moses is going to have a playmate.'

Jonathon gawped. He stared at her. 'But that's wonderful. How do you know? I mean, are you sure?'

'That's two questions. Which should I answer first?'

He dropped the cup and embraced and kissed her. James spotted the new arrivals and wandered over.

'Hey, hey, hey, what's going on here?'

'You're going to be an uncle,' said Jonathon.

'I'm already an uncle,' replied his brother-in-law picking up Moses and roughing the wee boy's curly red hair.

'An uncle again,' said Cate, 'which means even more babysitting work, brother.'

He laughed and kissed his sister. Moses tried to pat a sheep and failed. The dogs were given a drink while the warm sunshine quietly painted a few faces. Arrivals from that green and pleasant land were not used to so much sunshine.

They were having luncheon later that week when an unknown rider arrived. Jonathon came out of the cottage.

'Good day to you, sir.'

The rider dismounted. 'G'day. The name's Chisholm. The Governor has asked me and others to visit farms in the area and remind settlers the blacks are on the war path again.'

'What's happened?'

Cate, James and Moses came out to greet the visitor. Jonathon turned back to his wife. 'Can you prepare lunch for our visitor, my dear?'

She went inside and James played with Moses. Jonathon walked the rider away from the cottage.

'I don't want my family to hear any news about settlers being killed. It can be scary out here on our own.'

'Have you any weapons?' Jonathon nodded. 'Good because there have been more attacks elsewhere on the island; daytime raids on isolated farms. People have been killed. It seems they rarely, if ever, attack at night so at least you can sleep well.'

'How close to here have they come?'

'Nothing we know of since the massacre. You must have heard about that?'

'I discovered it.'

'What?' gasped Chisholm.

'I arrived at the farm after the aborigines left.'

'Hell, I didn't know. Are you the fella who saved the baby?'

Jonathon nodded and pointed to James playing with Moses. 'That's him with my brother-in-law.'

'Well, good on you, bloody well done.'

'Come and have some food and I'd ask you to play down or not even mention these attacks on farms.'

'Understood,' said the visitor and they went to the cottage.


Over lunch, Cate wanted the truth. 'Why are you here, Mr Chisolm?'

Enjoying the best fried eggs and potatoes he'd ever tasted, he replied. Jonathon held his breath. 'The Governor wants a survey of all the farms in the district, ma'am. How many people, size of flocks, state of buildings, et cetera.'

She seemed to accept his reply then asked a question.

'Have there been more clashes between farmers and aborigines?'

He shook his head. 'Only minor skirmishes. We think they've finally accepted good folk like you and your family.'

She didn't follow up but nor did she believe he told the truth or at least not the whole truth. Chisolm took his leave.

That night, in bed, Cate raised the subject with Jonathon.

'How much danger are we in?'

'We're fine, my darling girl. You take it easy and have your baby and ...'

'*My* baby? I didn't get pregnant on my own, Mr Sweeping.'

She raised the topic of the delivery. He declared it would be fine having the baby here on the farm. She wanted to say, "How on Earth would you know? You're a man."

He explained how many lambs and piglets he'd delivered. 'It'll be a piece of cake, Mrs Sweeping. Leave it all to me.'

Cate worried even more. She was on hand when Annie had little Hannah. The screaming—yes it was screaming—Annie made during the hours—yes, hours—it took to give birth, made Cate seriously want to be near people with experience in seeing a baby born.

'I want to say something,' she whispered, 'and I don't want you to interrupt me.' She paused and the silence lingered.

'You want to have the baby in Hobart Town, don't you?' he said.

Stunned, she lay there and, in silence, wept. His kindness and perception were never far from the surface.

He drew her close. 'We'll go this week but James will have to stay and look after the animals.'

'Will he be all right?'

'Of course and we'll have to take Moses.'

She fell silent. Her brother was nearly 17 and knew more about farming than many twice his age. The thought of him being alone on this isolated farm with aborigines still attacking settlers, stealing supplies, and even killing people, filled her with dread. Leaving him alone sent a chill through her body.

'Go to sleep,' he said and kissed her hair. 'Good night little Master Sweeping,' he added and that at least brought a smile to her lips.


They told James about Cate having the baby in Hobart Town. It was hard to pick his reaction.

'I'll take Cate and little Moses and they'll stay there till she has the baby. I'll come back as soon as she's settled.'

'Take your time,' he said. 'I'll have the dogs and we'll be fine.'

Out in the paddocks the day before they were to leave, Jonathon took his brother-in-law aside. 'Listen to me, Jimmy. If you have sight of aborigines, do not try and engage them; ever. Take the rifle and dogs and hide in the bush. If they steal supplies, let them. They won't stay. But you are not to challenge them, and God forbid you would even *think* about fighting them. Do you understand?'

James stared at his serious brother-in-law and nodded. 'Sure but when did we last see an aborigine in this area?'

There was no mention of the massacre on the nearby farm.

Jonathon tried to reassure Cate he'd given her brother strict instructions and a plan to avoid contact with any aborigines. She thanked him but found it hard to worry about anything when her waters seemed ready to break.

She sat on folded blankets on the cart to lessen jolts from the rough tracks. Jonathon hitched his second horse, Queenie, to the rear of the cart. Cate waved to her waving brother as they set off hoping they'd meet again next week.

The dogs ran around James celebrating his presence. He went inside and found ham. All three scoffed it with glee.

Jonathon didn't need to ask if Cate could stay with the McFarlanes. He held Moses' hand as Andrew helped Cate inside. Annie had found a new maid, Flo, to help with the McFarlane's daughter, Hannah.

With his family settled, Jonathon paid a fleeting visit to Mrs Hodgson and her boarder then went into town to visit a doctor. The gentleman agreed to call on Cate tomorrow and recommended a midwife, Mrs Cuddy. Andrew McFarlane, under instructions from his wife, had already sent their new maid Flo, to call on the woman.

Jonathon decided to stay overnight. Mrs Hodgson was delighted to see him. He insisted on paying and she insisted on refusing. She won. He was up early and knocked on the back door of the vicarage.

Flo opened it and fairly yelled. 'It's a boy!'

The next few minutes were a blur. Andrew rushed out and pumped Jonathon's hand. Moses became excited seeing his father.

Annie appeared with tears running free and kissed the new father. The midwife arrived, grinning, exposing her missing teeth.

'Mother and little one are doin' well, sir.'

Eventually he entered the bedroom and saw his wife sitting up in bed holding a mess of brown hair sticking out of a small blanket.

Cate looked at her husband. 'You were right again, Mr Sweeping. It's a boy.'

He approached gently, kissed her and looked at the baby. Its eyes were locked tight. 'He has my eyes,' he said and kissed the baby's head.

'I have a favour to ask, Jonathon.' He looked at her serious face. 'I want you to go home, now, right now.'

He understood. Again he kissed her and the baby and went to say goodbye to the vicar and his wife. He gave Moses a kiss, distracted him, and then slipped outside. The cart was parked in the back yard. He saddled Queenie, mounted the horse and trotted away. Clear of the town he urged her on. If the cart took four hours, riding Queenie, he'd be home in half the time; less.

He kept thinking about his life, from child convict to gentleman farmer with a wife and now two sons. James would be tickled pink to have a second nephew.

Queenie didn't need guidance. She knew the track to the farm and Jonathon urged her on. As he neared the cottage, he stood in the stirrups scanning the land for James. Nothing.

The dogs came alive and bounded towards him, shouting their welcome. Their noise would rouse James. No James. *Where is he?*

Jonathon dismounted, unsaddled the horse and yelled. 'James! Where are you?'

The calls went unheeded. He patted the dogs to settle them but kept looking. His heart went cold. His mind played nasty tricks.

*I've left my wife's brother alone and he's been attacked and killed. It's me; I've as good as killed my darling young brother-in-law.*

He ran to the cottage. The back door was open. He suffered a flashback to the house where the mother and daughter were inside, murdered. He yelled and found no-one. Back to the paddocks he went, still calling.

Now his breathing laboured. He couldn't yell as he choked. Tears appeared. Only then did he take note of the dogs. They were barking and jumping and moving back and forth towards the bush.

'Oh God, no, please,' he gasped and headed after the dogs. Jonathon knew he could handle death but telling his wife her brother was dead would be impossible. Her joy at giving birth would be shattered at the terrible news about her only sibling, the last of her family.

Jonathon entered the bush with the dogs leading the way.

*Why doesn't James reply? If he's here, and the dogs say he is, why doesn't he respond?*

The bush was thick, virgin bush, unexplored for millennia. Tall trees, massive trees surrounded by thick undergrowth. He yelled again and followed the dogs. They stopped behind a solid eucalypt.

Blinking back tears, Jonathon moved around the trunk and saw James. On the ground in a foetal position, his face screaming pain. Jonathon knelt and touched the body. It recoiled.

*Oh dear God, he's alive. But is he injured?*

'James, it's me. Are you hurt?'

The boy blubbed. 'I killed a man.'

'What man? Where is he?'

'They took him away.'

Jonathon glanced around and saw the rifle nearby. He helped James to stand, picked up the weapon and half carried him back to the cottage. The dogs were overjoyed.

# Chapter 41

James lay on the bed in the cottage. He sipped water then fell back. Jonathon's emotions went from despair to elation to deep concern.

'You're safe, Jimmy. Cate has a lovely boy and will be home soon. I'm here. We're all safe.'

The patient wept in silence. Jonathon wanted to help but reckoned talking about the attack might cause even more distress.

'I'll make lunch. You rest. I'll be back.' Knowing how meticulous the young man was, Jonathon threw in a schoolmaster-like question. 'Have you fed the animals?'

It worked. Always keen to please, James sat up and assured the "boss" he'd done his duty. 'I have, Jonathon, the hens, the pigs and the ...'

Jonathon laughed at the animal-lover. 'And the wombat?'

It did work as James struggled to prevent a small smile. Jonathon beckoned. 'Come on, let's have a bite to eat.'

They ate outside and James explained the incident.

'I was in with the pigs when these aborigines, about 10 I think, appeared out of the bush. I did as you said and hid. They went into the house and the shed and took food. They were leaving when one saw me hiding. He yelled and the others approached. One raised a spear so, without thinking, I pointed the rifle and fired. I only wanted to scare them but I think I hit the man holding the spear. The others carried him away and they all fled.'

James was back being deeply troubled. 'Jonathon, I killed a man.'

'You don't know that and if you hadn't fired, you may well be dead.' He paused and tried to lighten his sadness. 'Although you being dead with the pigs would have meant they'd have dined in style.'

James looked confused then understood and this time tried to grin. Jonathon described the new baby but when the subject was exhausted, James resumed talking about his painful experience.

'What I don't understand is why the blacks are so aggressive. What have we ever done to them?'

Jonathon studied his brother-in-law and decided he was genuine; ignorant but sincere.

'We stole their land.'

That's all he said and James wanted an explanation and to ask questions. Before he could speak, Jonathon continued.

'The aborigines were here in Van Diemen's land, who knows, for a long, long time before we Europeans arrived. They lived their lives catching fish, killing kangaroos and other animals, picking wild fruit, picking wild grasses to make their own flour to bake their own bread, and raised their families. They lived here. This was their home.

'We arrived and decided their laws didn't exist or ours were better or superior, and so we simply claimed the land for ourselves. "It's now our land," we said and built wherever we liked.'

He gestured to their farm. 'We built this,' then said what he believed.

'The aborigines walked across this land to hunt and find food and, in a trice there were fences herding sheep and cattle on what was their land for, God only knows, thousands of years. We arrived and stole their land.'

'But we were the first Europeans.'

'But not the first humans.' James wanted to understand. 'Let's pretend a ship with aborigines arrived in England, made a camp on someone's farm and claimed it was their land.'

'That wouldn't be allowed.'

'But that's what we did here.'

James argued. 'But they're killing settlers. They nearly killed me.'

'James, they're fighting back. European settlers, soldiers, sealers and convicts have shot and killed aborigines. Many aboriginal girls and women have been kidnapped, raped and even murdered by our people, by Europeans. What would you expect the natives to do? Run away and hide? They're defending their families and doing it with spears against our guns. They're outnumbered with inferior weapons but fight because their lifestyle and lives are being destroyed. What would you do if you were them?'

James breathed slowly. His experience with shooting a man troubled him deeply. Hearing certain home truths made it worse.

'What's going to happen?'

Jonathon shrugged. 'It's becoming a war and in war, usually one side wins and the other is defeated, sometimes destroyed. Unless there's a peace treaty, a lot more people are going to die.'

It was a sobering thought. Jonathon made a request.

'Listen Jimmy, I think it best we don't tell Cate anything about your business with the aborigines. She's got two little boys to raise now and I don't want to upset her or them. Let's keep this incident between the two of us. Do you agree?'

James nodded. 'I won't say a thing. And I'll ask the dogs to say nowt as well.' He grinned and Jonathon caught the grinning routine.

The next few days took forever. Jonathon worried about Cate and the baby longing to know how they were. James moped around doing his work still depressed about having shot a person. Hearing a detailed explanation about blacks and whites killing each other and what had been done to the aborigines only deepened his misery.

After three days, Jonathon decided.

'We'll go into Hobart tomorrow and fetch Cate and the baby. James looked scared. 'I said we. You're coming too.'

The young man's face changed. 'Thanks,' he said and meant it.

'We'll leave the dogs and ride Queenie. We'll leave before dawn so we don't have to stay the night.'

They set off before dawn. James fed the hens and pigs telling them he'd be back before long and to not misbehave. He was like that.

The dogs were ordered to remain. They looked sad but trusted their humans implicitly.

Queenie trotted well and they made good progress. Jonathon stopped once to collect as many wild flowers as he could find. James hopped down curious. 'What's happening?'

'I made this trip a year or more back when I proposed to your sister. I gave her a huge bunch of wild flowers, and she said, "Yes." I reckon a new baby deserves another bunch. What do you think?'

'So flowers are the way to impress a girl?'

'It worked for me,' replied a grinning Jonathon and appointed his brother-in-law the florist.

They reached Hobart Town well before luncheon wanting to get going. Annie insisted they stay for a meal. Jonathon's flowers did the trick again only this time Cate insisted they stay with the hostess.

Moses couldn't decide which man he wanted to hug first. He loved his Dad but Uncle Jimmy made him laugh.

The new mum looked radiant and Jonathon couldn't get over how beautiful she looked. The as yet unnamed baby was fast asleep and according to all, behaved perfectly most of the time.

'I thought new mothers were supposed to look tired and worn out,' he said to his wife. 'Why is it you look wonderful?' She purred. 'James and I are desperate to get you home so we can eat decent food again.'

James protested claiming his cooking was better than good and the laughter was such, little Mr No Name woke and started crying.

Andrew McFarlane interrupted. 'Before you run away back to the wilderness, it behoves me to ask about your son being christened.'

'Yes, Jonathon,' said Cate. 'Please let's do it before we go.'

Jonathon went to complain. He'd given no thought to such an occasion. 'But a church service will take forever.'

'Not in our sitting room it won't,' said Annie smiling.

'We can have Annie and James as godparents,' added Cate, 'and all we need do is agree on a name. I like Edward.'

'So do I,' said James. 'Our father would be so proud.'

Jonathon liked the name, and with all the adults urging him to get a move on, he smiled.

'Eddie it is,' he said and the mood lifted.

Not every new-born is christened in a parlour but all were sure God didn't insist on a particular building. Edward James Sweeping got his head wet just before tucker time.

Everyone except Cate, who was feeding the wee lad, then enjoyed luncheon and while James and Annie and new maid Flo helped Cate with her growing family, Jonathon and Andrew took a stroll in the garden.

'I'm not sure what you've heard, Jonathon, but reports of more violence on the farms keep arriving here every week.'

'Don't say a word of this to anyone but when I was here with Cate before the baby came, James was attacked by blacks.'

'What?' gasped Andrew, his face twisting with alarm.

'He hid, they found him and he claims he shot a man who was carried away.'

'So James wasn't hurt?'

'His mind took a beating. He's a sensitive lad and shooting another human made him sick.'

'I don't mind telling you, Jonathon, I'm worried. It's like a war and tit for tat killings won't stop unless something major happens.'

'Like what?'

Andrew shrugged. 'A peace accord is made or until we kill all the blacks.'

'Kill all the blacks? *All* of them? Are you serious?'

Andrew struggled to discuss the situation. 'I've been asked to join an Aborigine Committee which is to advise Governor Arthur. I'm torn because I fear the anti-aboriginal members want to push for harsh and punitive action.'

'You have to join, sir, if nothing else to try and stop the attacks.'

Andrew agreed. 'I think you're right. Now, are you okay on the farm? Do you have a plan if there is an attack?'

Jonathon hated thinking about the situation. Having discovered Moses as the sole survivor of an attack, he knew what could happen.

'We'll be okay and thanks for your concern.'

'I'll try and have the military do more patrols in your area.' They shook hands. 'Now, let's get you and your ever expanding family on the road.'

The trip home was slow. Nursing the baby, Cate sat next to Jonathon, and little Moses thought he was Christmas riding with Uncle Jimmy on Queenie. En route the married couple discussed life with their now larger family.

'Having the two boys sleeping in our room might be okay for a while, Jonathon, but having another bedroom would be better sooner rather than later.' He nodded. 'And especially if the family keeps growing.'

His head snapped around. 'Pardon?'

'You haven't forgotten what to do have you?'

He snorted a suppressed laugh and leant across and kissed her cheek. Little Eddie maintained his status as a perfect passenger.

Jonathon avoided any mention of the incident with James and the aborigines. It was getting dark when they arrived. Both men scanned the property looking for any intruders or damage to the buildings.

All seemed normal. The two canines were trying to outdo one another in giving the best welcome-home greeting.

James sorted the horses, fed the dogs and the animals while Jonathon helped his wife, Moses and their new-born son. It was an interesting first night.

Eddie's crying in the wee small hours woke Moses and both parents began the first of many nights of interrupted sleep. As Jonathon helped Moses, he spoke to his wife feeding the baby.

'I see what you mean about a second bedroom.'


James helped the former sweep turned carpenter as the brothers-in-law worked at building an extension. They were splitting timber when a cart came along the track. A man and two women were aboard.

Cate came out with the baby and everyone met everyone.

'My name's Gallagher,' said the man. 'This is my wife and daughter.' The unnamed females were Eleanor and Chloe.

Jonathon introduced his family giving each a name, even the youngest. Gallagher continued.

'We've taken over the farm where the previous family was killed,' said the neighbour.

'Not all the family,' corrected Cate. 'My husband rescued this little boy.' She pulled Moses close. 'And we'd appreciate you not talking about the incident, especially in front of the child.'

Gallagher didn't like the rebuke. His female family members remained mute.

'I wanted to meet you folks to learn what tactics or plans you have when those crazy blacks decide to attack.'

James wanted to be sick. Jonathon wanted to explode.

'Why don't your wife and daughter go inside for refreshments while you and I discuss the matter in the paddock?'

Gallagher copped another rebuke.

'Come on ladies,' said Cate. 'I've baked scones.'

The women went inside. Jonathon didn't want James in on the conversation only because it might reignite his depression. 'Jimmy, can you take Moses to find the wombat?' Uncle and nephew departed.

In the paddock, Gallagher counted Sweeping sheep. He wished he had a flock even half that size.

'So what's your plan?' he asked.

Jonathon worried; his neighbour's anger was out on show. Shoot first and take no prisoners being his preferred and only option.

'I've had first-hand experience with the blacks. I've even been in one of their camps.'

'They captured you?' hissed a fuming Gallagher.

'They invited me and gave me food and shelter then guided me safely back home.'

Gallagher was lost for words. 'What about the massacres?'

'Ours or theirs?'

Gallagher hit back. 'You already know they've murdered settlers like us.'

'As we've done the same to them, arguably worse.'

This conversation was not going well. Gallagher wanted a united front against the people he believed were savages.

'So you're not going to help me protect my family?'

'If I can help I will, of course I will. But if you're attacked, by the time you get word to me, the aborigines will be long gone. Even if you travel through the bush, it'll take you an hour or more to get here.'

Gallagher stared at Jonathon. 'Are you a free settler like me?'

'I'm free now but I arrived in chains.' His face remained expressionless. 'I'm a former convict.'

Gallagher fumed. He took off back to the house, called his womenfolk who obeyed as if slaves. James and Moses appeared having looked in vain for the wombat. James was close to the Gallagher cart and offered a hand to the daughter. She accepted his kind gesture and their eyes met for a fleeting moment. With both females on board, the driver gave his horse a whack and it turned and the party departed with not one human giving a backward glance.

Jonathon and Cate exchanged looks with raised eyebrows, and the carpentry chums resumed work.

# Chapter 42

The months rolled by. Christmas came and went. The New Year meant heat and sunshine in Van Diemen's Land. On the peace front, there was no peace. Europeans launched deadly attacks on aborigines who returned fire using spears and clubs. Governor Arthur came under enormous pressure. Local newspapers inflamed the situation.

"Notoriously savage" was one description of the aborigines in Van Diemen's Land. City folk demanded action believing sincerely they were superior humans, and the heroic settlers were being attacked without reason. What was worse, the colony depended on the food produced by the farmers. Kill them and the townsfolk die.

Out in the bush, the Sweeping farm offered accommodation for a growing family with *growing* the operative word.

With their sons asleep in their own room, Cate waited till her husband joined her in bed before whispering in the dark. 'Mr Sweeping, I am with child again.'

He lit a candle with fumbling fingers then looked at her face.

'How did that happen?' he asked with mock indignation.

Her grin set off his grin and they embraced.

'Perhaps you could build another bedroom before the baby arrives.'

'What's wrong with the one I've just built?'

'You can't put your daughter in with two rowdy boys.'

'Oh, so it's a girl is it? You said that last time.'

'And I don't want you taking me into Hobart.'

'What?'

'When I'm getting close, go in for supplies and fetch Mrs Cuddy the midwife who helped me with Edward.'

She called their son Edward but Jonathon stuck with Eddie.

They both slept well thinking about their growing family in the wilds of Van Diemen's Land. In the morning, James, Moses and toddler Edward were excited when told the news.

The Sweeping clan never saw or heard any aborigine as the weeks and months drifted by. Another bedroom was added and Jonathon's animal husbandry kept improving. James acquired so much experience he could easily have taken over from his brother-in-law. Two former Englishmen were now proficient farmers in a British colony. Cate reckoned she was due in a week or two.

Jonathon gave James instructions regarding any unwanted visitors, kissed his wife and children, and hitching Queenie to the cart, left for Hobart Town and the midwife. He went straight to her house. She was available and would be collected in an hour.

He purchased supplies, called in on Mrs Hodgson and Arnold Walker, and then made a visit to the McFarlane residence. Their daughter, Hannah, was up and about. They'd heard about Cate's latest pregnancy but the Sweepings didn't know Annie was expecting her second. Living in the bush without much of or any mail service meant news took an eternity to arrive, if at all.

'Congratulations, that's wonderful news,' beamed Jonathon. 'Cate will be delighted.' He enjoyed a light meal and kissed Annie as Andrew walked him to the cart.

'It's grim news, Jonathon.'

His face creased with worry. 'What's happened?'

'I'm on this committee dealing with the aborigines, and there are more reports of clashes with casualties on both sides. The Governor is talking about declaring martial law.'

Jonathon hesitated. 'I don't understand.'

'It's civil law replaced by military law. In this case, the Governor would declare aborigines need permission to travel in certain parts of the island, and if caught breaking the law, they'll be arrested.'

'But how will they know these laws? They don't even speak let alone read English.'

'Illustrated posters will be used with drawings of Europeans and Aborigines. The posters will appear in places on trees.'

Jonathon wanted to laugh. His sarcasm exploded. 'Why not put the posters in newspapers and have them delivered to all the camps?'

'I know, I know it sounds unfair.'

'Unfair? It's white men trying to justify their brutal behaviour.'

'And I'm sorry to say it gets worse. There may be a law which will see Europeans paid if they arrest an aborigine.'

Jonathon's face turned red. 'I get paid to capture an aborigine?'

'Hopefully more than one; they'll want as many as they can get.'

'You're making this up.'

'I wish I were.'

'The Governor is paying Europeans to murder aborigines?'

'Well the wording will not permit murder but if you claim the aborigine threatened you, then your word, a white man's word, is certain to be accepted. The document will say you are entitled to defend yourself.'

Jonathon thought about his neighbour, Mr Gallagher. That man and a gun equalled carnage.

'But the whites who hate the blacks will take this as permission to slaughter them.'

Andrew grimaced. 'Being in the bush with no authorities, no witnesses …' He shrugged. 'You of all people know what can happen.'

They walked to the cart, said their sombre goodbyes and Jonathon went to collect Mrs Cuddy, the midwife.

The trip home was uneventful with Jonathon wondering about life in the colony. Arrive, claim land, and kill the people living there.

*Do the English lawmakers know about this? Do they care?*

They rounded a bend of the track and stopped as two women were walking ahead of them. They heard the cart and turned. Jonathon knew them and stopped.

'Mrs Gallagher, Miss Gallagher, what are you doing out here alone in the bush?'

'We're going home,' said the wife. 'We were travelling when my husband saw aborigines and set off to deal with them. He told us to go home and wait there.'

'You might be safer at my farm. Oh, this is Mrs Cuddy, the midwife.' The women nodded.

'Is your wife having a baby?' asked Mrs Gallagher.

'She is. Please climb on the cart and we'll call at your farm. You can leave a note for Mr Gallagher and he can come and collect you.'

The daughter persuaded her mother. 'I think we should, Mother.'

Mrs Gallagher agreed. She didn't feel safe here on the track. She didn't feel safe anywhere, even in her own home. The women climbed on the cart and Jonathon turned off for the Gallagher farm, hating the thought of revisiting the scene of the massacre.

Mrs Gallagher went inside, wrote a note and returned. They set off and finally arrived at the Sweeping home. The dogs raced to greet them, then James carrying Edward, and Moses followed. Jonathon helped the midwife down and led her inside. He called.

'We're home my dear and Mrs Cuddy is here.'

The midwife went to the patient. Jonathon spoke. 'James, bring the ladies inside and offer them a cup of tea.'

Mrs Gallagher interrupted. 'Please, Mr Sweeping. We'll wait here till your wife is attended to. We're fine. You go, please.'

Jonathon thanked the Gallagher ladies. 'Jimmy, please look after our guests and the boys. I'll be right back.'

Jonathon joined his wife who looked decidedly pregnant. 'I thought you were never coming,' said Cate, now teary.

'We're all here, my darling girl. And the Gallagher ladies are here too waiting for Mr Gallagher.' Cate's worried face became more worried. 'It's all right. They were out on the track and I gave them a lift. Now, you relax and let me do the worrying.'

If there had been anything to hand, Cate would have thrown it.

Jonathon remembered being a child in London when his sister was born. He was all of six at the time and still remembered his mother's cries.

'Let's have a look, Missus,' said Mrs Cuddy.

That sounded too hard for the father. 'I'll check on our visitors my dear, and be right back.' The coward departed. Outside, he asked Mrs Gallagher if she'd be kind enough to sit with his wife. She happily agreed.

James kept one eye on the boys and the other on Miss Gallagher who seemed to enjoy playing with Moses and Edward.

Jonathon announced he would make tea. His sons were enjoying their new nanny.

'They're very well behaved, Mr Sweeping,' she said.

'Chloe's a brilliant babysitter,' added James. 'You and Cate should employ her once the new baby arrives.'

That stopped the conversation. Jonathon looked at his brother-in-law wondering what had happened, recovered and went to make tea. After a while he popped into the bedroom to be told to go away.

Darkness arrived and lamps were lit with still no news on the baby front. The dogs came alive and Jonathon went outside. A furious Seamus Gallagher drove his cart into the yard, and leapt down not caring about his horse.

'Where are they?' he thundered.

'Good evening, Mr Gallagher. Your wife and daughter are safe inside.'

Jonathon's calm and polite demeanour meant nothing to the irate farmer. 'I can look after my own family.' He bellowed towards the house. 'Come on, we're leaving.'

James came outside. Jonathon decided to hit back. 'I'll thank you to lower your voice, sir. My wife is about to give birth.'

The news flattened Gallagher a little. Then he was distracted by sounds from his cart. He walked to it and Jonathon followed. In the subtle moonlight you could see two aborigines, tied securely.

'Shut up,' snarled Gallagher and the prisoners fell silent.

'What this?' asked Jonathon, alarmed.

'I caught these bastards hiding in the bush ready to attack me.'

'With their bare hands?' asked Jonathon.

'They surrendered as soon as they saw my rifle.'

'What are you going to do with them?'

'There's a rumour around we'll get five pounds for each savage we catch.'

'What will happen to them?'

'Who cares? I don't give a shit. The Governor wants 'em gone, I want 'em gone, and I'll have the cash, thank you very much.'

Jonathon wanted to release the men but knew he'd have to fight his neighbour first. He clenched his fists and planted his feet.

'Seamus,' called his wife from the doorway. 'We need to wait. Mrs Sweeping's having a baby.'

Gallagher seethed. He hated not being in control. He set off for the house to physically eject his wife and daughter. Jonathon whispered to James then followed the bully inside.

'Right you two,' snarled Gallagher, 'out!'

The women rose and refused to defy him. As they headed for the door, Cate gave her best and loudest scream, the midwife shouted and Jonathon brushed past everyone to race to the bedroom.

The midwife handed the infant to the mother and the father stared in wonderment and pride. The baby howled. The mother smiled.

'You've done it again, Mr Sweeping,' she said. 'You now have three sons.'

'Out you go,' fussed the midwife pushing him into the kitchen.

'It's a boy,' said Jonathon and the female Gallaghers smiled, purred even and wanted to clap.

The male Gallagher exerted his control. 'Right, now you know, we're going. Get on the cart.'

The women left waving to the little Sweeping boys. Jonathon followed. Gallagher led and then exploded. He stared at his empty cart, screamed his fury and ran around looking for his cargo.

'They've gone,' he fumed and accused Jonathon. 'You untied them, you bastard.'

'I was inside with you as my wife gave birth. We all were.' He lied.

Gallagher thought the claim might be true. He knew trying to find the aborigines in daylight would be nigh on impossible; at night it *was* impossible. He jumped on his cart, snapped at the females who joined him. He pulled hard on the reins causing the horse to be alarmed, and drove away.

James appeared from the shadows. 'They spoke some English,' he said. 'As they fled, the older aboriginal said, "Thank you, Gubbah".'

'Good man,' said Jonathon, 'and your reward is another nephew.'

After the excitement of the new baby settled, and Mrs Cuddy retired, Jonathon sat on the bed and looked at his wife feeding the latest member of the family.

'We haven't discussed a name,' he said. 'I know you were keen on Beth and Daphne but I think it would be cruel to call the lad Doris.'

'Stop it,' whispered Cate. 'I'm glad it's a boy because there's one name I have in mind.'

'Oh yes?'

'It's Jonathon.'

The father sighed. 'You can't name him Jonathon. You'll call one of us in from the paddock, and we won't know who you mean.'

'Then he'll be Jon and you can be ... what's your name again?

He looked at his grinning wife and was never so happy.

# Chapter 43

Three sons under four equals joy, feeding frenzies and a lot of bottom wiping. The brothers-in-law worked outside almost as hard as did the mother/cook/teacher/cleaner inside. The men bred more sheep and pigs, operated the best vegetable patch in the valley, and with the apple trees planted by the Walkers now weighed down with fruit, the Sweeping family ate healthy, hearty meals. That was the good news.

Elsewhere things became worse. The Van Diemen's Land War, because that's what it was, a war, didn't have one huge battlefield with massed forces facing off in a grand Waterloo-type finale. It was a string of mini wars, skirmishes with depravity most foul.

Such conflict became inevitable. Land was settled, meaning the aborigines could no longer hunt where once they hunted. With their food supply reduced, starvation beckoned. To survive, they raided farms to get supplies. Farmers protested promising revenge.

Away from the towns, sex-starved European males went hunting for black females in order to fornicate. This enraged aboriginal men. Their women suffered appalling crimes being used and abused. Some were tortured, some murdered. Justice; what's that? Revenge was all that remained for the original inhabitants.

This Van Diemen's Land War overflowed with war crimes, despair and death. Observers would later invoke the word genocide.

It can be said to have started in 1804 at Risdon Cove when some 300 aboriginal men, women and children were driving a mob of kangaroos, their food supply. A convict reported the unarmed natives to soldiers who arrived with weapons. Despite offering no threat to the military, the soldiers opened fire and slaughtered the defenceless blacks. The exact number of casualties is not known.

Brutal incidents occurred away from prying eyes. Few, if any, witnessed the atrocities. And news took time to reach the authorities and the newspapers. It was a guerilla war being fought in secret.

Letters between the Colonial Office in London and Governor Arthur in Van Diemen's Land took forever to cross the seas. Decisions made in one country were not received elsewhere for months.

But still the anger sizzled and attacks continued which led to revenge attacks. It became a tit for tat killing spree.

Fear became widespread. Imagine living in the bush as did the Sweeping family or a nearby tribe of aboriginals. There were no rules of warfare. There were no warnings of an attack.

The aborigines almost always attacked by day. Settlers might hear an unusual sound in the bush. Hearts beat faster, guns were grabbed.

The Europeans generally attacked at night. The quality of mercy was seriously strained. Europeans would look for a fire glow at night then send a scout to survey the site. He'd walk in socks or bare feet to maintain silence and secrecy.

Then the troops would gather and, on a signal, open fire without warning. No discrimination between male and female, adult or child. Survivors were lucky if they bled to death sooner rather than later.

Farmers built huts to store goods—food, blankets, grain, tools. They would arrive at the store to find it empty or seriously depleted. Food and blankets were prized items for aborigines.

This was too much for the hard-working settlers. Their protests hammered the Governor. The Black War, the Van Diemen's War galloped to its fearful climax.

Chloe Gallagher grew into a lovely young woman who sadly lived on a desert island. An only child with a brute of a father and a battered wife of a mother, Chloe had vague and incomplete knowledge of life in general and human sexuality in particular and worse, no-one to speak to. Loneliness haunted her. A trip to Hobart Town meant she was chained to her mother and guarded by her father. Alone in bed at night she pondered her future.

*I will live here until my parents die. Then what?*

As the conflict between white and black increased, her father grew more unstable. He drank heavily, abused his wife and threatened his daughter. At first Chloe sensed great sadness for her mother although this sadness turned to disrespect believing her mother lacked a backbone in not standing up to her husband, the bully.

Life ebbed away on the Gallagher farm. It's as if a curse settled on the property after the massacre involving the family of wee Moses. Hope, if ever it lived here, fled to peaceful climes.

The idea of escaping slipped inside Chloe's mind. *Where will I go? How will I travel? What will happen if I am caught?*

She spent time outdoors. Feeding the hens became a legitimate excuse. Going for walks saved her sanity. Her father worked with his sheep and cattle and her mother ignored the fact her girl disappeared.

One afternoon Chloe reached the end of the western boundary and stared at the bush. Some trees tickled the clouds. She remembered the directions when they reached the end of their drive. Turn right for Hobart Town; turn left for the Sweeping farm.

Thinking about her idea took seconds. She climbed the fence and walked into the bush. A large fern blocked her way. Stepping around it she trod on a fallen branch, lost her footing and fell. Throwing out her hands she cut both on the spiky vegetation. It was easy to cry.

*Go back* shouted the voice in her head. She pictured her brutish father, and imagined her miserable future living with the tyrant. Up she stood and pressed ahead. Where was she heading? Hobart Town? Battling the bush was tough and her slim build copped a beating. Still she moved until an obstacle appeared and she knew all hope was lost.

The river was deep with a steady current. Swimming was a foreign activity to her. She sat on the bank and cried again. Seeing her like this would enrage her father and devastate her mother. Time passed and staying here in the dark would be terrifying; no, more terrifying.

She heard a sound behind her. Turning meant her fear exploded. Something headed in her direction. It was a creature she'd never seen; too big for a snake and too low for a dog. On its face was a huge bill like a duck. It moved low to the ground and swayed as it headed towards the river, making no sound other than disturbing the bush.

Chloe froze. The creature waddled or ran and loomed closer. About ten yards from the young woman, it veered to its right making straight for the human. Chloe panicked and leapt into the river to escape. The creature joined her, sliding into the river causing Chloe's panic to erupt. She faced the other bank and smashed the water with every ounce of energy in her body.

As a style of swimming, it was indescribable. As a method of reaching the other bank, it worked. She grasped vegetation, dragged herself out of the water, then turned back to see if the monster followed her.

It hadn't. It disappeared. Underwater, the giant and temporarily blind platypus burrowed its bill into the river bed hunting for food.

James inspected sheep and fencing in the far paddock. The afternoon sun dropped below the tree line and hunger pains kicked in. One of his sister's lamb stews with potatoes and carrots grown on their farm meant his stomach made noises. He was alone and called the dogs.

They ignored him and ran away. He called again. They barked. He followed them and stopped at the fence. It took him a few seconds to comprehend the reason the dogs reacted.

He leapt the fence and ran into the bush. A bedraggled, bleeding and soaked Chloe Gallagher lay exhausted beside a tree.

'Miss Gallagher,' he gasped and knelt to help.

She tried desperately to speak. 'I've run away,' she said and fell unconscious.

James put his arms around and under her and lifted. She was light and limp. He struggled through the bush and climbed the fence. The dogs ran ahead announcing the news.

Through the paddock they went. En route, James examined the sleeping beauty. Despite her bush adventure, he thought she looked beautiful. Her wet clothes clung to her body and he found himself not always staring at her face.

Once they reached the back yard, James called.

'Help! I need help!'

Jonathon flew out of the house with two of his sons in various stages of running and the third crawling. Cate appeared and picked up Jonathon Junior as she joined the crowd.

'It's Chloe,' said James, puffing.

Jonathon took the girl and carried her inside, the crowd of humans and dogs in pursuit. In the bedroom, Cate took control.

'She needs to get out of those wet clothes.' The adult males stood there thinking a variety of thoughts. 'Out,' ordered Cate. 'Both of you, out! And make the tea.'

They disappeared, the door was closed and when it opened, Cate appeared with an arm around Chloe who wore one of Cate's dresses.

'Where's the tea?' asked Cate. James hurried to pour it. 'Honestly, you men.' She guided the young woman. 'By the fire, Chloe, sit here and get warm.' She spoke to James. 'Put some rum in her cup.'

They fussed over the visitor. Three little boys gazed in wonder. Two *big* boys gazed in wonder.

'I'm so sorry,' said Chloe feeling ashamed.

The others protested. 'Stop that,' said Cate. You have nothing to apologise for. You can stay here for as long as you like.' She looked at her husband and brother. 'Can't she?'

What a stupid question. Both men agreed with élan.

'James, check the beds in the boys' room. Put Jon in with Edward and Moses.' He fled with nephews in trail. She called. 'And get more blankets from the cupboard.'

Mr and Mrs Sweeping waited for Chloe to speak. She sensed an explanation was required.

'I've run away. My parents don't know where I am.' She begged. 'Please don't make me go back. My father bullies me and my mother.'

'You can stay, Miss Gallagher. You're safe here. There are five fit and able males to protect you,' said Jonathon.

Three of the fit and able males came back with curious faces and Chloe smiled at them. Their combined ages would soon reach 9. This was the warmest and best feeling she'd enjoyed in ages.

'Your parents will be worried, Chloe,' said Cate.

Sadness returned with a rush.

'I know but I'm scared I'll be locked in my room and won't ever be allowed into town again.'

Jonathon worried aloud. 'Right now your parents will be wandering everywhere calling your name. They'll think you've been kidnapped by aborigines or are lost in the bush with wild animals.' He paused. 'I should go and tell them you're safe and well.'

Chloe's depression grew. 'But that'll bring my parents here and I'll be taken home by force. You don't know my father.'

She was wrong there. They all knew the ogre, Gallagher.

'You won't be taken anywhere,' said Jonathon. 'Your father won't even come here if I tell him a story.' Both women looked at him. 'I'll tell him I was in town and heard you're living with a family in Hobart, and are happy and want to stay there.'

That suggestion sounded possible and certainly nicer.

'Would you do that?' she asked.

He looked at his wife and her eyes told him to go ahead.

'I'll leave in the morning pretending I've come back from Hobart. I'll call in at your farm and tell them the news.'

Chloe was out of her chair and hugging Jonathon. James entered and suffered an emotional storm. *Why is Jonathon hugging my girl?*

Gallagher came in from the paddock on his farm. 'Where's Chloe?'

'I don't know, I haven't seen her,' said his wife.

He snarled. 'What do you mean, you don't know?'

'I haven't seen her since lunch.'

The brute seethed. At the back door he bellowed. 'Chloe, where are you?' The silence enraged him. He wandered outside continuing to call. Inside their cottage, Eleanor despaired. Which was worse; her daughter missing or her husband enraged?

No response meant Gallagher's blood boiled. He couldn't believe his daughter would defy him and run away. She must have been kidnapped by those filthy savages.

Being unable to hit back at daughter or aborigine, he took it out on his wife, blaming her for their missing child. Eleanor cowered in fear, his brutality appalling. What could she do, and who would help her out here alone in the wilderness?

His anger subsided and he collapsed on the bed. She sat in the darkness and contemplated killing herself. She didn't know how. Her husband's firearms were foreign to her. She couldn't bring herself to slash her wrists or throat. He snored and she fell asleep in the chair.

The Sweeping evening meal was unusual. They rarely had a guest to stay the night. Dining complete, Cate fussed with the dishes and gave her husband a certain look. He understood.

'Okay boys, bed time,' he said. They complained. 'Say good night to Miss Gallagher.'

'Please, Mr Sweeping,' she said, 'do call me Chloe.'

'Goodnight Chloe,' called the male chorus and disappeared.

James grew bold. 'Let me show you our resident wombat, Chloe,' he said. She smiled and headed outside. James looked at his sister who gave him a certain look. His heart skipped in time with his feet.

Everyone slept well, and next morning Jonathon was in the saddle with Queenie when his family sat down to breakfast. Chloe suffered an inquisition from three small boys. Cate interrupted.

'You should get going on your work routine, brother. Take the monsters with you.'

Moses was in charge of collecting the eggs with Edward always wanting to help. Jon kept asking if he could go too. The males left to find their footwear and the ladies chatted.

'Jonathon's gone into town for supplies and will call at your farm on his way home. That will help his tall tale. He can say he heard you were in town and has called in to tell your parents the news.'

'Thank you so much,' said Chloe. 'You've all been so kind.'

James entered and couldn't help himself. 'You're welcome to stay as long as you like, Chloe.' The nephews ran in from their room and heard the last comment. 'Isn't she boys?'

All three cheered although Edward posed a question.

'Will I have to sleep with Jon every night?'

'No, you won't,' said his mother. 'Moses, you can sleep in the shed with Uncle James.'

James would have preferred Moses to swap with Chloe.


In town, Jonathon bought soap, bandages, candles and medicine for Cate and wire and nails for himself and James. He stopped at the vicarage and lively sounds came from within.

He got and gave news. Andrew and Annie now had two daughters, the second called Dimity, while he and Cate had their three sons.

'You need a third daughter, Annie,' said Jonathon over tea. 'Then they can marry our three boys.'

Annie scoffed. 'Trust a man to tell a woman what to do. Why don't you have a go at being pregnant, Mr Sweeping?' More laughter before the visitor left and he and Andrew talked outside.

'The latest story is horrendous, Jonathon. Some settlers suggest putting poison in sacks of flour and sugar and placing them in unguarded sheds.' Jonathon's teeth hurt. 'The blacks are desperate for food, so will steal the flour and sugar and die a horrible death.'

'But that's murder.'

'Indeed it is, my friend. And some are urging the Governor to drive the remaining blacks out of Van Diemen's Land.'

'What?'

'Some believe the way to end the war is to remove the aborigines.'

Both men found their stomachs react. They were angry, furious. Depressed, the farmer mounted his horse and rode away.

Near the Gallagher farm, Jonathon's heartbeat accelerated. He dreaded lying to Chloe's parents. Gallagher would be furious and demand to know where his daughter was staying. More lies from Jonathon who would never grass.

He turned Queenie onto the track to the Gallagher cottage. The massacre memories came flooding back. But he had a job to do.

As the horse walked the last few yards, Jonathon saw no-one and reckoned the parents were out looking for their girl.

The silence sent a chill up his spine. 'Hello,' he called and slipped from the horse. He wandered towards the cottage and called again. 'Mrs Gallagher, are you there?' The back door was open. He knocked. Still nothing. Horrible memories of the silence he found here once before attacked his brain. *Where are the bodies this time?*

'Hello,' cried a voice.

Jonathon turned and saw Mrs Gallagher emerge from behind the chicken shed. She didn't move towards him so Jonathon set off.

'I have good news,' he called, approaching her. 'Chloe is safe and well.' The woman showed no emotion. 'She's living in Hobart Town. I didn't see her but someone who did said she looked happy and well.'

Jonathon struggled at the mother's lack of response. He wanted to ask if she understood his news but she spoke first.

'He's dead.'

That was it, those two words. Jonathon needed clarification.

'Sorry, who's dead?'

'My husband.'

Now shock gripped Jonathon by the lapels and slapped his face.

'What happened?'

'A few aborigines came and attacked him.'

'Oh Mrs Gallagher, I'm so sorry. Are you all right?' She nodded. She didn't look all right. He paused as it seemed surreal. This is the second time he arrived at this property to discover a massacre.

'Where is Mr Gallagher?'

She indicated behind her. He hesitated then moved to the shed, stepped through the door and there, surrounded by hens pecking at grain in the dirt, face down, lay Van Diemen's Land's leading bully.

The back of his skull with its filthy, long hair was a mess. Jonathon immediately thought of the club or waddy made and used by aborigines. Struck from behind, Gallagher didn't stand a chance.

There was a messy mass of blood on and beside the body and, when Jonathon looked around he saw even more blood on the back of an axe lying in the corner a few yards away. He looked at the widow.

Jonathon, with no experience as a government official, watchman or constable, and no belief in religion, made a decision on the spot.

'I'm sorry for your loss, Mrs Gallagher. The aborigines are brave in seeking revenge, and I'll be happy to tell the authorities Mr Gallagher died as a result of a native attack. In the meantime, with your approval, I'll dig a grave and bury your husband.'

He looked at her. She knew he knew the truth but his response sent a wave of relief to wash over her body. A good serving of joy joined the party.

'Thank you, Mr Sweeping. There's a spade outside.' She pointed. 'Perhaps the grave could be well away from the house in the bush.'

He smiled in a respectful way. 'I'd love a cup of tea, madam.'

The widow returned his smile. 'Come inside when you're ready. I made a carrot cake this morning.'

They parted and he dragged the body into the bush. The hens were glad to see it go, feet first.

In the bush, thanks to the abundant rain in recent days, the grave was easy to dig. He wanted it deep to keep wild animals from enjoying a midnight feast, and to leave no trace of the brute.

He placed the farmer on his back with his face staring up at the bush. His face screamed surprise. Fancy a timid, cowering female being so capable. Dirt landed on the corpse.

The gravedigger hid the location by flattening the ground and placing fallen branches and debris on the grave. He scuffed the area where the dragged body and his footprints could be seen. Jonathon would tell the authorities, if he ever got around to it, the aborigines carried off the body, never to be seen again.

A missing headstone was appropriate. Gallagher who?

# Chapter 44

The carrot cake was delicious. Jonathon stuck to his made-up story about Chloe living in Hobart Town.

'I will go and find her and bring her back,' he said. 'Stay in the house, Mrs Gallagher, and I'll be back later today.'

The widow thanked him and wept as her neighbour rode away. He thought about his speech to the daughter. If her mother decided to tell the truth, it would be her choice. For now, his lies were set. The aborigines killed the farmer. His daughter escaped to Hobart Town.

When Jonathon arrived, the daughter trembled. After the usual greetings, with the children outside, he asked Chloe to sit as he spoke in a calm voice telling the young woman her father had been killed. She showed no emotion although inside, her heart began to dance.

'I must go to my mother,' she said.

'I'll take you,' said James so quickly he even startled himself.

Cate foresaw difficulties. 'I think we should all go,' she said.

They did. James rode Queenie with the three adults on the cart seat and the three boys and dogs happy to ride in the tray.

'I told your mother you were in Hobart Town, Chloe,' said Jonathon. 'It's your decision, and you might wish to leave it at that.'

Chloe sat between the Sweeping couple with Cate's arm around the young woman who nodded.

'Thank you,' she whispered.

The Sweepings could only guess at Chloe's thoughts. The journey continued with the boys alternating between pointing at birds in the bush and returning fire when one sibling pushed or pinched another.

They turned onto the Gallagher track and Mrs Gallagher, having heard them, stood outside anxiously awaiting their arrival. James was off his horse and stood ready to help his sister and then Chloe to the ground. Once her feet landed she ran and embraced her mother.

'What do we do?' whispered Jonathon.

'We wait,' whispered Cate looking at Moses, wondering if he held memories of this place. Hardly, he was only days old when rescued.

The Gallaghers held their embrace for an age. The Sweepings and James stood still. Then Eleanor released her daughter and called. 'Please come inside.' The ice was broken and everyone moved. Eleanor said nothing about the whole Sweeping clan being there.

Cate asked her brother to do something. He protested.

'Oh, but why? They can play by themselves.'

Her stare spoke volumes and James collected his nephews and led them to the yard to explore. They were thrilled, he was miserable.

In the cottage, both Gallaghers fussed finding chairs and cups. The refreshments were enjoyed and the conversation steered well clear of the missing husband/father and the daughter's adventure. Jonathon tried to steer the conversation back to the current situation.

'Once you make your plans, Mrs Gallagher,' he said, 'I'll be happy to help with whatever needs doing.'

'We both will,' added Cate. 'And my brother is experienced too.'

'You're very kind,' said Eleanor. 'But Chloe and I can't possibly run the farm so we'll move to Hobart Town as soon as possible.'

Those words killed the conversation. Chloe didn't want to leave.

'Must we move, Mama?' she pleaded.

'Of course we must. The aborigines are dangerous. They killed your father. If a strong man can't survive, what hope do we have? I won't risk your life for a single second longer than necessary.' More silence from the gathering. Eleanor changed the subject.

'Where are your boys, Mrs Sweeping? Please invite them in for refreshments.'

'I'll go,' said Jonathon who hopped up and left. The women sat still and Cate tried to pacify a much-disappointed Chloe.

'Your mother only has your best interests at heart, Chloe.'

That comment only made Chloe feel worse. Before she spoke, scampering footsteps of three boys and two adult males ordering them to walk and to be quiet interrupted the tea party.

Ever so politely the lads entered having been taught good manners by their parents. Each was again introduced to the widow who became friendly in repeating their names. James was the last to be introduced.

'We've already met, Mrs Gallagher, when you called at our farm.'

'Of course,' she said. 'I do remember.'

Chloe passed around the scones for the boys.

James continued. 'Please accept my sincere condolences for the loss of your husband.'

The young man's sincerity and plain speaking impressed everyone. 'Thank you,' said Eleanor.

'And I would like you to know I'd be happy to help with any tasks on your farm which might need a man's touch.'

Cate put him straight. 'Mrs Gallagher and Chloe are moving to Hobart.'

James copped a hard slap across his cheek. His disappointment decorated his face. 'Oh but you can't.'

He didn't think but said what he thought, and in so doing, stopped the conversation.

'Can't?' replied Eleanor. 'I think you'll find, young man, I most certainly can.' James froze. He wanted to argue, state his case, declare his love for a certain young woman, and get his way but faced a now fiery foe. Eleanor didn't care what she said.

'Having been told what I can and can't do by a man for the last twenty years, I'm not about to take orders from another male, no matter his age.'

'Mother,' hissed Chloe, angry and embarrassed.

'Apologise, Jimmy,' said his sister using controlled aggression.

Without hesitation, James responded with humility. 'I apologise, Mrs Gallagher. I would never presume to tell you to do anything. However ...'

Everyone held their breath. Even the boys stopped eating meaning three young mouths were open revealing new, even baby teeth covered in jam and cream. James ploughed ahead.

'However, I would like to ask you something.' He took a breath while everyone else held theirs. 'Will you please consent to your daughter becoming my wife?'

His question was as unexpected as it was powerful. Chloe was the most surprised. Her body started shaking as she stared at her would-be husband. He stared at his would-be mother-in-law. Cate and Jonathon's frowns switched to beams, and their sons closed their mouths, kept chewing but watched, fascinated.

Eleanor sat in the spotlight. The others stared at her. Her feelings were in turmoil. Having broken free from her appalling husband, in a somewhat unconventional way, she now saw a new path, a new life before her. Her daughter married to a fine young man, their farm saved, and the possibility of grandchildren in a single simple request.

'Well,' she began, looked at her daughter and smiled. 'That might be acceptable.'

James reckoned "might be acceptable" sounded wonderful.

'Hey,' whispered Jonathon to his brother-in-law. James looked at Jonathon and saw him nodding towards Chloe. James twigged. In front of the entire population of this small part of Van Diemen's Land, he knelt before his beloved.

'Miss Gallagher, Chloe, please will you do me the honour of becoming my wife?'

It was a fine proposal, well written and well delivered. Chloe didn't hesitate. 'Yes, Mr Ramsay, James, I would love to marry you.'

The resultant embrace and kiss went down a treat with three young nephews applauding as vigorously as the adults. To say the mood changed would be a massive understatement. Eleanor Gallagher couldn't control her tears. From sadness, bitterness and despair, a brand new world of happiness and prosperity beckoned.

Now it could be reported, two young men from England became owners or operators of farms in a new colony.


Jonathon rode to the home of the Reverend Robert Knopwood who was delighted to pay a visit to the Gallagher, soon to be Ramsay farm and do the necessary. He arrived two days later. Mesdames Sweeping and Gallagher produced a feast for an army. The honeymoon, what honeymoon, was postponed and the new sleeping arrangements for Mrs Gallagher suited her fine. Mother and daughter swapped rooms.

Back at the Sweeping property, Jonathon and Cate lay in bed with their sons asleep in the next room.

'Well Mr Sweeping, there goes your right-hand man. It's time to promote one of your assistants.'

He smiled in the darkness. 'We'll be all right. In a few years, I'll be able to retire and let the mob next door run the show.'

Cate turned over and pulled the blankets higher. 'Of course if you'd fathered three daughters, they'd be running the place by now.'

# Chapter 45

George Augustus Robinson was an Englishman, a builder, who decided to travel. In 1824, he landed in Hobart Town, and being a go-getter, set up in business hiring staff for building projects. He was a joiner by trade and a joiner by nature becoming a leading light in the Bible Society and Mechanics' Institute.

The war with the aborigines was *the* topic of the time, and the newspapers gave it front page coverage. George took a keen interest.

The Governor was unpopular with almost everyone. Convicts hated his cruel and torture-rich prisons. Settlers hated his lack of action against aborigines. Newspaper editors deplored his nepotism and anti-free press rhetoric. He tried to win over his critics by declaring martial law.

Fortunately for the aborigines still alive, Seamus Gallagher wasn't. Others, like Gallagher, went hunting aborigines and being offered £5 for any adult captured was a serious incentive with £2 for an arrested child being better than nothing. But martial law flopped mainly because, as with the whalers and sealers, there were far fewer aborigines around, their population having been greatly reduced.

Despite this, the killings continued. Letters from London warned the Governor of the stain on Britain should further harm come to the aborigines. Governor Arthur wanted a solution with as little bad press as possible. He wanted the "problem" to go away. Mind you, this was the Governor under whose watch the number of churches quadrupled, and the number of hangings went from zero to hundreds. He encouraged Wesleyans to comfort convicts about to be executed. George advocated a strange mix of prayer and punishment.

He placed an advertisement in the local newspaper. "Wanted: A person to make contact with aborigines and bring about a form of peace." Enter the bible-believing builder.

George Robinson won the job and worked on it for years. His simple plan was to use aborigines to convince other aborigines to stop fighting Europeans, and to settle in an area where they'd be safe.

If the Europeans could place the original inhabitants in a secure location, the war would end, and the locals would be free to make money from their purloined paddocks. And with the aborigines secured, George could have them educated in the ways of the Lord.

But the other George, Governor Arthur, hedged his bets. If Robinson failed to round up the aborigines, Plan B might do the trick, and The Black Line was devised. This became a massive undertaking. The plan was to drive the aborigines in the east of the island to a reserve created on the Tasman Peninsula.

Men gave up their employment, formed a gigantic line and, like beaters driving the grouse from their hiding places, shouted, fired guns and blew bugles, trying to force the aborigines into the open, and from there to a secure compound. Once penned, they'd be transported elsewhere. Those caught could be given new names and new clothes and no longer kill or be killed. There would be peace because the aborigines would be under the control of the Europeans.

Both Jonathon and James were working on their respective farms when a military officer rode in. His message to both men was brief. 'You're needed.' For convicts and ticket-of-leave men it was a form of conscription. The brothers-in-law saddled their horse, said goodbye to their families and joined The Black Line.

Jonathon and James rode to a meeting place where many men gathered. A senior military officer gave instructions.

'We spread out when the terrain is easy but close ranks when the bush is dense. We are here to capture not kill. Is that clear?'

Jonathon and James exchanged glances.

'We arrest any blacks we find. They will then be re-settled on an offshore island. The Black War will end. Now, any questions?'

A settler responded. 'How long does this go on for? I've got animals and a farm to run. We all have.' Others supported him.

'Do you want the war with the blacks to end?' The rhetorical question brought no response. 'Carry out this search well and you'll never have an attack on your land, animals or family again. Now listen to your unit leaders and good hunting.'

Jonathon and James were in the same group. The instructions were clear and the operation began. The brothers-in-law were two in a total of more than two thousand—farmers, convicts, soldiers, settlers—most of the able-bodied males in the colony.

When the land was open and clear, the men were well apart. When they entered the bush, they came together. Those with experience on the land, in the bush, knew any aborigine could easily hide, wait for the searchers to pass then slip away. Such was the routine by day. By night, the natives could stroll through the line. They did.

The search was huge, lasted for many months, a massive logistical and expensive exercise all in the name of controlling the aborigines, thereby stopping them from attacking the white settlers, and giving those who believed in the Christian God the chance to bring the ignorant out of darkness and into the light.

The review of The Black Line did not make for exciting reading. Two aborigines killed. Two aborigines captured; a man and a boy.

It was a tragedy for the indigenous population, again, but in short, a monumental failure.

George Augustus Robinson ignored The Black Line. With a mixture of family, convicts, porters and aborigines—male and female—he traversed the island by land and sea, meeting aborigines from various nations.

When Robinson encountered some locals, he fell back sending his aboriginal mediators to parley with their kin. Later, the leader came forward bearing gifts and lived up to his title of Conciliator.

Those still living their ancient lifestyle were urged to re-settle. Many did and an area on Flinders Island, between Van Diemen's Land and Port Phillip was chosen. This would be the new home of the original inhabitants of Van Diemen's Land. They were removed from the land they occupied for tens of thousands of years.

On this new "reservation", a school was built where aboriginal children could be educated in English meaning another death blow, this time to the indigenous language and culture.

A local market was established where aborigines could buy and sell goods and thus learn the value of property. A potato plot was established with aboriginals encouraged to grow their own food; this for people who had survived for millennia.

For Lieutenant-Governor Arthur, this was the best of both worlds. The aborigine problem was solved, the bloodshed and terror stopped, and he could report the success to his masters in London, and to the other colonies on the mainland. He'd found the way to "fix the aboriginal problem".

Sadly, or more correctly tragically, the project on Flinders Island, like the project, The Black Line, became another colossal failure.

The busiest activity at the settlement on Flinders Island involved grave digging. Disease brought by the Europeans killed many of the locals. Teachers and missionaries trying to bring a way of life to a group of people with an ageless culture of their own, failed utterly. Replacing an ancient culture with one having a far shorter history and with a belief system totally at odds with the indigenous Dreamtime, was doomed from the start.

The few remaining indigenous survivors on Flinders Island were moved back to the mainland to a settlement south of Hobart. Not long after their arrival at Oyster Bay, the last full-blooded aboriginal in Van Diemen's Land, then Tasmania, died.

Robinson became a self-made hero. He commissioned a bust of himself, and convinced many of his handiwork. Sailing the world on the *Beagle,* Charles Darwin described George as, "an active and benevolent man". Not everyone agreed with the Devil's Advocate.

Robinson went on to prosecute his mission of converting aborigines in other parts of the mainland of Australia with the same singular lack of success, although without wiping out an entire race. He returned to England, finishing his days as a gentleman in fashionable Bath.

# The Family

## Chapter 46

Over the next decade, the Sweeping and Ramsay families continued farming with ever more success. The Black War was over. The aborigines were gone. James and Chloe started a family with a daughter, Georgina, followed by a son, James. The habit of naming a son after his father was catching. Grandmother Eleanor adored her grandchildren and the last dozen years of her life were full of happiness and joy.

Further up the valley, the Sweeping boys grew into strapping lads respecting their parents and working with their father. From both parents, each young man gained a basic education. The farm expanded, profits grew and the parents began to wonder if all three boys would want their own land. Moses, 20, raised the subject.

One night, after his brothers Edward and Jonathon retired, he asked his parents if he might have a word. It was summer and they sat outside in the cool night air.

'I've been thinking about the future,' said Moses. His parents were hooked. 'I'd like to move and tackle a career other than farming.'

'If that's what you want, my boy,' said Jonathon, 'we'll be sad to see you go, but we'll back you to the hilt, won't we, my dear?'

Cate responded with even more feeling. 'Of course, and if you find things don't work out, this will always be your home.'

Jonathon spoke his mind. 'There's a ton of land, here, Moses. There's plenty of room to build another ten houses. You and your brothers can build wherever you like. Find a wife and raise a family.'

Moses expected their answer. 'I thought you'd say that.'

Pauses slipped into the conversation.

'When are you thinking of going?' asked Cate.

Moses shrugged. 'No hurry, not tomorrow, but soon.'

'Where will you go?' asked Jonathon.

'I think to the colony at Port Jackson in New South Wales. I'd like to work in the world of business.'

'We'll give you money, son, a down payment on your inheritance.'

Moses went to protest.

'No argument,' said Jonathon. 'I'll ride into Hobart with you and arrange a bank account.'

Moses was overcome. His decision to raise this subject sent his anxiety levels racing. He loved his parents and worried his decision would hurt them. Their kind and loving response turned his nervous tension into raw emotion. Their kindness knocked him for six.

He let the night sounds of the bush fill the silence. When he next spoke, it was his parents who were knocked for six.

'Over the years, I've sometimes wondered why I'm different.' Jonathon and Cate sensed their bodies grow tense. 'I'm the only member of the family with red hair. My brothers are taller than me and look like you. I don't. Is there a reason for that?'

Years ago, Jonathon and Cate discussed what, when and even if they would tell Moses the story of how he joined their family. Their decision then was to say nothing unless it became necessary. As Moses grew into a happy, healthy boy, the subject, though never forgotten, never arose. Right now it became necessary.

When their own sons were born, the brothers grew to love Moses and he them. James was the perfect uncle being free to teach, help and entertain them. The origin of Moses Sweeping remained a secret—until now.

The parents looked at one another. A lamp from inside threw a little light on their faces. Cate gave her husband a look and an imperceptible nod. Jonathon understood and spoke.

'There's something we need to tell you, son.'

Jonathon told the whole truth, and did it well with love and simplicity. He began with the aboriginal attack, the death of Moses' birth parents and sister, and how the baby, later called Moses, was hidden, and then discovered by the man he knew as his father.

Despite the story rocking him, Moses barely moved or reacted. The facts of the brutal murder of his family, and the reason he was called Moses made his skin burn. His pulse accelerated.

His birth mother hiding him in the flour box, and the father he knew finding and saving him sounded fantastic; then wonderful.

He stood and moved to Cate. She stood. They embraced for a long time. He turned to Jonathon who stood. They embraced. Moses began to weep, to sob, but refused to release the man who carried him to Hobart Town in a basket, and later adopted him. Moses kissed his "father," once, twice and a third time and continued to sob. His "mother" joined them and all three could feel each other's heartbeat as the nocturnal animals in the surrounding bush rose up and their cries became their applause.

Cate retired leaving the men to bond. Having told Moses so much about his early life, Jonathon chose to explain his own beginnings.

'I copied my father when we adopted you.' Moses wanted more. 'My mother was about sixteen and a scullery maid when a wealthy man raped her. A stable hand working on the estate offered to marry my mother and so adopted me. That man became my father.'

Moses struggled with the amount and depth of information.

'Like father, like son,' he said. Jonathon smiled. 'So what happened to your parents? And have you always been a farmer?'

The amazing Jonathon Sweep story began covering the London slums, his life as a chimney sweep, the death of his parents, his flight from London with his sister, his life as a criminal, escaping from a prison hulk, transportation, and working as a convict labourer in Van Diemen's Land. Being gifted a farm, this farm, was a knockout punch.

The already strong bond between Moses and Jonathon grew stronger. The young man would never forget his beginnings for the rest of his life. They embraced again.

'I think, Dad, you should tell my brothers what you've told me.'

Jonathon paused. 'I'll think about it.'

Moses nodded 'You do that.' He walked to the shed, his room. Jonathon watched. Moses turned at the door.

'Good night, father.'

'Good night, son.'

The day dawned when Moses would leave. His brothers were cut to the quick. They were a unit. They grew up together, worked together, swam, fished and went camping together. Now the team was breaking up and as Moses was leaving the island, how could they ever meet again? Would they ever meet again? The farewells were fierce and moving. Cate wept freely.

Jonathon saddled two horses, now Benny and Mo, and would use the second as a pack horse returning with supplies.

The Sweeping dogs, Smokey and Ash, died of old age, and two new hounds, Rusty and Spike ruled the roost. They ran after the two riders and needed to be recalled by the younger brothers.

The riders naturally called at the Ramsay farm. More desperately sad farewells for Moses with his uncle and his family, and then the Sweepings headed for Hobart Town.

The next ship sailing to Port Jackson was in ten days. Jonathon took his son to the bank, arranged an account and made a deposit, then went to the shipping office and bought a ticket—a one-way ticket. There was a feeling of dread. Then they called on Mrs Hodgson.

Her sadness showed. 'Oh, Mr Sweeping, Mr Walker passed away.'

Jonathon copped a pain in his chest. Arnold was the person who gave him a start as a free man. More importantly, Mr and Mrs Walker gave him their property as thanks for the work he did on their farm.

'My boy, Moses, needs a room for a few days, Mrs Hodgson. Can you put him up?'

'What a silly question,' she replied and took Moses's bag.

'We'll call on Mr McFarlane and be back soon.' The men left.

At the vicarage, Annie McFarlane beamed, embraced the visitors and dragged them inside.

Andrew appeared and greeted the visitors. When he and Annie discovered Moses was leaving, a serious mood settled on their gathering. The McFarlanes' daughter, Hannah, looked a picture of health and a younger version of her attractive mother. Her sister, Dimity, had good manners off to a tee and a smile to light up a room. All the latest news was freely exchanged.

Andrew walked Jonathon outside. 'I don't suppose you've heard, but the mission for aborigines on Flinders Island ran into serious difficulties. All those efforts by George Robinson in moving the aborigines from Van Diemen's Land have failed.'

'I don't understand.'

'I'm afraid we Europeans have a belief that our religion, our culture and our way of life is superior. We seem to think the so-called uncivilized people of the world must follow our God if they are to be truly happy.'

Jonathon's mind raced. 'I'm confused, sir. Should a vicar, a Christian clergyman be saying those things?'

Andrew grimaced. 'The Europeans who arrived in Van Diemen's Land, took the land owned by the aborigines, raped their women, shot and killed far more of them than they killed Europeans and now, as our penance, we shipped them offshore where our diseases finished them off.'

Jonathon shook his head in disbelief. 'Are they all dead?'

'The last few have been moved to Oyster Bay, south of here but God only knows if they'll survive.'

Jonathon blew air. 'It's hard to believe in two or three generations, a whole race of people has died.' The men looked at one another.

'And their culture too. Who knows what damage has been done? Their way of life might be gone forever.'

It was a sobering thought. These two men first met a quarter of a century ago. They saw Hobart Town expand; they married, fathered children, and came face to face with the horrors of war.

Now their lives were changing. Jonathon's son was leaving Van Diemen's Land and Andrew's interest in local politics gave him a new challenge in life.

'Jonathon, I want the Governor to persuade Westminster to stop transportation; no more convicts.'

'I agree with that. I'll support you.'

'There are brave men here in Hobart talking about independence. If you were closer to town, I'd persuade you to join the movement.'

Jonathon shook his head. 'Not me, sir, I'm flat out on the farm.'

'The problem is many of your fellow farmers want transportation to continue. They benefit from the convict labour.'

'Because it's free.'

'Exactly.'

Jonathon remembered. 'I was once a convict labourer.'

'And look at you now; a free man, a landowner, successful farmer, father of three strapping boys, and a credit to the colony.'

Jonathon offered his hand. 'I must collect Moses and get going.'

Andrew lost his smile. 'Oh and I suppose you heard the Reverend Knopwood has died.'

'I did. He was the man who encouraged me to teach children and helped me propose to my wife.' Jonathon and Andrew shared a moment of sadness mixed with happy memories.

'Time marches on, sir,' added Jonathon.

He collected Moses and took him back to Mrs Hodgson's house. He gave his son his ticket and a well-wrapped package containing twenty pounds. He hugged the young man he picked out of a box of flour two decades ago.

Riding away, Jonathon fought hard not to turn and wave. He did and both men allowed tears to flow freely.

Back home he told the family his news about Moses, the McFarlanes and the death of people they knew. Cate was desperate to hear if Moses seemed okay.

'He was fine. You've done a grand job in raising him.'

'Did he get cold feet when you said goodbye?' asked Edward.

'No, why should he? He's not a soft Mummy's boy like you.'

A small portion of mashed potato flew across the table scoring a bullseye on Jonathon's nose.

Cate interrupted. 'All right, enough.'

The potato war was cut short although the ribbing continued.

'So what's been happening during my absence? Have you two managed to ruin the estate?'

Young Jon was curious. 'Now Moses has gone, will Eddie and I have more responsibilities?'

Everyone paid attention.

'That's a big word, son,' said his father.

'What are you getting at?' asked Edward, his eyes on his brother.

Jon continued. 'We're a man down, Dad. How about you employ someone to give us a hand? The number of lambs this year will be bigger than ever.'

Again the others were shocked and impressed at the thinking and language of the lad.

'Where did all this thinking come from,' asked the senior Jonathon. 'Are you planning on becoming a gentleman farmer?'

Jon gave a sort of shimmy and smiled. 'And what if I am?'

Cate cleared away the plates. 'That's all we need; a toff in the family.'

They laughed and tucked into the best apple pie in the Apple Isle. Cate's cream from their two cows meant orders for seconds were in line before the bowls were empty.

# Chapter 47

Jonathon and his two sons were in the large paddock inspecting ewes. Counting those expecting meant mustering and marking. The dogs, Rusty and Spike, adored the work.

'Check those over there,' said Jonathon. 'I'll get more dye.'

The sons did as told while their old man headed for the shed for supplies. As Jonathon approached, he heard sounds. They came from inside his shed.

He hurried and went to grab the door. It flew open and two men came out in a hurry. They looked terrible; unshaven, unwashed and wore filthy clothes more like rags. They seemed young, in their 20s, although being filthy and bedraggled made it hard to tell.

Jonathon yelled. 'Hey!' He grabbed the first man and they fell on the ground. The second joined the struggle. Jonathon leapt to his feet grabbing both men. The farmer's shouting sounded the alarm. The sons and dogs came running. This wasn't a fair fight; two against one. But as the intruders grabbed the farmer in holds that incapacitated him, the scene changed.

'Stop!' screamed a voice and all three males turned to see the only human female on the property pointing a rifle in their direction.

The two intruders backed up quick smart and surrendered in fear. The husband of the savage-looking warrior couldn't believe his eyes. *What is she doing?* His wife hated guns, never fired one and refused to even learn how to load it. He was surprised she had it pointing in the right direction. Their sons arrived out of breath, the dogs not sure if they should celebrate or attack.

Jonathon took the firearm and made the men sit on the ground.

'What's going on?' he asked.

'We're hungry,' said the first man.

'We only want food,' said the second.

'Why not ask? If you need a feed, we'll feed you.'

'We have no money.'

'We don't charge for helping people in distress.'

The men were not expecting that reply.

'Are you convicts?' asked Edward.

The men replied with their eyes, haunted, grim, and desperate.

'When did you escape?' asked Jonathon. No reply. 'Were you at Macquarie Harbour?' Neither spoke. 'Port Arthur?' More silence. 'I heard it's impossible to escape from both of those prisons.'

Finally the first man spoke. 'We were lucky. We were on a road gang. They make us work for hours, hardly any water, and the sun's bloody hot, no rest, and if we stop, they beat us.'

The second man took courage from his mate. 'We took off and have been runnin' ever since. Three days and two nights ...'

'Four,' corrected his partner.

'We're starvin'. We knew the first one of us who carks it will be the other bloke's breakfast.'

The Sweeping family wanted to vomit.

'You get a hundred lashes for a minor mistake, and they make the prisoners flog their own,' said the first.

'And if you don't flog hard enough, the convict doing the flogging gets flogged himself.'

On a sunny day in the beautiful bush surrounds, the atmosphere became gruesome.

Jonathon looked at his sons. 'Fill the tub and get some of the working clothes and boots Moses left behind.' To his wife the orders kept coming. 'It's time for an early lunch, my dear, if you please.'

His family left. He looked at the men. 'I'll feed you and give you clothes. You can sleep in the shed. In return, you'll not steal anything, do no harm to my family and tell no-one, especially the Governor's spies, that I helped you. Do we have a deal?'

Both convicts were on their feet, shaking Jonathon by the hand.

'Thank you, sir, and we can do whatever work you need.'

'We won't let you down, sir,' said the second man.

'Right,' said Jonathon. 'Your first job is to scrub yourself clean. You both stink.'

It was an interesting evening meal. There were six for dinner. The convicts, Paul and Ralph, looked a sight with their clean bodies and new clothes. One was much taller than Moses meaning the convict displayed plenty of skin. Jon had taken over the shed after Moses left so moved back inside leaving the convicts their own quarters.

The brothers had never seen this side of their father, how he treated the visitors, and wondered how the situation would end. They learnt soon enough.

'Now gentlemen, I want you to know this is a temporary situation. As it happens I could do with extra hands during lambing season but please understand, your visit is not permanent.'

'We understand,' said Paul. 'And we're really grateful.'

'We are,' added Ralph, '*very* grateful.'

'You're the first people we've met since landing who've showed us any sort of kindness, any basic human decency' said Paul.

Ralph nodded. 'He's right and I'm curious, Mr Sweeping. Why are you doin' this for us?'

Jonathon hesitated. His wife knew his background. She'd had a recent refresher history lesson when Jonathon told her about his chat with Moses. But his sons were ignorant. They grew up on a prosperous farm with parents who loved them and an older brother and an uncle in a happy family unit. With little knowledge of the life of their parents, the boys were in for a shock.

'I know what you've been through,' he said and everyone stopped. 'I came to Van Diemen's Land as a child convict.'

His sons and his guests were hooked. Their eyes widened. They stared at the speaker. Cate endured a sliver of fear not wanting to learn anything new that might upset her and especially not her boys.

'You never told us, Dad,' said Edward.

'You never asked,' replied Jonathon.

'You were a child convict?' gasped Jon.

Jonathon nodded. 'I was and a few years younger than you are now when I landed in Hobart Town.'

Edward looked at Cate. 'Mother, did you know this?'

'I did and I still married him.'

The atmosphere buzzed. The guests already held a high opinion of the farmer and now their opinion climbed higher. He was a convict like them.

'Is that why you're helping us, sir?' asked Ralph.

Jonathon nodded. 'I know what you've been through. I worked as a convict for a family until I received my ticket-of-leave.'

'We'd love one of those,' said Paul.

'Then I moved here and the elderly husband and wife who owned the farm treated me like the son they never had. Eventually the old lady died, the farmer retired and moved into Hobart Town where he told the authorities I was the new owner.'

'He gave you the farm?' asked a stunned Edward.

Both his sons were in shock. They grew up on this property thinking their English parents came to this land, married and became successful landowners.

'I'm sorry, Dad, but can you tell us why you were convicted?' asked Jon, worried the father he loved was a murderer.

'My parents died in London, I was about 10, starving, and so I stole a silk handkerchief.'

'Is that all?' asked Paul.

'I was imprisoned on a wreck of a ship on the river Thames but because I'd been a chimney sweep as a little child, I could climb through small spaces.'

'You were a chimney sweep?' asked a head-shaking Edward.

The sons and escaped convicts found it easy to let their jaws drop.

'I squeezed out of the side of the hulk, unlocked the hatch and helped two men escape. I was caught and thrown on a ship bound for Hobart Town.' He slapped his hands on the table. 'And that, gentlemen, is all there is. Here endeth the lesson.'

Heads were shaking, faces contorting, and hearts racing.

The host stood. 'I'll show you to your quarters, gentlemen,' said Jonathon, 'and have a word to the dogs about their bedroom behaviour with guests.' The trio left.

The sons besieged their mother with questions.

She waved her hands shushing them. 'You know as much as I do. Now who's washing the plates tonight?'

The convicts earned their keep. Having two extra workers made lambing much easier. On their third night, it was decided the men would leave. Jonathon suggested they get on a ship disguised in their "new" clothes. He would take them to Hobart Town on the cart as he needed supplies. Departure would be the day after tomorrow.

Next day they were out in the paddock working hard. Jonathon called time for lunch and all five headed for the cottage. They passed the grazing horses when a kangaroo bounded out of the bush and scared them all. The horses reacted and Edward ran to calm them. Benny was okay but Mo panicked. She reared. Jonathon shouted.

'Leave her, son, let her go.'

But Edward worried she would take off and injure herself. He reached up for her bridle, grabbed it trying to calm the animal. She bumped Edward knocking him to the ground.

'Let her go!' screamed Jonathon running to his boy.

Terrified, the horse dropped its front legs on the fallen young man, smashing his right kneecap, then reared again and trotted away.

Jonathon dropped beside his son whose face screamed pain. Shock gripped his body. Blood oozed through his trousers.

'Lie still, lie still,' said Jonathon as the others ran to help.

'I can't breathe, Dad,' gasped Edward. 'And my leg hurts something awful.' Tears welled in his eyes.

Jonathon spoke to his fit son. 'Blanket, bandages and towels, go!'

'What can we do?' asked Paul.

Jonathon was inspecting his son, trying to think, and having haunting flashback memories of his father minus a foot thanks to an accident with a horse. If life has its happy and sad moments, this one was tragic. He stared at Edward in despair.

'We'll get you inside, son, give you some medicine and fetch a doctor. Please be brave.' The convicts looked on helpless. Time dragged. Jonathon looked up and saw Jon and Cate running with their arms full. 'Look, here come the troops.'

Cate was ready to weep but carried on not missing a beat. She knelt and kissed her son's head.

'Spread the blanket beside him,' said Jonathon. They did so. Jonathon wrapped a towel around his son's right knee. 'Now we lift and place him on the blanket.'

The four men crouched either side of Edward. Jonathon knelt by his son's right leg. He looked for a way to support it causing the least amount of pain.

'After my count of three,' he said. 'One, two, three,' and they lifted him onto the blanket. Edward's scream of pain struck terror in his parents' hearts. 'Right, a corner each and again, lift on three.'

The walk took forever with Cate holding her son's hand and telling him anything she could think of to give him comfort and courage.

He lay on his bed. They cut his trousers and undid his shirt. There was a horrible bruise on his chest and his kneecap and lower leg were bloodied and broken.

They made him drink rum and bandaged his leg to stop the bleeding. The parents spoke in the kitchen.

'Sit with him,' whispered Jonathon to Cate.

She whispered back. 'What will you do?'

'Take him to hospital. I'll take the convicts and they can sit either side of him in the cart. Jon can stay here with you. As soon as he's settled, I'll be back.'

'I want to come.'

'No, Cate, you can't do anything.'

'If he's going to die, his mother will be there holding his hand.' That was the end of the conversation. She went to get her hat.

Jonathon took the convicts and Jon outside. 'Jon, I want you to stay and look after the farm. Gentlemen, this is your chance to start a new life. My wife and I will take Edward to Hobart in the cart. You're welcome to travel with us but when we get there, you're on your own.'

'Thank you, sir,' said Paul. 'I'll be honoured to help your son on the trip.'

Ralph hesitated. 'I'd like to stay, sir, at least till you return. I can help Jon with the farm and keep him company in this tough time.'

Jonathon looked at Ralph and his son. Jon nodded.

'Thank you,' said Jonathon to Ralph. 'If you're staying, you'll be paid a proper wage.' Ralph almost bowed so great was his gratitude. Jonathon addressed his namesake. 'Get the cart ready, son.'

Loading the patient on the cart was a nightmare. They placed straw making a bed for Edward. Jon was hugged by his parents who then both grasped Ralph's hand. Cate and Paul were either side of the injured passenger. The journey began and Jonathon looked for ruts on the track trying to make the ride as smooth as possible. Hobart Town was a long way away.

# Chapter 48

The journey seemed to take forever. At the Colonial Hospital in Liverpool Street, Paul helped Jonathon and two orderlies carry Edward inside. Cate was a mess. Once the staff took over, Paul said goodbye and set off to start a new life.

After an age, the surgeon came out to speak to Jonathon and Cate. They were close to tears, ready to break down.

'Will he live?' asked Cate, begging for good news.

'He has terrible injuries. We can bind his ribs and, in time they should heel, but his leg is badly broken in two places. I'm sorry but he has to lose it.'

Cate cringed, her pain acute. Jonathon buried his grief and kept an arm around his wife. 'Do you mean just his foot?'

The surgeon shook his head. 'No, above the knee.'

A cry of anguish from Cate caused people to turn and stare. Jonathon gripped her tighter. 'And when will you operate, sir?'

'Now, the sooner the better. He's sedated but if you wish to see him before we operate, you can go in now.'

He indicated and the parents found their way to Edward's side. He was drowsy and his smile lacked energy.

'Sorry, Dad, but it looks like you're a labourer short.'

Cate clasped his hand.

'Don't think you're getting off lightly, sonny Jim,' said Jonathon, and father and son grimaced as their grins were overtaken by tears.

'We'll be waiting outside,' said Cate kissing her son with feeling.

'Chin up, my boy,' said Jonathon and squeezed Edward's arm.

At the door to the ward, they turned and the sight of the patient and the thought of what was to come, started a fire in their chests.

They waited at the hospital ready to rush in if things went badly. What could they do? Sit and wring their hands, wipe their eyes, ask Andrew McFarlane to say a prayer? Jonathon went out to check on the horse. He returned and looked at Cate for any news. She shook her head, and they sat beside one another holding hands.

'I'll need to make changes at home, make it easier for him to get around,' said his father.

Cate despaired. 'What can he do? All the farm jobs need a person who is fit and strong. He'll feel useless and become depressed.'

Jonathon remembered his father's drinking and self-pity once he lost a foot.

'Let's cross that bridge when we get to it.'


In those days, setting broken bones was a medical skill yet to be acquired. Broken legs weren't set but severed. Doctors weren't called Sawbones for nothing. It didn't take forever to perform the operation. The surgeon came out and the blood on his apron turned the stomachs of the parents.

Cate and Jonathon hurried to him. 'He's come through okay. He's in serious pain but he's brave. You have a fine young man.'

Cate lost control and Jonathon supported her. 'Can we see him, Doctor?' she pleaded.

'I'd wait awhile. He's been sedated and when he wakes the shock is usually as bad as the pain. Come back in an hour or so. I'll keep an eye on him.'

His smile reassured them a tad and they left. In the cart, they drove the short distance to the vicarage and scared the living daylights out of Andrew and Annie McFarlane.

Their daughters Hannah and Dimity were lovely young women with their mother's natural beauty and charm.

The terrible news dominated the conversation.

'You must stay here,' said Annie brooking no argument. 'Hannah please ask Flo to prepare the spare room.'

'Certainly, Mama, and I'm truly sorry about your son, Mr and Mrs Sweeping.'

'Having Moses and young Jonathon running the farm must be a relief,' said Andrew having forgotten Moses had left. Annie reminded her husband and embarrassed, the vicar apologised profusely.

The Sweepings drank tea then headed back to the hospital.

'I can't leave him alone,' said Cate. 'He'll have to stay in Hobart until he recovers and he must have someone to care for him. You'll have to make do without me at home.'

'I'll stay too, for a while anyway.'

They reached the hospital and went into the ward. All 12 beds were occupied. They spotted Edward and moved to him. He was drowsy but recognised them.

'Hello my darling,' said Cate. 'How are you feeling?'

'Sore,' he said, 'oh and lighter.'

His mother cried although his father smiled. 'You should have been on the stage, son,' said Jonathon and gripped his son's hand.

Cate took over. 'We're staying in Hobart, darling, with Mr and Mrs McFarlane. We'll be here every day to care for you and bring whatever you need. What can we get you?'

'A wooden leg and a pair of crutches would help.'

The parents were thrilled with Edward's attitude. They half expected him to despair, to drop his bundle but his first reaction was so positive and encouraging.

Jonathon talked shop. 'Paul has gone to find a ship but Ralph stayed and is helping Jon run the farm.'

'Good for him,' said Edward and winced.

Jonathon gave his wife a look; time to go. She kissed her son. 'We'll see you in the morning, darling.'

Jonathon gently squeezed his boy's arm. 'I'm mighty proud of you, son. You're a bloody champion.'

The parents left and took their tears with them.


The discussion with the McFarlanes about Edward was long and detailed. After supper, Andrew and Jonathon strolled in the garden.

'I know this is the wrong time, my friend, but you won't have heard of the progress made here in Hobart, and elsewhere on the island. We're setting the colony free from Westminster.'

'You mean home rule for Van Diemen's Land?'

'I do and many want to change our name as well.'

'A new name?'

'They want transportation abolished and reckon having the word Diemen, which sounds like demon, reminds us of the terrors we inflicted on the aborigines and, more recently, on the convicts.'

Jonathon's mind was elsewhere. He couldn't stop thinking about Edward but hearing news of the colony he arrived in soon after it was founded proved a distraction.

'Have they got a new name?'

'Tasmania.'

Jonathon pondered the new name. 'Tasmania?'

'It comes from the chap, Tasman, the Dutchman who we think was the first European to make landfall here.'

'The aborigines arrived well before Tasman and the other Europeans. Why not an aboriginal name?'

Andrew thought about the suggestion. 'Having wiped them out, I think the authorities will not want any reminder of their murderous regime.'

'We were a part of that, Andrew. In our lifetime, the aborigines have gone from landowners to survivors to ... to oblivion.'

Both men fell quiet. Both thought of the killings, the rapes and the theft of land. Andrew was keen on the new political movements.

'And all these proposed changes lead me to ask a question.' The pause pushed up the tension. 'Will you consider standing for the new government?'

Jonathon's eyebrows shot up. 'Me? A member of parliament?'

'Why not? You're a local, a self-made man. You know the colony, you arrived not long after Hobart Town was born. You've brought prosperity to the island and you know the needs of the place.'

'And its tragic and terrible history.'

'Yes, Jonathon, I know we made a God-awful mess dealing with the aborigines but let's not continue the mistakes. Let's put a stop to the slavery racket with the transportation of convicts. Let's give everyone the right to vote. And with our own parliament we can do that. We can do good for the people. What do you say?'

'You mean do good for the white people.'

Andrew couldn't answer. There was a feeling of anger between the two men. 'I know, I know, it's too late for the aborigines.'

They looked at one another in silence. Andrew looked at the man he admired and respected. 'Let's talk some more in the time you're here before you take Edward home.'

Jonathon grimaced. The mention of Edward plunged him back into misery. He wished he could take his son's place.

# Chapter 49

There was joy in seeing Edward survive but despair in thinking of his future. After a week, Cate stayed in town while Jonathon left the cart behind and rode home to check on the farm. He trusted his youngest son but barely knew Ralph the escaped convict.

Cate was always at the hospital. She helped feed Edward and performed various tasks usually done by staff. Some locals reckoned patients received better care at home. She talked about how he could find new work and even find a girl and settle down as a married man.

'If she had one arm, Mother, we'd be able to work well together.'

His humour was natural and while it cut deep inside his mother's heart, she played along with his quips.

The doctor wanted to get Edward out of bed as soon as possible. His muscles were getting little exercise, and a defeatist attitude could creep in and make his recovery so much harder and longer.

'I have these crutches for you, Mr Sweeping,' said Dr Bedford. 'Let's have you give them a try.'

Cate's heart worked overtime. 'What a wonderful idea, Doctor,' she said. 'Come on, son, I'll give you a hand.'

Edward wasn't keen. Despite coming through the amputation horror, depression about his future continued to attack his mind. But what even half-decent son could deny his mother? With helpers galore, Edward placed his foot on the floor, and positioned himself on the bed. He was helped to put the crutches in position.

'Take your time,' said the doctor. 'We'll lift you and keep holding you so have no fear of falling.'

He spoke the truth. Cate held her breath as two able-bodied males each took one of Edward's arms and lifted him. He would have fallen, forwards or backwards, had not the men kept a firm grip. Edward settled. Now he saw life as a challenge. Now he relished the fight. He moved the top of each crutch into his armpits and put his weight there. He stood proud and tall. So pleased and proud was he, a grin automatically flooded his face. His mother smiled and cried at the same time.

'Well done,' said Dr Bedford. 'Now, how about pushing down on the crutches and moving your foot.'

Edward looked at him thinking it was a joke. The medical man was never more serious. Everyone watched. The two helpers maintained a firm grip on an arm a piece. It seemed like an eternity as Edward asked his brain, or was it the other way around?, to do what seemed the impossible.

The pain under his arms kicked in as the pressure mounted. Then it happened. He moved his foot, lost his balance and started to fall. His mother gasped but relaxed as the two helpers held him fast.

Everyone in the ward applauded including fellow patients. Edward was guided back to his bed and copped a kiss from his mother.

It was a small step, almost a nothing step but the most important movement he ever made.

Over supper with the McFarlanes, Cate couldn't stop gushing about her son's mighty achievement.

Jonathon reached the farm fearing the unknown. His doubts vanished when both dogs bounded towards him and his son and the new labourer appeared wearing dirty clothes and big grins.

'So, the place is still standing,' he said climbing down. Ralph took the horse and led it away to be unsaddled, watered and fed.

Jon saw his father watching. 'Best labourer in the whole of Van Diemen's Land, Dad. How's Eddie?'

Jonathon hugged his namesake. 'Not too bad; not too bad at all.'

Jon had been thinking about his father's childhood for days.

'So he's got his old man's fighting spirit then?'

They went inside and ate lunch as Jonathon told the sorry saga of Edward's amputation. It put a massive dampener on the mood.

That night, after Ralph retired, father and son got serious.

'Dad, will Eddie ever work on the farm again?'

His father took a deep breath. 'If he learns to walk, he'll want to come home. But if he believes he's a burden, he'll be living in hell just being here. Can you imagine at lambing and shearing, we're working 12, sometimes 15 hours a day while he hobbles about trying to pick up a single fleece?'

'He'd hate that,' said his brother.

'I told your mother I'd return to Hobart as soon as I was sure you hadn't managed to set fire to the place.'

Jon expressed mock anger. 'I see, and *are* you sure?'

'You've done a brilliant job, my boy, brilliant. Jon's body coursed with pride. He had a new admiration for his father after recent family history revelations. 'Mind you, having a wash more than once a week wouldn't hurt.'

They laughed.

'Dad, Ralph's a great worker. I know it sounds a rotten thing to say but if Eddie can't work again, Ralph is the perfect replacement.'

Jonathon nodded. It was good news yet made him feel worse.

'Oh,' added Jon, 'and he's teaching me to play cricket.'

'Cricket?'

'Back in England, he played for the Players against the Gentlemen at Lord's Cricket Ground.'

Jonathon looked at his son thinking his youngest spoke a foreign language. In Bermondsey, cricket, gentlemen and St John's Wood were never discussed. The men chatted then retired.

Two days later, Jonathon rode away from the farm feeling confident his son and Ralph would have the property running as well if not better than if he were there.

Rather than head straight to Hobart, he turned off to what was now the Ramsay farm. His brother-in-law James struggled of late.

Jonathon's arrival brought great joy. Living alone in the bush meant contact with the outside world varied between rare and non-existent. Loneliness became a constant activity. James and Chloe had two children growing like the mighty trees on the farm. Their grandmother adored them and they her.

After the warm greeting and the inevitable tea and scones, Jonathon broke the news about Edward.

The family collapsed. Spirits dived into despair.

'Will he ever come back to the farm?' asked James.

Jonathon paused. 'It's difficult and right now I don't know. If ever I get to Heaven, the first question I'll ask God is, what did the aborigines do to deserve being driven from their land? And second, why did my father and son both have to lose a limb?'

His seriousness cast a pall over the others. Jonathon saw how his behaviour hurt them. 'I'm so sorry,' he said and stood. 'James, come and show me the work you've been doing.'

The men went outside where it was obvious the farm faced problems. Rather than tell his brother-in-law his farm was in need of attention, Jonathon made a positive suggestion.

'Would you like a fit and capable labourer?'

James' eyes lit up. 'Really? Who? How?'

Jonathon explained the situation about Ralph, the convict escapee and now Sweeping farm labourer, being an outstanding worker.

'Him being a fugitive doesn't worry me at all,' said James.

Jonathon explained. 'Without Moses and now Eddie, I need him but I have Jon whereas you only have your youngsters.'

'They're learning fast,' said James.

'But right now, Ralph would be a godsend for you.'

James knew this was true and reckoned it the best news ever.

'Thanks,' he said and meant it.

'I don't know how long I'll be in Hobart,' said Jonathon. 'You can wait till I return or go to my place yourself. Tell Jon and Ralph I'm happy for Ralph to switch farms, and see how they react.'

'I'll go today.' James leaked enthusiasm.

'Mind you,' interrupted Jonathon, 'the man must be paid a fair wage. None of this slavery rubbish.'

James pumped his brother-in-law's hand. 'Of course, and I think you're worried I'll turn out the better farmer.'

They laughed and went back inside.


After Jonathon continued his journey to Hobart, James left for his sister's farm. Ralph agreed to the switch but only when Jonathon returned and gave the move his approval in person.

Riding to the hospital, Jonathon's guts gave him hell. What could he say or do to help his boy? The young man had his whole life ahead of him. Whatever answer entered Jonathon's brain, two reasons popped up to knock it down.

He thought about calling on Andrew and Annie first in case Cate was there but instead went straight to the hospital. Not having any news, even bad news, gnawed away at his insides.

Prepared for the worst, he steeled himself as he walked through the hospital. In the corridor he stopped when Cate stepped out of a wash room.

'Cate,' he exclaimed.

She looked surprised. 'Jonathon. When did you arrive?'

'Just now. How's Eddie?'

'Not too bad.'

Worried, he moved to her. 'Not too bad? What's that mean?'

She ignored him and called. 'Edward, your father's here.'

'Oh, what does *he* want?' called the bored patient, still unseen.

Jonathon looked at his wife. Her blank expression said nothing. Then Jonathon looked up as his son walked, well in his unique way, out of the ward and headed towards them. He'd mastered the crutches and one-leg routine and could even smile at the same time.

'G'day Dad,' he said as his father's eyes filled with tears.

Jonathon didn't know how to hug his son but managed. Cate stood there having a quiet weep herself.

Jonathon stepped back to admire his son. 'This is bloody marvellous,' he said.

'Fancy a race round the ward?' asked Edward who winced as a new pain kicked in.

'Okay, enough,' said Cate. 'Come and sit down.'

For all three Sweeping family members it was an uplifting occasion. Edward's pride, Jonathon's happiness and Cate's pleasure created enough energy to heat the entire hospital. They swapped news and then reached the critical decision. Jonathon desperately wanted Edward home but hated the possibility the disability would kill the boy's spirit.

'Everything's settled, Mr Sweeping,' said Cate to her husband. 'Edward's being billeted here in town and will receive treatment to build his strength. We'll check on him every few weeks and make decisions depending on his progress.'

Jonathon blew air and sensed relief flood through his body.

'Are you happy with that?' asked Jonathon looking deep into his son's eyes.

'More than happy,' said Edward who found his new mobility both a challenge and a serious boost to his attitude to life.

They made plans to return in three weeks. 'Two,' said Cate and she won—again. The farewell hugs were powerful and long.

All the way home, the couple talked non-stop. That was a first.

'And James and Chloe and the others are all right?'

'They're fine,' he said, 'and so are we.'

They turned into the path leading to their farm. As always, the dogs bounded towards them followed less enthusiastically by the two chaps supposedly running the farm. They weren't caught in the back paddock mustering sheep. They were in the back yard.

Ralph tossed from one hand to the other what looked like a ball, and Jon carried a piece of wood that looked like a homemade cricket bat.

'Welcome home,' called Master Sweeping. 'How's Eddie?'

The news was quickly conveyed, the kettle boiled and the tidying of the cottage began; naturally by the only female.

Ralph wanted to discuss the recent visit and offer from James, and obtain Jonathon's opinion on the swapping farms suggestion.

Jon protested. 'But you can't go, Ralph, until I've mastered the cover drive.'

The parents looked at one another. Their youngest son held court giving his parents an education in the art of spin bowling and fielding in slips. Oh dear, he'd become a cricket fanatic.

Despite several additional coaching sessions, two days later Ralph packed a bag containing hand-me-downs and whatever from the Sweepings, and he and Jonathon rode a horse each to the Ramsay farm. Here they all shared a meal before Jonathon wished the escaped convict well and left. James employed a new hand and the Ramsay property improved no end.

Two weeks later, Cate and Jonathon returned to Hobart and were directed to a small cottage on the outskirts of town where they found their son. His landlady, a widow, was not at home.

Mrs Laidlaw has made me feel so welcome,' said Edward. 'You'll like her.'

'When will she return?' asked Cate anxious to meet the old lady.

'Ah, not till tonight. She's helping the new convicts in the Cascades Female Factory.'

The parents exchanged glances. Jonathon switched topics. 'You're looking grand, my boy. How's the mobility?'

'Great and I'm having less pain but best of all, I'm able to help Mrs Laidlaw with domestic chores around the cottage.'

Cate cut to the chase. 'So how do you feel about coming home?'

He went all wishy-washy. 'Ah, I'm not sure, Ma. Mrs Laidlaw has shown me how helping others less fortunate can be so rewarding. She invites female convicts home here for a meal, and I've heard fascinating stories about life back in England.'

The parents shared another glance being both unsure and yet pleased Edward seemed so full of life.

'Let me make tea,' he said, 'hopping up.' Cate was on her feet. 'I can do it.'

He stopped and gave her a look. She understood and sat.

Jonathon whispered. 'I told you not to mollycoddle the boy.'

Cate raised her eyebrows and meant to ask what the word meant.

They stayed for an hour and shared all their news. Edward thought his young brother playing cricket was a hoot. 'There's a team here in Hobart and I'm thinking of joining.'

The conversation stopped when he saw their stunned expressions.

'As the scorer,' he said. They sighed with relief. 'Although if I did have a bat, I'd need a runner with two legs.' They were sucked in again until his smile appeared and his parents laughed.

Mrs Laidlaw remained absent and the parents decided. Edward looked great, his spirits were sky-high, and there was no need to take him home. They promised to return in a few weeks.

'Don't hurry,' he said and walked out to their cart. 'Give my love to the cricketer and Uncle James and his crew.'

He watched as they drove away, heading to the vicarage. Cate looked back and couldn't believe it. 'He's waving with one of his crutches.'

'Thank God for Mrs Laidlaw and her charity work. Has she taken on Edward as one of her projects?'

'Looks like it, and who are these females she's inviting home? Is our boy being seduced by loose women from London?'

'Half his luck,' said Jonathon and copped a whack.

# Chapter 50

On the Sweeping property, life returned to normal—almost. Jonathon and Jon worked well together. Cate kept thinking about her other sons, and her brother and his family. Jon insisted on his father throwing cricket balls at him on the long summer nights.

'If you won't help me practise my batting, Dad, I'll ride over to Uncle James and have Ralph give me a hand.' Father was no bowler.

The weather can get pretty warm during summer in Van Diemen's Land and the signs of a forthcoming belter were in the air.

It was easy to rise early and work before the hot sun did its worst.

After a good morning's work, father and son headed back for lunch when a cart appeared heading down their track. Cate came out and nearly died.

A man and woman sat on the seat with the driver none other than Edward Sweeping. Cate shrieked she was so pleased and surprised. Her curiosity though was at fever pitch.

Seated beside her son and his crutches was a young woman with a bonnet under which was hair to take your breath away. As the cart stopped beside the cottage, the residents saw the young woman and her beautiful smile.

Jonathon and Cate couldn't believe Edward had found a girl.

'Hello,' cried Edward and skillfully climbed down. The woman handed him his crutches. He kissed his mother and hugged his father and brother before turning to help his companion to the ground.

'Mother, father, Jon, I'd like you to meet Victoria, my landlady.'

Shock exploded. This is the elderly widow who helps destitute female convicts? Hands were shaken and everyone moved inside out of the heat. Jonathon and Cate now understood why their boy was reluctant to leave Hobart. He'd found a stunning sweetheart.

It took a while for the shock to fade only for it to roar back to life when Edward spoke again.

'We wanted you to be the first to know that last Saturday, Victoria and I were married.'

Now had a mob of kangaroos burst through the front door, bounced around the kitchen and hopped out the back door, their presence would have created less of a response than did the impact of this announcement.

Cate stifled a scream, Jonathon gasped, and Jon grinned and embraced his brother. The handshakes which greeted the former widow on her arrival became hugs and kisses, albeit chaste.

Edward's explanation took time and only when all the details were delivered did the shock begin to fade.

Victoria spoke. 'I wanted to have you all attend the ceremony but Edward insisted we marry and managed to persuade the Reverend McFarlane to read the banns and hold the service. I chose three bridesmaids from the Female Factory and my son, Stephen gave me away.'

The images created sent Jonathon's and Cate's minds in a spin. Jon rejoiced. Open mouths became catching.

'You do realise, Ma,' said Edward, 'you're now a grandmother.'

Before anyone could speak, Victoria explained. 'Stephen's only four and we thought the long trip might be too much for him so he's staying with the McFarlanes till we return to Hobart.'

"Knock me down with a feather," best described the visit. The parents had suffered on-going despair over Edward. They feared the loss of his leg might plunge him into depression and worse, an early death. Instead, a few months later, he returned home with an angelic wife, an instant family, and a smile to gladden any heart.

He was in love and his life transformed.

Edward explained. 'Victoria owns the cottage you visited and her late husband has provided funds for her to continue helping female convicts find their way in the colony. I'm able to help with the record-keeping and letter writing.'

His parents shook their heads in wonder, their hearts delirious.

'It's all thanks to you teaching me to read and write, Dad. All those years ago when Moses, Jon and I were little, you'd have us sit at this kitchen table as you hammered the alphabet into our heads.'

More head shaking from his parents although Jon was impressed but not as involved. That was about to change when Edward added more information.

'And you won't believe my latest activity. I've become the scorer for the cricket club in Hobart.'

Jon leapt in the air. 'Cricket!' he yelled. 'I'm playing cricket. Can I play for your club?'

It took a while for Jon's latest craze to be explained and to have all his questions answered. The young man enthused.

'Hang on,' said his father. 'I started out having three sons to help me run this place. One's gone to the mainland, another's moved to Hobart, and now Jonathon Junior here fancies himself as a famous gentleman cricketer. What about me?'

It was half said in jest and certainly provoked a few funny remarks. But the bottom line saw the parents thrilled, Jon super excited, and Victoria over the moon to be accepted so well by her husband's family. Edward purred, his life surging in a new direction.

At night, after a smashing meal, Jon willingly moved to the smaller third bedroom giving the newlyweds his room. In their respective bedrooms, the two couples whispered well into the night.

Cate couldn't stop chatting. 'I love the name Stephen Sweeping.' Her husband wanted to sleep.

Jonathon turned his back on the missus. 'Goodnight, Grandma.'

She smiled in the dark and when she finally drifted to sleep, the smile was still on her face.


Jonathon travelled into town with the new Mr and Mrs Sweeping. His horse trotted along behind their cart. They first called on the McFarlane residence.

Jonathon knocked on the door and daughter Hannah answered. 'Mr Sweeping, and Mr and Mrs Sweeping, please come in.' She called. 'Mother, it's the Sweepings.'

Annie smiled but looked sheepish. 'I've been dreading this moment. Andrew tried to persuade these lovely people to delay the wedding but Edward insisted.'

'I did,' said Eddie, 'and I'd do it all again.'

Jonathon brushed aside the matter and explained the couple's arrival at the farm, and Cate's consternation and celebration.

'Annie, please, all's well that ends well and Cate and I are delighted. And Jon's beside himself hoping to play cricket in town.'

'But you haven't met young Stephen,' said Annie.

Right on cue, Hannah and Dimity entered holding the little boy's hands. He ran to his mother.

Jonathon stared at Victoria's little boy. 'Darling,' she said, turning her son. 'This is your new Daddy's Daddy, your grandfather.'

Jonathon held out a hand and the lad took it and spoke beautifully. 'Hello, sir, I'm very pleased to meet you.'

The boy displayed manners to die for.

It was a melt your heart moment. Jonathon struggled because he knew when he got home his wife would ask him a hundred questions about the lad.

Andrew McFarlane was due home but rather than wait, the Sweepings decided to make their move. With the young boy on the seat between his mother and stepfather, and with Grandpa Sweeping trotting along behind, they said farewell to Annie, Hannah and Dimity and set off for Victoria and Eddie's cottage.

Once there, after refreshments, Jonathon gave his son advice on fixing the dilapidated back fence then prepared to say farewell.

'Someone's left a note,' said Victoria to her new husband.

'Ah,' said Edward reading. 'There's a match here on the 21st. You'd better tell the cricketer in the family, Dad.'

Jonathon nodded then said goodbye. He bought supplies and headed to the vicarage in the hope of seeing the vicar.

In recent years, Andrew enjoyed watching the building of a new church, and it became the best looking and best attended in Hobart. In fact Anglicans made up about 52% of the local population although the figure would be challenged when the potato famine brought many Irish Catholics to the island.

Andrew was home and he too offered profound apologies over the wedding sans family. It was again dismissed and he and the farmer went into the street.

'It's great news, Jonathon,' said Andrew.

'Indeed; Cate and I are thrilled.'

'No, I mean besides Edward and Victoria.' Jonathon didn't understand. 'We're getting our own parliament. We're getting self-government.'

Andrew buzzed with excitement. Jonathon didn't. Would the subject of him standing for office be raised again? It wasn't. Andrew could read people. He knew the former child convict turned farmer was happy doing what he did and so let the subject slide. They shook hands and Jonathon headed home.

Travelling alone gave Jonathon the chance to think about his family and his life. His feelings were mixed. His life was full of challenges. Yes he was getting older and perhaps this is what happened to someone in their autumnal years. Two of his sons were gone from the family property and probably would never return. His youngest was all he had left. He knew Jon would make a good farmer but what if he too discovered the wanderlust. Surely this cricket passion would pass but without his youngest, Jonathon would struggle to run the farm. He could and should employ a convict as he was once employed.

He reached home, greeted his family and offloaded the supplies. Cate was desperate for news. Jon too wanted instant answers.

'Yes, son, Edward wants you to know there's a match in a fortnight and will ask about you having a game.'

The youngest son struggled to keep a lid on his happiness. 'Thanks, Dad, that's brilliant.'

Jon attended to the horse leaving the parents alone.

'Well?' asked Cate demanding news.

'Andrew and Annie were embarrassed about going ahead with the wedding without us but I told them not to worry.'

'And?'

And what?'

'Oh come on, Jonathon. What about the cottage, the Female Factory convicts, Edward's work and our new grandson?'

'Oh you'll love him, he's a real little gentleman. Beautiful manners and is as handsome as his mother is pretty.'

'That's not enough. I want to know what he said, what he wore, how he walks, everything.'

'Yes dear,' said Jonathon thankful he'd stored as many facts as possible. It was going to be a long night.

# Chapter 51

Life settled back into a sort of normality with Jon helping his father and both finding it tough going with only the two of them. Not so long ago Jonathon had all three of his sons to help him. And with summer arriving in a rush, being outside made maintaining your water intake essential.

Over tea, wife and son made their case for a trip to town.

'The match is on this Saturday, Dad, and you know I have to go,' said Jon.

'And I must meet my grandson,' added Cate.

Jonathon responded. 'When you say *my* grandson, I assume you mean *our* grandson.'

Jon piled on the pressure. 'I'll finish all the tasks on Friday so we can leave early on Saturday morning, and I'll ride Benny so if the match goes late, you can leave without me.'

The head of the household was boxed in and accepted his fate. Jon was true to his word and worked like a navvy on the Friday. That night he was exhausted.

'If they ask you to play, you'll be too tired,' said his mother.

'Not me,' replied Jon. 'This will be a day to remember.'

They departed early, the cart with the parents and dogs, and the budding sportsman on his horse. They arrived at Edward and Victoria's cottage mid-morning.

The newlyweds were delighted to welcome the visitors and Cate and little Stephen hit it off from the start. Edward's mobility seemed effortless as he moved around the cottage and outside in the garden. He showed his father the work he and little Stephen did on the back fence.

Jon pestered Edward about the cricket match and only settled when told the game didn't start for another hour and yes, he'd arranged for baby brother to play in the match for the Hobart team.

After lunch, the brothers set off to walk to the ground. The family promised to come and watch later although the blazing sun made going outside a daunting task.

Cricket started in Van Diemen's Land pretty much as soon as the colony began in 1803. Soldiers and settlers as well as convicts were familiar with the English game and friendly matches became popular.

Today's game featured a group of soldiers against the local club recently formed in Hobart.

Jon couldn't get over how well-liked his brother had become since volunteering to become the team's scorer.

'Gentlemen, this is my baby brother, Jon, and he loves his cricket.'

Jon disliked the "baby brother" reference but glowed inside as the other players shook his hand and slapped his back.

'Welcome, Jon, I'm Tobias, the captain. Are you a batsman or bowler?'

Shyness and modesty encircled Master Sweeping. 'Ah, I like batting and can bowl accurately.'

'Good show; we'll get you involved and remember, we have to beat these pompous military chaps.'

The others supported their skipper and after the toss, Hobart found themselves in the field. It was hot, damn hot. Entomologists have long known that flies were born to disrupt anyone playing cricket. The spectators settled under any tree they could find. Edward sat at a small portable table and made sure his pencils were sharp.

The Military Eleven took the game seriously. They weren't having a bunch of convict oiks—most were free settlers or their offspring—beating them at anything. Jon fielded in the outfield far from the pitch. It was suspect with bumps and cracks making the underarm bowling tricky but soon the runs began to mount, and Edward's pencil worked overtime.

In the early days of cricket matches, and certainly in far-flung Van Diemen's Land, bowlers mostly bowled underarm, overs consisted of only four balls, and there was no boundary fence. A batsman couldn't hit a four or a six; everything was run.

With the temperature climbing, all players sweated encouraging the batsmen to hit out or get out. You didn't want to be stuck in the middle for too long. The military lads made 73. Jon didn't get to bowl but fielded a few balls and threw them back well. The refreshment tent beckoned.

'Sorry you didn't get a bowl, young Sweeping,' said the skipper.

'That's okay, sir,' panted Jon, 'I'm happy just to be playing.'

'But your fielding was excellent and you'll bat at number 10.'

Jon's excitement bubbled, and then took off when he spotted his family with a group of other spectators.

Andrew McFarlane and his family were with the Sweeping clan. 'See, the Conqu'ring hero comes,' cried the vicar, and Jon tingled.

He was introduced to those he met a long time ago but one caught his eye. Dimity McFarlane was only a year or two younger than Jon. *If playing cricket means meeting pretty girls*, he thought, *I'll be here every match.*

'Jon, you're batting at number 10,' said his brother.

'Yes, the skipper told me,' said Jon revelling in the game's jargon.

His parents made eye contact reacting to the new language being used by their sons. The boys' happiness washed over their parents.

Despite the heat, the jovial mood continued and the Hobart team began their innings. The soldiers were more advanced and bowled round arm. The run-up and action of the bowlers looked ferocious and a few deliveries hit the batsmen who reacted as the pain kicked in. The crowd reacted with audible groans. Now Jonathon and Cate worried. Their boy was no gladiator.

The score mounted slowly as did the fall of wickets. With the Hobart score on 69, the eighth wicket fell, and young Jon Sweeping was the next man in. His stomach entertained butterflies while his face entertained flies. One wandered inside his nose.

The result was in doubt. Two wickets for the bowling side, five runs for the batting side with Jon Sweeping now at the crease.

Perspiration trickled from his forehead making him blink to keep the sweat from his eyes. He worried the flimsy protective equipment he wore might not save him from a nasty blow. Playing in the backyard with Ralph and then his father held no fear. Now a burly brute of a soldier, armed with a cannonball, was breathing fire and steaming towards him, about to aim the ball at the batsman's head.

A voice yelled from the crowd. 'Knock his block off, Geordie,' which was exactly what the lumbering bowler intended to do.

The round arm action of the bowler confused the inexperienced Jon. He saw the ball at the last split second, pushed forward and the ball leapt and thudded into his ribs.

The fielding team screamed an appeal and Jon's mother gasped. 'Not out,' said the umpire and Jon's ribs told him they were sore.

He refused to show his distress and faced again. In ran the bowler. This time a full toss flew straight towards Jon's middle stump. He didn't defend, he attacked. A short back swing and a straight bat saw the ball fly along the ground out on the leg side.

'Run,' yelled the other batsman haring towards Jon who scampered up the pitch. Back they came for a second and Jon wanted to celebrate although confusion clobbered him when his partner screamed and hared down the pitch calling for a third run.

'Yes,' he yelled and Jon had no choice. He ran and made it although the fielding team roared their delight.

Jon spun around to see his partner had run himself out. Only two of the three runs would count. The Hobart team was 9 out for 71. Two runs to tie, three runs to win but only one wicket left.

It was the end of the over and Jon would take strike. The last batsman walked to the centre of the ground. He was short and rotund, a kindly clerk, an office worker who loved cricket and wore thick spectacles. Jon worried and his battered ribs didn't help.

If Jon couldn't hit the winning runs, the blind-as-a-bat batsman would face the bowling and that probably equalled disaster. Jon approached his new partner. 'Be ready to run,' he said.

The players and spectators knew the situation. Edward announced the score as the game crept to its conclusion. 'Three runs or one wicket to win.'

'Two runs to tie,' added a spectator who knew about cricket.

Out in the middle of the sunbaked ground, Jon's mind raced. His first match and he could be a hero. His family was there to watch. *And how can I talk to that girl, and what sort of a name is Dimity?*

The new bowler had barely a run-up. He bowled slow balls which spun. He used guile and trickery not brute force. Jon prepared to face.

'You can do it, Jon,' yelled a voice from the crowd. It was his namesake, the old man. The pressure kept building. Talk about tense.

Up stepped the bowler bowling underarm. The ball floated high and looked like a gift. Jon took a huge swipe and missed. The ball bounced and spun missing the wickets by a coat of paint. Jon survived. It was still three runs or one wicket to win.

'Come on, Razor,' yelled the fielding side. 'Finish 'im orff.'

Jon told himself to stay calm. Razor bowled again and this time tossed the ball even higher. Jon fell for the same trick, tried to hit the ball into the River Derwent, missed and overbalanced. Lying on the ground, the opposing players taunted him. Sledging was a part of the game. Jon struggled to stand. Even some in the crowd were laughing although not the Sweeping clan; never that family.

Then, to an already tense situation was added a new and unusual factor—smoke. In the height of summer, the land gasped for a drink. A grass fire came alive. Smoke drifted towards the cricket ground.

The third ball was bowled and Jon learnt his lesson. It was a full toss, easy to hit and the batsman played a dead bat. He patted it back to the bowler. He survived but missed a golden opportunity to score the winning runs. One ball left in this over.

The heat and tension was joined by drifting smoke. A match might be abandoned because of rain but fire? One wicket, three runs; it couldn't be much closer.

Jon knew he must get at least one run from the last ball or else his shortsighted partner would be facing the demon fast bowler in the next over.

In stepped Razor and, trying to trick the batsman, bowled a fast, low ball. Jon played a forward defensive stroke, and set off yelling, 'Run.' A single would mean he would be facing the next over. A run out would mean game over and victory to the military lads.

His partner was asleep. It took him a second to start running. He was still yards from the crease when the fielder swooped on the ball. A simple underarm throw to the keeper would affect the runout and win the match for the soldiers.

But the fielder, trying to make a name for himself, heaved the ball hard. It missed the keeper and the stumps and set off to the other side of the ground. They could make a second run, an overthrow.

'Yes,' screamed Jon, who was halfway down the pitch. His partner, like a huge warship turning on a sixpence, took an age to stop and turn. He finally set off with Jon already at the same end. A fielder retrieved the ball a long way from the pitch. The scores were tied. Jon watched his partner reach the other end and decided.

'One more,' screamed Jon who waited till his partner set off. The number 11 batsman had trouble walking with speed, so his running didn't inspire. Once Jon saw his partner start, he set off for the far end. They crossed.

Jon turned back to see the worst batsman in the world stumble and fall flat on this face. The fielder threw the ball to the keeper. The fallen batsman struggled to his knees and thrust his bat towards the crease. The keeper caught the ball and smashed the wickets with every fielder screaming their joy.

Silly them because if the last man was run out, the result would have been a tie. But the soldiers' cheers were flattened when the umpire declared, 'Not out.'

The Hobart side had won and their celebrations were extraordinary. And guess who was carried from the ground by his overjoyed teammates? In his first game of cricket, Jon Sweeping became a hero.

# Chapter 52

As he accepted back slaps and kisses, Jon revelled in his moment of triumph. He hoped the vicar's younger daughter might have offered him even a smile but she was lost in what became a sense of panic.

The grass fire exploded and now headed straight for the ground. Spectators grabbed their belongings and hurried to the middle of the oval. Players joined locals who were fighting the blaze. The cricket ground became a safe area although the smoke smelt and tasted terrible.

A lack of fuel and the work of the firefighters eventually killed the blaze. People regrouped and made plans. Jon was on fire. Not from the burnt surrounds but with passion for his cricketing success and a certain young female. He approached his parents.

'Ma, Mrs McFarlane has invited me to have tea with her family. You go ahead without me.'

'I don't want you riding home in the dark,' said Cate.

'He'll be all right,' said his father torn between not wanting the last of his sons to fly the nest while wanting him to spread his wings.

'It's okay, Ma. Victoria and Eddie said I can stay at their place.'

There was nothing more to say. Jon was the youngest son and now the latest to possibly leave home. Jonathon and Cate were happy and sad at the same time. They said farewell to their sons, new daughter-in-law, grandson and the McFarlanes, and pointed the cart for home.

Because of the heat, they travelled slowly, stopping to give the horse and dogs a drink. Despite the long summer days, it meant the last couple of miles were in the dark, and even then the weather was oppressive.

Some British and Irish arrivals in the colonies found the heat a reason to return to the land of their birth. The Sweepings, in the coolest colony in Australia, adapted but longed for the autumn.

When they turned into the home drive, the dogs jumped from the cart and raced to the cottage, barking. Cate grabbed Jonathon's arm in fear. 'Stop,' she whispered.

He pulled up the horse a good fifty yards from the cottage.

'What?' he asked, confused.

'There's a light in the house.'

He saw it and worried.

Living in the bush as they did, neighbours were as good as living on the moon. You could go weeks, even months without seeing another human. If you left your home and property, empty except for the animals, you would return to an unoccupied home. Not now. Someone was there.

'Wait here,' said Jonathon who climbed down and worried because the dogs ran ahead to confront the intruder but stopped barking. They could see in the dark so why did the dogs stop barking in the night? If there was a person in their cottage, the dogs tipped off the visitor or visitors.

Jonathon trod softly wishing his firearm was to hand. He couldn't even remember where he left it ever since the aborigines were wiped out in Van Diemen's Land.

He decided to make the first move. 'Hello,' he called. 'Who's there?' Cate climbed down and followed her husband at a distance.

The lantern disappeared from the window and the house went black. Then the lantern appeared outside with a person beside it.

The person spoke. 'What sort of a welcome do you call this?'

Jonathon froze not believing the voice. Cate knew who it was and ran, yelling as she passed her startled husband.

'Moses!' she cried and raced to hug the prodigal son.

Jonathon took off and made it a three-way embrace. It was awkward with the lantern interrupting the movement of bodies but eventually all three made it inside. The dogs were delighted.

Jonathon remembered the horse and dashed out to the animal. The patriarch wanted all the news from his boy. 'Don't you start without me. Wait till I come back.'

As he fled, Cate gave her son another long hug. 'Let me look at you,' she said lighting a second lantern to improve the light.

'You've grown and put on weight and ...'

'No Ma, the only thing different is the beard.'

'It suits you, makes you look dignified. So sit down and I'll make you a meal.' She fussed.

'No Ma, I've already helped myself and for which I will pay you.' He took coins from his pocket.

His mother turned, angry. 'Don't you dare! Since when has one of my sons ever paid me for anything?' He backed off.

'So where are my brothers? Don't tell me they've run off and left you and Dad alone.'

'Right now they're both in Hobart and will be furious they weren't here to greet you.

'And you and Dad are well I see.'

'Indeed we are,' said Jonathon entering having run back to the cottage once he set the horse free in the paddock. 'Come here, you.'

He hugged Moses, again for a long time. Then they sat, drank tea and the conversation began. Moses wanted to hear their news first and what a mixture it was. He delighted in hearing about Jon and his cricket but wept at Edward's accident and loss of his leg.

'But he's married and happy and has an adopted son like me?'

'Indeed,' said Cate, 'but enough from us. We're desperate for your news.'

He paused. He looked well. Surely he had good news to tell. His job, his marriage and possible family, his desire to come home, and something unusual were all thoughts entertained by his parents. But when he spoke, he flattened them.

'I've found my birth family.' They gasped. Of all the topics he might have raised, the one they weren't expecting hit the hardest. On the one hand they were thrilled and on the other, a sense of unease seeped under their skin.

'Tell us everything, please,' said Jonathon. Moses did.

'It wasn't my goal; I genuinely wanted to see what the world had to offer. In Hobart I checked with the government land grants register and found their names—mine too and my sister's. Then from the shipping office I discovered my birth parents arrived in New South Wales before they came here. With their names, I went to Sydney and discovered their last address in England. It was a small village in Derbyshire. I wrote a letter addressed to the family of Brendan and Maree Cole.' He shrugged. 'It was the only thing I could think of.'

'So your birth certificate reads Cole,' said Cate.

'Joshua Cole,' he said.

'Joshua, Moses,' said Jonathon. 'We were pretty close.'

They laughed but not for long.

'And what happened?' asked Cate on the edge of her seat.

'I received a reply. It seems I have three aunts, an uncle, two grandmothers and a tribe of cousins.'

Cate clapped her hands and cried with happiness. 'Oh Moses, how wonderful you've found your family and discovered the names of your parents.'

'True but to me, the names of my parents will always be Jonathon and Cate.' They wept. 'Without my father rescuing me and my mother feeding and caring for me, I would have died with my family.'

They hugged him and cried. Finally, Cate managed to speak.

'What was your sister called?'

'Esther.'

The parents wiped their eyes and rejoiced in the reunion. The sadness ran deep but the appearance of Moses and the news which gave so much meaning to his life meant so much to all three.

'What are your plans?' asked Jonathon.

'I want to say goodbye to my parents and brothers before returning to England to meet my other family.'

'You'll like Eddie's wife,' said Cate, 'and if I'm not mistaken, Jon has found a sweetheart too.'

Moses reacted. 'What's the matter with me?' he asked. 'My brothers have found a girl, and here I am, a miserable old bachelor.'

They laughed and chatted into the night. Moses could see his parents were tired so they all retired buzzing from their reunion and news.

Moses insisted on sleeping in his former bedroom, outside in the shed. It was still oppressive and he found it hard to sleep. Around 2 am he woke and went outside. The breeze worked hard to become a wind. The night sky was its usual black with diamonds as stars but away to the south, it changed colour—a reddish yellow. It grew bigger.

Moses panicked and ran inside. 'Dad, wake up,' he called banging on their open door.

Both parents were up and out of bed. 'What's happened?' asked Jonathon.

'Come and see.'

All three went outside and saw the sky lit up. 'That's a bush fire,' said Jonathon and it's heading towards James' place.' Calling, Jonathon ran inside. 'Get dressed, son. We need to help your uncle.'

'Be careful, Jonathon, it's dangerous,' cried Cate.

He dressed as they argued. 'If nothing else, we can take you and his family to safety. Now hurry.'

She dressed while the men ran to hook the horse to the cart and saddle Benny.

'You ride Benny and I'll drive your mother. Follow us and don't go riding off on your own.'

It was a mad scramble. The wind grew muscles and the sky glowed red. Tall trees tried to stand still but lost their hats as the bullying wind attacked. The horses neighed in fear. Jonathon ordered the dogs onto the cart; no second invitation required. The party left.

It was terrifying driving as fast as they could. Dawn was two or more hours away but the light from the fire was eerie. Native animals burst out of the bush frightening the horses. By going to the Ramsay farm they were heading towards the approaching fire. They arrived with James and Ralph running out to meet them.

James looked terrible having the responsibility of protecting his wife, mother-in-law and children and could hardly muster any shock at the sight of Moses. Jonathon took control.

'Put the women, children and all the dogs on our cart. Cate can drive. She'll head to Hobart. We'll do what we can then use the horses to escape if we have to.' James froze. 'Go!' yelled Jonathon and his brother-in-law got busy.

Cate trusted her husband. This was no time to argue. He told her straight. 'Head for Hobart. If you reach the river and think the fire is too close, get everyone in the water and stay there till the fire passes.'

He helped her up on the seat. 'What about you?' she yelled.

'We'll follow.' He helped the others into the cart then slapped the horse's rump. 'Now go!'

He watched the cart for a while then ran to James and Ralph. 'Open the paddock gates and let the sheep into the bush. If the fire arrives they'll die in the paddock. Let loose they may have a chance. Get the horses and bring them here. Go.' James and Ralph took off. He grabbed Moses. 'Come with me.'

Jonathon and Moses collected buckets, saucepans, chamber pots, anything they could find and filled them with water then placed them about three yards apart around the cottage facing the fire. Jonathon thought they'd be next to useless if the fire roared through.

You could see the flames racing across the roof of the bush. You could hear and feel the powerful wind, and the crackle of burning branches and undergrowth grew louder. Fleeing animals burst into the open. The smaller, slower animals lumbered along their chance of survival in the lap of the gods.

James and Ralph returned with the terrified horses. They were tied to posts ready to be ridden if necessary.

Jonathon shouted above the wind, fire and animal cries. 'We fight for the cottage. First, cover as much of your skin as possible then soak a towel and drape it over your head. Grab another towel and wet it well.' They looked at him. 'Go!' he shouted at Moses as well. The trio ran inside.

Jonathon wet himself and a sheet he grabbed off the washing-line. The others came out looking strange with towels over their heads.

'We make a stand here with one aim to save the cottage. If the sheds go, leave them. If it's hopeless, we grab a horse and ride like hell. Stick together so if one's in trouble, the others can help him. Understand?'

James, Ralph and Moses nodded. They trusted Jonathon but reckoned death for all of them was now a real possibility.

There wasn't a sound like it. The wind howled and burning embers broke free, and raced ahead of the flames dancing in the sky. In the pitch black before dawn, the heavens lit up like a giant lantern. The horses threw their front legs in the air wanting to break free.

Jonathon thought of his wife and James' wife, children and mother-in-law. Were they safe? Could they reach Hobart? He knew wild and domestic animals and crops and fences and sheds and houses could be destroyed. Mother Nature was miles bigger and stronger and actually looked for victims as the fire sprinted through the tree tops.

Because the bush was well cleared around the cottage, the men had space around the building. This is where they stood to fight. Speaking was useless as the wind turned up its volume and trees fifty yards away burst into flames. Many trees exploded into fireballs.

Burning embers were joined by burning branches. They landed in the yard and against the cottage. The quartet attacked these spot fires with their feet and towels.

A fire exploded on the cottage roof. Moses grabbed a bucket of water and heaved its contents. It killed the danger only for another fire to start on the other side. This time James did the water throwing and again with success. But it was no use. The heat was enough to kill you, let alone the flames. Jonathon decided. He screamed and waved.

'Get the horses. Let's go!'

Everyone ran to untie their horse. Jonathon struggled. The others were in the saddle ready to ride, their charges desperate to flee. Jonathon put his foot in a stirrup. James looked up and shouted, 'Look out!'

A burning branch snapped, broke free and plummeted to earth. Jonathon saw it falling, leapt aside and landed on his back. His horse took off. The main trunk of the branch smashed into the ground missing Jonathon by inches. Had it struck him, he would have been crushed. Smaller branches, burning fiercely, fell and one struck his head. James, Ralph and Moses were off their horses and dragging Jonathon free. Their horses galloped away in fright.

In the ghostly glow of the fire, Jonathon's scratches drew blood but the catastrophe, his real problem were burns; horrible burns to the right side of his face. It screamed in agony while the victim remained mute.

'Get water,' yelled James and Moses ran returning with a kitchen pot. James and Ralph gently lifted Jonathon's head and found their supporting hands wet. Moses sprinkled water over his father's face. Jonathon fought hard not to scream. When James and Ralph laid the fallen man's head back on the ground and withdrew their hands, they were covered in blood. 'Jesus,' whispered the brother-in-law.

The three helpers died inside. 'We need the horses, at least one,' said James, and Moses and Ralph ran searching and calling. James knelt. 'We'll get you out of here, Jonathon. Keep still. The fire's behaving in a strange way, but we're staying to help you.'

James held Jonathon's hand and they both watched, expecting to see the cottage burst into flames. It didn't. Why not? The wind was as loud as ever but different, strange different. The wind changed direction. That was the something strange.

It shifted, made a turn to the left, sending the fire north. It raged, even stronger but now in another direction. Moses and Ralph returned holding the reins of the horses.

'Tie them,' said James then help me carry your father inside.

'The fire's going in another direction,' cried Moses.

'Hurry,' shouted James.

They lifted Jonathon who made not a sound, carrying him inside and placing him on the bed.

Jonathon looked fine if you studied his left profile but the right side of his face was a mess, and the blood on the back of his head was scary. His left eye escaped the flames but his hair, ear and cheek on his right side were singed. The pain must have been excruciating.

'Stay with your father,' said James to Moses, and then gave Ralph a look and they went to the kitchen. They returned with pieces of cloth used to dry plates. One was dipped in water and James gently dabbed Jonathon's burns. Then the others lifted the farmer's head so James could place a cloth as a bandage against the back of the skull then tie it over his forehead. The pillow was red.

Through all this, the former sweep turned farmer made no sound. He winced and his body tensed but throughout his life, Jonathon saw many people in pain, in agony from wounds and disease. He saw his parents and then his son writhe in tortuous agony. He saw children fall out of chimneys, watched convicts being flogged on prison hulks and on long sea voyages and felt the sting with each lash of the cat. Now it was his turn. Now he lay still as his skin screamed pain.

James took control giving orders to the others. 'Get the cart. Take the bedding from the other room. Harness the mare. If there are any sheep still in the paddock, close the gate then come back here as quick as you can.'

Moses and Ralph fled.

Jonathon tried to speak.

'Don't speak,' said James. 'For a change, we're looking after you. The fire's heading north so the ladies will be fine heading to Hobart. We'll go there, get you to the hospital and have the doctor treat your wounds.'

Time seemed to fly and then stand still. They lost track of it. They used a blanket as a bed and carried Jonathon to the cart. They tied the other horses to the rear.

James took the reins. 'You two hop in with the boss and help him drink.' He whispered. 'Don't let him fall asleep.'

They left. The fire was now behind them and streaks of daylight crept above the trees. James could see the track and urged the horse on. Of course the ruts and bumps made the journey even harder for Jonathon but time was vital.

It was impossible to know Jonathon's thoughts but James knew, apart from thinking about his wife and his demise, his brother-in-law would be wondering about his own farm. With the change in wind direction, was the Sweeping property soon to be consumed by fire?

As the day dawned bright, they drew closer to Hobart. James would look back and exchange glances with Moses who would nod grimly but when they saw the first buildings, tears decorated the cheeks of Moses. James pushed harder towards the hospital.

They stopped outside the front door. 'Stay there,' said James as he leapt from the cart and ran inside. He returned with three orderlies. Using the blanket, all six lifted Jonathon and took him inside.

James grabbed Moses. 'Where will your mother be?'

James shook his head. 'Eddie's place perhaps but I don't know where he lives.'

'The McFarlanes will know. Take a horse. Tell them what's happened but find your mother and bring her here.'

Moses didn't want to ask if his father would survive but did.

'Of course,' said James. 'Your father's invincible. Now go.'

Moses rode. James asked Ralph to wait while the brother-in-law entered the hospital. He found Jonathon surrounded by a doctor and several orderlies.

'Doctor,' said James.

An orderly whispered and escorted him out of the ward. 'Wait outside. The doctor will talk to you directly.'

James paced the corridor but it wasn't long before people arrived. Cate hurried in with Jon and Edward. Then Andrew and Annie McFarlane arrived followed by Chloe and Moses. A brotherly reunion took place under terrible circumstances.

James began to cry when he saw his wife safe and well. He tried to give more details. His news scared them and broke Cate's heart. To say the mood was sombre would be an understatement.

The doctor appeared and discovered the family. He spoke in a calm voice but laid it on the line.

'The burns are bad and will leave scars. But the problem is the injury to the back of his skull. He's hit a rock or something solid, and lost a lot of blood.' He paused. 'I think you should prepare for the worst.' Cate strangled a cry. Moses and Jon stood either side of their mother each with an arm around her. 'I'm sorry,' said the doctor. 'We've made him comfortable and given him something to dull the pain.'

'Thank you, doctor, but we have to see him—please,' said Cate.

'Of course, but not too many at once.'

James spoke on behalf of the others. 'We'll wait here.'

Cate went to the ward with her three sons. Jonathon looked better than when he arrived but it was a huge shock for Cate, Edward and Jon. Jonathon's head was swathed in bandages.

'Hello Mr Sweeping,' said Cate fighting hard to control her tears. 'I can't leave you alone for five minutes and look what you do.'

Jonathon smiled with half his face. 'So you made it then?'

'I course we made it. Now you're to stay here until you're better and then we'll come and take you home. No arguments, Jonathon.'

As if. Moses stepped in. 'Did you know the wind change saved the Ramsay farm, Dad.'

'I thought *we* saved it' he said with another weak smile on the working side of his face.

Moses had more to say. 'I hope you remember what I told you last night. My family in Britain is my second family. You and Ma and Eddie and Jon are my first family. You are my father.' He paused. 'Do you understand ... father?'

Jonathon tried to nod. Moses leant in and kissed the patient's forehead then broke down which didn't help the atmosphere.

Eddie wanted to tell his father his news. 'I would love to help you keep the farm in tip-top condition, Dad but until this other leg grows back, I'll have to restrict my visits to birthdays and Christmas. I know you reckon it's a pathetic excuse but my heart's in the right place.' He too paused but had no hesitation in continuing. 'I love you, Dad.'

He kissed his father and, like Moses, couldn't stop his tears.

Jon was next but seemed distracted. 'Hey! Dad, listen! Can you hear that?' They stopped and tried to concentrate on anything other than the man in the bed. 'That's rain, Dad.'

'Heavy rain,' said Edward.

'It'll kill that bloody fire, Dad. The farm is safe and waiting for you and me to get stuck in again.' Jonathon nodded and reached out to his youngest. 'There'll always be a Jonathon Sweeping on our farm, Dad, always. I've found a girl and, who knows, one day we'll get married and have a son and call him Jonathon. What do you reckon?

Jonathon struggled. 'You getting married sounds scary.'

The others wanted to laugh but couldn't. Jon moved in and his warm embrace and kiss made everyone weep even more.

Moses looked at his brothers. 'Let's give Mum a chance to chat with Dad,' he said and his brothers followed him out.

Cate pulled a chair in close and held his hand in two of hers. 'It's true what Jon said. He's only been in town a day and already claims to be walking out with Andrew and Annie's girl, Dimity. Talk about like father like son.' Jonathon looked confused. 'It's where you proposed to me, you great lummox.'

Out came his half smile. Jonathon struggled to speak. 'It was the huge bunch of flowers that did it.'

Cate couldn't speak. A solid lump lodged in her throat. She squeezed his hand so hard it replaced the pain from his burns. 'Thank you, Mr Jonathon Sweeping,' she croaked. 'I've always loved you ... and I always will.'

She looked into his eyes as they started to fade. The rain began a crescendo so loud it drowned out her loving words as well as the last breath of Jonathon Sweeping, the former English chimney sweep and convict who became a bloody good Australian farmer.

*****

# The Detective Joanna Best Mysteries

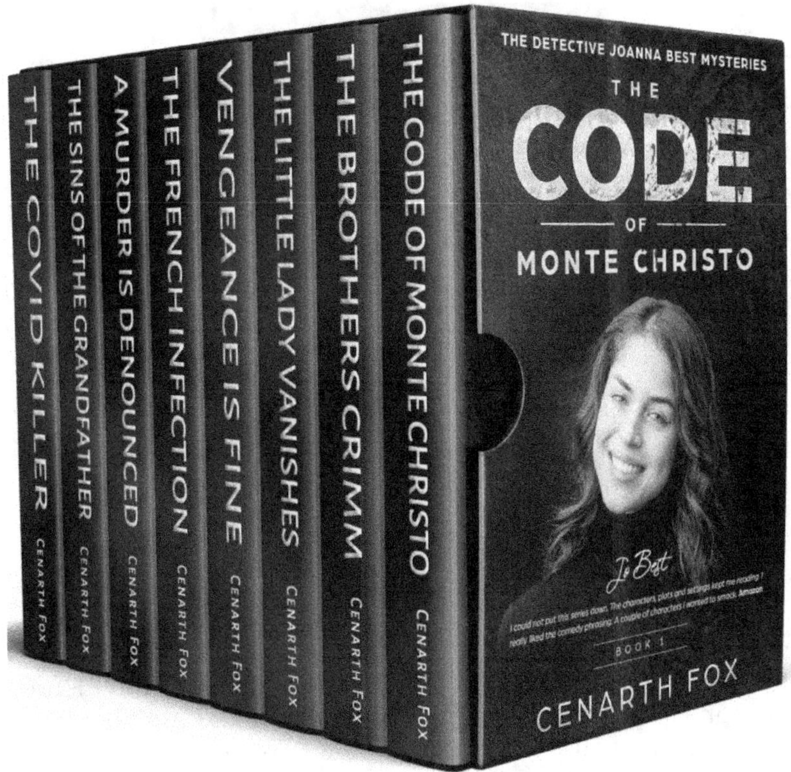



www.cenfoxbooks.com

Joanna Best is the youngest homicide detective in town. Smart, feisty and gorgeous, she's brilliant at cracking cases and rubbing people up the wrong way. Some jealous colleagues are desperate to undermine her. Certain criminals want her dead. Juggling a career with Victoria Police, having three men madly in love with her, and a strange family, Jo Best's adventures will drag you in. Her second banana is an Australian born Chinese IT guru who makes computers sing. Her best pal is a female 60ish police surgeon, a forensic genius and chocoholic.

*I could not put this series down. The characters, plots, settings, kept me reading. I really liked the word comedy phrasing. A couple of characters I wanted to smack.* **Amazon**

# Sherlock Holmes

The great man is soon to retire. On his last night at Baker Street, the loyal landlady drops a bombshell. Holmes is staggered. Mrs Hudson has done what!? Sherlock Holmes never panics—until now. Dr Watson arrives and is stunned. It's their greatest challenge. Sir Arthur Conan Doyle is furious. A famous author turned WW1 counter-intelligence spy is on the case. *The Strand Magazine* smells a scoop. Inspector Lestrade from Scotland Yard plans revenge, and at stake is the brilliant reputation of the world's most famous consulting detective. His only hope is to 'play the game'.

www.cenfoxbooks.com

*A delightfully imaginative pastiche. Recommended.* **Peter Blau BSI**
*An extraordinary book, one of the most enjoyable pieces of Holmesian fiction I've read in a long time ... a complex, ingenious and deliciously funny story of intersecting realities, and the conclusion is entirely satisfactory. I love it!* **Roger Johnson**
**Commissioning Editor: *The Sherlock Holmes Journal***

# Three World War Two Thrillers

In 1939 Germany is smashing through the Low Countries and the British, Belgian and French forces are trapped at Dunkirk. Louise Wellesley is a gorgeous and aristocratic young Englishwoman desperate to become an actress. But her upbringing demands she go to finishing school, the Buckingham Palace debutante ball and remain at home until the right chap comes along. Such young ladies most definitely do not cavort semi-naked upon the wicked stage. But war brings change. People tell lies. Rules are broken. So when you're in a foreign country and living by your wits while facing arrest, torture and death from the French police, Resistance, Gestapo and a double-agent, you bloody well better remember your lines, act out of your skin and never ever bump into the furniture. Oh and it helps if your new best friend is Edith Piaf.

*A Plum Jewel is the third in the series about a beautiful young actress turned spy. In the opinion of this reader it may be the best. Cenarth Fox has loaded this tale with so many twists and obstacles the reader may feel the need to take notes. Mr. Fox's knowledge of the working of wartime Britain and France is remarkable. The reader is right in the middle of the action. I can't recommend this book strongly enough.*
**Scott Skipper**

The Plum Trilogy – www.cenfoxbooks.com